THE
SPEEDICUT PAPERS

Book 1 (1821–1848)

THE SPEEDICUT PAPERS

The Memoirs Of Jasper Speedicut

Book 1 (1821–1848)

Flashman's Secret

Edited
by
Christopher Joll

authorHOUSE®

AuthorHouse™ UK
1663 Liberty Drive
Bloomington, IN 47403 USA
www.authorhouse.co.uk
Phone: 0800.197.4150

Published by AuthorHouse 10/25/2017

ISBN: 978-1-5462-8388-1 (sc)
ISBN: 978-1-5462-8389-8 (hc)
ISBN: 978-1-5462-8387-4 (e)

For

PAX

Who will probably disapprove of every line of this
book... if he ever gets around to reading it

CONTENTS

NOTES ON THE EDITOR

After serving time at Oxford University and the Royal Military Academy Sandhurst, Christopher Joll spent his formative years as an officer in The Life Guards, an experience from which he has never really recovered.

On leaving the Army, Joll worked first in investment banking, but the boredom of City life led him to switch careers and become an arms salesman. After ten years of dealing with tin pot dictators in faraway countries, he moved - perhaps appropriately - into public relations where, in this new incarnation, he had to deal with dictators of an altogether different type.

From his earliest days, Joll has written articles, features, short stories and reportage. One such piece of writing led to an early brush with notoriety when an article he had penned anonymously in 1974 for a political journal ended up as front page national news and resulted in a Ministerial inquiry. In 2012 Joll wrote the text for *Uniquely British: A Year in the Life of the Household Cavalry*, an illustrated account of the Household Cavalry from the Royal Wedding to the Diamond Jubilee, and in 2017 he published *The Spoils of War*. His yet to be published memoires, *Anecdotal Evidence*, promises to cause considerable consternation in certain quarters should it ever appear in print.

Since leaving the Army in 1975, Joll has been involved in devising and managing charity fund-raising events. This interest started in 1977 with The Silver Jubilee Royal Gifts Exhibition at St James's Palace and The Royal Cartoons Exhibition at the Press Club. In subsequent years, he co-produced 'José Carreras & Friends', a one-night Royal Gala Concert at the Theatre Royal Drury Lane; 'Serenade for a Princess', a Royal Gala Concert at the Banqueting House, Whitehall; and 'Concert for a Prince', a Royal Gala Concert staged at Windsor Castle (the first such event to be held there following the post-fire restoration).

More recently, Joll has focused on devising, writing, directing and sometimes producing events primarily for military charities. These include in various different roles the Household Cavalry Pageant (2007); the Chelsea Pageant (2008); the Diamond Jubilee Parade in the Park (2012); the British Military Tournament (2010-2013); the Gurkha Bicentenary Pageant (2015); the Waterloo Bicentenary National Service of Commemoration & Parade at St Paul's Cathedral (2015); the Shakespeare 400 Memorial Concert (2016); The Patron's Lunch (2016), the official London event to mark The Queen's 90th Birthday and *The Great War Symphony* to be premiered in 2018 at the Royal Albert Hall. In 2017, Joll was appointed Regimental Historian of the Household Cavalry.

INTRODUCTION

The determination of modern biographers to strip-off the shoes and socks of their subjects and expose their feet of clay is well established. However, the revelation in *Book 1* of *The Speedicut Papers* that Brigadier General Sir Harry Flashman VC, one of the greatest heroes of the Victorian age, was nothing more than a Paris-based remittance man and a plagiarising fraud will come as a shock to many, as will the disclosure that for two hundred and fifty years there has existed a secret society at the heart of the British Establishment dedicated to intervening in the affairs of the nation.

These facts only emerged with the unearthing of a box buried in a Leicestershire field. But had it not been for the coincidence that I am a fan of *The Flashman Papers*,[1] and that for twenty years I was a public relations consultant specialising in the property sector, *The Speedicut Papers* would not have come into my possession and I would not have recognised them for what they are: the hitherto unpublished record of the life and times of Colonel Sir Jasper Speedicut, soldier, courtier, bi-sexual and reluctant hero who, throughout his long life, was the friend of the *soi disant* national hero, Harry Flashman.

The story begins when, some years ago, my public relations company won the account of Swat International Developments Ltd, a real estate development company based in Pakistan. One of Swat's first acquisitions with which I had to grapple was the site of a former Army barracks on the outskirts of Ashby-de-la-Zouch in Leicestershire. Thanks to my company's expertise, Swat's steel and glass structure achieved its planning consent and the clearance of the site commenced. Some weeks later, I received an urgent call from my client to get up to Leicestershire without delay, for it appeared that one of the demolition company's diggers had unearthed a human skeleton.

---

[1] Editor's Note: *The Flashman Papers* is the collective name for the 13 volumes of the previously unpublished private memoirs of Brigadier General Sir Harry Paget Flashman VC KCB KCIE, which were expertly edited and annotated with extensive historical notes by George Macdonald Fraser and published between 1969 and 2005.

By the time I got to the site I was told by the police that their forensic expert had already established that the bones had not been buried recently. However, there were certain aspects of the human remains that were giving the police cause for concern. In particular, there was a large compression at the base of the skull, the lower arm bones had been joined behind the spine by a rusty set of iron manacles and there were a number of other unusual items found with the skeleton, including what appeared to be the blade of a dagger, a broken mace and a large sealed box.

Some weeks later the Coroner's Court announced that the remains were of a man who had been buried sometime in the early years of the 20th century. The Coroner returned a verdict of 'unlawful killing of a male in his early nineties, identity unknown, by person or persons unknown', and the case was closed. The bones were consigned to be cremated and the artefacts found with the skeleton were sent to the archives of the New Walk Museum in Leicester.

In the course of the police investigation, the sealed box had been opened. It was found to contain a large quantity of letters and other documents, which were arranged in bundles and appeared to cover the period from the second quarter of the 19th century to the first quarter of the 20th century. The letters were from someone who signed himself 'Speed' and were addressed to 'Flashy' – a close associate judging by the tone of the letters, so the Inspector said. The police had read a couple of the letters but then rejected them as evidence and resealed the box.

Given all the other issues with which I was grappling on behalf of my highly emotional client, I gave no further thought to the Ashby find. It was only in mid-2010 that my thoughts returned to the cache in the Leicester museum's storage department and I requested permission to examine them. It quickly emerged that, taken together, they were a detailed account in the form of letters, reports and newspaper cuttings stretching over eighty years or so, of the life of the man signing himself 'Speed'. I also recognised that at least some of the narrative and the references in the letters bore a striking resemblance to the accounts of his life given by Brigadier General Sir Harry Flashman in *The Flashman Papers*.

From that discovery, it was easy for anyone who, like me, had read either *Tom Brown's School Days* or *The Flashman Papers*,[2] to hazard a good guess that 'Flashy' was Harry Flashman, the Rugby School bully and 'Speed' was his partner in crime, Speedicut. The narrative which follows in this and the subsequent volumes of *The Speedicut Papers* draws principally upon the Leicestershire find but is supplemented by additional material I unearthed from a cache of Speedicut papers.[3]

Originally published in letter format as *The Speedicut Papers (Books 1 – 7)*, in response to popular demand I have re-edited the published volumes and *Books 8 & 9* into a narrative text. I have also omitted from the main text in this first volume the utterly deplorable early letters written by Speedicut to Flashman from Rugby School. However, for those readers of a prurient turn of mind, I have included them (with some editorial notes etc) in Appendix B. Finally, in the interests of clarity, I have annotated the text with dates and historical or explanatory background material.

CHRISTOPHER JOLL
www.jasperspeedicut.com

---

[2] Editor's Note: *Tom Brown's School Days* by Thomas Hughes, was first published in 1857. It is an account of Rugby School in the second quarter of the 19th century which included as a central character the ace cad, drunkard, bully and teenage womaniser, Harry Flashman and his sidekick Speedicut. Thomas Hughes (1822-1896) was a lawyer and an author. There is a statue of him in front of the Temple Reading Room at Rugby School. He had two daughters, Mary and Lilian; Lilian perished on the RMS *Titanic*.

[3] See Appendix A.

PRINCIPAL CHARACTERS IN ORDER OF APPEARANCE

Any similarity to persons now dead is <u>entirely</u> intentional

Jasper Speedicut – an officer and a gentleman, known as 'Speed'

Harry Flashman – a friend of Speedicut, known as 'Flashy'

Dr Thomas Arnold – the reforming headmaster of Rugby School

Miss Molly Theakston – a randy barmaid

Master George Arthur – a Rugby schoolboy and the object of Speedicut's adolescent affections

'Scud' East & Tom Brown – Rugby school boys, friends of George Arthur and enemies of Speedicut

Miss Letitia Prism – a governess and paid companion

Mrs Lydia Wickham – *née* Miss Lydia Bennett, a merry widow

The 3rd Marquess of Steyne – millionaire art collector, influential Establishment figure and head ('Great Boanerges') of a quasi-masonic secret society called 'The Brotherhood of the Sons of Thunder'

Lieutenant Colonel Parlby - Commanding Officer, Tenth Royal Hussars

The Hon Dudley Fortescue – a libertine and son of the Viceroy of Ireland

Mrs Rosanna James – *née* Gilbert; brothel keeper and, later, a notorious courtesan

Mr Sweeney Todd – a barber

Mrs Lovett – a baker

Captain Sir Richmond Shakespear – imperial adventurer and member of 'The Brotherhood of the Sons of Thunder'

Muhamad Khazi – a Kizilbashi irregular cavalryman with oriental morals

Captain Count Pavel Nikolayevich Ignatiev – a Russian aristocrat

Nikolai Pavlovich Ignatiev – the son of Count Ignatiev

The Rev Joseph Wolff – a Christian missionary of German-Jewish origin

Lance Corporal Frederick Searcy – a riding instructor in the 2nd Life Guards

Mrs Dora Empson – the unwilling wife of an elderly Major of Artillery

Captain Horace Blight – a former officer in the Royal Navy, later the Master of SS *The Pride of Poonha*

HRH Prince Albert of Saxe Coburg & Gotha – husband of HM Queen Victoria

HRH Prince Heinrich of Reuss – a minor German princeling

Johannes, Count von Schwanstein – an elderly Bavarian courtier

Mitzi, Countess von Schwanstein – Count von Schwanstein's much younger wife

HM King Ludwig I – the King of Bavaria

HRH Princess Alexandra of Bavaria – King Ludwig's youngest daughter

Signor Brunoni – also known as George Pennyworth, a travelling magician and illusionist

Mrs Lucretia Cazenove – the lusty wife of a City financier

Lady Mary Steyne – the only daughter of the 3rd Marquess of Steyne

Cornet George Heald – a young officer in the 2nd Life Guards

CHAPTER ONE: THE SHINY TENTH

As that scribbling spinster Jane Austen should have written, and as the pages which follow more than adequately illustrate, a fellow with a tolerable phiz, well-filled britches and understanding creditors should never lack for adventures between the sheets. But I anticipate. The story of my own steady, if at times dangerous, climb up the greasy *schwanzstucker* of life started on 20th December 1821 with my birth into an upper-middle class family which, for several generations, had been based at the Dower House, Acton Park, near Wrexham in north Wales. As my early years of soiled nappies, involuntary nocturnal emissions and bruised knees are of no interest to anyone, other than our then laundry maid and my late nanny, I'll skip over them and go straight to the end of my last term of imprisonment at Rugby School, a Spartan establishment to which I'd been sent at about the time my nuts started to drop.

As schools go Rugby wasn't a bad school, which is to say that, thanks to Flashy who was a term or two ahead of me, I didn't get much of a classical education. But I did get a very thorough grounding in drinking and fornication until, that is, my partner in debauchery was expelled towards the end of 1838. After that, whilst Flashy fossicked in Cardigan's fashionable 11th Hussars,[4] things at Arnold's Rugby went from tolerable to unbearable.[5] The slide down the slippery slope towards my own probable expulsion was a consequence of consecutive interludes of rogering involving a local barmaid called Molly Theakston and a school fag called George Arthur. This latter dalliance was followed by the unsolicited and

---

[4] The Earl of Cardigan (1797-1868) was at this time the Commanding Officer of the 11th Hussars.

[5] The Revd Dr Thomas Arnold (1795-1842) was educated at Corpus Christi College, Oxford. He was a zealous Anglican cleric, although distinctly anti-High Church, and a proselytising educational reformer. He packed a great deal into his relatively short life including making, whilst Headmaster of Rugby School, an indelible change to the principles of English secondary education, starting the Broad Church reforming movement, holding the chair of Regius Professor of Modern History at Oxford University and fathering seven children.

unwelcome intervention of two 'come-to-Jesus' second-years called Tom Brown and 'Scud' East.

Not long after I had put a temporary stopper in Brown and East,[6] the school broke up for the long Summer holidays, which I was destined to spend with my family in north Wales. It was not what I would have chosen but, after the dire end to the Summer Half, time spent at the Dower House at least afforded me opportunities to exercise *droit de seigneur* with the better-looking members of my Papa's domestic and stables staff, whilst I worked out how to avoid the carnal desert awaiting me when I returned to Rugby in September.

I was riding around our small estate one afternoon, shortly after I'd returned home, when the answer came to me. My Papa was a mean old devil and – so I reasoned - he might be pleased not to have to pay any more school fees. As I was clearly not destined for any of the varsities or the professions, I thought he might listen to reason and let me join Flashy in the 11th. Once I'd handed my nag back to our groom, I lost no time in putting this idea to Papa. After the usual outburst along the lines that I was a 'useless, lazy, good-for-nothing wastrel' etc etc, he said he would give it some thought. Where he was concerned that usually meant throwing a leg over Emily the parlour maid before taking a decision; Papa was a man who kept his brain in his balls.

Sure enough, later that afternoon, as I was loafing around the stables, I saw her descending from the hay loft pulling straw out of her hair, followed shortly after by my Papa, who gave me a most unpleasant look. The upshot was, as far as I could gather later from Mama, that the old boy seemed to think that pulling me out of Rugby wasn't such a bad idea and, thanks to some help from our neighbours, the old skinflint bought me a commission in the Shiny Tenth.[7] Mama was over the moon at this development, as

---

[6] See Appendix B.

[7] The Tenth Hussars probably had more nicknames than any other regiment in the British Army: The Shiny Tenth (because of their glittering uniforms), the Chainy Tenth (because of their unique chain-link cross belts), The Shiners, The China Tenth (because they were accused of being 'precious') and Baker's Light Bobs (after a famous, and later notorious, Commanding Officer, Valentine Baker).

I was to be based at Hounslow from where, so she said, 'the Regiment regularly escorts Her Majesty'. I wasn't sure what the escorts entailed but I was reasonably certain that Hounslow was a swamp on the outskirts of London. However, so Papa said, the following year the Regiment was to move to Northampton where the hunting couldn't be bettered.

It wasn't initially clear when I was to join, but there was a lot to do before that blessed day. Our neighbour, Lady Cunliffe, who had been Presented at Court in her youth and knew her way around Town, said I would need at least two nags, one for parade and one for hunting, and tons of kit for me and the horses. This, she advised, I should acquire in London as I would get a better fit and longer credit. I dropped a note to Flashy, who was based in Canterbury, telling him the good news and suggesting that we met up in Town.

· · ·

Editor's Note: There is then quite a significant gap in The Speedicut Papers, but it seems reasonable to assume that Speedicut probably met up with him in London, got his uniform and – sometime before Christmas 1839 or in early 1840 – reported for duty at the Cavalry Barracks in Hounslow for service with the Tenth Hussars, before moving to Northampton in March of that year.

· · ·

Meanwhile, whilst Flashy was attempting to lay the entire female populace of Canterbury end-to-end, I was in Northampton with the Tenth, where life was pretty relaxed, although some of the old timers complained that herding rioting Chartists wasn't at all the same thing as royal reviews, Court functions, and months and months in Brighton with nothing more to do than getting togged-up and parading at the Old Ship Rooms, the Pavilion or rogering the local Cyprians.[8] But for my money – or rather the old man's – anything was better than Rugby where I would have been listening to that prize booby Arnold's tiresome sermons.

---

[8] During the Regency, the Tenth Hussars were stationed wherever The Prince Regent happened to be.

As counties go Northamptonshire, which was dotted with grand estates, wasn't bad and the fences out with the Quorn were so good that the Regiment organised a grand steeplechase,[9] followed by a monumental party in the Mess. This was only marginally spoilt by the rumour that we were to ship out to Ireland later that year. I wasn't at all sure that policing stinking bog trotters was quite what I'd hoped to do in the Army, but it appeared that there was much fun to be had in Dublin. Anyway, the subalterns all prayed that we would be posted to Ireland's dingy capital and not sent to some wind-swept hell hole on the west coast or, worse still, that Horse Guards would have a change of mind and send us to Glasgow, where the Regiment had been posted some years previously. Apparently, in the opinion of my older colleagues, the second city of Scotland was an open sewer peopled by dwarves in skirts and raw-boned Presbyterian mamas with about as much humour as my charger's hindquarters.

Meanwhile, there was the proposal that Flashy had made when we'd met up in London: to induct me into a secret society he'd joined called 'the Brotherhood' or some such.[10] I couldn't see any reason not to accept, providing it didn't cost me too much as, having paid the bills for my kit, my Papa was in no mood to shell out any more rhino on my behalf. Besides which, I had no money of my own at that time – excepting my meagre Subaltern's pay which didn't amount to a hill of beans. Of course, there was always the chance that Papa would snuff it or I could persuade Mama to prize open his purse for me again.

However, of more immediate concern to me was a certain Mrs Lydia Wickham. I've already mentioned that we had a riot of a party in the Mess

---

[9] The Grand Military Steeplechase was first run in 1840 near Northampton. It is now run at Sandown Racecourse.

[10] Editor's Note: This is the first mention of 'the Brotherhood'. On first reading, I had assumed that it was a Masonic lodge or something similar and gave it no further thought. There was nothing unusual in Flashman, who had at least six months' more service than Speedicut, already having been inducted into a Masonic lodge, nor was there anything unusual in him inviting his closest friend to join. Some further clarity as to the nature, but not the identity, of 'the Brotherhood' emerged in the next batch of letters, which I have interspersed with some extracts from Mrs Speedicut's journal.

after the steeplechase; being the most junior, I was the Picket Officer on duty and Mrs Wickham, who was the widow of some johnnie in the Militia who had had his head blown off in a duel in Newcastle a few years before, was very much in evidence. According to Scudder the Riding Master, she's was a semi-permanent fixture around the garrison and the object of considerable interest on the part of a number of the senior officers. Pretty in a mature sort of way, during the aforementioned party she was gliding around the ante room, flirting mildly with the Field Officers, in a low-cut bodice that showed off her jugs to their best. I hadn't given her much thought and, anyway, I was deep in conversation with General Lygon - that's to say I was helping the old boy to stay upright - when who should sidle up to us but the woman herself.[11]

"Oh, General Lygon," she purred, "won't you introduce me to this new young officer?" Lygon – who could hardly stand let alone speak – belched out that I was called Deepcut and promptly keeled over.

"Poor man, he is obviously quite overcome by the heat! Perhaps we should make him more comfortable... Could you give me a hand, Captain Deepcut?"

Before I could tell her that my name wasn't Deepcut and I wasn't a Captain, she had one of his arms and I had no choice but to grab t'other. Thank God, we weren't in full view of our Commanding Officer, Colonel Parlby, or I might have been doing extras until the following Easter for, as we both bent down together, my nose went straight between her tits. She gave a little squeak of surprise, but at the same time I felt those two warm balloons tense and it was as much as I could do to extract myself without leaving behind half my newly grown 'tash.

At that moment, I heard the clock strike the hour and I remembered that I had to inspect the Guard, so I rather regretfully made my apologies and legged it off to the Guard Room. Anyway, about half an hour later I was sauntering back to the Mess, having done my duty for the evening and

---

[11] The Hon Henry Beauchamp Lygon (1784-1863), later 4th Earl Beauchamp and Colonel of the Tenth Hussars.

wondering what to do once the party closed, when I felt two gloved hands cover my eyes from behind.

"Coo-ee! Guess who?"

As I'd already had my nostrils force fed with her perfume, I recognised who it was immediately. But before I could say a word, she had pulled me behind an empty carriage, despite the fact that there was a coachman by the horses' heads. Thank heaven it was a dark night for, without so much as a 'by your leave' she prized open my britches, sank to her knees, flipped out my principal asset and started to give me – well, I don't need to spell it out, do I? Anyway, the woman was an expert. Just as she was about to bring me to the point of no return, I heard footsteps on the other side of the carriage. I froze, but Mrs Wickham was too busy with my 'midlands' to hear anything and carried on regardless.

"Climb-up, m'dear," I heard Colonel Parlby say to someone, followed by a creaking of carriage springs.

God, I thought, any moment now the coachman will be getting-up on the box on our side of the carriage. I tried to pull Mrs W off but, even though my prick was shrinking rapidly from the fear that was now coursing through my body, she remained fixed to it like a limpet. In a desperate attempt to avoid catastrophe, I swung my cloak around her kneeling form. At this point the wretched woman must have realised that something was up, for she detached her lips.

"What's going on?" she asked. But afore I could tell her to shut-up, the Colonel intervened.

"Who's that?" Judging by a further creaking of coach springs, he then leant out of the window on my side of the carriage.

"You, sir," he called out, "who are you and what are you doing?"

I had no choice but to turn on the spot, hoping and praying that Mrs W would have the sense to stay put and that she would remain hidden under my cloak.

"It's me, Colonel - Jasper Speedicut…"

"Speedicut? I thought you were inspecting the Guard."

"I was, Colonel," I replied, as I saw out of the corner of my eye the coachman approaching from the direction of the horses.

"So, what are you doing in the bushes?"

"Err, nothing, Colonel, just takin' the night air."

It was the best I could think of at short notice and anyway the coachman was staring at me over his shoulder as he climbed onto the box.

"A likely story," the Colonel reposted. "See me in the morning!" He then ordered the coachman to whip-up and the carriage pulled away.

In that moment, I saw my whole life collapsing in ruins about me. The coachman was bound to tell Parlby what I was sure he'd seen and I'd be drummed-out of the Regiment before the next day was over. Meanwhile, Mrs Wickham had crawled out from under my cloak. To my surprise she said nothing but, with considerable coolness, pulled a mirror from out of her reticule – which she angled to catch the light from the torches on the porch – smiled and then dabbed her lips with the edge of a gloved finger.

"Don't forget to adjust your dress, dear," she said, "and do close your mouth or the Colonel will think you've just been down on me!"

Then she turned on her heel and marched off to the gate whilst I staggered back to the Mess and headed straight for my room, where I lay on my bed staring at the ceiling. All I could think of was not why Mrs Wickham had singled me out for her favours, but the certainty of my disgrace the following morning. I slept not a wink and shortly after First Parade, with my stomach in such turmoil that I couldn't face breakfast, I made my way over to Regimental Headquarters. Baird the Adjutant looked up as I entered the outer office.

"Ah, Speedicut, come to see the Colonel, have you?" I nodded. "Well, he's told me to deal with you. It's a week's extras for piddling in the bushes. Now bugger off!"

And that was it. No drum head Court Martial, just a week of extra Orderly Officer duties after which I'd be free to see more of the randy widow. I nearly fainted with relief.

In October, the Order finally came through that we Shiners were off to Ireland in the New Year to maintain 'good order and discipline' amongst the reeking Celts and other assorted heathens. But the destination, thank God, was Dublin, so there would be plenty of parties and routs to fill in the time between stringing-up assorted bog trotters. To celebrate our departure to the land of rain-soaked peat, and despite the fact that 'the Tenth don't dance',[12] a ball in the Mess was organised for after Christmas. I wrote to Flashy, inviting him as my guest, and to my Mama to ask if my sister Lizzie could come. In due course, the news from the Dower House was that Lizzie could only attend the ball if she was chaperoned by her governess, Miss Prism. That was a bit of a poser, for the Prism woman was about as much fun as a wet week-end in Glasgow. Hey, ho, I thought, perhaps I could palm her off on Scudder, who was unmarried and about her mark. I'd get him to show her the 'horse with the green tail',[13] as that would get her out of Lizzie's hair for an hour or two.

But before the post-Christmas festivities, I and the other new Subalterns were sent on a week's course with the Tins to brush-up our ceremonial drills,[14] in preparation for the escorts we would have to provide in Dublin

---

[12] At a ball in Dublin in 1824, given by the Lord Mayor and attended by most of the eligible daughters of the burghers of the city, the aristocratic officers of the Tenth Hussars - in order to avoid being presented – declared that "the Tenth don't dance". This was widely, and sarcastically, circulated around the rest of the Army.

[13] Editor's Note: "Do you want to see the horse with the green tail?" is an old seduction 'line' used by cavalrymen with naïve, wide-eyed young lady visitors to cavalry barracks. It almost invariably leads to a 'fate worse than death'.

[14] One of the nicknames for either the 1st or 2nd Life Guards, usually at this time based in London or Windsor, and – then as now - the acknowledged experts at mounted ceremonial.

for the Viceroy. A spell in London would also give me a chance to catch up with Flashy and find out some more about his 'Brotherhood', which sounded like fun even if it was a bit mysterious. All that Flashy had told me at this point was that the 'Brothers' were all men of influence, which rather begged the question as to what he was doing in their company.

On the night before I left for the capital, I had dinner (again) with the widow Wickham. She was really a bit too old for me, but she was an 'education' in the bedroom department - and there wasn't much choice around Northampton anyway, other than overweight barmaids and a couple of the senior officers' wives who'd been trying to catch my attention.

Needless to say, the week in London was even more exhausting than a night with the widow Wickham. Quite how I managed to get on my horse the morning after I'd dined with Flashy was a mystery. Luckily the other chaps were also in a fair state of disrepair, so we all looked and performed about the same on the Row. Nonetheless, I heard one of the Tins' Corporals – who were a very superior lot and insisted on being addressed as 'gentlemen'– make some pretty sharp remarks about the 'lack of standards in the line cavalry'. This was damned cheek from a bloody Cheesemonger,[15] albeit rather a good looking one.

The afternoon after our debauch on Piccadilly, Flashy introduced me to his Brotherhood chum, the Marquess of Steyne. He was charming, rather intimidating and not exactly forthcoming about the society he headed: he said that I had to 'commit' before he would 'reveal'. Well, if thought, if Flashy was happy to join on those terms then so was I, although it would mean having to work on Mama to get the old man to stump up

---

[15] Editor's Note: The two Regiments of Life Guards traced their origins back to the mounted bodyguard raised by King Charles II from amongst his friends prior to the Restoration in 1660. To the present-day officers in The Life Guards address all their NCOs and ORs collectively as 'gentlemen' and the rank title of Corporal, rather than Sergeant (meaning 'servant') as in other regiments, is used. One of the nicknames of the 2nd Life Guards arising from the fact that, at this time, many of the officers' families were reputed to have made their fortune 'in trade'. The 1st Life Guards was an altogether more aristocratic regiment.

the necessary moolah to pay my entrance fee. But, I thought, being able to tell her that the show was run by a Marquess will help.

It did and, thanks to Mama's best efforts, my guv'nor decided that my joining the Brotherhood was not such a bad idea after all and sent me a bag of sovs, with a letter saying that I was never to call on him again for money this side of the second coming and that the less of me he saw at Acton the better. Fortunately, I'd had the foresight to tell my Mama that I needed rather more than Flashy had told me was required, so I was able to pay my sub and settle both my Mess bill and the debit side of the betting book. Even so, I knew that I would have to be more careful going forward, particularly as the widow Wickham kept dragging me past a jeweller's shop in Northampton. I didn't think it was a ring she was after, but rather something she could pop once the Shiners had crossed over to the Emerald Isle.

In the meantime, there was the Regimental Ball to be enjoyed. I took well-separated rooms at the George for Flashy, Lizzie and the Prism crone and wrote telling him that I'd also laid on a carriage to get them all to and from the Mess.

. . .

Editor's Note: Whether or not Flashman heard from Speedicut before setting off for Northampton is unclear, but it seems that he did get to the George Inn before the Speedicut party in Lady Cunliffe's barouche, as the following letter from Miss Prism to Mrs Speedicut makes clear.

. . .

Madam

You asked me to inform you of our safe arrival in Northampton and this I can confirm.

Mr Jasper had to leave for the barracks as soon as we arrived, but his friend Mr Flashman, who was already installed at the inn, was most amiable and saw us safely into our rooms, which are most comfortable.

However, this morning when I awoke I discovered that the publican's lady – a most superior person from, she tells me, Bow – had misallocated the rooms and that I have the view and Miss Elizabeth has none. So, I have arranged for our bags to be moved after breakfast. Miss Elizabeth protested that this was not necessary, but our new Rector, Dr Chasuble, who quite by coincidence is staying at the George on his way to London, came to my assistance and persuaded Miss Elizabeth that she should indeed have the room with the view! So that is now all settled and our bags have been moved.

Mr Jasper and his friend Mr Flashman are to take us for a drive later this morning and then I will ensure that Miss Elizabeth rests before the Ball this evening.

Respectfully yours,

Letitia Prism

But there was trouble brewing as a letter from Speedicut to his mother, probably written in some haste the morning following the ball, reveals:

Dearest Mama

I send this brief letter to you by Elizabeth's hand.

Although the ball was a huge success, and Elizabeth was much admired by all, there was an unfortunate incident later last evening for, some time after Elizabeth and Miss Prism returned to their hotel, an intruder broke into Miss Prism's room and attempted to assault her. She cried out and the publican came to her assistance. Her assailant got away, but enquiries are now being made.

Needless to say, Miss Prism was most distressed, which is why I have returned her to Acton with Elizabeth without delay.

Your loving son,

Jasper

CHAPTER TWO: FLASHMAN'S DISGRACE

It didn't take much imagination to understand what had happened: dear old Flashy, ever the randy womaniser, had clearly selected Lizzie as his next prey – of course, I'd have had to call him out if he'd succeeded - but did not know that Miss Prism had swapped rooms with her earlier that morning. One can easily imagine the shock to the Prism woman's nervous system when confronted with a priapic Cherrypicker in the early hours of the morning.

Unfortunately for him, Flashy's base instinct to flee betrayed him and the truth of what had happened soon dawned in Northampton. Baird was ordered by the Colonel to make enquiries which resulted in the landlord of the George identifying the culprit, who had compounded matters by leaving the inn without paying. The upshot was that Baird was ordered to send a report to Lord Cardigan, who – so it emerged - was decidedly unhappy to say the least and minded to cashier Flashy then throw him to the Peelers. Fortunately, Lord Steyne intervened and was able to square away the 11th on the condition that Flashy resigned and left the country to avoid the larceny, assault and attempted rape charges that had been filed against him. Whilst all this was fizzing away, I received a note from Steyne requesting a date on which to induct me into the Brotherhood. As it happened, I had a week-end leave coming up before the Dublin embarkation, so I tooled down to London to sign on the dotted line and hand over my bag of ill-gotten gold to his nibs.

As to what happened next, I'm not sure that I will ever forgive Flashy, who must have been wetting himself with mirth in Paris, in the full knowledge of what was in store for me. But I anticipate. In his letter, Lord Steyne had told me to be 'on parade' exactly at midnight at his palace in St James's Square. In order not to be late, I arrived in the square in good time and hung around by the house until I heard the local church clock start to strike twelve. On the last chime, I lifted the knocker but, before it fell, the door was opened by a flunkey who, without a word, led me across the hall and into Lord Steyne's study, which was dimly lit but warm and welcoming with a blazing fire in the hearth. A moment or two later Steyne himself entered.

"Mr Speedicut," he said without further ado as he wagged my paw, "are you ready to be inducted into the Brotherhood of the Sons of Thunder?" I said that I was, although I still had no idea what it was really all about. "In that case I must ask you to prepare yourself for the rites. Behind that screen," he said, indicating one in the corner of the room, "you will find a silk dressing-gown and a hood. Please remove all your clothes, then put on the gown and the hood. When you are ready, please say so."

That was a ball out of deep cover, as all that I was expecting to do was to hand-over the subscription, sign the members' book and get back to my lodgings. But I did as he told me and walked over to the screen. Behind it I found a chair and a small table. Folded on the chair was a black silk dressing-gown and a matching black hood with a draw string, not unlike the bag that's put over a condemned man's head just before he takes the 'long drop'. I didn't much like the idea of the bag but, once I was stripped and in the gown, I put it on anyway. It all seemed a bit bizarre, but after all, what harm could I come to? A few minutes later I called out that I was ready.

"Please confirm that the hood is over your head, it is drawn tight around your throat and that you can see nothing." I said that was the case. "Then remain where you are."

I heard a door open and close and, sometime later, I heard it open again. There was a rush of cold air that did nothing to make me feel more comfortable and then, without warning, I felt two sets of hands grip me by each of my upper arms. In shock, I was silently propelled rather than led to what I assume was the centre of the study. We stopped and, without a word of warning, I was spun on the spot until I was so dizzy that I could hardly stand up. Thoroughly disorientated, I was then again propelled forward and, judging from the icy flags that now replaced the warm carpet under my bare feet, we had moved into another room. A few paces into this new chamber we halted and the hands released me. It was horribly cold. My skin rose into goosebumps and my teeth started chattering from both the icy air and, I'll admit it, an un-named fear that was starting to overcome me.

Just as I was wondering what was next in store for me, I heard the muffled notes of an organ and, at the same time, I felt a pair of hands undo the dressing-gown's chord around my middle and then another pair of hands slipped the gown from my shoulders. I was now standing naked, save for the bag over my head, and I instinctively covered my family jewels with my hands.

"Remove your hands from there and keep them by your side," boomed out a voice that I did not recognise. But I did nothing. "I say again, Mr Speedicut, remove your hands. Obedience is the first requirement of a Brother."

Rather reluctantly, I did as I was told. Meanwhile, the organ droned on in the background. The effect was even more chilling than the cold of the room.

"Mr Speedicut," the voice said again, "you have been invited to become a member of the Brotherhood of the Sons of Thunder and you have agreed to join. Is that correct?" I said that it was, although this came out as a squeak rather than a proper response.

"I have said already," the voice went on, "that obedience – blind obedience – is the first requirement of a Brother. There is a second requirement, which is to take the Oath of the Brotherhood.

"However, before you take the Oath, your obedience must be tested. If, at any point, you fail to obey my orders, you will be removed from this place and you will have no further dealings with the Brotherhood. If you satisfy the Brothers here assembled and our leader, the Great Boanerges, on the first requirement, then and only then will you be invited to take the Oath. Is that absolutely clear?"

I squeaked that it was, whilst all the time wishing that I had never listened to Flashy and that I was, instead, miles from Steyne House safely tucked-up in bed with Mrs Wickham.

"Very well," said the voice. "On my word, you will take three – and only three – paces forward." There was a pause. "Now!"

I moved first my left, then my right foot. Nothing happened. But, as I was lowering my left foot for the second time, I stepped into a void. Instead of landing on the floor, however, I plunged feet first into icy cold water. The shock was so great that it knocked the wind out of my body and I didn't – indeed I couldn't – even let out a cry of surprise. However, the pool wasn't deep and in a moment my feet hit the bottom leaving me with my head and shoulders out of the water. The bag now clung to my face, but still I could see nothing. Panic rose in my chest and without thinking I made to remove the bag.

"Keep your hands by your side!" roared the voice.

Now, whilst every instinct in my body told me to drag the bag off my head and flee from the room as fast as my feet would take me, I lowered my hands back below the water. Perhaps it was the discipline that I had so recently learned in the riding school, perhaps it was just fear, but I seemed now to be behaving like an automaton rather than as a rational being.

"Walk three paces forward." I did so, stubbing my toes on what I assumed must be the other side of the pool. "There are three steps to your front. Climb them."

Rather shakily, I did so, conscious that I must have looked a sorry sight to whoever else was in the room, with my wedding tackle – I was sure - reduced by cold and fear to the size of a couple of hazelnuts and a small gherkin. I stood there shivering, dreading what was to happen next.

"Mr Speedicut," said the voice again, "you have passed the test of air and water. Only the test of fire remains. Are you ready?" I nodded feebly, for

I seemed to have lost the power of speech. "Then stay exactly where you are." Two things then happened almost at once.

First, the muffled drone of the organ suddenly rose to an almost deafening blast of full-throated music. The effect on my already battered senses was quite terrifying and I nearly passed out. At the same time, I felt the air around me starting to change. Instead of the penetrating cold, a warm breeze was blowing around my nether region. At first it was rather pleasant and welcome, but as the music grew louder so the temperature rose. In a matter of minutes, it was almost unbearable. Instead of air and water chilling me to the bone, it was sweat that now coursed down my body. I was about to cry out in pain and scream to be released, when the music and the infernal blast subsided together. A short while later the music had stopped and the air temperature reverted to its previous chill.

If, at that moment, I could have got my hands around Flashy throat he would not have lived to see the dawn. Whatever the benefits offered by the Brotherhood, in that instance I most sincerely wished that the bugger had never mentioned it to me. But if I thought that the initiation was over I was wrong. The directing voice broke the silence.

"Mr Speedicut, you have done well and you have completed the three tests of air, water and fire to the satisfaction of the Brothers here assembled and the Great Boanerges. There remains but the Oath. Are you now willing to take the final step?" Well, I thought, I've got this far, so what the hell?

"Yes," I replied in a voice that, to my surprise, was far firmer than I felt.

"Good," said the voice. "Mr Speedicut, raise your arms." God, I thought, what next? Then the voice said: "Robe him!"

But, instead of being put back into the silk dressing-gown, I felt a heavy robe being manoeuvred over my hands and head whilst at the same time my feet were eased into soft slippers. Once the robe was in place, a pair of hands then undid the bag and removed it from my head. Blinking in the light, I looked around me and found myself standing in a high-vaulted, heavily gilded circular room lit by candles. It resembled the inside of a

Catholic chapel. In the centre of the room was the pool into which I had so recently tumbled. Around the perimeter of the room were black robed figures, each armed with a naked sword held point down, their heads completely encased - save for eye holes - in tall conical caps of the type worn by the Inquisition. It was the most menacing environment in which I have ever been and I almost shat myself in fear.

The figure nearest to me, whose robe was heavily embroidered with gold thread, stepped forward and extended his hand, on which there was a red-stoned gold ring, and led me quaking across the floor to a black-draped table which bore a gilded mace, a roll of parchment, a quill pen and a dagger. The figure took up a position on one side of the table and ordered me to stand opposite him with the table between us. Meanwhile the other figures had left their positions around the chamber and formed a semi-circle behind me. The air of menace, that already had me nearly crapping myself with fear, deepened.

"Step-up to the table," ordered the figure and I recognised the voice of Lord Steyne. "Open your robe."

The robe had a row of buttons from the neck to the waist, so I opened them. This done, Steyne picked up the dagger and rested its point just above my exposed left tit; with his other hand, he handed me the parchment scroll. At the same time, the figures behind and around me raised their swords and rested the points around my exposed neck. If I had moved I would have been impaled on one or more of their points – in any event, I was pretty sure that if I faltered I would be impaled anyway.

"Please read the Oath aloud,[16] Mr Speedicut," said Lord Steyne and I proceeded to do so. Steyne then took the parchment back from me and, taking my right hand in his left, he moved the point of the dagger from my breast and, hardly before I knew it, sliced a small cut in my 'walking out' finger. [17]

---

[16] See Appendix C.

[17] Editor's Note: 'walking out finger' is Army slang for the middle finger of the right hand.

"Sign the Oath with your blood," he said quietly and, this done, he went on: "In my capacity as the Great Boanerges I welcome you, *Brother Speedicut*, to The Brotherhood of the Sons of Thunder."

At these words, the sword points around my neck vanished, the Great Boanerges and the rest of the figures removed their hats and, suddenly, I was being patted and congratulated. My head in a whirl, all I could think was that I wouldn't be able to use that finger in any of the local tarts or toughs for a week or two until it healed.

The ceremony over, we all filed back into Steyne's study where there was a tray loaded with champagne. He told me to get dressed but to put the robe on over the top; he also said to leave the subscription, about which I had completely forgotten, on the table behind the screen. Once changed, I walked over to the fire where Steyne, or the Great Boanarges as I had to call him, introduced me to the rest of the Brotherhood. He explained that a number were not present as they were 'out in the field' as he put it. He then took me to one side.

"Brother Speedicut, you are now a member of a most significant group of people who, since the formation of the Brotherhood, have had a hand in many of the great events of history: to give you but one example, Napoleon's defeat at Waterloo would not have been possible had not one of our Brothers tampered with the Corsican Corporal's wine. Much will be expected of you."

Well, that was a big statement and I wondered if it could be true? Anyway, in the heat of the moment - as it were - I asked him why, with so many heroes-in-the-making in the Brotherhood, he had taken on Flashy and me.

"It takes all sorts to make the world go around, Brother Speedicut." And that was it. I wondered whether the Brotherhood was running a bit short of heroes and the right answer should have been 'any port in a storm'.

About half an hour later we disrobed and the party broke-up. As I was leaving, the GB said that he had something in mind for me and that he would be in touch. Meanwhile, I was to get on with Regimental soldiering.

...

Editor's Note: There is a break in the narrative which recommences at the Cavalry Barracks, Dublin Castle in July 1841.

...

Dublin wasn't bad and our quarters in the Royal Barracks were pretty decent, but there wasn't a great deal to do, beyond looking forward to the opening of the hunting season in September and I was starting to think that, perhaps, I was mis-spending my youth in a round of far too innocent pleasures when I was asked to dine with the Viceroy. I had met Lord Ebrington before this,[18] as he had held a reception for the officers of the Tenth when we first moved-in, but I hadn't seen much of him since. He was a pretty decent old cove and, with the Shiners to adorn his rather dreary Court, has taken to asking the Picket Officer on the Castle Guard to dine with him and his missus whenever he's in residence – and my turn had come up.

So, I pulled on my best Regimentals and rode over to Viceregal Lodge in Phoenix Park. The dinner was a fairly dreary affair, enlivened only by the presence of the Hon Dudley Fortescue,[19] Ebrington's youngest son and a well set-up, good looking chap just a year older than me. After dinner, he suggested we take a turn around the garden and we fell to talking about the delights or otherwise of Dublin. I said that I had found it to be a pretty dull sort of dump and he said that, *au contraire*, it had some 'hidden charms – if you know where to look.' The upshot was that we agreed to meet the following evening for a 'tour of the town'.

At six pm the next day, Fortescue turned up at the Mess in a closed carriage and off we set. Now, I may have been in Dublin for five months but, to be honest, there hadn't been much time-off outside barracks and, anyway, with Young Irelanders lurking around every corner – or so the politicals

---

[18] Viscount Ebrington (1783-1861) later 2nd Earl Fortescue. Viceroy of Ireland 1839-1841.

[19] The Hon Dudley Fortescue (1820-1909) was a Liberal politician. He married his first cousin – they had no children.

told us – there hasn't been much incentive to stray off the straight and narrow.[20] But Fortescue was clearly an old hand and got the carriage to drop us at the end of Montgomery Street – an area we had been warned-off as being full of rancid bog trotting thugs, so this was my first visit.

"Welcome, Speed, to the Monto!" Dudley announced and proceeded to take me down what the Doctor would have called 'the route to the pit of damnation'. For Montgomery Street, or the Monto as the locals called it, turned out to be just one enormous knocking shop – that is to say, it was a whole street of pleasure. Fortescue told me that there were more than two thousand tarts working the pavements and that it was the biggest whorehouse district in Europe.[21] On reflection, I'm not surprised that we were told to stay clear of the place, although not for the reason given.

Fortescue clearly knew his way around, for he steered me about halfway up the street to a small door on which he knocked three times. A young tart opened it and we were shown into a very over-decorated parlour, all plush and gilt, with the curtains drawn and some lamps in corners. It took a while, after the fading daylight outside, to get accustomed to the gloom and, before I did, the door at the far end opened and a middle-aged, rather overweight man, whose paunch was threatening to break loose from his velvet waistcoat, sidled in with a small cigar in one be-ringed hand and a glass of fizz in the other.

"My dear Dudley," he drawled in a soft Irish accent, "and who have you brought to see your old granny this evening?"

"This, my dear Fingal, is Cornet Speedicut who is with the Tenth Hussars at the barracks. Speed, this is Mr Fingal O'Flahertie who owns this, err, establishment." We shook hands, that is to say I gripped his and it nearly dissolved in mine, so soft was it.

---

[20] The Young Irelanders were the forerunners of the Fenian Brotherhood and the Irish Republican Army (IRA). They were dedicated to gaining Irish independence through violence against the British; they staged an unsuccessful uprising in 1848.
[21] Speedicut's description of this extensive red-light area is largely correct. It was cleaned up at the start of the 20th century but not before it had been visited, in the late 1880s, by the future King Edward VII and his son the Duke of Clarence.

"Ooh," the old queen purred, "well, she's *very* welcome – as are you, you *naughty* boy!"

Now, I take my pleasures wherever I find them, but I must say that I found the Irishman's manner quite hard to stomach and I was feeling less than comfortable. However, before I could tell Fortescue that I would prefer to go elsewhere, O'Flahertie piped up:

"Now, Mr Speedicut, you must tell me what takes *your* fancy. I know what Dudley likes, which is why he has probably brought you to this palace of the pleasures, but as for you... we have boys, girls, boys and girls, girls and girls, or boys and boys – you can watch or you can take part – or you can do *both*. The only thing that my humble little establishment does NOT provide is the more *brutal* forms of pleasure. For *that* you will have to go to Mrs Rosanna James's further up the street. [22] So, just have a peek in here and let me know what you fancy."

He drew back a curtain with a flourish and revealed a window into the room next door. What I saw there completely took my breath away.

---

[22] Eliza Rosanna James (1819-1861), *née* Eliza Gilbert, started life in Ireland, married a British Army officer and moved to India with him, but in 1840 she left India without him. This is the first published evidence that she returned to England via Dublin.

CHAPTER THREE: A CLOSE SHAVE

Through the window I could see that the room was full of boys and girls in various stages of undress but all with one thing in common – a square of material tied to their arms with a number on it.

"There you are, dearie, take your pick. Guests go first! The even numbers are ten bob and the *odd* numbers – if you'll forgive my little joke – are seventeen and six. That's by the hour of course; I'll give you a discount if you want to stay the night, but we don't serve breakfast and we don't take cheques – *do* we, Dudley!"

Well, it'd been a few months since I had last spent an evening of fun and games – and that had been with the widow Wickham – so I decided, for old times' sake, to have a mixed bag of sweets and chose a black-haired boy, with the number three around his arm, and a red-haired girl, who reminded me of Molly Theakston of not-so-sacred memory, with the number sixty-nine around hers. Dudley picked out a couple of boys and O'Flahertie showed us up to separate rooms on the first floor.

"That's right, dearie, make y'self at home. There's a wash basin over there in the corner, but all my boys 'n girls are clean so you don't need to worry on *that* score."

And with that he pulled off the cover of a large bed in the middle of the room, lowered the lamp and withdrew through the door, blowing me a kiss as he went.

No sooner had I dragged off my kit and thrown myself on the bed than the two I had chosen slipped in through the door, dressed in no more than a thin cotton gowns. In no time at all, we were down to business. I won't bore you with the details but I will tell you that they had more tricks in their boxes than either Molly, the widow Wickham or any of my other previous experiences had prepared me for. An hour later, and feeling as though I had just been point-to-pointing on a pulling nag, there was a tap on the door and O'Flahertie's voice called out:

"Time's up, dear, unless you want a change of entertainment. If not, there's a glass of bubbles waiting for you in my parlour as is *naughty* Master Dudley, who never takes long, poor love."

With that my partners grabbed their robes and slipped out of the room without a backward glance. Well, they were professionals. I pulled on my togs and headed down the stairs.

"How was it?" asked Fortescue, with a leer on his face. "Time for dinner?"

I nodded, drank the cheap fizz in a couple of pulls, handed O'Flahertie the price of the evening and headed back out into the street hard on Fortescue's heels. We found his carriage waiting for us at the end of the Monto and, in high good humour, we headed off to a tavern he knew on the other side of town. Over dinner we talked about mutual friends – he had been to Eton and was presently up at Oxford, so he knew some of the Rugby crowd – and then he mentioned that he knew old Steyne who had told him to look me up. I thought nothing of it at the time, but I have wondered since if Steyne knew quite what Fortescue would be introducing me to.

And that was the start of my real life in Dublin which, thanks to Dudley Fortescue, developed rapidly into a constant whirl of race meetings, balls at Dublin Castle, dinners at Viceregal Lodge and further debauchery in the Monto. But you can have too much of a good thing and by September I was practically on my chin strap with tiredness. Fortescue, who seemed to have a quite insatiable appetite for fleshly delights, tried to drag me off to the Monto practically every night and usually headed for O'Flahertie's, which was frankly becoming a bit of a bore.

So, one night, just for variety, I tried Ma James's. Once I'd worked out the 'drills', I found it to be a lot more fun than even O'Flahertie's finest had to offer. To be fair to the old queen, his boys and girls were better looking than Ma James's tarts but their range of skills were extensive but somewhat conventional. Ma James herself was a damned fine-looking woman of about my age and reputed to be married to a soldier who she has dumped in India. She was very outspoken, and some of her views were bordering on the treasonable, but that didn't seem to bother her clientele for whom she specialised in the more painful end of the business. Now, after four very odd years at Rugby, I had had more than my fair share of being on the receiving end of the cane, so the opportunity to redress the balance was welcome – to say the least – and I spent a couple of evenings giving as good as I'd received from Arnold and others. As I was leaving a few evenings later, Ma James promised to let me lay into a local Catholic schoolmaster client of hers, who had apparently been told by God that he must receive two strokes for every one that he administered at his seat of learning. So, I tooled round there on the next night in the expectation of being able to pay back Arnold, albeit by proxy.

The James establishment was not nearly as plush as O'Flahertie's. In fact, it was decked out more like a prison or a prep school than a palace of the pleasures. The bedrooms were about as stark as a cell for the condemned with bare floors and plain iron bedsteads liberally festooned with manacles. Ma James told me on arrival that night that my schoolmaster was already in position and awaiting my attention. I wasn't sure exactly what to expect, so I hung my cloak and tile on a peg in the hall and followed my hostess's swaying rump up the rickety stairs to a room just off the landing on the second floor. It was rather smaller than those I had used before, the window was shuttered and barred and the only source of light was an old oil lamp on a chest of drawers, on which there also lay a cane 'schoolmasters for the use of' as the Quartermaster would have said. There was also a decanter of what looked like the local firewater with a glass next to it. There, in the middle of the room, was the usual bedstead and, sprawled on it face down and stark naked save for a hood over his head, was what – judging from his musculature – appeared to be a reasonably young man.

Ma James whispered to me that my victim liked the blows to be administered at fairly lengthy intervals and that his buttocks were the preferred target area. Should I wish to admonish him for his sins before administering the punishment that would be welcome and he was expecting at least two dozen of the best. It seems that his pupils had been particularly unruly earlier that day... As she slipped out of the door, Ma James said that she had left the whisky to provide me with the refreshment that she felt sure I would need in the course of my duties.

It'd been a tiring day, so I poured myself a large shot before stripping off my coat and giving the whip a few preliminary flicks to judge its weight and flexibility. As it swished through the air, I saw my victim's buttocks clench, presumably in anticipation of the pain to come. As this seemed to be part of his pleasure, I decided to keep him waiting a while longer. After a couple more pulls on the whisky – which had a rather strange taste that I ascribed to it being the Irish rather than the Scots-variety (neither holds a candle to French brandy, in my opinion, but then why should the Celtic fringes to produce anything better than distilled cat's piss?) – I approached the bed quietly, raised the whip over my shoulder and administered a cut that should have drawn blood. It didn't. Instead, the beak let out a moan of pure pleasure and started, would you believe it, to roger the mattress.

Despite the fact that I had given him only one stroke, and the whisky decanter was still half full, I was starting to feel quite light-headed, so I threw my waistcoat on top of my coat and set-to with a will, declining like a banshee and reciting 'amo... amas... amat' as I brought each blow down on his quivering and reddening posterior. It seemed to be appropriate (after all he was a schoolmaster), it was all the Latin that I could remember at short notice – and I was damned if I was going to copy Arnold and recite the Lord's Prayer.

I think I had got as far as 'amamus', and was really starting to enjoy m'self, when the room started to spin, my eyesight became blurred and I blacked out. The next thing I knew, I was coming-to in what seemed to be the same room. But, instead of the prostrate and writhing form of the naked beak manacled to the bed, it was me who was lying face-up staring at the grubby, fly-blown ceiling, chained at wrist and ankle. Judging from the shocking draught around my nether region, I too was in the altogether without even the benefit of a bag over my head.

As my noodle started to clear, I tried to puzzle out what had happened. My first thought was that this was Ma James's idea of fun – or perhaps Dudley was having a joke at my expense and had told Ma James that, despite my assertions to the contrary, I had a taste for being on the receiving as well as the giving end. Whatever had happened, and I did at least work out that the whisky must for some reason have been drugged, I was not afraid and I waited patiently for the situation to resolve itself. I had no sense of time but, as there was no light seeping through the shutters, it seemed that it was still the evening and, as my stomach wasn't rumbling, it also seemed fair to assume that it was still only a matter of hours if not minutes since I had arrived.

But nothing happened and, after a while, I must have drifted-off again into an untroubled sleep in which I was administering some well-aimed cuts with the flat of my sabre at the Doctor's scraggy rear-end, whilst Mrs Wickham was caressing my shoulder and practically suffocating me with her scent – and two badly dressed men just behind her were arguing about whether or not I should be sent to Todd's for a shave and how I would taste in one of Mrs Lovett's pies or some such nonsense. Well, it was a dream. Then I felt a smooth hand shaking me awake and I looked up into the eyes of my redoubtable hostess.

"I say, Rosanna, what's going on?" I spluttered as my eyes once again became accustomed to the light in the room. "Get me out of these clamps and give me my clothes. This is not at all my bag, as I thought I had made clear, and…"

"Shut up!" she cut-in with her faint Celtic accent, "and, if you value your life, listen to me."

I started to protest again and struggled to free my hands from the cuffs, but she clamped one paw over my mouth and with t'other she gave my nuts a painful twist.

"Be quiet and listen to me. You have become a pawn in a game you didn't even know was being played and, if you don't want to end up being removed from the board, you will co-operate and help us in the way we require." Ice was rapidly forming in my stomach and it was not the result of the draught I had felt earlier.

"I want you to meet my friends Mr Thomas Davis and Mr John Dillon..." and at that two shabbily dressed men stepped forward from behind Ma James and stared down at me.

"You won't have heard of them, so let me introduce you: Mr Dillon," and she indicated the man on her right, "is the editor and Mr Davis," she pointed to t'other, "the sub-editor of the *Morning Register*."[23]

Damned scribblers, I thought, what are they doing here? Was this perhaps some plot to embarrass me and discredit the Regiment? But before I could develop this thought she went on.

"Now whilst these gentlemen are *bona fide* journalists, they are also the leaders of a group which your government seems determined to suppress."

The ice in my stomach formed into a solid block that, in the north Atlantic, would have posed a hazard to shipping. For these were clearly Young Irelanders, who were about as dangerous a group of thugs and cut-throats as you could have found this side of Seven Dials – and, in my somewhat addled memory, I seemed to remember hearing their names mentioned in a briefing we had recently been given by a political.

"Mr Speedicut," said Dillon, "although most of Dublin hereabouts knows you to be little more than a young man with an overactive member, oi and my friend here know that, as well as being randy, you are also rich. And it is that attribute, not the one that seems now to have shrunk to the size of a button mushroom, which is of interest to us."

I started to protest through Ma James's fingers, but she gave my nuts another vicious twist that turned my protest to a yell which, if it hadn't been muffled by her hand, would have awoken the whole street.

---

[23] The *Morning Register* was a nationalist, Catholic newspaper.

"I suggest you lie still for a moment and listen to what Mr Dillon has to say," she said with a most unpleasant look on her face.

"Mr Speedicut, oi'll be brief," went on the cove who Ma James had identified as Dillon. "Moy organisation is badly in need of funds and we think that you are just the man to solve our problem.[24] So here's what you are going to do: in a moment, Mrs James is going to release your right hand – you are right handed, oi believe?" I nodded. "When she has done so, you are going to sign this letter which is addressed to your Commanding Officer. Oi will read it to you, because oi would nivver ask a man to sign a document unread. If you do not soign it, Mrs James will administer to you the same treatment you were so recently handing out to my fellow countryman, although she will be applying it to the front of your person rather than the rear. She will continue to administer the treatment until you agree to sign. Is that clear?" Again, I nodded as my bowels gave an ominous gurgle. "Very well, this is the letter to which oi hope, for your sake, you will shortly append your signature."

Dear Colonel

I am in the hands of the Young Irelanders who require a ransom for my safe return. The sum demanded is £1,000 in gold.[25] The money, which my father will provide, should be placed in a small, water-tight barrel and dropped off the Ha'penny Bridge across the Liffey by Merchant's Arch at midnight next Sunday week. If the barrel is safely recovered and its collection not pursued I will be freed. If neither of these conditions is respected, it will be my body which will float down the Liffey and the circumstances of my ignominious capture, whilst debauching myself in an establishment in Montgomery Street, will be sent to The Times of London.

On the head of my Mother I beg you to do as they demand,

Jasper Speedicut, Cornet

---

[24] Editor's Note: This was certainly true. It was only the arrival in the Young Irelanders of Davis and Dillon, who set about restoring the organisation's finances, that saved it from collapse.

[25] The equivalent today of about £200,000.

Ma Gilbert had removed her hand from my mouth, whilst keeping the other in place, and I thought for a moment before replying. If I signed then my reputation within the Regiment would be stained beyond repair, there was no guarantee that the guv'nor would stump-up the brass (in fact, I was certain that he wouldn't) and I would be sent on a watery voyage to the hereafter. And if I didn't sign, I would be flogged and then killed or worse. I decided to try and play for time and employ a technique which had worked well with Arnold. So, I started to blub. It didn't work and I stopped immediately when the bitch James released my nuts, picked up the cane and whacked me across the sole of my right foot. The pain was excruciating and drove all other thoughts from my brain.

"All right, all right!" I cried through clenched teeth. "I'll sign. Just release my hand and give me a pen and some ink."

The deed done, the murphys each gave me a stiff little bow and headed for the door. Ma James did not, but instead continued to stand over me with the cane in her right hand and a look of considerable pleasure now on her face.

"Well, Mr Speedicut," she leered, "at least you showed some common sense in signing. The question now is: what are we going to do with you whilst we wait for the barrel – or you – to drop into the Liffey in ten days' time?"

I didn't have an answer for that, but the prospect of remaining bollock naked and chained to a bed for the best part of two weeks was not an appealing one.

"It's clear we can't release you, but perhaps I should make you more comfortable." And with that she turned, grabbed my coat off the floor and threw it over me. "You'll be wanting some food too, I dare say, but I think first that another drop of Liffey water is called for – so be a good boy and drain this glass."

I knew what would happen if I swallowed the puggled firewater, but I also knew that, hog-tied as I was, there was little to be gained from resisting, so I took the glass with my free hand and drank. In no time at all I was back in la-la-land.

Sometime later, and it can't have been that long as the drugged brew seemed to be quite short-lasting, I came-to again to find that my right wrist was back in the manacle, but the bitch had put a smelly pillow under my head and my coat had been replaced by a rough blanket. As my head cleared I started to think. Trussed as I was, escape was out of the question and, anyway, I was naked and my clothes had disappeared from view. Release seemed unlikely as the prospect of the guv'nor stumping-up the fee was remote in the extreme, which just left rescue. At which I started to think hard. My absence would not go unnoticed and, at the latest, my failure to attend First Parade the next day would surely sound alarm bells, even if Dudley had failed to make an earlier report? Dudley also knew where I had been and would, surely, tell the authorities – at least I hoped to God he would – and in all probability the Peelers would search the James establishment. But if I could work all that out, then surely so too could James and her Celtic revolutionaries? The likelihood was that I would be moved and that was when I might, just might, be able to make a break for freedom. Oh, God, I prayed, if you give me that chance I will never sin again.

However, I'm not the religious type and whilst that prayer was heartfelt, it was offered-up with no real hope of being answered. So, it was shocking in more ways than one when, right on cue, the door burst open and in stumbled one of Ma James's customers, a tall cove with a ruddy face dressed in a gaudy red coat with the flap of his britches hanging open. He saw me, belched and said in the unmistakable tones of the truly drunk:

"Ho, ho – what have we here?"

But before I could answer, Ma James, who had clearly been right behind him, grabbed his collar, flung him out of the room and, from the clatter and groans which followed, either kicked or threw him down the stairs. Moments later she returned to the room, shutting the door firmly behind her.

"You are awake again, are you? Well, we've decided that you can't stay here – as has just been proved by that oaf who will shortly be rolling in the gutter outside with a knife in his ribs – so we're moving you to a friend of ours. He's a barber, so at least he'll keep you looking clean." This last remark reminded me of something that I thought I had heard earlier, but I couldn't remember precisely what.

"I'm going to release you now and you can get dressed, but you will take care not to make a false move or you will be joining your new friend in the Monto's sewer, with a neat hole in your back for good measure."

And I saw out of the corner of my eye that she was brandishing a small pistol. She then reached forward and unlocked my right wrist, stood back and threw the keys onto the blanket whilst all the time keeping the gun pointed at my chest. It would clearly have been foolish to disobey her, so I unlocked myself from the bed, rubbed my wrists to get the circulation going and then pulled on my clothes, which had been stacked neatly next to a chipped and soiled jerry under the bed. In all this time, I uttered not a word, for there seemed to be nothing to say.

Once I was up, she indicated the door and told me to move onto the landing and down the stairs. Could I, I wondered, make a break for it once I got to the street door and risk a bullet between the shoulder blades? But the bitch had anticipated me and friend Dillon and his partner, Davis, were positioned one inside and one outside the door, with a carriage drawn-up as close to the house as the overhang permitted. Davis pushed me into the conveyance, the door was slammed shut and, with a lurch, it made off down the street. With no real hope, I tried the doors and the windows, but the handles had been removed and I was locked-in. My prospects of release plunged as I realised that neither Dudley nor the authorities would have any clue as to my location once I was away from the Monto.

For what seemed an eternity, but was probably not more than half-an-hour, the carriage rumbled over the cobbles and then started to lurch from side to side as it hit what I assumed to be a rutted turnpike. I supposed we were leaving Dublin and, with it, any remaining hope of rescue. My spirits plunged still further and I did what Arnold would have expected of me:

I started to pray. I had just repeated for the twentieth time my promise to the Almighty never again to err from the straight and narrow if he would only intervene, when the carriage pulled up abruptly. The door was wrenched open by a grubby looking cove with sunken cheeks and long, dirty hair falling over his collar, a cocked pistol in one hand and a lamp in the other. He beckoned me out onto the muddy road and then, without a word, pushed the pistol into my chest, indicating with the lamp a low wooden gate in a rickety fence. Beyond this was a short path leading to a tumbledown hovel of the sort that the Irish think passes for a house. It was not unlike many that I had seen when out hunting, which were usually infested with rats, waifs with rickets and their slatternly mothers in rags.

Just as I got to what passed for the front door, with my escort's pistol now firmly wedged between my shoulder blades, it creaked open and I was met by a short middle-aged woman with rather a kind face, in a floured apron and brandishing a meat cleaver from which blood was still dripping. With a faint smile she beckoned me into a hot, dimly candle-lit room that at first glance seemed to serve as parlour and kitchen.

"Mr Speedicut, my name is Mrs – actually, that's of no concern to you. We have been expecting you. Please take a seat."

She pointed politely with the cleaver to a heavy looking, high-backed wooden chair. Next to this was a trestle table on which were a half-butchered carcass of what I presumed was some animal, although it was difficult in the dim light to tell, and a neat row of raised pies ready for the oven. I sat, whilst the pistol-toting oick who had shown me up the path half-turned to close the door, the weapon still levelled at me.

"No, leave it open, Sweeney," she snapped at him, "or we'll all suffocate in here once the oven's ready for baking."

He did as he was told and through the doorway I could see the coach with the driver on his box waiting for I knew not what. The woman was well-spoken and, from her accent, she wasn't Irish, which gave me a momentary glimmer of hope so I started to protest. In an instant, she had raised the cleaver and in a flash of candlelight, with a sickening thud she embedded it in the arm of the chair between the second and third fingers of my left hand, missing them by a fraction. If there was ever a time in my life up to that point at which I should have shat my britches, it would have been then, but I think I was too shocked even for that involuntary response.

"Listen very carefully to me, young man," she said in a surprisingly level voice, although her face was now set in the same way the Doctor's used to be just before he gave one a thrashing. "You have been sent here by friends of ours to sit-out the response to their demands. You can have it easy or you can have it difficult; the choice will be yours. My friend here is now going to cuff your wrists and your ankles to the chair and tie a kerchief around your mouth. If at any point in the coming days you attempt to escape, it will give me great pleasure to use one of these knives," and she pointed to a row of blades on the wall, "to remove the kerchief, cut out your tongue and bake it in a pie, like one of those in front of you. Do I make myself clear?"

I nodded in shocked disbelief as the bile rose in my throat. She then went on, as though now addressing a group of elderly dowagers.

"In the unlikely event that help even threatens to reach you before the hour appointed for your release, I will cut your throat, dismember your carcass and your mortal remains will be on sale in Mrs O'Miggins's pie shop on the Monto within the week. For make no mistake, whilst my friend may be a barber and knows how to wield a razor, my father was a master butcher and my mother a cook. As you can see from what remains of another who recently crossed this hearth, I learned my trade from them – and I learned it well."[26]

With a spasm of horror, I realised that what I had taken to be a butchered animal on the table in front of me was part of a human corpse – and I

---

[26] Editor's Note: Judging from this narrative, it is possible that Speedicut had been consigned to the care of the murderous barber Sweeney Todd whose lover, the baker Mrs Lovett, converted his victims into meat pies. From 1846 the couple operated from Fleet Street, London; given Todd's first name it is probable that they were originally based in Dublin.

puked up the entire contents of my stomach. Ignoring this reaction, she continued, once again smiling.

"Now be a good boy and give the nice gentleman no trouble whilst he applies the manacles…"

With that my still silent escort handed the pistol to the fiend in the frock, opened a cupboard next to the open door from which he drew four sets of steel cuffs that were not dissimilar to those in use *chez* James, from where they had undoubtedly come, and secured me hand and foot to the chair. As he was pulling a grubby rag from one of his jacket pockets, presumably to bind my mouth, despair finally gripped me and I must have passed out.

CHAPTER FOUR: THE GREAT GAME

I came to some while later to find myself, for the second time that evening, chained hand and foot. The murderous dame was busying herself beside an oven in the corner and my other jailor was puffing on a reeking pipe over by the open door. Suddenly, outside a shot rang out. I heard the coachman groan and I thought I saw him tumble from the box. Quick as lightening, the woman slammed the door shut and wedged a chair against it. She then pushed her accomplice towards the back of the room.

"Scarper, Sweeney, I'll join you in a moment!" she said, whilst lunging for one of the murderous looking knives on the wall.

I tried to yell as she advanced around the table towards me but no sound came out of my gagged mouth. Before she could reach me, the door crashed off its hinges, another shot detonated almost in my face, she dropped the knife and careered out of the room whilst there stood, framed in what remained of the door surround, the drunk in the red coat who had staggered into my room *chez* James not an hour or more previously. He was clearly not drunk now – and he had a smoking pistol in his hand.

"Ah, Mr Speedicut," he said in what would prove to be the understatement of the year to date, "it would seem that you are in need of release."

He bent down and, with what must have been a skeleton key, unlocked my shackles and then removed the gag. I rose unsteadily to my feet, conscious that my knees were knocking together uncontrollably and that my shirt front was covered in vile-smelling vomit.

"If you would be kind enough to follow me I have a carriage waiting to return you to your barracks."

I meekly followed him out of the house to a waiting town coach drawn-up behind my earlier conveyance and surrounded by a small group of mounted men with carbines resting on their hips.

"With the compliments of the Viceroy…" intoned my saviour, pointing to the door. "You will, I trust, excuse me a moment," and with that he called across to his colleagues.

"Gentlemen, the birds have flown but our customer is safe. Time enough to round them up later. We return to Dublin."

Then he stepped neatly into the carriage beside me, tapped on the roof with the muzzle of his pistol, and the carriage moved off accompanied by the clatter of hooves and the jingle of harness as our escort trotted alongside us.

"Permit me to introduce myself," he said in a pleasant accent that placed him as a native of Wales, "I'm Evans of the political service."

He put out his hand and shook mine as though we had just been introduced at a Dublin Castle reception. In a croak, for the drugged whisky and the fear seemed to have affected my vocal chords, I asked him for an explanation.

"Ah, well, Mr Speedicut, I'm not sure that I am permitted to give you a full answer to that question. Let's just say that we have been keeping an eye on Mrs James and her nationalist friends. When Mr Fortescue reported to my office that you had not joined him as arranged for a drink after, ahem, your rendezvous with the Reverend O'Connor, we tightened our watch on Mrs James's establishment.

"As you may recall, I effected an entry onto the premises in the guise of a customer and, when you left, we followed… the rest you either know or can surmise. Shall we leave it at that? I have a clean shirt somewhere here…" he said as he rummaged in a bag, "…perhaps you might like to relax with this on our journey back to the city… and I should also return this to you."

He placed a shirt on my knees and then pushed gently into my shaking hand a flask of brandy and a letter. A quick glance in the light from the carriage's lantern, showed me the letter was the one I had signed earlier in the evening. I thanked him as best I could. It seemed churlish to ask this superman how he had acquired it, so I slipped it into the pocket of my britches, drank the contents of the flask to the last drop and then exchanged my soiled shirt for the clean one he had provided. We continued the journey in silence.

When he dropped me by the Guard Room, Evans gave my arm a reassuring squeeze and murmured that, whilst he would have to inform the Colonel of the night's events in outline, he did not think that Parlby would need to know the details, beyond the fact that I 'had been saved from the clutches of a nationalist gang whilst enjoying my time off-duty'.

Once in the Mess, which was deserted, I made my way to my room and collapsed onto my bed just as the sun was rising over the trees. When I awoke around lunchtime it was to find a message from the Colonel instructing me to go to his office once I was in a fit state. So, I shouted for my orderly, washed, pulled on my kit and made my way over to headquarters.

Parlby's not a bad old stick, but he has a rather disconcerting way of munching his whiskers when he has difficult news to convey. He was in danger of munching them off when I marched into his office in the approved manner. I remember every word of what he then said.

"Speedicut, I am pleased with the way that you handle your men on my parades and your Troop officer says that you are shaping up well. However, last night's incident has confirmed my view that you are spending, munch-munch, rather more of your time in the town than is perhaps, munch-munch, advisable for an officer of this Regiment – or any man who has a care for his health. Moreover, Major Evans tells me that your continued presence in this city would also not be conducive to your well being, although he did not see fit to explain exactly why.

"Now, around the time of that unfortunate incident earlier this year with that officer in the 11th – Fastman wasn't it? – I received a communication from Lord Steyne, with whom I believe you are acquainted. He most generously offered to provide you with temporary extra-Regimental employment in the political service should your presence with the Tenth prove to be an embarrassment. As we know, thanks to prompt action by Lord Cardigan, the unfortunate affair soon blew over and Fatman is now, I understand, a civilian and living abroad. I was happy to keep you here as, clearly, other than an error of judgment in your choice of friends, the fault did not lie with you.

"But, in light of your, munch-munch, predilection for the, munch-munch, fleshpots of Dublin, I have decided that a period of enforced abstinence is in the interests of both the Regiment and yourself. So, even before the unfortunate affair of last evening crystallised my decision, I wrote to Lord Steyne asking him if his offer was still open and I heard yesterday that it is. It seems that Lord Steyne has need of you in India. Accordingly, you will report to him in London at your earliest – mark, sir, your *earliest* – convenience. If your service in India is satisfactory, I will be pleased to welcome you back to the Tenth. That will be all, Mr Speedicut."

What could I say? It wasn't exactly a dismissal from the Regiment – but India! And for how long? And to do what? This news pushed all the horrors of the previous evening out of my head. And I was damned if I knew what 'employment in the political service' meant but it didn't sound like much fun to me. And to think of all the trouble my Mama had gone to with the guv'nor in order to keep me away from Company service. Anyway, I told Fortescue, to whom I was most definitely indebted for my life, what was happening. He was shortly headed back to the 'groves of academe', so we agreed to share a cabin over to Liverpool and take the Mail together to London, but after that…

Somewhat to my surprise, my saviour Evans was on the pier from which we embarked (I think he was there to make sure I got on the boat). He told me that Ma James and my jailors had fled Dublin leaving no trace.[27] I wondered where they would next emerge and made myself a promise that if the James woman ever crossed my path again I would have my revenge. She may have been a looker, but she kept bad company and had a vicious

---

[27] According to her biographer, Bruce Seymour, in his book *Lola Montez* published in 1996, Lola Montez (aka Mrs James) arrived in England in early 1843.

streak the width of the Thames. As for the barber and his cooking friend, I vowed to steer well clear of meat pies unless I knew exactly what was in them.

Once I got to London it wasn't long before I knew my fate as, one grey October morning in 1841, I pitched up at St James's Square where I was shown into Steyne's study by a liveried flunky. Despite the fact that it was the middle of the day, the curtains were drawn and the great man had donned his black robe. The Brotherhood's mace and dagger – on which I could see there were still what looked like traces of my blood – were arranged on the table between us.

"Are you aware, Brother Speedicut, of recent events in Kabool?"

I wasn't a great reader of the rags when I was young, but even I'd heard of the trouble out there – though I'm not sure I could with any accuracy have placed Kabool on the map.

"The Brotherhood," he continued without waiting for a response from me, "is most concerned that the nation's honour is at stake in Afghanistan. A British expeditionary force is encamped in Kabool but under serious threat from the Afghan tribes. In addition, one of our Brothers, Colonel Charles Stoddart,[28] is at risk of his life in pursuit of our aims having been held captive since the middle of 1839 by Nasrullah Khan, the so-called Emir of Bokhara, who is one of the brigands who rule that lawless and God-forsaken land. Her Majesty's Government and the Board of Control seem unable – or unwilling – to do anything about the plight of our forces in Kabool or Brother Stoddart's imprisonment. From accounts reaching us, both are in peril. In addition, Brother Stoddart has on his person an item that belongs to the Brotherhood which I am anxious should not be lost. Given all the circumstances, the Brotherhood has decided to act.

"Your tasks are, first, in the days prior to your embarkation for India, to fully familiarise yourself with our nation's interests in Central Asia. For

---

[28] Lieutenant Colonel Charles Stoddart (1806-1842), a British intelligence agent in Central Asia.

that purpose, you may use the Brotherhood's extensive library which is housed here. Second, on arrival in Bombay you will make contact with Brother Shakespear who will familiarise you with the situation as he sees it.[29] Third, you are then to proceed to Kabool where you will compile for the Brotherhood a full account of the current situation there. This report you will send to me via our agent in Paris, Brother Flashman, who from now onwards you are to consider as your superior and controller. On completion of this task you are to put yourself at the disposal of Brother Shakespear for, at this very moment, Brother Conolly is on his way to Bokhara to effect Brother Stoddart's release.[30] If Brother Shakespear decides that he or Brother Conolly need further aid and assistance, you will provide it. Finally, you will return to me the item that Brother Stoddart is holding. Do you have any questions?"

As you can imagine, I had a thousand and five, but I needed time to gather my wits – such as they were - before asking them. There was, however, already one question on my mind which was: why me? What had I done to be thrown into the jaws of hell, other than to poke myself silly and then be frightened half to death by Irish nationalists and their associates? If I could have said there and then 'thank you very much, GB, but this isn't what I signed-up for', I would have done so. But the presence of the dagger was a sharp reminder that I had already surrendered that right. Oh, well, I thought, I've never been east of London and, with any luck, it will all be over before I get there, so I rather reluctantly nodded my assent.

"Very good," said the GB. "You will stay here as my guest until the date of your departure. My staff will make you comfortable, my secretary, Barrett, will provide you with the funds you will need to equip yourself for India

---

[29] Captain Sir Richmond Shakespear (1812-1861) first came to prominence in 1840 for his virtually single-handed rescue of 416 Russian slaves held by the Khan of Khiva. Shakespear delivered them, after an epic journey, to the Russian authorities in Orenberg – a feat which a 5,000-strong Russian military expedition had disastrously failed to pull-off earlier in the year. He was knighted for this achievement. Shakespear's first cousin was the author W M Thackeray.

[30] Presumably this was Captain Arthur Conolly (1807-1842), another British intelligence agent in Central Asia and an officer in the British East India Company's 6th Bengal Light Cavalry.

and your passage is already booked. If you have any questions you have only to write them down, give them to Barrett and I will deal with them as my time permits."

It was clear that I had had my marching orders so I did a smart About Turn and left the study. Hovering outside was the GB's secretary, a rather disagreeable type with a most superior look on his face who introduced himself as 'Mr Barrett'. With my traps being carried ahead by another flunky, he showed me up to my quarters on the second floor and pretty well appointed they were too. Once my kit was stowed, he showed me back to the ground floor and into an octagonal library towards the back of the house where over the coming days I did my best to get my head around who the hell were Brothers Conolly, Stoddart and Shakespear. I also had to figure out what was called the 'Great Game'.

As far I could discern, after a great deal of reading, the Great Game was a sort of Yankee Poker involving bluff and counter-bluff,[31] which was being played by Russia and Britain for the control of Central Asia and the gateway to India. It was also a game in which we Brothers seemed to have more than a chip or two. I'd just about got my head around all this when it was time to leave for the East.

Thanks to the GB and his influence with the Navy I got to India in the fastest time possible, on a series of express brigs and via the overland route to Suez. Most poor devils making the trip had to sweat it out for up to four months via the Cape, but I got there in just over half that time. I can't say I was much taken with Bombay, which was damned hot and full of stinking natives – it was just one big human ant hill. But the British quarter wasn't too bad, although the messing arrangements at the Fort were pretty primitive and the food was unfit for a dog. Everything was swamped in a foul-tasting brown sauce that deadened your tongue for a week; it was called curry, or some such, and apparently it was supposed to cover the taste of the rancid meat. It was quite a change from Dublin Castle and Viceregal Lodge, I can tell you.

---

[31] The card game, Poker, was invented in the USA around 1829.

But to business. There was a courier waiting for me with a message from Brother Shakespear, who'd recently been appointed Military Secretary to General Pollock,[32] who was putting together a force to relieve General Sale in Jalalabad.[33] Brother S was already on his way to Peshawar and my instructions were to join him there as soon as I could. Quite how I was then to get to Kabool to make my report for the GB was unclear, as was how I was supposed to recover the Brotherhood's precious 'item' from Brother Stoddart, if he was still held by the Emir of B; the GB made a particular point about this 'item' again just before I embarked, so clearly it was something important.

...

Editor's Note: Whilst Speedicut was en route *to India the situation in Kabool, which the British had occupied in August 1839 as a forward defence against a possible Russian invasion of India, had deteriorated dramatically. The collapse of the East India Company's control of Afghanistan started with the murder on 2nd November 1841 of the political officers, Sir Alexander Burnes and Major William Broadfoot, by a Kabuli mob. The already precarious situation rapidly went from bad to worse with the brutal dismemberment of Sir William Macnaghten and his staff on 23rd December by Akbar Khan. This happened whilst they were negotiating with Akbar to install him in place of the British puppet ruler, Shujah Shah Durrani, in return for which the British could remain in Afghanistan.[34]*

...

By the time I got to Peshawar everything in Afghanistan, including the nation's honour and a fair few of our troops, has gone totally tits-up, as Brother S informed me on my arrival. Nonetheless, he said that I should write a full report for the GB after talking extensively to Dr Brydon, who

---

[32] Major General (later Field Marshal) Sir George Pollock (1786-1872)

[33] Major General Sir Robert Sale (1782-1845) was the second-in-command in Kabul but had taken his Brigade from there in late-1841 to try and re-open the lines of communication from Kabul to Peshawar. He and his troops got as far as Jalalabad where they were trapped. Lady Sale was left behind in Kabul and was eventually taken into captivity during the retreat.

[34] Akbar Khan was the son of Dost Mohammad, who the British had deposed in 1839 and replaced with the weak Shujah Shah Durrani.

was the sole survivor of Elphinstone's disastrous withdrawal from Kabool and his Army's subsequent massacre in the passes,[35] which I did.

Brother S was a strange character. He was only a couple of years older than me and already has a knighthood. Tall, thin – wiry even – he had a messianic look in his eye and a humourless approach to life. For him, everything was business, and I suspect, he saw himself as something of a 'verie parfit knight', put on this earth to rescue fair maidens from dragons.[36] The ideal prefect so beloved of Arnold, the type who Brown and East probably dreamt about and then had to have their sheets changed by the skivvy in the morning. Not the ideal boss, I think you will agree, as his sort are prone to sending their minions on reckless tasks with hopeless outcomes.

In the meantime, and I should've known this was coming, Brother S told me that I was to affect the rescue of both Brother Stoddart *and* Brother Conolly. Apparently, Brother C had got to Bokhara and started negotiations with the Emir for the release of Brother S. For his pains, he had been slung in a dungeon along with the man he was supposed to have saved. To spring them from their smelly prison, in which they were doubtless chained hand and foot, I was to have only a guide, the disguise of a local bandit and my guardian angel to help me. When he briefed me, Shakespear implied that *he* would not have needed the guide…

Anyway, no sooner had I got the grime of the bazaar into my skin and the smell onto my clothes – and I can tell you that I smelt worse than my Troop lines after a week on field manoeuvres – than Brother S told me to take a bath, get back into uniform and report to Pollock's HQ. This was more welcome news than being told by the sawbones that I didn't have the pox.

---

[35] Major General William Elphinstone (1782-1842) was the hopelessly incompetent commander of the British Army in Afghanistan. He was known as 'Elphy Bey'.

[36] Thackeray wrote of his cousin: "His kind hand was always open. It was a gracious fate which sent him to rescue widows and captives."

It turned out that Pollock had orders to move from Peshawar to relieve Jalalabad, which was being besieged by slavering tribesmen, and I was to serve on his staff under Brother Shakespear. Quite what my duties were to be was not explained – so nothing new there then – and towards the end of March 1842 we set off, forcing the Khyber Pass on the last day of the month with very few casualties. Pollock, who was as sharp a commander as India could boast, had decided to play the locals at their own game and seized the heights in a smart flanking manoeuvre.

Two weeks later we marched into Jalalabad, pipes playing and colours flying to the strain of some Scotch song called, I think, "Oh, but ye've bin lang a' coming." It sounded like a thousand cats being strangled. Not content with relieving the dump, which, in my view, wasn't worth the shoe leather or the few lives lost – but which Brother S said is a key stronghold on the route to India – it then appeared that Pollock was keen to march on to Kabool to 'recover the honour of the Crown' or some such nonsense.

The result was that the march on Kabool turned into a race with General Nott,[37] who had just relieved Kandahar, and both brass hats were now keen as mustard to be the first to retake Kabool and collar a peerage for their pains. Brother S told me that, actually, they were under orders from the new Governor General, Lord Ellenborough, to withdraw immediately but they both decided that the shortest route back to India was via Kabool. Look at the map if you want to see the logic of *that* decision.

Anyway, the result was that we set off for Kabool, retracing Elphinstone's retreat. It was sickening. There were skeletons, both human and animal, all the way along the route and because of the narrowness of the track we just had to ride over them. As you can imagine, our boys started to get very over-excited by the growing evidence of what had happened and there wasn't an Afghan who was safe from our 'righteous wrath'.

Pollock tried to stop it, principally I think because it delayed the advance, but to no avail. In one village en route, that had just surrendered, the lads lined up every male inhabitant and shot them, then systematically worked

---

[37] General Sir William Nott (1782-1845).

their lusty way through the native bints – who I personally wouldn't have touched with the tip of my sword let alone my middle leg – and finally shot them too, along with those children who hadn't had the sense to hop it to the hills. It was not a pretty sight, and certainly not one that did us any credit, but I still think that the hill tribesmen only understood that kind of language.

It took us thirty days to fight our way through to Kabool, getting there on 13th September, but, as I was safely tucked away amongst the other staff officers, I never had to draw my sword or cock my pistol. Kabool was deserted when we got there. We set up camp on the old racecourse that Elphinstone had apparently built three years before, and the next day - without even firing a shot - we rode into the Bala Hissar, which made Windsor Castle look like a cottage and loomed menacingly over the rest of the dump. It was eerie and many of the lads lost their taste even for potting the locals, had there been any to pot. There was an uncomfortable silence over the camp that night. More out of morbid curiosity than anything else, I went with Brother S to look at where Burnes and Broadfoot had been shot then hacked to death but, other than the blackened shell of a house riddled with bullet strikes, there wasn't much to see.

Whilst the Generals decided what to do next, for Nott and his bravos had just arrived from Kandahar, Brother S took me to one side and said that he was under orders from the GB to 'recover the nation's honour' by rescuing the remnants of Elphinstone's Army and other sundry unfortunates, including Sale's wife, who had all fallen into the tender grasp of the Afghans. He didn't mention Brothers Stoddart and Conolly, but from what he had said earlier, I knew that they were also on his list of future heroics. Whilst I got my orders, the rest of the Army prepared to blow up the Kabool bazaar and 'put the city to plunder', which was a pointless act designed to administer a firm slap to Johnny Afghan; as if he cared.

As the smoke rose over the soukh, Brother S, with yours truly as his gallant second-in-command, set off at the head of a motley band of six hundred Kizilbashi irregulars (who put the fear of God into me, I can tell you).[38] Our route was across countryside that was said to be infested with twelve thousand slavering tribesmen, who were ready to slice us up in the most painful way possible.

What we didn't know was that, whilst our Generals were racing each other to seize Kabool, old Lady Sale had taken matters into her own hands,[39] bribed the guards, kicked Akbar out of his mud fortress at Bamian (where he had marched her and the rest of the hostages from Kabool at our approach), run up the Union Flag and was levying taxes from local travellers! If you don't believe me, look it up in *Britannica*. Much to my relief, it was in consequence a walk-over and the worst we had to deal with were fleas, hysterical mamas who wanted milk for their new-born babies – and a sergeant with steam coming out of his ears because his missus had run off with an Afghan, who clearly had a bigger lance than he did.

I was starting to think about the road home and wondering whether or not it would be possible to find some fun en route. My Kizilbashi orderly, Muhamad Khazi, a handsome ruffian with a pointed beard, hooked nose and the eyes of an eagle, had already suggested his younger brother, a lad with a grin a mile wide, but I didn't think it's wise to mix business with pleasure, so I had politely declined. They were a randy lot, those Afghans and, as their religion keeps their women off-limits afore marriage, they had no hesitation in taking their pleasure with whatever came to hand – even a watermelon, if a pair of olive-hued buttocks aren't available. Anyway, just as I was pondering what the prospects were of having my way with a certain Miss Pankers, or her younger brother George, who I had met briefly on my way through Bombay, I was summoned to Brother S's temporary office in the former home of Akbar.

"Brother Speedicut," he started – for we were alone – "we may have accomplished the first part of the Great Boanerges's mission, but there still remains the plight of our Brothers held in Bokhara and the recovery of the Brotherhood's property held by Brother Stoddart. Their rescue and

---

[38] Native cavalrymen in the part-time employment of the British.

[39] Lady (Florentia) Sale (1790-1853): judging from her actions and her portrait she was an indomitable old battle-axe who feared no one.

its recovery will not be achieved with anything like the ease of the last few days..."

For a start, I thought, they don't have Florentia Sale with them.

"As I originally briefed you, the only hope lies in stealth. I cannot move from here, for I am now too well known, but you can. I propose, therefore, that tomorrow, after dark, you and your orderly Khazi – who I know to be a competent scout with a good knowledge of the passes between here and Balkh – slip quietly out of town and, in native garb, make your way to Bokhara. You already have all you need, save this..." and he slipped a small, heavy leather pouch into my hand which, from the sound and weight of it, contained gold coins.

Meanwhile, the bells sounding my death knell had started to play in the background as I desperately tried to think of a way out of this madness. An instant dose of the trots, perhaps?

"If at any point you are stopped, or have to engage with the locals, Khazi will assume the part of a lance-for-hire on his way to join the Emir's irregular cavalry – and, as you have yet to master the local tongue sufficiently well, you will assume the role of his mute Circassian slave. It will, if necessary, explain your fair hair and skin. In any event, you will shave your head and stain your beard with henna before you leave."

The next thing he'd be suggesting, I thought, was that I cut out my tongue to complete the disguise.

"I estimate that it will take you less than a month to make the journey if you travel light. Once you have reached Bokhara, spy out the lie of the land and the situation of our Brothers. Then – if you can – effect their release if they are alive and return by whatever means possible to Peshawar, to which I am returning at the earliest moment possible. I wish you God speed – and may the spirit of the Great Boanerges go with you!"

Or to put it another way: 'Right Turn, to your death, Quick March!' That had put the vermin back in my armpits and no mistake. A crazy two-man crusade deep into territory that was crawling with blood-thirsty natives, whose women stood ready to cut off your pecker at the first available opportunity, before toasting you alive over a fire and feeding you to the vultures for supper. Why the hell hadn't the silly sod asked Florentia Sale to rescue them? It was too bad – and all for having spent too many hours pleasuring m'self silly in the Monto. Flashy had been condemned to a lifetime in the fleshpots of Paris for trying to throw a leg over the Prism woman, whilst I was sentenced to the prospect of a lingering and painful death. There was clearly no justice in this world.

So, the following night Khazi and I slipped out of camp. Fortunately, I had several weeks' growth of beard, now stained a revolting shade of orange, and, as I take colour easily, I just about looked the part – provided my golden locks didn't grow back too quickly under my turban, blond natives, even Circassian ones, being about as rare as a virgin in the Haymarket. I had also bought some robes from the least verminous looking Kizilbashi I could find and I now reeked as high as Khazi.

If you look at a map you'll see that there's a not-insignificant mountain range between Kabool and Bokhara called the Hindu Kush and, as I studied the lie of the land, I thought that Brother S was being hopelessly optimistic about the time it would take us to get there on foot and horse, but he knew the terrain and I didn't. Stinking like a tramp's hose, Khazi and I set off on a pair of sturdy Afghan ponies with an extra one apiece to carry our bags and as a back-up.

All went well until we got into the foothills of the Kush and then our pace slowed as we had to follow a single-file pass that Khazi knew, often on foot leading the ponies. To my surprise and relief, we saw no one except for the occasional goatherd. The fact is that, through the mountains, the biggest problem I had to deal with was Khazi, who insisted that we would stay warmer at night if we shared the same blankets. Of course, he was right – but it came at a price… Oh well, I thought, I'd had worse encounters and if it meant that he didn't leave me in the middle of the mountains to fend for myself, or deliver me trussed to the Emir, then the discomfort was worth it. So, I put it all down to experience. Besides which, I was – after all – playing the part of his slave and practice made perfect.

Between the western edge of the Kush and Bokhara lies a plain that is bisected by the Oxus river. Khazi said that our safest way into the enemy camp would be to join a camel train and this we planned to do in a fly-blown dump called Balkh, which I later found out was one of the oldest cities in the world. It certainly smelt like it. At first sight Balkh seemed to be composed almost entirely of mosques, including one with a green dome and another with nine of the buggers. The town was walled, but the fort and citadel were outside the walls on a mound to the north east. We entered after dark through the west gate, passed under three arches and made our way cautiously to the main square, which also served as the caravanserai. A few slovenly dressed soldiers were loafing about, but took no interest in us, although Khazi hissed to me that we needed to be on our guard and I should keep my mouth shut. As we sank down by the side of a fire, on the other side of which were a group of merchants and their bearers, I nearly had a seizure – for two of them were jabbering away in French.

CHAPTER FIVE: BOKHARA

Now, I may not have learnt much at Rugby but I did take on board a fair amount of the language of our garlic-eating neighbours – largely because I thought it might come in useful if I was ever let loose in Gay Paree. Anyway, the last thing I expected to hear around a camp fire in the middle of some God-forsaken hole in Central Asia was the language of fun and frolics. But I was not mistaken for, sure enough, an older man who was dressed – as far as I could see – as a prosperous merchant was jawing away in French to a young boy, probably his son or his catamite, I couldn't at that stage tell which. But why was 'oo-la-la' being spoken in this caravanserai? I listened in.

The boy was asking his papa in a childish, rather whiney voice – for that relationship became clear with his first words – when he would be back in Saint Petersburg to start his schooling at the Corps des Pages. Now I didn't at that stage in my life know much about Russia, but I did know that in this neck of the woods the Russians were definitely not on our side, that the Corps des Pages was the top school for young aristos and that all educated Russians spoke French as their first language. These two were clearly Russian aristos, which almost certainly meant that papa was military. Putting two and two together, and given that – like me – he was not in European dress, it seemed highly likely therefore that papa was up to no good, leastways as far as Britannia was concerned. This piece of, for me, quite monumental logic was quickly confirmed when another man joined the group and, again in French, asked if 'Monsieur le Comte' had any further request for the evening. He said that 'no' he didn't and that they should all get some rest before setting off on the 'morrow for Bokhara. And that was it. Making a mental note that Khazi and I would definitely not be joining the Count's party, I rolled myself up in my blanket and dropped off to sleep.

Now I don't know about you, dear reader, but if I ever dream about school it's not of its pleasures but its pains. Whether it was the trip through the mountains, Khazi's attentions, the surprise of hearing French, the filth we had just eaten or all of these things, I dreamt that I was in Arnold's class and that he had caught me being given a seeing-to by Molly, or it may have been Mrs Wickham, under the desk. He dragged me out of my seat by the ear, with my britches around my knees, and marched me to the front of the class where he ordered me to recite the Lord's Prayer in French whilst he thrashed the arse off me. I started screaming for mercy but, unfortunately – yes, you guessed it, and as was immediately evident – I had actually been screaming my head off in English. And I woke to find myself staring into the beady eye of the Count and that of a pistol pointed straight at my forehead.

My first thought was that Khazi would jump to my rescue, but out of the corner of my eye I saw him slinking away into the deep shadow of the arcade that surrounded the square. That's all the thanks I get, I thought, for keeping you warm in the mountains.

"It seems," said the Count in near faultless English, "that introductions are called for. I am Captain Count Pavel Nikolayevich Ignatiev and this is my son, Nikolai Pavlovich.[40] And with whom do we have the pleasure of sharing this delightful spot?"

Bluster was out of the question, so I told him that I was the Reverend Jasper Speedicut on an errand of mercy to my countrymen held in jail in Bokhara. Well, it was the best I could do at short notice, the Doctor was on my mind and I have always found that it's easier to remember a half-truth than a lie.

"Mr Speedicut, you are in luck for my son and I are on our way to see His Excellency the Emir and we can give you a personal introduction to him so you can plead your case."

It was clear that he didn't believe me and he ordered the cove I had seen earlier, who seemed to be his ADC, to truss me up like a chicken and

---

[40] Captain Count Pavel Nikolayevich Ignatiev was an aristocrat at the Court of Tsar Nikolai I, highly favoured for his loyalty during the revolt of 1825. Grand Duke Alexander (later Tsar Alexander II) stood sponsor to Nikolai Pavlovich Ignatiev (1832-1908) at his baptism.

then sat over me breathing a mixture of garlic and goat that was enough to make one puke.

Needless to say, I got not a wink of sleep and, as the local cocks started to shout the odds, my guard poured some stale water down my throat and bundled me onto the back of a donkey, which he then led from his camel. Even if I had had any thoughts of escape – or, miracle of miracles, rescue by Khazi – it was clearly impossible as friend Ivan positioned his mount in the middle of the party, all of whom were armed and also mounted on the smelly brutes, save for the Count's son who was astride a second donkey.

We'd been riding for most of the morning, with only a brief stop or two, when Nikolai edged his donkey over to mine and started questioning me about England, how I came to be in the area and so on. When he turned to face me, I noticed the damndest thing – one of his eyes was bright blue and the other was dark brown. That will mark you out from the crowd in later life, I thought. Anyway, I told him what I could, which was not much, of ecclesiastical life back home but he soon got bored and rode off to join his papa, who was heading the party.

If the trip through the mountains had had its moments, the tedious four-day journey to Bokhara had none beyond, that is, the squelching sound that came from my belly: it was in turmoil at the prospect of finding out what had happened to Brother C and Brother S in a way that I had neither foreseen nor planned.

Few of my readers – if there are any of you - will have been to Bokhara and I certainly don't recommend you making the trip. However, no matter the depths of despair into which one can be sunk, and I was wading armpit deep in the slough of despond, the first sight of it fair took my breath away: the architecture was monumental. On our way to the citadel of the Emir, which was itself a structure that would dwarf the Tower of London, we passed well built and maintained (which was rare in these parts) mosques, minarets, squares and public buildings, the like of which I have never seen anywhere else. But, unfortunately, this was no sight-seeing trip for, as the citadel drew closer, my heart sank lower. If I had formed any kind of a plan for scouting out the situation in Bokhara, it had certainly not included being marched-up the front steps of the Emir's palace at the point of a gun with most of my cover blown.

The main gate of the citadel was well guarded by the Emir's equivalent of the Life Guards in spiked helmets, mail and back-'n-breastplates, mounted on large ponies. The Count seemed to be expected, for the guard saluted and waved us through. Inside, the party halted in a large courtyard and the Count, young Nikolai, friend Ivan (who prodded me none too gently off my donkey with the point of his sword) and I were escorted deep into the fortress by a dismounted detachment, who had been waiting for us and clanked along beside us in fine Guardee style. We went up a grand staircase, along a wide corridor lined with the Emir's Foot Guards. At the end, a pair of slit-eyed flunkeys in sumptuously embroidered robes threw open a pair of brass-studded doors and we found ourselves in a richly carpeted room. Opposite the door, on a raised dais, sat the Emir, flanked by a man I took to be his Vizier, a couple of courtiers and yet more guards.

I hardly got a glimpse of the Emir, who like most middle-aged men in those parts was stout, bearded and over-dressed, before friend Ivan pushed me forward, then kicked my legs from under me, leaving me face down on the carpet. For good measure, he pinned me in place with his sword tip between my shoulder blades like some damned butterfly specimen. The Count stepped forward and spoke, this time to my great surprise in English, which was translated into the local lingo by the one I took to be the Vizier.

"Excellency, I return, as promised, with news of the British attack on Kabool, which has fallen to them, but also with this young Englishman, who I found in disguise at the caravanserai in Balkh. He says he is a priest and on a mission to beg you to release his fellow countrymen. You can judge whether he tells the truth or is, as I suspect, a spy."

The Emir farted, grunted and then said something that was not translated, whilst I lay face-down on the floor.

"Would your Excellency like me to remove this carrion from your presence?"

"No, Count, His Excellency will not put you to the trouble," translated the Vizier, "but he thanks you for this most unexpected gift, who might serve well in his harem. But, before he is prepared for that task, His Excellency thinks he should join his fellow cleric. Ahmed, put him with the other in the pit. Now, Count, to business…"

Before I could work out who this 'fellow cleric' could be, I heard the guards running forward, I was lifted bodily off the ground and carried out of the room in less time than it takes to tell. The brutes dropped me, then dragged me none too gently back along the corridor and down what seemed an endless flight of stairs lit by burning torches in brackets. At the bottom of the steps we halted in a circular chamber, with a large iron grate in the middle and what looked like prison cells set into the walls. Two warders lumbered forward, there were more incomprehensible grunts from my guards and then the warders lifted the grate in the floor and I was thrown forward into a pit about six feet deep. I landed in a pile of stinking straw, hit my head on something hard and passed out.

When I came to, I was flat on my back. I opened my eyes and found myself staring up through the grate into the chamber above. Then I heard shuffling sounds and sensed, rather than saw, someone crawling towards me. I instinctively shrank back and must have given a yelp, for the figure spoke – in English, albeit with a heavy German accent.

"Who are you?"

Well, in a morning that thus far had been a litany of horror, an English voice – even with an accent - was like a bottle of water in the desert.

"M'name's Speedicut," I replied, "and who are you. Not Stoddart or Conolly?"

"No," he said, "I am the Reverend Joseph Wolff.[41] I came here to rescue Colonel Stoddart and Captain Conolly – but, alas, I was too late. They are dead."

Thank you, Brother S, I thought. All this way for nothing – and with God only knew what else in prospect.

With my eyes getting accustomed to the semi-darkness, I saw that Wolff, who looked as though he was in his late fifties, was dressed, not like me in native garb, but in full canonicals, although he and they were looking somewhat the worse for wear. Over the next hours and days – I'm not exactly sure how long, for you soon lose track of time in dungeons – Woolf told me his story. It emerged that he was a German Jew who had converted to Christianity, taken the cloth and dedicated his life to finding – and if I hadn't been in a topsy-turvy world already, it would have beggared belief – the Lost Tribes of Israel! Along the route, which had stretched from Cairo to Calcutta, he'd heard that 'two Christian souls' were being held by Nasrullah Khan, the Emir of Bokhara. Undaunted, and entirely on his own initiative, he had decided that sweet reason would secure their release and had quite simply marched into the citadel, demanded to see the Emir and then asked for the release of our two Brothers.

Wolff was quite obviously barking mad – and it seems that the Emir thought so too for, according to Wolff, he just roared with laughter and then had the poor sap thrown into the delightful hospitality accommodation in which I had now joined him. Amongst Wolff's other skills he had mastered the local lingo and, whilst passing the time of day with his guards, had picked up the story of how our two Brothers went to join their Maker.

"As you may know, Colonel Stoddart was captured by the Emir in 1839 but, despite converting to Islam – the alternative being death – he was not

---

[41] The Rev Joseph Wolff (1795-1862) was known as the Eccentric Missionary. It was previously thought that he did not arrive in Bokhara, on a self-imposed mission to rescue Conolly and Stoddart, until mid-1843; *The Speedicut Chronicles* would seem to indicate that in fact he arrived earlier. The Rev Joseph Wolff remained a captive of the Emir of Bokhara until the following year when he was inexplicably released.

released and was, indeed, held for a time in this very cell. Captain Conolly, to whom the Emir had permitted Colonel Stoddart to write, attempted to negotiate his release at the end of 1841. However, it was a trap, for the Emir's agents had been tracking Conolly – who was in communication with the Emir's great rivals the Khans of Kiva and Khokand – and the Emir wanted to remove what he saw as a threat to himself.

"With the situation in Kabool deteriorating, Nasrullah Khan decided that he could safely dispose of his two unwelcome guests. It also seems that the Emir had written to Queen Victoria and was in a fury that he had received a reply from her Governor General, an event that he regarded as a great insult. So, last June, fearing no retribution from your Army following the Kabool *debacle*, the Emir had Stoddart and Conolly brought from this dungeon into the great square before the citadel. There they were forced to dig their own graves. Stoddart was beheaded first, then the executioner turned to Conolly and told him that the Emir would spare his life if he would convert to Islam. Well, Conolly was a devout Christian, God rest his soul, and had already seen that conversion had not spared his brother officer – so he said as much, stretched out his neck and shortly afterwards his head rolled next to that of Colonel Stoddart. The bodies were thrown into the grave, the earth was heaped in and then flattened. You probably rode over their resting place on your way here."

Words cannot express how I felt at that moment, for what Wolff had told me meant that my whole mission had just gone up in smoke: Stoddart and Conolly were dead and buried and the GB's prized 'item', whatever it was, along with them. Worse still, and besides sharing a stinking, rat-infested pit with a raving, Bible-bashing lunatic, I was faced with a one-way ticket to the hereafter. But then a chink of light appeared 'midst the encircling gloom, for had not the Emir mentioned something about putting me to work in his harem? That sounded like my kind of employment and, with time-off for good behaviour, I might even find the opportunity to slip away and get myself back to civilisation, assuming of course that I wasn't so knackered by my harem duties that I couldn't walk.

But this ray of hope soon dimmed as one day gave way to another with no sign of liberation. Worse still if that were possible, there was no place in our stinking pit for me to escape from Wolff's endless sermonising (converts, in my experience, are always the worst). Then, just as I was about to give up, turn my face to the wall and pray for the end, two things happened. First, whilst scrabbling in the muck for a crust of bread that had just been thrown down to us, my fingers touched a loose metal object. It felt like a ring and, when I raised it to my eyes and rubbed off the grime, I saw that it was indeed a heavy gold ring set with a polished red stone. It reminded me of one I had seen before, but I couldn't place it. Anyway, without thinking, I slipped it on my finger turning the stone into my palm. Wolff had been too busy feasting on his bread to notice anything and I made no mention of its discovery to him. Such was my mental state that it never occurred to me that it might have been his. A couple of mornings later, there was suddenly a great bustle in the dungeon above, the grate was raised and I was hauled out before I could even say a 'fond' farewell to Wolff. Two guards pushed me over to the wall, literally ripped off my robes, which anyway were hanging in rags, and threw several buckets of water over me. One of them then threw me a rough blanket and signed that I should dry myself, which I did.

Then, with no further ceremony and wearing not a stitch, I was dragged, for I could hardly walk, back up the way I had come all those days – or maybe it was weeks – before. The sun in the courtyard nearly blinded me and I could still hardly see when I was thrown, once again, onto the rug in the Emir's audience chamber.

"Get up!" ordered a voice.

I did as I was told and stood shivering from fear, acutely conscious of the fact that I had become an object of interest to the group in the room.

"Your skin and your hair are fair. Are you really an Englishman?" asked the Vizier, for it was indeed he. I replied that I was. "And what is your purpose here?"

"I came to beg for the release of my fellow Englishmen." It was the truth - and I thought that telling him I was another vicar on an errand of mercy would arouse righteous oriental wrath.

"You lie. You came to spy on His Excellency for your Queen!"

I blustered that I was doing no such thing. I was just starting to burble that the Queen had told me herself how much she respected the great Emir, when I was cut short.

"Enough of this rubbish, scum. The Emir, who knows of your Army's reoccupation of Kabool, has decided to be merciful and offers you two choices. You may convert to our faith, in which case you will be released – or you may work in His Excellency's *seraglio*. Decide – and quickly!"

I'm no fool and I can spot a trap when I see one. Wolff had said that Stoddart had converted and a fat lot of good it had done him. Anyway, the prospect of working with a load of bare-titted oriental bints was not a bad one. So, I said with as much dignity as I could muster, that I chose to serve in the harem.

"Good. Prepare him!"

With that, the two smelly brutes standing behind me seized my arms and held me tight. Now this was odd, because I had been expecting, having already had a rough bath, to be given a set of robes and packed off to work for the assembled Mrs Khans. Instead of which – well it looked like treachery whatever it was.

"You have chosen to work in the harem," said the Vizier, "so you must be adapted for the work."

With that he stepped up to me and ran a smooth, podgy little hand over my chest and then down to my crotch. The touch was gentle but infinitely disgusting. And then, suddenly, he grabbed my wedding tackle with his left hand and pulled a murderous looking dagger from his belt with his right.

"A pity," he murmured, "such a waste; these could have been a source of great pleasure..."

And then it dawned on me: harems are staffed by eunuchs! I screamed blue bloody murder and tore myself loose, not just from the Vizier's warm grasp, but from that of the guards too. I tried to run, tripped over the edge of a carpet and went headlong. But afore I could stir, I was flattened by about a dozen of the brutes.

"Turn him over," ordered the Vizier. "So, you have changed your mind? Very well, do you accept the law of God and the teachings of the Prophet Mohammed, blessings and peace be upon him?"

"I do," I whispered back.

"Excellent. There remains but one thing to be done."

He bent over me brandishing his knife. No, I thought, it's more treachery and he is about to slit my throat. But the effort to struggle, or even to cry out, had left me and I lay there limp fearing the worst.

CHAPTER SIX: EN ROUTE TO BOMBAY

But instead of pulling up my chin to expose my throat, I felt his soft, warm hand gently pull the end of my pecker, there was a flash of steel in the air and I felt as if my prick was on fire. As I passed out, my last thought was that life wouldn't be much fun without it.

I came to, not in the dungeon, but lying on a wooden cot in an airy, white-washed storage room with tiered shelves and a single, barred window through which sunlight was streaming. There was a pillow under my head, an embroidered native rug over me - and my prick was throbbing badly. But I was alive and seemingly almost in one piece, although it was too early to judge the extent to which I had been maimed. Then, for some reason, my mind went back to my bouts with Khazi in the mountains and I realised that, far from losing my wedding tackle, I had been circumcised. It still bloody well hurt and who was to say that it was just my foreskin that the bastard Vizier had removed?

I was starting to get my bearings and wondering whether or not my injury was too severe for me to move, when I heard bolts being drawn back and a bearded and turbaned old man came into the room, with two of the Emir's guards behind him, armed to the teeth as usual. The old man signed to me to lie still, pulled back the rug, gently removed the dressing, inspected the damage, wrapped it up again and nodded. He then made a sign to one of the guards, who turned on his heel and returned a few moments later with a pile of cloth on top of which was a platter of dates and a water skin. Then, without a word, they left me, the door slammed shut and I heard the bolts being slid back into place.

Well, I thought, this was better than the festering sewer I had so recently been sharing with the raving rector – but, despite the Emir's promise, I was clearly not free. So, I lay there for a while and then my stomach reminded me that I hadn't eaten in an age. I gingerly lowered my feet to the floor and, finding I could move without pain, made my way over to the platter that the guards had left on a wooden stool. I quickly tucked into the dates, which were tender and juicy, and washed them down with the water, which was brackish and goat-flavoured but drinkable. The inner man at least partly satisfied, I examined the cloth under the platter to find it was a thick cotton robe of the type worn by the locals. As I pulled it over my head I was starting to think that matters might have been worse, when I once again heard the bolts being drawn, so I nipped back to the bed.

This time it was not the old man but the Vizier and another brace of guards.

"Englishman," he leered down at me, "you have been more fortunate than you may think, for, instead of being returned to the 'pit of despair' to await your fate with your fellow countryman, His Excellency has granted my wish that you become my slave." I sat bolt upright at this.

"What the devil?" I stammered. "The Emir promised that I was to go free if I converted." But he pressed me back onto the pillow.

"It is only in God, and his Prophet Mohammed, blessings and peace be upon him, in whom you should trust. No, freedom is not for you. Once your wound has healed you will be taken to my palace where you will join the Circassians who comfort me in my leisure hours. It is an easy life that you may even grow to enjoy..."

Then he slid his revoltingly silk-smooth hand, which had so recently been grabbing me lower down, over my face, around my neck and down my chest. His meaning was only too clear and I involuntarily recoiled: it's one thing to takes one's pleasure with the likes of Arthur, or even submit to Khazi's carnal demands, but to become the catamite of a fat, greasy wog who reeked of scent and garlic was a prospect worse than death. I could see that the Vizier had correctly read my thoughts for he removed his hand.

"Of course, if you so wish it," he said, "I can return you to the dungeon and arrange a date for you with our most excellent executioner. The choice is yours. You do not answer? I will give you this night to think about it and I will return tomorrow when you can give me your decision. Ponder well, Englishman, and have sweet dreams."

He turned and swept from the room followed by the guards, leaving me with my mind in ferment. Yes, I thought, I had escaped emasculation but it seemed that I was now condemned to be prostituted to an oriental grease ball or, if I refused, join Brothers Stoddart and Conolly under the sandy sod of the town's main square. Both choices were so horrendous that neither bore thinking about.

As I sat in a daze unable to contemplate the future, the light in the room started to fade and I suddenly realised that I must have been sitting there for hours doing and thinking nothing. This won't do, I told myself: I had a few hours to seek a way out or it would be goodbye Piccadilly and hello to a life that would make a cabin boy blush. Whilst there was still light, I took stock of the room. It soon became clear that it was some sort of linen store, for the shelves were piled with lengths of white cloth that looked like sheets or window coverings. An idea started to form in my brain and I turned to the barred window. Looking through the grid of iron bars I guessed, judging from the houses opposite, that my room was probably only two or three stories above the square. If only I could remove the bars. I gave them a rattle and saw that the mortar around them was quite loose. Typical shoddy native work, I thought. Surely a few good pulls would work them free?

The moon was up before I started to make real progress and, by then, my arms were aching and my palms were raw from the metal, but eventually I found I was able to get some considerable movement into the grid. Just as I was about to try, by main force, to lift it out altogether I dimly heard heavy footsteps outside. Quickly sweeping the debris into a corner, I made it back to the cot just in time to hear the bolts being slid back. Through my lightly closed lids I saw that my new visitors were a couple of guards accompanying the old man, who carrying a lamp in one hand and a small steaming bowl of scented water in the other.

He gently shook me until I opened my eyes, signed for permission to lift my cotton robe and then proceeded to clean the wound. His touch was soothing, in stark contrast to the Vizier's. As I was being treated, the guards, who had positioned themselves at either end of my bed, glowered menacingly at me. I was hoping and praying that they would continue to concentrate on what was being done to me, when the most fearful commotion broke out in the square below. The soldier nearest the window went over to see what was happening. If he touched the bars I knew that I was done for, as he could not fail to notice that they were very loose. To my horror he stretched out a mailed hand but, before he reached them, the old man straightened himself up and spoke. He must have said that he was done, or some such, for the guard dropped his hand, turned, grunted something in Arabic and then kicked the leg off the end of the bed on his way out. As I fell to the floor, I heard the two guards laughing as they shot the bolts.

When I was sure that it was quiet again outside my room I returned to the bars. In the minutes that the old man had been ministering to me some of my strength must have returned for, with one almighty heave, I lifted the iron grid out of the window. It was heavy, damned heavy. I crashed back onto the bed with it - and the remaining three legs collapsed under our combined weight. The noise was frightful and I think my heart actually stopped for a moment. But there was no sound of running feet outside my door so, after a couple more minutes, I put my plan into action and, sweeping the lengths of cloth off the shelves, I started to knot them together to make a crude rope. The problem was how long to make it.

Now, I'm not a good judge of distance and I certainly didn't pay much attention in the maths classes at Rugby. To make matters worse, when I leaned out of the window, I found that - with the moon behind it - the building was casting a deep shadow so I couldn't see the ground. But, relying on my first assumption that I must be about thirty feet up, I used the collapsed bed as a rough guide (I reckoned it must be about six-foot-long for I am just under that height) and tied together five bed-lengths, secured one end to the iron bars, and having checked that there was no activity in the square below, with a prayer I threw the rest out of the window. Then I checked the square again, climbed into the window, got a good grip on the makeshift rope and gently lowered myself into space.

I must have dropped about four feet before the window bars jammed themselves into place, but it felt like much further, the jolt damned nearly made me lose my grip and the noise should have woken every guard for miles around. Yet again I froze, with my heart somewhere just behind my tongue, but nothing happened. It was agony clinging to that rope. So, deciding that if I didn't move I would fall off anyway, I started to lower myself down counting the knots as I went. When I got to the last knot my feet were still swinging in fresh air. Knowing that I had just six feet or so before the rope ended, I paused. What if I had seriously misjudged the distance? How far would it be from the end of the rope to the ground? There was only one way to find out and, as I had no intention – even if I had had the strength – to return to my cell, I carried on down.

Just as I felt the end of the rope sliding past my crotch, I heard a noise below me. Looking down I could see nothing but, from the clank of armour and equipment, it must have been at least a couple of guards, probably patrolling the citadel's perimeter, who had stopped right below me for a jaw. Would I be able to hang on long enough for them to move off? What would happen if they looked up? But these questions were banished by a most ominous sound of ripping fabric above me. I felt myself dropping in short jerks, then suddenly there was a prolonged rip, a longer jerk, I lost my grip and hurtled earthwards.

The next thing I knew I had landed right on top of the guards, whose bodies buckled underneath me, breaking my fall and their necks, for they uttered not a word, not even a groan. It took me a couple of minutes to get my breath back and realise that nothing was broken, although from the pain in my left ankle, which was now considerably worse than the ache in my prick, I realised that I must have sprained it. It could have been worse, for the spike on one of the guard's helmets was protruding between my toes; a fraction of an inch either way and my foot would have been skewered. I looked up to see the trailing end of my rope about fifteen feet above me. My trigonometry may be crap but I was free and almost uninjured. But I realised it was now imperative that I get out of sight before the dead guards, the rope or both were discovered and the alarm was raised. I dimly remembered that the souk lay across the square and

I was reasonably sure that I could lose myself there. So, I pulled-off one of the guard's mail tunics, put it on, jammed his tin pot on my head, and then half-walking, half-crawling, I made my way in that direction hoping my disguise would hold in the dark.

I had just stumbled into a street overhung with baskets and rugs and dimly lit with oil lamps, when I felt a firm hand on my shoulder and I was pulled into the nearest doorway. 'God, what now?' was my immediate thought. But instead of a bazaar ruffian intent on theft or worse, it was Khazi, God bless him. In short order, he told me that he had followed me to Bokhara and then kept a daily watch on the citadel, assisted by a number of street urchins. He was about to give up and head for home when he had spotted my rope and guessed, correctly, that it was me who was making a break for freedom.

In answer to my string of questions, he said that he still had our pistols, my spare kit, the ponies and some of the gold that Brother S had given me for the journey, which I had tucked under the saddle of my pony, and that – if we were careful – we should be able to make our way back to civilization in one piece. There was only one problem that he could foresee and that was how to avoid the inevitable hue and cry when my escape was discovered. He paused for a moment, his eagle eyes fixed on a distant point.

"Sahib, you will travel as my wife! The Emir's curs and scum will never dare to look behind the veil, particularly with me riding at your shoulder."

And that was precisely what we did. That night Khazi got me togged-up as a native bint, veiled from head to foot (God it was hot; I don't know how or why their women put up with it). But Khazi's idea for the disguise undoubtedly saved my life, for the following morning when we set off we were endlessly stopped by patrols and checkpoints who were clearly looking for me. However, Khazi's faith in the religious scruples of the Emir's soldiers was well placed and they paid me no attention.

We had decided not to try breaking back to Peshawar, which would have meant crossing the mountains again. Instead, we joined a Russian-free camel train to Teheran. It was a long journey, mercifully without incident and I've since found out that it was a distance of about seven hundred miles. Not surprisingly, it took us the best part of a month during which time Khazi was not slow to assert his marital rights, but we got there in the end sometime before Christmas 1842.

The Minister at our Mission to the Persians in the city seemed to think that it would make sense for me to make my way down to Bushire and get a coaster from there to take me back to Bombay in time for the New Year. At my request, he wrote a report to Brother S telling him of my recent adventures (the sanitised version, of course) and informing him that I was on my way back to India. Once I got there, I supposed I would have to make my way to Peshawar to get my next orders from Brother S. I prayed that they would be a quick 'About Turn and Quick March' back to Dublin and the warm embrace of the Shiny Tenth. And speaking of warm embraces, whilst in Teheran I made two early New Year Resolutions: the first was to take Khazi with me as I'd actually grown rather fond of the rascal. Even if he had given me my fill of the 'vices of the Greeks', he had, in the end, saved my life. I also had to choose the right moment to see if the rest of me was still in working order now that the scabs had come off.

However, the first of these good intentions was not to be. Khazi slipped away on the dockside in Bushire and that was the last I saw of him, which I rather regretted as he would have looked perfectly splendid hovering in attendance on me with the Shiners. What Parlby would have thought was another matter altogether. As to my second resolution, I was able to put that into effect in Bombay. But, yet again, I anticipate.

Anyway, our Minister in Teheran was as good as his word and his report to Brother S must have arrived in Peshawar long before the tug boat I was on docked in Bombay. For, on my arrival at the Fort, where I dutifully reported to the Governor, General Arthur,[42] there was a letter waiting for me from Brother S. Rather typically, it was short on praise and long on directions. However, to my considerable relief, it said that I was to return to London and there report to the GB, to whom I was to hand-deliver 'the

---

[42] Lieutenant General Sir George Arthur, Bart (1784-1854) was Governor of the Bombay Presidency 1842-1846.

enclosed document', which I assumed was Brother S's own report on the prize cock-up of the century: Kabool and God knows how many troops lost, the country's honour and reputation dragged through the dust and two prominent members of the Brotherhood gone to their Maker. It could have been worse, for it might have included my serving the Emir's bints without my tackle or having joined Brothers Conolly and Stoddart at the Heavenly Gates (or, more likely, the other place). As it was, it seemed that the minor amendment to my principal asset was – as you will see – proving something of a gain rather than a loss.

Having received my orders from the Governor, who was a kindly old soul with receding wispy white hair framing a beaky nose and rather prominent eyes, he said that I should stow my kit (such as it was) in the Fort's Mess, to where, to my considerable relief, Brother S had sent the uniforms I'd left in Peshawar at the start of this whole ghastly saga. The Governor told me to make myself as comfortable as I could and to wait for the departure of the next homeward-bound boat, for which he handed me a ticket and the date of the next sailing to England several days hence.

So, I tooled over to the low built house on the other side of the Fort's square that served as the Officers' Mess for the garrison. I was met there by a Mess waiter, a rather superior being who introduced himself as 'Corporal Frederick Searcy, late of Her Majesty's Second Life Guards' (God knows what a junior NCO from the 2nd Battalion was doing in Bombay, I thought to myself. Presumably, back home he had been caught with his hand in a till, a tart or someone's unspeakables and, in consequence, had ended up in this hell hole). With a bow, a scrape, and a rather knowing look in his eye, Searcy showed me to a white-washed cell overlooking the sea, which passed as officer's accommodation and where my kit was already neatly stacked in a corner.

"Luncheon, sir, is served at two o'clock and dinner is usually at eight. However, tonight there is a party in the Mess to bid farewell to the Battery Commander, who will shortly be leaving the garrison. I am instructed by the Mess Secretary to inform you, sir, that you are most welcome to join the party."

Searcy then turned on his heel and returned to his duties, leaving me with the strange feeling that we had met somewhere before. Well, I was never one to miss a party and, with my uniforms safely returned to me, a healthy tan, not an ounce of fat on my frame, my hair back to its usual luxuriant self, my whiskers positively blooming and a bounce in my step, I intended to cut a dash with the local memsahibs and find an opportunity to test-run my courting tackle under combat conditions, having already established that all was well under training conditions, if you get my drift.

I spent the rest of the morning sight-seeing. In Bombay, that means taking a turn around the parapet of the castle, which on one side had a sheer drop into the sea. Built of a local blue stone it had a certain charm – providing you were not down-wind of the native quarters, which sprawled all around the fortifications. About the only thing of any note during my stroll was a gate which opened onto a flight of steps that led down to a small beach. On it was a small notice announcing that, 'By Order of the Adjutant', sea bathing was strictly prohibited on account of sharks. Frankly, the amount of filth floating near the shoreline should have been enough to put anyone off dipping even the ferule of a gamp into the heaving swell, let alone indulging in full body immersion.

Although it was winter in India it was still pretty warm once the sun was up, so after I had been around the parapet a couple of times, I decided to rest in the cool of my hermit-like cell before the evening's entertainments. As I rounded the corner to my room I saw Searcy emerging from it with a pair of my boots in his hand. I don't quite know why, but I was instantly uncomfortable that he should have been in there.

"What the devil were you doin' in my room?" I shouted sharply to his retreating back, "come here and explain yourself."

He stopped, turned rather reluctantly on his heel and approached me with a half-smile on his boyish, rather handsome face.

"I was just making-up your bed, sir, and – as you don't have a servant – I have also laid out your uniform for this evening."

"That's very thoughtful of you," I replied in a kindlier tone, "thank you. Are you proposin' to attend to me during my stay or will you find me a native bearer?"

"That's up to you, sir," he replied, "but I am perfectly willing to attend to your *every* need, if that is what you would like..."

This last was said in such a way as to leave me in no doubt that his services would extend well beyond tending to my uniform and probably could stretch to servicing what lay beneath it. This was presumption of a high order and I decided to pretend that I had not caught his meaning.

"I am very happy for you to look after me, Corporal Searcy, but if you can find me a native who won't burn a hole in my britches or sell my epaulettes in the bazaar, then that might be more satisfactory. In the meantime, please carry on. I would appreciate it if I could have my boots back by seven and then you might give me a hand getting' dressed?"

"Sir!" was all he replied as he bowed, turned and made off towards the hall, throwing me a backward glance just as he rounded the corner at the end of the passage.

Letting myself into the room I saw to my surprise that Searcy had unpacked my bags, laid out my brushes and razors and done his best to make the room more of a human habitation than a cell. Throwing my jacket into a corner, I loosened my stock and collapsed onto the bed. The next thing I knew there was a sharp rap on the door, which woke me from a rather pleasant dream that involved several bare titted and veiled memsahibs of various ages gyrating around me to the music of a brass band being conducted by Khazi. It was dark, but there was Searcy with my boots, now gleaming in the light of an oil lamp in his other hand, which he placed on the native-made chest that served as a dressing table.

"I have a jug of hot water for you outside, sir, and I would be pleased to shave you before you dress, if you would like that?"

Rubbing the sleep from my eyes I grunted my assent, got up, stripped off my shirt and sat in front of the chest on which there was a mirror. In no time at all, Searcy had whipped a towel from off the end of the bed, draped it around my shoulders, lathered me up and started to scrape a day's growth off my chin.

"You know, sir, we have met before," he said casually as he scraped away, his face rather closer to mine than was strictly necessary.

"Really?" I parried.

"Yes, sir, you were on a riding course with my late Regiment and I had the privilege of instructing you." And then I remembered where I had seen him before: he was the insolent Cheesemonger who had made such disparaging remarks about line cavalry drill when I had been sent to London to brush up on ceremonial, afore embarking for the Emerald Isle. It seemed like a lifetime ago.

"It so happens," he continued, "that I believe, sir, you are also acquainted with my father and my younger brother?"

"Surely not?" I replied, whilst at the same time trying to keep my voice light and unconcerned as I feverishly trawled through my memories.

"Well, sir," he went on, his tone as light as mine, "unless I am much mistaken you were at Rugby School before you joined the colours."

"Yes," I replied with some firmness, "and what of it?"

"You see, sir, my father is the school porter and is assisted in that task by my younger brother. They often spoke to me about you and your friend Mr Flashman…"

I felt the customary chill in the pit of my stomach that always signals danger for me and which had nothing to do with the temperature in the room; but, then I thought, so what? I had never laid a finger on either, although the boy had narrowly missed connecting with the toe of my boot on more than one occasion.

"Yes, I remember them both well," I said with an attempt at a laugh, "and I hope that they are both in good health."

"That they were, sir, the last time I saw them before embarking for the East."

"Excellent," I said, "and I hope that you will give them both my regards when you next write home."

"That I will do, sir," he almost whispered as he wiped the last of the soap from my face, "…and would you also like your regards to be passed on to Master George Arthur, who my brother writes is now head boy? Or perhaps to Mrs Jones, who you may remember as Miss Molly Theakston?"

I was stunned into silence, for this highly unexpected conversation was clearly a sinister and thinly disguised preliminary to blackmail, an invitation to debauchery or both. I couldn't tell which but, either way, it was not good.

CHAPTER SEVEN: ILL MET BY MOONLIGHT

After my experiences in Afghanistan and Bokhara, I was attuned to danger signals and Searcy was signalling danger like a semaphore. I decided to keep my tone unconcerned and then parry with a shot of my own when he was least expecting it. I didn't have to wait long.

"Corporal Searcy, I would be most grateful if, when you next write home, you could send my salaams to everyone at Rugby, includin' the Head Master, Dr Arnold. Oh no, of course you can't do that as the great man has moved on to greater things. Well, just the boys and the staff, then. And now, can you help me into my uniform? I have so enjoyed this chat about the dear old school. Perhaps, when we have more time, we can resume it. But now I have a party to go to, so let's get on with the matter in hand, shall we?"

We both fell silent whilst he helped me into my regimentals, brushed away a few non-existent specks of fluff and then stood to one side as I admired myself in the glass on the chest. As I made for the door, which he opened for me, I tapped him on the chest with a gloved finger and gave him a steely look straight into his baby blue eyes.

"I would also much like to hear why you, a respected member of the 2nd Life Guards' ridin' staff, are in this God forsaken backwater. Perhaps, Sir George will tell me if I ask him?"

Then I marched firmly out of the room in the direction of the ante room. I hoped this last remark would put Searcy firmly back in his place. Although it was an uncomfortable revelation to know that my past was an open book to him, I pushed it to the back of my mind as I applied myself to an evening of pleasure and, possibly, seduction.

I'm told that, in the previous century, white women in India were a rarity, which with hindsight was probably a blessing, but well before 1843 they had been arriving in droves – and the likes of that old harpie Florentia

Sale had ruled the roost ever since. As I could quickly see, there was certainly no shortage of Florentia look-alikes at the party in the Mess. Admittedly most of them wouldn't have been allowed in through the gates of the Tenth but, amongst the nettles, the occasional wild orchid could be glimpsed. On the other side of the room, by an open window, one in particular caught my eye. She was not above twenty-five, blond, pretty with an upturned nose, piercing blue eyes and wearing a dress that showed rather more of her finer features than was strictly decent or necessary. She was hanging on the arm of a ruddy-faced, dewlapped and bewhiskered old Major of Artillery, who I assumed to be her papa, and was deep in conversation with the Governor. Well, I thought, that would ensure me a decent introduction.

Squaring my shoulders and thrusting out my chest, I gave my 'tashes a quick curl and bore down on the group, whilst noting the admiring glances of a number of fillies, both old and young, as I made my way across the crowded chamber. Clearly, there was a reserve eleven to be called on if I got bowled out on the first ball.

"Ah, Speedicut!" cried the Governor as I hove into his line of sight, "glad you could make it. May I introduce you to Major Empson, in whose honour this party is being held, and his charming wife?" Wife, eh? I thought; that's a pity - or perhaps not. Anyway, as he did not name her, I assumed that the old boy had forgotten it, and as I wagged their paws the Governor went on:

"Despite his parade ground appearance and cavalry dash, Mr Speedicut has recently returned from arduous and extremely dangerous service in Afghanistan and elsewhere, during which time he was disguised as a native, taken captive by the Ruskies and delivered by 'em into the murderous clutches of the Emir of Bokhara, from whom he barely escaped with his life." Mrs Empson gasped in the approved manner.

"Never let it be said that the role of cavalry is merely to add tone to what would otherwise be a vulgar brawl, eh what?" he said giving me a friendly dig in the ribs.

"Anyway," he continued, turning to Mrs Empson, "he will, I am sure, dear lady, tell you of his exploits if you press him hard enough – but, m'dear, I must warn you to have your smelling salts ready to hand, for it is a fearsome tale…"

I couldn't have introduced myself better and I could see, from the gleam in Mrs E's eye, that we might be half-way to the bushes already. But the niceties had to be observed first and so, whilst the Governor kept expanding on my story at every turn, I gave the Empsons a sanitised version of my recent adventures, pausing for effect whenever the Governor or danger intruded into the story. Just as I was about to tell them about the raving rector, my companion in incarceration, danger of an altogether different sort sidled-up to us bearing a tray loaded with drinks. It was Searcy, his lips set firmly in the best below-stairs manner.

"Thank you, Corporal Searcy," said the Governor as he exchanged his empty glass for a full one, "I hope you are seeing that our gallant hero," indicating me, "is being properly cared for whilst he stays with us?"

"That I am, sir," replied Searcy in his most servile tone.

"Good, good," beamed the Governor at him, "well be off with you!" As Searcy turned to go, I said loudly enough for him to hear:

"Interestin' fellow, that young Corporal, Sir George. He was tellin' me as I was dressin' that he had taught me mounted drill when I was last in London. Can't say I remember him, but how come a well set-up chap like him should end-up in Bombay?"

I saw Searcy's shoulders stiffen as he moved back into the crowd with his tray and, slightly to my surprise, I could have sworn that Mrs Empson gave a quick gasp as well.

"No idea, Speedicut, but out East we don't ask too many questions. We are just grateful when the Company gives us someone who doesn't have two left feet. Now, you were telling us about that dreadful dungeon…"

And so, I resumed my story, noticing with some satisfaction that Mrs Empson's blue eyes were brightening still further. Eventually the tale was told, Mrs Empson revived herself with a maidenly sip of her drink and it was time to move on. The Governor, who knew a good thing when he heard it and was now treating me like the prize-winning bull at a county fair, steered me around the room to repeat my adventures to each and every group. By the time we had completed the first circuit I was starting to wish myself back in the Emir's dungeon – no, I shouldn't exaggerate, the Teheran Embassy more like – and what with the heat of the room and the booze I was downing to keep my vocal chords oiled, I decided that it was time for some fresh air. With a grateful bow and a murmured apology to Sir George, I slipped out of his grasp and made for the verandah.

"Brave boy, that," I heard him say to the crowd as I headed for the verandah.

Once outside, I rested my hands on the iron railing as I stared out towards the lights of the harbour. Mercifully, the breeze was from the north and so I was able to take in a couple of lungsful of reasonably unfoetid air as I viewed the scene I had surveyed earlier in the day, which was much improved by moonlight. Just as I thought it was time to return to the party, I heard a rustle of skirts behind me and, before I could turn, my upper arm was gripped by a gloved hand and I heard the slightly common tones of Mrs Empson.

"Mr Speedicut," she said in an accent that was surely not the one she had been born with, "I think you are *quite* the bravest man I have *ever* met." Well, I wasn't going to deny that. "And I *very* much hope we will be able to see more of you." Ah ha, what's this leading to, I wondered?

"It will give me great pleasure to keep you company whilst I wait for my passage home," I replied, "and I do hope that, in the time remainin', I will be able to get to know you and the Major."

"Sadly," she replied, without a trace of sadness in her voice, "Joseph departs for the frontier tomorrow, but if you would care to take tiffin with me one day? Of course, I can't *invite* you to my quarters, but all the families may use the Mess for tiffin, so perhaps we *could* meet next week?"

I let her question hang in the air before telling her that would be nice, despite the fact it was not at all what I had in mind. At that moment, there was a crash from the ante room and we both rushed inside to see that someone had collapsed. Closer inspection revealed that it was her husband, who appeared to have succumbed to the heat, the booze or probably both, and was lying on his back, his face the colour of a well-boiled beetroot. In short order, his wife was on her knees, tearing at his collar and screaming, in an accent I had suspected but not heard before, for iced water and fresh air. When neither materialised, I took a few quick strides to the nearest sideboard, grabbed a pail in which a bottle of wine was cooling, threw the bottle to the nearest Mess waiter and then dashed the pail's contents over the apoplectic Major's face.

The effect was almost instantaneous for he quickly, if rather damply, revived. Mrs E's cries for help, and her accent, instantly turned to more refined shrieks of gratitude as she somewhat hysterically seized me around the legs and poured out her thanks. Had it not been for the swift intervention of Corporal Searcy, who lifted the distraught woman to her feet, I was in imminent danger of joining her husband on the floor. As it was, Mrs Empson's inadvertent attempt at a footer tackle, Rugby style, told me rather more than she had done moments earlier on the verandah. Deciding to play this game long, I discreetly backed away from the situation into the surrounding crowd, but not before I heard the Governor say:

"... and resourceful, too."

Which I think I rightly assumed referred to me. The commotion seemed to signal the end of the party and first the Governor, and then the other guests, made their farewells to Major Empson, who was now rather soggily seated in an armchair by the door, his wife beside him. It wasn't long before the Empsons, myself and the bachelor officers – apart from those who hadn't been invited on to dinner by any of the prune-faced memsahibs - were left in sole occupation of the ante room. I decided that the smart thing to do would be to wish the Major a hearty *bon voyage* and to give his wife my respects and a lusty leer if no one was looking. Both tasks achieved, I joined the other bucks as they filed into the dining room whilst Mrs Empson helped her husband into his cloak and hat and then set off back to their quarters across the square. I thought I saw her stop in the hallway and have a quick word with one of the waiters but, in the half-light, I couldn't be sure.

By the time the wine and brandy fuelled dinner was over and I had, yet again, recounted my adventures to the open-mouthed subs, I was ready for bed and I wasn't altogether surprised to find Searcy waiting in my room to help get me out of my togs.

"That was very quick witted of you, sir," was his opening line, "the Major might be mutton by now if you hadn't revived him."

"I think that's overstatin' it," I said, "but he certainly did seem to be in trouble."

"I should think that Mrs Empson will be very grateful to you – leastwise, unless she was looking forward to widowhood and a Company pension…"

I chose to ignore this last remark and, by now ready for the mattress, I thanked him and bid him a firm goodnight. As I lay staring at the bugs on the ceiling I thought that, whilst the evening had not gone entirely to plan, I had at least laid the ground work for some future fun and games and, with that happy thought, I drifted off into a well-earned sleep. Sometime later I was awoken by a rough shaking of my shoulder.

"Wake up, sir, wake up – you have a visitor…" It was Searcy.

"What the devil?" I spluttered as I came out of a deep sleep, but he said not another word.

Instead, as I could see from the lantern he was holding, he put a forefinger to his lips, then threw me my gown and beckoned me out of the room. I decided to follow him, although I was puzzled at what this was all about and not a little nervous at Searcy's involvement. But, throwing caution to the winds, I followed him nonetheless.

It must have been late, for all the lights were out. But shafts of blue-white moonlight streamed through the windows we passed as I crept down the passage behind Searcy, who led me back towards the ante room and then out onto the same verandah I had been on earlier. I sensed rather than saw a form in the shadow cast by the awning but, before I could grab the lantern, Searcy had scuttled away and, seconds later, a cloaked woman threw herself at me, her lips locking onto my mouth and a hand scrabbling for my crotch through my night shirt. It was Mrs Empson.

Quite how she had got there, or what Searcy's involvement was, were questions – important though they were – that were driven momentarily from my mind as her tongue and her fingers explored me in a way that would have shamed a Monto whore and were certainly most unexpected from the wife of an elderly Major of Artillery. Well, mine to reason why later, I thought. Finding that under her cloak the shameless hussy was wearing no more than a slip, I disengaged her from my nether regions where, judging from her murmurs of delight the modification was bringing pleasure rather than disgust, and lifted her into the Horse Artillery position (which, under the circumstances, seemed appropriate) and firmly, but swiftly (for there was no privacy to our sport) brought us both to a satisfactory conclusion. Before I could say anything, she had disengaged and was flitting back across the ante room and out of the building. With a smile a mile wide, I made my way back to my room which, mercifully, was empty and dropped back onto my bed and into a deep sleep of contentment. For not only had it been a most pleasurable if short lived experience, but it had also proved – once and for all – that the Vizier's knife had done me no lasting damage and possibly even handed me an advantage.

The sun must have been well-up the following morning when, after a peremptory knock, Searcy sidled into my room, drew back the muslin curtains, placed a cup of tea next to my bed and enquired after my well being, in a manner that gave no indication that he had had anything to do with the previous night's antics. Indeed, as he busied around my room tidying away my kit, his manner was entirely different to that of the day before. It should have set me on my guard but it didn't. He maintained this air of normality for the rest of the day and it was only when I was dressing for dinner that evening that I decided I could stand it no longer.

"Corporal Searcy," I said as he eased me into my overalls, "would you care to provide me with an explanation for your conduct last night?" If this came as a surprise to him, he concealed it well.

"I'm not sure I know what you mean, sir."

"I mean," I said with some asperity, "your conduct in wakin' me in the small hours and leadin' me to an assignation with a certain lady whose acquaintance I had made earlier in the evenin'."

"Oh, that… well, it's really quite straightforward, sir. As she was leaving the Mess with her husband, the lady in question told me that she was particularly keen to show you her appreciation for saving her husband's life. I asked how I could help and she said she would return later, told me to wait up for her and then alert you to her presence, which is what I did. As I think you may have observed, I did not see it as my place to linger whilst she showed you her 'appreciation'… Does that answer your question, sir?"

Of course, it did – but if Searcy thought for one moment that I would believe he was not fully aware of what had transpired next, then he must have thought me a fool, which was possible but unlikely. I waited for what I was sure would be a demand for money to keep his mouth shut, but instead he said nothing and nor did I, although the silence between us lay heavy in the air. It was only when I was heading for the door and dinner that he spoke.

"There is something else, sir. Both Mrs Empson and I have a favour to ask of you… but it can wait until tomorrow."

As you can imagine I didn't sleep well when I finally hit my scratcher, for I was convinced that this was a preliminary to blackmail. Of course, there was nothing I could do about my Rugby reputation and, anyway, I didn't think that Searcy really had much to go on, other than servants' tittle-tattle, but to have allowed him to be complicit in the pleasuring of a brother officer's wife. What can I have been thinking? This was undoubtedly going to cost me dear and, short of pitching him into the harbour, I could see no way out. As dawn broke I decided I could wait no longer, so I pulled hard on the bell cord. Within a few minutes, Searcy tapped on the door with a steaming cup of tea in his hand.

"Up early, are we, sir?" he said with just a hint of insolence as he placed the cup beside me. "And how were you planning to pass today? Will you be wearing civvies or uniform?" he continued, as he started to tidy the room.

"Enough of this nonsense," I growled sitting-up straighter in bed, "I want to know the meanin' of your remark last evening – about you and Mrs Empson needing a favour. What can you possibly have to do with an officer's wife and why do either of you need a favour? Now, out with it man, if you value your hide."

"Well, sir, it's like this…" I had caught him off guard and he paused for a moment, shuffling his feet and looking from the window to the door, indeed anywhere but at me. "You see, sir… Mrs Empson is my twin sister."

CHAPTER EIGHT: SHARKS

Of all the things he might have said, that was a pill out of the wrong side of the scrimmage and it was now my turn to be wrong footed. Was it possible that Mrs E was Searcy's sister? I certainly didn't remember ever having seen a skirt around the Porter's Lodge – leastwise not one you'd look at twice – but a quick glance at his face, and his eyes, told me that it was probably true.

"I see," I said playing for time, "but what can this possibly have to do with me and how can you imagine for one moment that I would ever countenance doin' you and your sister a 'favour' as you put it?"

"It's a long story, sir, but the short of it is this: when Major Empson was on his last furlough he decided that he wanted a wife. It was his habit, when in England, to stay with Dr Arnold, who was a friend of his from university days. While on this leave some two years ago, the Doctor happened to mention that my old dad, who you remember as the school porter, had a pretty young daughter of marriageable age who lived with a maiden aunt well away from the school and possible harm."

So that's why I'd never seen her, I thought: he was no fool, that porter. Searcy continued:

"The Major entered into a transaction with the old rascal and bought her. I knew nothing of it at the time as I had long since joined the Life Guards in London. The first I knew was a letter from Dora begging me to stop the wedding but, by the time I got that, it was too late and Major Empson and Dora were already on their way to Bombay.

"Over the months that followed she wrote me several letters begging me to rescue her. When I could stand it no more, I handed in my whip and shipped out, using my savings to procure the price of the passage. On my arrival here, the Company were keen enough to sign up an ex-soldier with a clean record and I've been in Bombay ever since, trying to work out how I could affect her release. And then you turned up, sir."

"Well, Searcy," I said, "it's a pitiful tale but I can't see how I can possibly help – or indeed why I should."

"I thought you might say that, sir," he replied, "and it's like this: as to how you might help, well that's up to you, sir, although I do have an idea. But as to why – meaning no offence, sir – I am sure that, if it were known that you had seduced a brother officer's wife, you would not be basking in your present glory..." He let the prospect of a duel, disgrace or worse rise up like an avenging ghost to hover over the bed.

So, neither the prostitution of the dratted Dora nor Searcy's earlier and thinly veiled offer of his own person were an attempt at bribery. Their attempt to blackmail me for help put rather a different complexion on the matter. Thinking furiously, I decided that, as before in such circumstances, what I needed was time.

"Now look here, Searcy," I said, "I will overlook your impertinence and the quite disgraceful allegation you are makin'. But I am willin' to give some thought to a way-out of the unfortunate circumstance in which your sister finds herself. Now, you said you had an idea: what is it?"

"Well, sir, you will shortly be returning to England and, as the hero of the hour, if you were to request that I should accompany you as your servant, who could refuse you?"

"So how does that help your sister?" I responded.

"Easy, sir. Immediately before you embark, I change places with Dora. You must have noticed how similar we look and in my clothes, with her hair tucked-up under a cap, who would not take her for me? And think of the fun you will have on the long voyage home..."

It was clever, I will give him that, and clearly he and the wretched Dora had thought it out, but I could see a flaw in the plan already.

"Alright, Searcy," I said, "let's for one moment assume that I will go along with this hare-brained scheme, answer me this: what happens to you and how do we avoid a hue 'n cry set-up by the Major when he eventually hears at his new post that his beloved wife has gone missin'?"

"The first is easy, sir. I lie low in the native quarter until the next boat home. Then I sign-on as a deck hand under another name and work my passage back. As to covering Dora's disappearance, well I thought you might have an idea about that."

"Did you, indeed? Well I don't."

"But I'm sure if, *under the circumstances*, you gave it some thought, sir, that you *will*." he replied. "Now, sir, can I help you to get dressed?"

So that was it: work out a way to cover Dora's disappearance and sneak her back to England as my servant or else. It could have been worse and at least the scheme, which did have a pleasurable upside in prospect, would not hit my purse. As to what happened once we got back to England, and whether or not I could ever throw off the wretched Searcy, were problems for another day. So, I got up, allowed the fellow to dress me and tooled off to breakfast. After the bowl of the revolting curried soup that passes for the first meal of the day in India, helped down with a burra peg of the Emperor's best, I set off around the ramparts to collect my thoughts and seek inspiration. It wasn't slow in coming. I had paused half-way around the fortifications to light a cheroot and was leaning over the parapet, looking out to sea, when I saw a couple of boats full of native children just off-shore. They were playing a game that involved a sort of relay race between the craft, which were about thirty feet apart. Just as I was about to turn away from this charming scene, I heard a shout.

There were two kids in the water and their playmates had started screaming and pointing. At first, I thought this was encouragement but, shading my eyes, I saw a fin powering through the waves behind the two in the water; the kids in the boats had seen it too, hence the furore. Before I could even blink, the fin disappeared and, a second later, so too did one of the children, to be replaced by a swirl of pink-stained bubbles. Feeling faintly queasy, I turned away and resumed my walk; but an idea had started to form in my mind. After luncheon, I returned to my room and rang the bell. Moments later Searcy was standing in the doorway.

"Come in," I said. "I may have a solution to the flaw in your plan. But, before I tell you what it is, there is somethin' that is troubling me and to which I require an answer."

"Sir?"

"If Mrs Empson so dislikes her present situation why, in heaven's name, did she carry on in the way that she did when her unbeloved husband nearly expired at the party t'other night?"

"That's quite simple, sir, she had no choice. It was important to our plan for her escape that there could be no question of Dora being anything other than a devoted wife. The Major's fit was unplanned, but she's a bright girl and she immediately seized the opportunity to establish beyond doubt that she was totally committed to him."

"I see. You've both thought this through and so have I - and I am willin' to help you." Searcy let out a sigh of relief. "And I think I may have a plan to cover your sister's disappearance. I leave for Cape Town on Thursday; on Wednesday, your sister will book herself into the Mess for tiffin."

...

The rendezvous with Mrs Empson, over yet another ghastly meal in the Mess, arrived as I had planned.

"You know," she announced to the table as the glutinous curried fish and rice muck was being removed by Mess servants, "it's such a lovely day that I have a most uncommon desire to be rowed around the point. Who would like to take me?"

Right on cue I said that it would give me great pleasure, providing I could find someone to do the hard work of rowing. There was a cough behind me.

"Begging your pardon, sir," said the voice of Searcy, "I've had some experience with row boats and would be pleased to take on the job."

"Good man," I said over my shoulder. "Well, that's settled then, Mrs Empson. Once tiffin's over we can go in search of a skiff." Searcy coughed again.

"Begging your pardon again, sir, I know where to find one."

"Excellent. You're a handy man to have around, Corporeal Searcy. We'll meet you by the entrance just as soon as we have finished here. Now, gentlemen," I said to the assembled officers, "how about a burra peg or two of firewater to wash away the filth we've just eaten and to celebrate my departure tomorrow?" There was a murmur of appreciation around the table, although the Adjutant said that he had to get to his office with a clear head, got up and left. "Corporal Searcy, be a good chap and bring us the best the cellar has to offer."

Why, you ask, was I being so generous to a roomful of people I hardly knew? The answer is that I'd didn't want any of them to get the idea into their heads that it might be a good idea to join our boating party. Several bottles later there was no danger of that happening as, in turn, each young officer rose unsteadily from the table and made for a wicker chair in the ante room. Once they were all snoring, Mrs E and I made our way out to the hall where Searcy was waiting for us.

"All set?" he asked his sister. She replied that she had everything they needed. Ten minutes later she and I were being rowed around the point by her brother.

"I think this would be a good place," I said, pointing at a short stretch of pebble strewn shore line that was sheltered from prying eyes by a clump of palm trees. Searcy pulled towards the place I had indicated and the prow was soon held fast by the stones.

"Time to change," I ordered Mrs E.

"Right you are," she said as she took off her frock, to reveal underneath that she was dressed in a pair of her brother's cotton drill uniform trousers and an open-necked shirt. Then, whilst Searcy artfully ripped the bodice of the dress, Mrs E tugged from her bag a pill box cap and a large green medicine bottle. After she'd pulled on the uniform cap, into which she tucked her hair, she then unstoppered the bottle and poured its contents over the top of the dress.

"Pig's blood, just as you ordered, sir," said Searcy.

"Perfect. Now put the dress into the shallows, give us both a good soaking and then be off with you to the native quarter."

"Sir!"

Half-an-hour later Mrs Empson and I, she looking remarkably like her brother, staggered into the Adjutant's office leaving a trail of sea water behind us.

"What the bloody hell?" he exclaimed looking up from his desk.

"There's been a terrible accident," I managed to splutter, whilst Mrs E covered her face with her hands and sobbed.

"Good God, man, what on earth has happened?"

"As you know, at her request I took Mrs Empson for a row around the point. We'd just passed the end of the breakwater when Mrs Empson thought she saw her husband, stood up and waved at him with her hat. I told her that it couldn't be him as he'd already left for the frontier but, at that very moment, a wave hit the boat, she toppled in and… and…"

"And what?"

"Well, Corporal Searcy and I both jumped in to try and save her, but… but…"

"Yes?"

"Well she was screamin' and flailin' about, what with the weight of her dress pulling her down, I suppose, and it must have attracted the attention of a…"

"Of a what, man?"

"A shark. But before we could get to her the brute got there first…"

"Good God! What did you do then?" Mrs Empson then piped up in a choked voice muffled by her hands.

"He tried to save the lady, sir… But… but, I pulled him back… It was too late… There was nothing Mr Speedicut could do." I looked at the floor at this point.

"You shouldn't have done that, Corporal Searcy," I said quietly. "You should have allowed me to try and prise poor Mrs Empson from those terrible jaws…"

"It's just as well, Speedicut, that the Corporal here prevented you from becoming a victim too. Typically heroic of you, and all that, but the Service needs men like you." I said nothing but stared hard at a crack in the boards. "Hmm, so what did you do next?"

"Fortunately for us," I almost whispered, "the shark was so preoccupied with Mrs Empson that we managed to swim to the boat and, as there was nothing we could by that time do for her, we climbed back in, managed to row back to the Fort… and here we are."

"That's simply appalling," he said. "I'll send the Guard to see if we can, err, can… find any remains. Then I'll have to get a message to her husband. In the meantime, is there anything I can do for you?"

"Well, as a matter of fact there is," I replied. "I know it sounds a bit heartless to bring up the subject at a time like this, but I'm off tomorrow and, given what has just happened, I wondered if you would release Corporal Searcy into my service?"

"What? Searcy? Yes, of course. Meanwhile, I must tell the Governor about this terrible tragedy."

Later that morning the Guard returned with Mrs E's waterlogged, ripped and blood-stained dress which, as I'd planned, they'd found on the shore line. It was laid in the Fort's morgue as there was (not surprisingly) nothing else of her to lay out.

The following day, Thursday 13th January 1843, I left India a hero and with the profound sympathies of everyone, from the Governor downwards, 'for the truly shocking incident'. The first leg of my journey home, with Mrs Empson in tow, was from Bombay to Cape Town on the good ship *Pride of Poonha*, said to be the latest in steam and sail power with '10 First Class cabins luxuriously appointed and with all modern conveniences'. However, in reality its charms were strictly limited, as were those of Dora Empson which, four days out, were starting to pall. She may have been an enthusiastic rattle on the Mess verandah, but her repertoire in my cabin was sadly limited and she seemed reluctant to take lessons. Lower-middle class prudery is always the worst: give me a duchess or a barmaid any time in preference to a grocer's or a porter's daughter any day.

Before leaving, I hadn't given much thought as to how we would maintain Dora's disguise throughout the long journey back to England, although I did have the foresight to order Searcy to pack some of his clothes with mine so that his sister would have something to wear. However, once on board, the solution presented itself in the shape of the Purser who, with a hand-wringing apology, said that unfortunately there was no spare accommodation in the servants' cabin and 'would it be possible for my man servant to sleep on a cot in mine?' Of course, the answer was 'yes' and I quickly agreed with Dora that she would confine herself to our quarters. But, after four days, *I* decided that this was an arrangement that would have me in Bedlam if it continued all the way home. So, I agreed with her – leastwise I gave her no choice – that I would leave her in Cape Town with enough money to wait for another ship back to England. While in the Cape, she could resume her female identity under an assumed or her maiden name. She wasn't altogether happy with this, but I was firm and, anyway, in reality she had no choice.

The ship's passenger accommodation was full of Jewish box wallahs from Bombay. They may have been rich but they were deadly dull, so I quickly found myself with a dilemma: to remain in my cabin with the increasingly tiresome, and unremittingly common Dora, or be bored to sobs in the saloon. It was with some relief, therefore, that I struck up a friendship with the elderly Captain Horace Blight, late of Her Majesty's Royal Navy and, for some years past, the Master of the good ship *Pride of Poonha*.

Blight, a grizzled, one-eyed old salt in his early sixties, had served as a junior officer on the *Victory* at the battle of Trafalgar in 1805, and had been one of the matelots who had helped to carry the ridiculously vain Admiral to his death bed in the scuppers.[43] Blight's retelling of the story, which was a regular after-dinner occurrence, always brought a tear to his one remaining eye and invariably ended with Nelson's instructions to Hardy about Lady Hamilton, for whom Blight clearly had a sentimental spot.

On several occasions, I tried to draw Blight on the subject of La Hamilton, but – unlike his Trafalgar reminiscences – he would always clam-up if there was an audience. However, one evening a couple of days before we were due in Cape Town, we were taking a late stroll on the deck and he suddenly opened-up on the subject. It seems that he had known the

---

[43] Presumably, Vice Admiral Horatio Nelson, 1st Viscount Nelson & Duke of Brontë KB (1758-1805) who was famous for always wearing his orders, decorations and a diamond aigrette in his hat – vanity which may have cost him his life, as it is widely believed that his decorations drew the fire of the French sharp shooter who killed him.

redoubtable lady since Nelson had first met her in Naples back in '98, when Blight was a junior Midshipman on the great man's boat.

"There's no other word for it," he sighed, "she was absolutely gorgeous then: the real Queen of Naples. Beautiful, charming, voluptuous and a look in her eye that none of her portraits have ever really quite captured. She had the whole world, and the Admiral, quite literally at her feet. Before we sailed for Aboukir Bay she came on the flagship and struck some of her 'attitudes'.[44] Not many of us slept sound that night, I can tell ye, what with the thoughts of what lay beneath her muslins and gauzes... later, of course, I hear she got quite stout, but I believe she never lost her charm.

"Y'know the great Nelson was completely besotted with her and she was never far from his thoughts. On that terrible day when he saved England at the cost of his own life, it was of her that he thought at the last. There's been a lot of nonsense talked about his last words – but I can tell ye what they really were, for I was right next to him, cradling his head."

"What did he say?" I asked.

"He said: 'kiss *her* for me, Hardy'."

"I thought he said, 'kiss *me*, Hardy'."

"That's just nonsense, Mr Speedicut. You see, once he'd gone, everyone in the Admiralty tried to paint Lady Hamilton out of the nation's memory and those last words didn't suit the case at all. So, the Admirals ordered Hardy and the rest of us to swear that it was 'kiss me, Hardy'. Damned stupid: as if the hero of the hour wanted to be kissed by a man! Of course, once he went to his Maker, Hardy did plant a kiss on his forehead, but

---

[44] Lady Hamilton (1765-1815) caused a sensation at the British Minister's house in Naples with her 'Attitudes', which were actually classical character poses that her audience were challenged to identify. Earlier in her career, then still only 15, she had developed an altogether different reputation when, after dinner at Uppark, she danced nude on the dining table for the entertainment of her 'protector', Sir Harry Featherstonehaugh, and his friends.

that was out of respect for the greatest sailor since Drake. But there's no telling anyone different now.

"As for Lady Hamilton, well, she was left to starve, she who had looked after him in his darkest hour – and that old gorgon, Lady Nelson, and that pious booby of a vicar, his brother, reaped his glory. There is no justice in this world, Mr Speedicut, no justice at all." And with that he turned on his heel and headed for the bridge.

The following day we were all gathered in the saloon before luncheon – at least what passed for luncheon on the heaving tub – when Blight announced that he had a treat for us before our arrival at Cape Town. It appeared that one of our number had asked the Captain if we could cruise past a barren rock called Dyer Island on which, it seemed, there were an uncommon number of fur seals, some of whose pelts the wretched box wallah was hoping to buy in Cape Town. So, as a treat and to help relieve the boredom of life aboard, Blight had decided to hug the coast and bring the good ship *Pride of Poonah* down the channel between Dyer Island and another bird-shit covered rock called Geyser Island.

"Y'll all be interested to know," he explained, "that the presence of the seals means that there are plenty of great white sharks around the islands. If ye've never seen one, they're quite a sight: some can grow to twenty feet or more with teeth the size of cutlasses. Ay, they're the most murderous beasties in the ocean and, if we heave-to and throw some offal in the water, ye'll see that I'm no spinning ye all a yarn."

The next morning Blight brought the ship much closer-in to the shore and, sure enough, a couple of bare-arsed rocks gradually came into view. As we got nearer I could see that they were covered in seals, penguins, birds and their shit; it was really quite extraordinary how much wildlife was crammed on there and how much filth they had accumulated. True to his word, Blight slowed the steamer virtually to a halt between the rocks and we took up positions on the platforms either side of the starboard paddle wheel, with just a chain between us and the briny. There was a gentle swell and, as we were more than ten feet above the sea, I felt quite safe. Then, on Blight's order, one of the stewards tipped a bucketful of bloody guts into the water.

At first nothing happened, then – and it came as one hell of a shock – a large fin suddenly broke the surface and powered towards the offal as the current took it away from the side of the boat. I could just make out a huge dark shape in the water when suddenly a great triangular black head, with a white underside and a gaping maw full of enormous serrated teeth, broke the surface, looked at us for a second with a dead black eye, devoured the muck and sank below the surface. As it swam past the side of the boat it seemed to be at least fifteen feet or more in length. It was a completely thrilling and terrifying sight.

The box wallahs couldn't get enough of it and begged Blight to get more offal into the water. For myself, I would have preferred to push on for Cape Town: one great white shark was quite enough for me. But no, they must have a second sighting and so another pail was called for. Somewhat to my surprise it was carried over to the platform by Dora, whom I had assumed to be safely battened down in our cabin, but who must have come up on deck to see what all the fuss was about. With a show of mock respect, she offered the bucket to me, but I pushed her and the filthy stinking slops away.

Quite what happened next, I will never know: one minute she was there and the next, or so it seemed, she'd slipped on some offal on the platform, slid under the chain and fell into the water with an ear-piercing scream. As she hit the foam her cap came off and her long hair spread itself out on the water's surface, along with the reeking contents of the bucket.

"My God," shrieked the box wallah next to me, "it's a woman! Someone save her!"

And by that he meant someone other than himself. But before I could decide that, whoever it was, it wasn't going to be me, I felt a hand on my back, the ship pitched and, before I could cling to the chain or recover my balance, I was over it and flying through the air towards Dora and my doom. I hit the water with a great splash, briefly submerged – my

God, it was cold - and then rose to the surface. Spitting water out of my mouth and clearing the hair from my eyes, all I could see in front of me was Dora, surrounded by offal, waving her arms in the air and screaming fit to wake the dead. Behind her, some twenty feet or so and closing fast, was a large black fin.

Before I could even reach out a hand towards her, the grotesque head of the shark rose once again from beneath the surface, the jaws caught her around her chest, cutting off her yells as blood spurted from her open mouth, and then, as though she was a rag doll, the shark threw her into the air, caught her, threw her in the air again, caught her for the last time and then sank beneath the waves leaving a spreading ripple of red foam.

It had all been so quick that I'd had no time to be scared, but now fear gripped me in a vice as tight as the shark's jaws, for in no time at all I knew that it or one of its friends would close-in on me. At that moment, I felt an appalling pain in my left shoulder and I had the sensation of being lifted bodily out of the water. This is the end, I thought, and blacked out.

CHAPTER NINE: REVENGE IS A DISH…

When I came to some minutes later, it was not in the belly of the shark, but on the deck of the steamer in a puddle of my own blood. Blight was trying to pour brandy down my throat and someone had thrown a coat over me.

"We'll get the surgeon right along to fix your shoulder, Mr Speedicut, but it's a small price to pay for your safety," said Blight. I must have looked bemused, for he went on.

"Had it not been for the quick action of Mr Sassoon in snagging you with a boat hook, you would have gone the way of your servant – for the great beastie was back soon enough looking for his second course." I mumbled my thanks to the nearest box wallah, took a serious pull on Blight's brandy and sunk into a deep stupor.

I was out cold until we tied up in Cape Town harbour a few hours later, at which point I was stretchered off the boat and taken to a run-down hotel on the edge of Cape Town harbour, prostrate with shock. But how, you may ask, when the bloody foam had subsided, did I account for the presence of a woman in my cabin and who, indeed, was she? The fact is that I didn't really have to do any explaining at all. As we had left Bombay shortly after Dora Empson's first (fictional) fish-feeding experience, no one on the boat had heard anything about the loss of an Artillery Major's wife. Her second (terminal) close encounter with the jaws of hell might have called for explanations had it not been for my own 'heroic' attempt to save her – leastwise, that's what everyone thought I had tried to do. In the event, Blight, who as the ship's Master had to make a 'report to the appropriate authorities', took the view that the matter was best hushed-up and put it about that I was as shocked as everyone to discover that I had been harbouring a woman in my cabin for all those weeks. Well, truth is often stranger than fiction and the story was accepted. Blight recorded the death of 'one person, true identity unknown, travelling under the alias of Frederick Searcy' and the file was closed at least as far as the authorities were concerned.

But if I thought or hoped that was the end of the matter as far as I was concerned, I was to be disappointed, for I had left Searcy himself out of my calculations. You will remember that I had last seen him on the Bombay shoreline, heading for the reek of the native quarter from where he planned to work his passage back to England. That, of course, was just what he did. However, one day as I ventured forth from the sanctuary of my hotel in Cape Town to take a glass of the local red infuriator at a sea-front establishment, which I had noticed seemed to have a well-titted barmaid lurking in its nether regions, there he was. I saw him before he saw me, but I was not quick enough. Before I knew it, he was standing before me.

"Mr Speedicut, sir," he said giving me a mocking bow, "I did not expect to see you here, sir. I thought as you and Dora would be well on your way back to England by now, so what are you doing here, sir – if you don't mind me asking? And where's Dora?"

There was nothing for it but to tell him the truth. Then I thought again. The story of Dora's date with destiny was unknown outside of a tight group of officials, with whom he would have had no contact; the sailors on the *Pride of Poonha* had long since departed back to Bombay; and the passengers were now on the high seas headed to who knew where. The point was that no one in Cape Town knew about the gruesome fate of his sister and, for some unfathomable reason, I didn't think it was entirely in my best interests to tell him.

After a moment's hesitation, I said that I had decided to stay on in Cape Town for a few weeks to enjoy the climate but that Dora had been 'anxious to return to hearth and home' and had prevailed upon me to buy her a ticket on the next boat to England, which she had boarded ten days previously under the assumed name of Mrs Smith. This was the best I could think up at short notice, but he believed me. At least I thought he did.

Deciding that there was nothing to be gained from snubbing the man I asked him to join me for a drink, which he readily accepted. Now, under normal circumstances, I would have poured some booze down his throat and then left him to make his way back to England. However, Searcy's mind had clearly been working even faster than mine. Over a bottle of the best that the Cape had to offer, which is not saying much, I gathered that he had not enjoyed his time 'afore the mast' and was anxious not to repeat the experience on the homeward leg. Indeed, he had already enquired at the best hotel in town whether any gentleman bound for England was looking to engage a man servant, but so far had had no takers. He proposed that as I was now lacking a man servant... I could see no immediate or compelling reason to deny him and it occurred to me that there were plenty more sharks in the sea.

We boarded the next steamer bound for England, a Frog-owned rust bucket of a boat called *La Reine Marie*, apparently named after Mary Queen of Scots and with a saloon full of French novels, presumably there to relieve the boredom. I took care to ensure that Searcy had a cabin to himself, well below the water line, whilst I had a shady stateroom on the saloon deck. I was already far too compromised with Searcy to risk him adding his own favours to the list of leverageable assets he held over me and I did not wish to have to explain the partly-healed wound on my shoulder. He continued to attend to me, but well within the bounds of propriety. We docked at Tilbury in late May 1843 and made our way back to London. Searcy said that he was off to Rugby to track down his errant sister, so I gave him the price of the mail coach, wished him good luck and offered-up a small prayer that that would be the last I would see of him.

My first stop on the morning of our arrival in town was Steyne House. Fortunately, the GB was in residence, so I handed over Brother Shakespear's report and settled down to await developments. It was hard to judge from the GB's impassive expression precisely what Brother S had written. But eventually he put down the report and looked over his wire-rimmed glasses at me.

"You have done well, Brother Speedicut. I am pleased with you. We may have lost two members of the Brotherhood and, with them, the item I told you to return to me but that was not your fault, and Brother Shakespear reports that you showed considerable resourcefulness and courage in executing your mission. Your escape from the clutches of the Emir of Bokhara would, under normal circumstances, merit public recognition – but, alas, as with so much of our work, it must remain beneath the rose.

"However, I will ensure that your Commanding Officer is informed of your conduct and there may be something else that I can do for you, but let's wait and see. Meanwhile, Barrett will show you to your former quarters whilst we decide where and in what way you can be of further assistance to the Brotherhood and your country."

As I was leaving the GB's study he called to me to stop. What now, I thought? Has he suddenly seen something in Shakespear's report that he had over-looked? Steadying myself for an earful, I turned slowly.

"What is that you are wearing on your left hand?" he demanded.

I looked down at the ring I had found in the Emir of Bokhara's best guest suite. I had been wearing it ever since, as it was a good bit of jewellery and my Papa had yet to give me a signet ring. Anyway, I had long-since forgotten that I had it on.

"This ring, sir?"

"Yes. Please show it to me." I eased it off my little finger, walked forward and handed it to him.

"Where did you get it?" he asked, so I told him.

"And why didn't you mention this ring to Brother Shakespear?"

"Well," I replied, wondering what was coming next, "why should I have done?"

"Because, my dear Brother Speedicut, this is a ring that was entrusted to Brother Stoddart and was the very object I tasked you with recovering for the Brotherhood!"

I was completely stunned, for it had never occurred to me that the 'item' held by Brother S was a ring. The GB had never told me what I was to return to him, hoping I suppose that Brother S would simply give it to me. I, on the other hand, had assumed - if I had thought about it at all which, once the fun had started, I hadn't - that it was a document that had probably been buried with Brother S in the main square of Bokhara. I said as much to the GB, who was now looking as delighted as I was surprised. And then I remembered where I had seen the ring before: it was the twin of the one that the GB had worn at my initiation ceremony. Quite what it meant to him or the Brotherhood he didn't explain but without further ado he slipped it into his waistcoat pocket and I could tell from his beaming phiz that he was as pleased as Punch.

"I think, Brother Speedicut," he said still beaming, "that despite the early hour this calls for a celebration! It may have been by accident that you have restored to the Brotherhood one of its most valuable heirlooms, but that does not diminish the importance of its return." He rang the bell and ordered a bottle of fizz from the footman.

A bottle of Dom Perignon later, I was politely dismissed by the GB to my quarters and, whilst a flunkey unpacked my togs, I sloped off to St James's Street to make contact again with civilisation. Sure enough, who should I see outside Boodle's but Baird, the Adjutant of the Tenth. He looked a bit surprised to see me, which I put down to five months' growth of beard and a healthy tan, but nonetheless he asked me in for a drink and some luncheon.

Over the meal I gathered that, during the eighteen months I had been away 'on detachment' as he delicately put it, nothing much had happened to the Shiners in Dublin and, indeed, Baird was back in England enjoying the Season and with no immediate plans to return. I gave him an account of my own adventures in which I was careful to play-up the danger, play-down the hardship and omit any references to the Brotherhood. Clearly there was more to me than he had originally thought for he gave me the impression that he was impressed.

As we finished our luncheon, he asked me if I would like to join him and some friends at Her Majesty's Theatre that afternoon. The plan was to watch a rehearsal of a sensational new dance act to be performed by some Spanish beauty with raven hair, a bouncing bust and, if you could afford it, a trick pelvis, who had been taken up by his friend Lord Malmesbury.[45]

Having nothing better to do, I agreed immediately and, after we had punished a bottle of port, we made our way rather unsteadily across St James's Square to the Haymarket. There under the portico was Benjamin Lumley, the greasy impresario and manager of HM's Theatre, and a group of haw-hawing bucks gathered around the tall, bewhiskered and unmistakeably aristocratic figure of Lord Malmesbury.

"...and she's the most extraordinary woman," the Earl was saying as I approached with Baird. "I met her on a train coming back to town and she told me her story. She said she was the widow of the recently executed Don Diego Leon, who as we all know staged an unsuccessful rising against the Spanish Queen, but had stayed to face the consequences. His widow was now, as a result, a penniless exile and had come to London to sell some property and to give singing lessons.

"I took pity on her – well who could look on her beautiful face and not do so – and arranged a benefit concert for her at my place in the country, at which she sang some of her native ballads. The concert was such a success that I thought Lumley, here, might be interested in her as a special *entre acte* feature and, once he had seen her perform, he readily agreed, didn't you Lumley?"

"That I did, my lord, and, as your friends will shortly see, Dõna Montez – or Dõna Maria Dolores de Porris y Montez, which is her full name," he said taking a squint at a grubby card, "will, I am utterly confident, create a sensation that will be highly beneficial to my investors including, of course, your lordship. We have engaged her for a month."

---

[45] James Howard Harris, 3rd Earl of Malmesbury GCB PC (1807-1889).

This was no bad way to pass the afternoon, for it was clear from the nods and winks that Lumley and Malmesbury exchanged, that Dõna Montez was probably as fake as a well-hung grouse in July. It was 'her charms' not her skills which would be the main attraction. Baird introduced me to Malmesbury as we made our way into the dimly-lit theatre, but he gave me scarcely a glance as he his party made their way to the front of the pit. For some reason, I decided to hang back and take a seat in the shadow under the grand tier. It was just as well that I did.

Some minutes later the curtain went up on a fairly bare stage on which, in the centre and towards the front, was a folding screen. A chandelier was already alight above but a stage hand quickly lit the footlights and I heard rather than saw a pianist take his place in the pit. After a moment's silence, the pianist struck-up a Spanish dance tune and, from behind the screen, castanets in hand, and with a black lace mantilla hanging from a tall comb on her head, stepped... Mrs Rosanna James.

I was so surprised I nearly cried out. As it was, I almost fell off my seat in shock. For, despite the outlandish Spanish costume and some excessive make-up, it could be none other. But how she had, in eighteen months, transformed herself from a brothel-owning Irish independence sympathiser into a distressed Spanish aristocrat was beyond me.

Once the initial shock had passed I watched the act closely. Now, I know nothing about Spanish dancing but, as she cavorted and strutted around the stage, it was immediately plain that neither did Mrs James. What she did know, however, was how to give the audience brief but frequent glimpses of bits of her body that would normally have remained under close wraps. Dancers at the opera show their ankles, but Mrs James practically showed her crotch; and her corseted dugs were permanently threatening to break loose from their moorings as they bounced up and down to the rhythm of her stamping feet and the frenzied, but uncoordinated, clashing of her castanets.

When she finished, with a flourish that seemed certain finally to release her principal assets, there was absolute silence – and then the bucks broke into wild applause. Lumley, who was sitting next to me, merely smiled. He clearly knew a good thing when he saw it, for Mrs James promised to be the sensation of the Season.

As I made my way back to Steyne House, a growing sense of unfairness and injustice started to well-up inside me. Thanks directly to the hell cat who I had just seen practically showing off her nipples on London's leading stage, in what was sure to be a performance that would establish her in the highest echelons of London society, I had been to perdition and back, faced murder, been kidnapped and imprisoned, narrowly avoided castration, suffered circumcision and been frightened out of my wits more often than was decent for one lifetime, let alone a few short months. By the time I arrived *chez* Steyne I had only one thought on my mind: revenge.

Now, as I've already recorded, I found the GB intimidating and I always hesitated to approach him but, as a footman let me into the house, I happened to see the great man making his way from the library to the stairs and I called out a greeting. He stopped, turned on his heel and bore down on me.

"What have you been up to, Brother Speedicut?" he asked in tones that for him were positively avuncular. As he led me into his study, I told him of my meeting with Baird and our subsequent visit to Her Majesty's Theatre.

"Are you absolutely certain," the GB asked, "that this woman calling herself Dõna Montez is the same person who you encountered in Dublin?" I said that I was totally confident that she was one and the same person.

"I see. Well, we have been wondering for some time what had become of her. As you know, Major Evans lost her trail in Ireland, but he was reasonably sure that she had fled abroad. It now seems that she went to Spain, for where else could she have picked-up her present skills?" I was not about to dispute this as my concern now was not where she had been but what happened to her next.

"Brother Speedicut," the GB went on, "I propose that you leave this one with me. Mark me, sir, I do not want you to return to Her Majesty's Theatre or make any attempt on your own behalf to address this situation.

Is that clear?" I nodded meekly. "Tomorrow I may have some other business I wish to discuss with you, so please meet me back here before luncheon."

This was clearly the end of the interview, so I thanked him and made my way back to my room. As the GB hadn't invited me to dine, and having had a heavy day, I decided to spend the night in. I told the footman serving my room to bring me supper on a tray: the meal that arrived a couple of hours later was so lavish it took two of the liveried buggers to carry it into my room. The following morning, I was back in the library at the appointed hour. After indicating a chair and clearing his throat the GB went straight to business.

"First, I have come to the conclusion that it is not appropriate that you should stay here other than as a purely temporary measure. I have, therefore, spoken to Brother Verulam,[46] who has recently established a club for his friends and other gentlemen at 54 St James's Street. He is happy to take you as a member and you can stay there whenever you are in London. Indeed, if it is not inconvenient, I propose that you move there as soon as you can.

"Second, although I have already told you that your activities on behalf of the Nation cannot be publicly recognised, nonetheless His Royal Highness Prince Albert has expressed a wish to hear at first-hand your experiences in the East and your impressions of the situation there.[47] Next Wednesday I will accompany you to Buckingham Palace; that should be time enough for you to get your uniform in a fit state for your presentation. You will, of course, make no mention of the Brotherhood during your audience with His Royal Highness.

"Lastly, I will have more to tell you about Mrs James in a day or two. Meanwhile, I repeat my instruction that you are not to go near the theatre. Is that clear?" I nodded my head in assent and that was it.

---

[46] James Grimston, 1st Earl of Verulam (1775-1845).

[47] HRH Prince Albert of Saxe-Coburg & Gotha (1819-1861).

Somewhat to my surprise, a pleasant one this time, I discovered on my arrival there that the Verulam believed in modern luxury and old-fashioned service. It was just up from White's and Boodle's, around the corner from Savile Row and the hell holes of the Haymarket, and was a most conveniently located base from which to prepare for my encounter with royalty. Thank heavens I knew where to find Baird again, so that I could check out with him the appropriate order of dress in which to be Presented at Court. Fortunately, most of what I had was still current except for my shako. Baird told me that, whilst I was in the clutches of the Emir, the Shiners and most of the rest of the light cavalry had finally abandoned the old leather lids and replaced them with black sable-skin busbys. And damned fetching they were too, besides being a sight more comfortable than the upturned leather buckets I had been used to. Mr Locke in St James's was able to kit me out with the necessary fur tile and so it was in reasonably good order, and with a newly shaved chin, that the GB and I bowled over to the palace in the Steynes' best town coach.

The drill at the palace was fairly straightforward: sentries saluted as we approached, the carriage pulled-up to the Privy Purse Entrance – although there was no sign of either a privy or a purse – where a fawning footman relieved us of hats and swords and then handed us over to the ice-cold clutches of a 'member of the Household', in this case the Prince's Equerry, a most superior being in the tight green tunic and black overalls of the 60th. We were then led along endless corridors into a rather grand room at the back of the palace which overlooked the gardens. Here we were asked to wait and, a couple of minutes later, a pair of double doors at the far end of the room were silently opened by liveried footmen with powdered wigs and the Equerry ushered us forward into the Presence.

Standing in front of the fireplace was Prince Albert, our esteemed monarch's husband, effectively sewn into a double-breasted and wasp-waisted frock coat, his ample whiskers flowing over the edge of his stiffly starched shirt collar. Next to him was a diminutive woman who looked not unlike a housemaid and was no more memorable; quite what she was doing there was a mystery to me. Perhaps, I thought, she was a Kraut niece come to hear of my deeds of daring-do. Anyway, we had been instructed by the Equerry to take three paces into the room, halt, bow and then walk forward another three paces, bow again and then lightly grip the outstretched hand of royalty. As the Equerry announced 'the Marquess of Steyne and Cornet Speedicut', to my considerable surprise the niece stepped forward in front of Albert.

CHAPTER TEN: ... BEST EATEN COLD

Before I could say 'what the hell?' the GB was murmuring 'Your Majesty' as he took the proffered lace-covered fingers in his gloved paw. So, this was Victoria, Queen of the United Kingdom, Defender of the Faith and gallop to the stuffed shirt on her left. In a week full of surprises, that was perhaps the greatest: she was quite the most unremarkable figure in authority I had ever – up to that point - met. At least, that was my first impression. Turning her attention to me, the Queen opened in a high-pitched voice with an accent that sounded like a curious mixture of German and Cockney, spoken with great intensity and seriousness.

"We *understand* that you have been engaged on behalf of *our* Crown in action of a *most* secret nature in central Asia, Mr Speedicut. *Do* please inform *us* of your adventures."

So, I did. Meanwhile, Albert was already deep in conversation with Steyne about the situation in *mittel Europa* or some such. With each new horror I related, the Queen's eyes widened further and her gloved hand eventually came to rest permanently over her lips. Of course, I moderated the retelling of the more intimate assaults on my person and played up the heroics. When I got to 'incarceration vile' with the Reverend Joseph Wolff her questions came thick and fast: was he really a German Jew, had he made any progress in tracking down the Lost Tribes and could anyone be so reckless as to just walk into the Emir's palace? The answer to the last was easy, since that was just what I had done, albeit under an armed guard and anything but willingly.

"Albert – *Albert, my dear*, are you paying attention to this *most thrilling* of tales? Mr Speedicut has shown *such* braveness on our behalf that we must *reward* him in *some* way."

Ho, ho, I thought, it will be out with a sword and 'arise Sir Jasper' any moment now – but I caught Albert raising a quizzical eyebrow to Steyne who made an almost imperceptible gesture of negativity in reply.

"Ma'am," interposed the GB, "much though we would all like to see this gallant young man's exploits properly recognised, the exigencies of the service, the delicate situation with Your Majesty's Russian cousins, to say nothing of a general desire to play down the unfortunate events in Kabool, mean that no such public gesture is possible. Given what I know about Mr Speedicut, I think I can say with some confidence that there will be plenty of future opportunities for the light of Your Majesty's gracious countenance to shine upon him…"

Not if I can help it, I thought. Our dear little Queen, however, was pouting like a child deprived of chocolates.

"Well, Lord Steyne, we find it *most vexing*," she said, now with a dangerous look in her eye, "most vexing *indeed*."

And that should have been the end of it, had not Albert probably decided that, for the sake of peace, quiet and his next frolic in the four-poster with HM, he had better intervene.

"Zer ist a way, *meine liebschen*, in vich you could show your apprreciation," said the tailor's dummy in an accent that hailed from deep within the caverns of Gotha. "As Commander-in-Chief ze matter of prromotions lies entirrely in yourr hands…"

"Oh, Albert, you are so *clever*," she gushed, all ill humour instantly forgotten as she bounced up and down on her little feet, "what *should* I do without *you*? Now let me think… Mr Speedicut, you are a Cornet?" Before I could answer she raced on.

"It is our *pleasure*, that you are promoted for 'meritorious service in the field' to…" - a Major, I wondered, a Colonel even - "to… Captain! There it is *done* and we are *most pleased*. It shall be gazetted *tomorrow*."

With royal honour satisfied she immediately seemed to lose interest in me and took Steyne off to one side, from where I am sure he was keeping one ear open on my conversation with HM's esteemed consort. Albert took over the role of Grand Inquisitor but, after some further enquiries about my health under trying circumstances, or some such nonsense, his questioning took an entirely unexpected turn.

"Tell me, Captain Speedicut, do you haf any Gerrman relations?" That was a poser and no mistake.

"No, sir, I don't believe that I do."

"Hmm," growled Albert, "it ist just zat you bear a quite remarrkable rresemblance to mein cousin, Prinz Heinrich of Reuss-Lobenstein-Ebersdorf.[48] Of course he is zumvat older than you, but you could be his yonger brozzer. Anyvay, I am sure I would not haf remarked on it had I not seen ze Prinz in London zis verry veek. Vell, the vorld ist full of zuch strrange coincidences. Now tell me, are you to rreturn to yourr rRegiment in Dublin?"

"To be honest, Sir," I replied, "I have no idea, although I am sure that someone will tell me my future at some point…" I ended rather lamely.

"Vell, notting changes in our Arrmy it zeems."

And, with that, the audience was over. Victoria had re-joined her husband and, before I knew it, Steyne and I were propelling ourselves backwards out of the presence, heads bowed in the prescribed manner.[49] Once back in the carriage, Steyne was all smiles:

"Well done, Brother Speedicut! That really went off better than I could have hoped. Her Majesty's Presence was a most unexpected surprise that you handled well – and, as to your promotion, well, my congratulations! I will write to the Tenth this evening so that they hear it from me rather than read it in the Gazette. I was, in any event, going to write and ask that you

---

[48] HRH Prince Heinrich LXXII (1797-1853), hereditary prince of Reuss-Lobenstein-Ebersdorf, a German principality amounting to 165 square miles.

[49] Editor's Note: This is a completely different version of the tale told by Flashman in Volume 1 of *The Flashman Papers* in which he imagines he is decorated by Queen Victoria for his 'gallantry in Afghanistan'. We now know this to be very thin fiction based upon Speedicut's report of the true facts.

should be on loan to me for a while longer. I have a job for you that will, I believe, be particularly well suited to your brand of resourcefulness – and a certain unique asset which even the Prince remarked on." He had lost me there. "In any event, I understand from Evans that it is definitely *not* in your interest to return to Dublin now or, indeed, at any point in the near future.

"Speaking of Evans and the Irish situation," he went on, "you may be interested to hear that Mrs James's engagement at Her Majesty's Theatre was what is, I believe, called a 'one-night stand'." I must have looked surprised for he raised an eyebrow. "But, of course, you saw the redoubtable lady in rehearsal and doubtless are wondering why a performance of such bravura should not have run for months? I agree with you. I attended her first night and it certainly 'brought the house down',[50] for there was a stampede from the back to the front of the pit to get a better view.

"I saw Malmesbury as he was leaving the theatre and mighty pleased he was too, not only with his protégée but also with the future prospects for his investment in the theatre. However, what I told him did not please him at all and I believe that he went straight round to the back of the theatre and ordered Lumley to take her off the bill: the theatre's a fickle world.[51]

"Of course, I don't believe that will be the last we will hear of Mrs James, Dõna Montez, or whatever alias she chooses next, although I am determined that it will be the last she is heard of in this town. However, that is not enough and I intend to ensure she is consigned to oblivion once and for all – and, thanks to a remark made just moments ago by His Royal Highness, which confirms a view I had already formed, I think I can see a way to achieve it. Would you be so good as to call on me tomorrow morning and I will tell you more," he ended as he dropped me off at the Verulam and then proceeded on his immensely grand way to St James's Square.

...

---

[50] 3rd June 1843.

[51] Editor's Note: This account is a completely in keeping with the known facts.

In the 1840s, London was the easiest town in which to make a complete pig of yourself for little coin and less risk. Most of the establishments had the Peelers in their pockets, the madams weren't too greedy and, providing you steered clear of the stews and the shambles – and particularly that area around Seven Dials – the tarts were mostly clean, well clean-ish anyway. After I'd dragged off my Regimentals and had a soak in the Verulam's steam room I decided on a relaxing kip followed by a quick dinner before setting off to see what the 'dilly had to offer.

I poked my nose into a couple of the establishments I'd sampled with Flashy, but I didn't take an immediate shine to anything on offer. Then, on a whim, I made a smart Right Wheel into Clarges Street and headed for the delights of Shepherd Market. There was nothing of much interest playing at the theatre over the market, so I loafed into the pit bar to see if anything would turn up and, just as I was about to give up and call it a night, a pair of young lads caught my eye. It was clear from both their dress and their manner that they were new boys in town, so I sidled over to see if there was any fun to be had in that direction.

As I approached, one of them turned full-face on to me and I realised, with a start, that it was East and Brown, that simpering pair of 'come-to-Jesus' ninnies so beloved of the Doctor at Rugby. Quite what they were doing hanging around one of the better dives was a mystery which, as they were sure to cut me, was likely to remain unsolved. But not a bit of it.

"It's Speedicut, isn't it?" queried Brown (or was it East) staring hard at me and tentatively extending his hand.

At that moment, I couldn't remember which of the blond-headed prigs was which and, of course, neither had seen me with cavalry whiskers. I nodded and Brown/East carried on.

"We heard that you were at Kabool, but no one seemed to know what you were doing there."

"So, what are you both doin' in town?" I drawled, ignoring the question and parrying with one of my own.

"Oh, we've both joined the Company and are up in London to get our kit before shipping-out for duty in India.[52] Scud's joining Gardner's Horse," - well now I knew which one was which - "and I'm joining Skinner's."[53]

It seemed that, despite the past, they were minded to be civil. So, I bought them both a drink. Over the next two hours we did considerable damage to the stock of brandy behind the bar. That is to say I ensured that they both had a skinful and I had just enough to inure me against their endless tales of admiration for the dratted Doctor, Rugby and a lot of other tedious nonsense besides. Finally, when it was clear that if either of them had any more they would sleep where they sat, I gently enquired where they were lodged, only to discover that it was barely a few paces around the corner at the Running Footman.[54] However, whilst I could have manhandled one, two strapping lads were beyond me – and I required both to achieve the revenge that had been forming in my mind. For I had neither forgotten nor forgiven their high-handed treatment of me in my last term at Rugby. Just as I was thinking to ask one of the roughs hanging around the bar to give me a hand, a familiar but unwelcome voice sounded in my ear.

"Do you require some assistance, sir?" It was Searcy.

"Where have you sprung from? I thought you were in Rugby lookin' for your sister," I spluttered.

"That I was, sir, but it seems she never went there. So, I'm back in London to try and pick up her trail. Meanwhile, it appears that you might be needing some help to get these handsome young gentlemen back to their beds."

---

[52] The East India Company was usually referred to as 'John Company' or just 'the Company'.

[53] 2nd Lancers (Gardner's Horse) was formed in 1809 and 1st Duke of York's Own (Skinner's) Horse in 1803.

[54] 'I am the Only Running Footman' public house was established in 1749 but was renamed in the early 19th century when the lease was acquired by a retired running footman. The pub is still there today.

I could deal with the problem of Searcy's re-appearance later; but I certainly needed assistance immediately for the two bravos were now slumped unconscious in their seats.

"If you could take that one," I said pointing at East, "I think I can deal with Master Brown. We've only got to drag 'em as far as Charles Street."

By the time we got to the inn, with minimal assistance from the pair themselves, it was all closed-up and they were both out for the count. Dropping Brown none too gently in the gutter, it took me a good fifteen minutes of banging on the door and throwing stones at various windows to wake the landlord. Finally, he emerged in a night cap, gown and with a candle in his hand. He was in a surly mood, but softened somewhat when he saw that I was on an errand of mercy with two of his customers. On enquiring which were their rooms, he pointed up the stairs and said that they were the two on the right of the landing. He then took a couple of keys off hooks behind the door, handed them to me with the candle and gruffly told me to put the keys back through the box when I left. He then padded back up the stairs still complaining.

"Let's get 'em up," I said to Searcy, who still had East hanging from one shoulder. "If we drop 'em both inside, we can then carry each of 'em up between us."

Searcy nodded agreement and dragged East over the doorstep and dropped him on the flags in the hall. I tugged Brown out of the gutter and did the same with him. Some five minutes later we had them both laid-out on the floor in the first room. Now there arose a problem, for to complete my plan I needed them both off the floor.

"Tell you what, Searcy," I said, "let's put them both on the bed. It'll save draggin' that lump next door," I went on, pointing at East. In no time at all they were both laid-out on the coverlet, dead to the world and snoring like billy-o. "Thank you, Searcy, you have been a great help. Here's a half crown for your trouble – and may I wish you all the best with your search to find Mrs Empson?"

Searcy was, I think, reasonably sure that there was more fun to come, but my dismissal had been firm and he slunk out of the room with a curt 'goodnight'.

What followed was not altogether easy. I quickly and roughly stripped-off their clothes, noting with pleasure that nature had not been over-generous in her endowment of either of them. Next, I dragged East around on the bed so that his feet were on the pillow. I then pitched each of them onto his side so that they were facing each other, nose to tail as it were, then I placed East's limp left hand between the cheeks of Brown's arse and did the same with Brown's.

The tableau complete, my only regret was that there was no way of capturing the enchanting scene – but I wedged the door open with one of their coats, put the candle at the head of the bed so as best to illuminate the pair of them and, well satisfied that mutual embarrassment if not outright scandal would be the result, I walked out of the room, felt my way down the stairs, through the front door, which I locked as requested, and sauntered back to the Verulam, mightily pleased with my night's work. On the voyage back from Cape Town, I had read a penny dreadful called *Mathilda* by a French scribbler by the unlikely name of Susan or some such. Anyway, a particular phrase, in what was otherwise a dull book, had obviously stuck in my mind and now returned to me as I crossed the 'dilly: *la vengeance se mange très bien froide.*[55] And that applied in spades to East, Brown – and Mrs James.

---

[55] 'Revenge is a dish best eaten cold' first appeared in *Mathilde* by Eugène Sue, published in France in 1841 and first published in English in 1846. Speedicut had clearly read the original version.

CHAPTER ELEVEN: CONTINENTAL AFFAIRS

I slept well that night and awoke refreshed and ready to receive my next orders from the GB, hoping and praying that they wouldn't take me back to the lion's den. I smiled at the thought of the scene at the Running Footman and regretted that I could not be a fly on the bedroom wall. Ah, well, it's greedy to want everything as nanny used to tell me. Fortified by a couple of chops washed down with some claret – fortunately the Verulam has old-fashioned ideas about what constitutes a proper breakfast – I breezed into Truefitt's for a chin scrape and a general tidy-up and then made my way over to St James's Square.

The GB was waiting for me in his study. Without any preamble, he gestured me into a gilt armchair and took up his customary position behind his desk.

"Brother Speedicut, I mentioned to you yesterday that the Brotherhood has determined that Mrs James's presence in London is unwelcome but also, as I think I said, that we are determined to ensure that she poses no further risk to our interests. Now, as you know, I was successful in getting her engagement at Her Majesty's terminated and there will be much adverse publicity on the subject of her dancing, which will appear in the press over the coming days. That should deal with her here.

"But I have now heard that she is to dance at a benefit concert at the Covent Garden Theatre on 10th July. Because of the charitable nature of the event, I think it is unlikely that I will be able to halt that performance, but I remain determined to see the back of this besom, and I believe there is a way that will both draw her out of the country *and* so ruin her reputation that her only recourse will be to seek exile in the colonies."

He paused but did not invite me to comment.

"You may recall that yesterday His Royal Highness remarked on the extraordinary similarity between yourself and Prince Heinrich of Reuss.

I had, indeed, already remarked on the likeness – for I have known Prince Heinrich for many years past – although it was your growth of facial hair whilst you have been in the East that made the similarity particularly striking; it is less so now that you have shaved your chin. The Prince also, unlike you, has a receding hairline and not a little grey in his hair. However, these differences can easily be rectified with time and some artifice. The greatest difference between the two of you is the absence on your left cheek of a duelling scar."

Now hold on a moment, I thought, I don't know what barking-mad scheme you have in mind but I'm not having my face slashed for anyone.

"May I ask, Great Boanerges, where all this is heading?"

"Be patient, my dear Brother Speedicut, and I will explain. Whilst in London, Prince Heinrich has been paying court to Mrs James. He returns to Ebersdorf at the end of the month, but Mrs James won't know that, as no announcement has yet been made. If he were to appear in a box at the Covent Garden benefit concert and pay particular attention to her, following up his enthusiasm with a large bouquet of flowers in which will be concealed some jewellery and an invitation to Ebersdorf, I think it highly likely that the lady would take the bait, don't you?" It was a question that didn't invite a reply.

"Once out of the country I can ensure that she is never allowed to return, and the humiliation she will suffer in Ebersdorf - which will of course be widely covered by journals from Saint Petersburg to the Sublime Porte - will render her, at best, a laughing stock and, at worst, a social pariah.

"All I require you to do, after some appropriate attention from one of Lumley's make-up artists, is to appear in the box at Covent Garden at the benefit concert and make sure that Mrs James notices you. Now what do you say?"

What could I say? At first sight, it seemed to be about as risk-free a venture as I had yet embarked on for the Brotherhood. I would get to play a Prince for a day and, hopefully, be part of a plot that ensured the total eclipse of Mrs Rosanna James. And, from the sound of it, the disguise could be effected without any proximate harm to my own precious carcass. Without any further ado, I agreed and my subsequent impersonation of HRH Prince Heinrich of Reuss at Covent Garden was an outstanding success, helped no doubt by the diamond bracelet the GB had given me to conceal within the flowers.

Mrs James, or perhaps I should now refer to her as Dõna Montez, took the bait 'hook, line and sinker' and announced to the world that she was off to Ebersdorf at 'my' invitation. That's another success chalked-up for the Brotherhood, I thought, and I could now enjoy some well-earned leave. Unfortunately, the GB had other ideas for me. For, at the eleventh hour, he spotted the flaw in his plan: if Dõna Montez took the bait, how would Prince Heinrich deal with her on arrival? Clearly the last thing the GB wanted was for the Prince to announce that his letter was a forgery.

However, as quick as lightning and thanks to the Brotherhood's courier service, the GB had not only confessed all to Prince Heinrich, but had also got his agreement to continue the subterfuge and deliver the requisite humiliation. Quite what hold the GB had over the Prince I never did know, but it was enough to do the trick. Perhaps it was the guarantee of several rolls in the royal silk sheets with La Montez or several bags of sovs that did it. Whatever it was, Prince Heinrich, however, demanded a price for his co-operation: the presence at his Court of a representative of the GB to ensure that nothing went wrong and that the impact of any acts of *lèse majesté* by Dõna Montez be kept to the minimum. And the GB's selected victim – well, worst luck, it was of course me.

I protested to the GB as forcefully as I could that Dõna Montez knew me, quite literally, in the buff and that no disguise would be sufficient to stop her uncovering the truth and unmasking me - or worse. The GB, whilst sympathising with my unwillingness to put myself within range of the hell cat's claws, nonetheless was of the view that I could pull it off and when I continued to protest he reminded me quite sharply of my oath.

"Assuming she accepts the invitation, Dõna Montez cannot be in Ebersdorf before the end of July but we can get you there well ahead of her. I have agreed that you will join His Royal Highness's staff in the guise of a French officer on detachment as a temporary Equerry. That will cover your lack of German. In the uniform of a French Lancer, with some false pigtails of the type so beloved of those intrepid horsemen, your whiskers trimmed to the appropriate French cavalry-style and with a black patch over one eye, there is no reason – if you give Dõna Montez a reasonably wide berth – why you should not be able to maintain your disguise."

It seemed pointless to protest that I would be skating on very thin ice, so with the best possible grace I agreed. Two weeks later I was in Ebersdorf, which is about the size of Rugby. Prince Heinrich, who was known locally as 'Serenissimus', seemed to have sired at least half the local population, for it would be no exaggeration to say that many of his subjects looked exactly like him.

Hard on my heels arrived a letter to Prince Heinrich from Dõna Montez announcing her arrival in Leipzig, from where 'she hoped' the Prince would convey her 'in State' to his realm. The Court went into a positive frenzy of preparations and the six-horse gold State coach with a small mounted escort trundled off towards Leipzig to collect the bitch.

It returned several days later, rather incongruously piled high with luggage, madam on the box holding the ribbons and smoking a cigarette - and the royal coachman nursing a black eye (it emerged later that she had belted him with her fan when he had refused to let her drive). I know it sounds incredible, but it was all true. Not content with this unconventional arrival, she allowed the Prince to kiss her hand and then proceeded to inspect the Guard of Honour. From there it went from bad to worse. One night in the royal bedchamber was clearly enough for Dõna M, who proceeded the following day to regale the Court with 'humorous anecdotes' of Serenissimus' technique – or lack of it – between the sheets. She then adopted his dog, Turk, cut the heads off his best blooms in the palace garden with her whip and then wove them into a daisy chain, which she hung around the neck of Prince Heinrich's favourite horse. He was not a happy man, no matter how fetching the horse looked.

Meanwhile, as one horror succeeded another, I found myself on the receiving end of the Prince's royal wrath. By the end of the third day he was begging me, almost on bended knee, to get rid of the woman. I already knew enough about royalty to realise that they always need humouring, so I put my head together with the Court Chamberlain, a tiny little man who saw his career (and all its perks) coming to an expensive end. In no time at all, and with the agreement of HRH, we devised a plot based around a *fête champêtre* at the Prince's hunting lodge at Weidmannsheil on the following day.

The Combined Band of the Foresters and Miners, an uncouth group of rustics accompanied by their ragamuffin children, was ordered to provide the musical backing, whilst the Court disported itself on assorted bearskins and cashmere rugs in a shady glade in the lee of the hunting lodge, to await the arrival of Serenissimus and his, by now, most unwelcome guest. However, *noblesse oblige* is obviously the watchword of continental royalty, for the Prince himself drove La Montez from Ebersdorf to Weidmannsheil in a phaeton he had recently acquired in London.

At first all went well but, after half-an-hour of ear-splittingly discordant 'music' from the band, the children finally broke into the Principality's National Anthem. La Montez jumped to her feet and screeched: 'Get rid of that rabble!' Now, during the whole visit thus far, I had been careful to keep well in the background but, for some reason, the Prince decided that it should fall to me to dismiss the tuneless brats and the yokel band.

Unfortunately, La Montez clearly thought that I wasn't doing my job fast enough for I suddenly heard her scream: 'Get him!' Before I knew it, I had been bowled over and pinned to the ground by Turk, his slavering jaws mere inches from my collar and his rancid breath nearly suffocating me. Just as I thought my last moment had come, the Prince himself dragged the brute off me and, summoning all his regal authority, he rounded on La Montez whilst I lay completely winded on the grass:

"That won't happen again, Madame! I am the master here!"

To the astonishment of everyone present, cool as a cucumber she replied:

"And I am the mistress!"

That was too much even for Prince Heinrich and he stormed-off back to Ebersdorf leaving me to discharge the second part of our plan. Now you won't credit this, but the Court, which had risen at the Prince's exit and were following him to his carriage, were ordered back and told to proceed with the feast, which they all did. In no time at all, the party was going with a real swing and La Montez was the centre of attention, dancing a series of fandangos with some of the younger and better-looking aides. And all I could think of was a phrase that had been doing the rounds of the clubs as I was leaving London: 'How unlike the home life of our own dear Queen'.[56] Barking, I know, but that's Ebersdorf.

Of course, the principal reason for this party at Weidmannsheil, and why the Prince had ordered his Court to stay, was to get Montez out of Ebersdorf and to ensure that she never returned. When I thought that she had quaffed enough champagne to be reasonably certain that she wouldn't recognise me, I marched over to her rug and, with the appropriately florid greeting so beloved of our garlic-eating cousins, I presented her with two letters.

"Thank you. Now I do hope," she said in what she imagined, wrongly, was passable French, "that your encounter with Turk," whose slobbering jaws were at that very moment resting on her lap, "has not put you off dogs? He really is a harmless pussycat." Well, that was a laugh. "He is also completely devoted to me; as you have seen he does just whatever I say." And with that she snatched the letters from my hand.

I would have liked to be well beyond the range of Turk's jaws before she opened the first letter, but protocol demanded that I remained rooted to the spot, with the dog's beady eye on me and a faint growl now escaping the slobber and foam from around his prominent teeth.

---

[56] The remark was made by one of Queen Victoria's Ladies-in-Waiting shortly after a performance of Shakespeare's 'Antony & Cleopatra'.

Reaching for a knife in her belt, La Montez slit open the first letter, which was emblazoned with the Prince's coat of arms and addressed, she cannot have failed to notice, to 'Mrs James' – a touch of my own that I at that point rather regretted. She quickly scanned the letter, which I knew contained her marching orders, put it to one side without a word and opened the second, which was a letter of introduction to the Kapellmeister of the Court Theatre in Dresden, in nearby Saxony. To my utter astonishment, she rose to her feet and announced to the Court:

"That's not such a long trip!"

Then she grabbed me by the upper arm and, with Turk at her side, propelled me to the nearest coach. She pushed me in, fell to her knees to bid a tender farewell to the dog, which left her bust covered in its slobber, jumped in beside me and ordered the driver to head for Dresden.

When we got to the border she ordered me out, rummaged in her reticule for a moment, drew out the castanets she had been playing earlier and shoved them into my hands through the window with the words:

"Here, a souvenir of my visit to your corner of the world! Send my bags on to the Hotel de Wein…"

Then she told the driver to whip-up and left me standing in a cloud of dust, feeling about as foolish as I can ever remember. As I made my way back to Ebersdorf, courtesy of a nag I requisitioned from the customs officer, I wondered if she had recognised me? I thought at the time it was unlikely, for why had she not used her dagger on me in the carriage?[57]

No sooner had old mother Montez taken the high road from Ebersdorf to Dresden than it was made clear to me that my own esteemed presence was now *de trop* in the Principality and that it would be much appreciated if I could make arrangements to ship-out *pronto*. Pleading, through the good offices of my friend the diminutive Chamberlain, that I could move nowhere without further orders, I was obliged to sit out my time in a rat-infested garret over the palace stables, whither my kit had been moved even before the dust had settled on the road to Dresden. In due course, the orders arrived in the form of a letter. After the most perfunctory thanks for my efforts, the GB said that my task was by no means concluded for, by shifting La Montez to Dresden, I had actually perpetuated the problem. His letter went on:

> *You are to abandon your present disguise and adopt that of a short-sighted English gentleman of leisure engaged on the Grand Tour. You will follow Mrs James at a distance and report her movements to me. To affect this new persona, adequate funds are at your disposal chez Rothschild in each of the cities you visit. Under no circumstances will you make direct contact with Mrs James but, whenever the opportunity arises, you are to use your initiative to blacken her name.*

Serenissimus, on hearing that my traps were packed and that I was headed for the capital of Saxony, was gracious enough to command my presence and bid me a *bon voyage*. I had thought that he might bestow upon me the

---

[57] Editor's Note: Somewhat remarkably, Speedicut's version of Lola Montez's short visit to Ebersdorf is accurate in almost every respect. It is interesting to speculate whether this letter or *The Prisoner of Zenda*, a copy of which Speedicut sent to Flashman shortly after it was published in 1894, was the basis of the latter's wholly fictional Ruritanian-style adventures as related in *Royal Flash*. In any event this incident would seem conclusive proof that Flashman's adventures, as related in *The Flashman Papers* were nothing more than an outrageous and blatant piece of gross plagiarism – and that his military rank, his honours, achievements and reputation, which rest entirely on his memoirs, were nothing more than a fraud. QED.

Reuss equivalent of the Bath 'for services rendered' in disposing of his unwanted guest. However, he implied that, in reality, it was the GB who should be sending *him* an expensive bauble – or another large draft – to cover the expense and inconvenience that had been caused at the GB's request.

Once in Dresden, and confident that Baron Rothschild's coffers would be deep enough, I took a room on the first floor of a smart new hotel, just across the street from the Hotel de Wein where I knew La Montez had set herself up. With some relief, I shed my French disguise and most of my whiskers and, as instructed, adopted that of a foppish and bespectacled English gent on the Grand Tour.

On my first evening in town, I found myself at a loose end and decided to see what the lobby of the hotel had to offer. Sure enough, not five minutes after I had settled into one of the deep leather armchairs, a glass of Napoleon's finest at my elbow, a lady hove into view through the front doors with an ageing gentleman on her arm whom I assumed, at the time, to be her father. I watched as she consigned him to the care of one of the porter's boys, who led him up the stairs towards, presumably, his room and then – with barely a glance in my direction – she settled herself down at a small table to which a tray of coffee was soon delivered.

In any company, she would have been an arresting sight, but in provincial Dresden her fashionable dress and the sheer beauty of her face made her stand out from the crowd. I was immediately smitten and, as I hid behind a week-old copy of *The Times* in which Miss Montez's various antics were lovingly reported, I started to think furiously about how I could affect an introduction. I needn't have bothered, for in reaching for my brandy I saw over the top of the paper that she was up and heading in my direction.

"I am so sorry to disturb you," she said in near-perfect English when she got near, "but I couldn't help noticing that you were reading an English newspaper and I do so long for news of my friends in London. Please permit me to introduce myself, I am the Countess von Schwanstein."

I was on my feet faster than a greyhound out of the trap. Giving her a deep bow, I introduced myself as the Honourable Jasper Thynne, offered her the newspaper and a seat.

"How very kind of you, Mr Thynne," she said, "but I really should not disturb you. All I want to do is to catch up with the goings-on in the London Court Circular and then I will leave you to your brandy."

Nonetheless, she gently lowered her delicious rump into the seat opposite me and made no attempt to open the paper. Hmm, I thought, this is a most unusual Countess. In no time at all we were chatting away as though we had known each other for years, which was not as surprising as it might seem for, having spent a couple of Seasons in London, she knew many of my contemporaries including my fellow Shiner, Francis Leigh. She was about my age, blond, fair-skinned and quite tall for a woman, but without the hideous great bust and backside that disfigured so many of her sex in those days. She was, I admit it, rather boyish in her looks – but there was nothing of the 'tomboy' about her. Emboldened by her friendliness, I asked if she had already dined, was told that she had not and – taking the plunge – I tentatively asked her if she would join me in the hotel's dining room. Without a moment's hesitation, she accepted and the rest is, as they say, history.

Of course, it wasn't as straightforward as that. For a start there was the Count, but Mitzi (for it soon emerged that was her Christian name) said that he, Johannes, was quite happy for her to do as she pleased providing that he was not left out of the daytime activities. It turned out that Mitzi was a member of the immensely rich and grand Bavarian noble house of Thurn und Taxis but, as the youngest daughter of a younger son, she had to marry as well as she could. Because of this, she rather sensibly chose the ageing Count von Schwanstein, an hereditary Court official to the Wittelsbach rulers of Bavaria, who was responsible for the upbringing of the junior members of the clan. Schwanstein was delighted to have captured such a pretty young thing and she clearly saw her husband's fortune, amiability, advanced age and Court appointment as opportunities not to be missed. In other words, it was a perfect marriage. When I met him the following morning I found him to be a jolly old soul, not nearly as ancient as I had taken him to be the night before and excellent company.

Anyway, after our second bottle of claret at dinner on that first evening, and with Mitzi giving every indication that she wanted to get to know me better, I decided that it would be much simpler to bring her into my confidence – particularly as, at the time, I spoke scarcely a word of German and I badly needed outside help if I was to carry out the GB's orders. She instantly forgave me for my initial deception and, in no time at all, she was effectively in charge of operations. And how long was it before Countess Mitzi cuckolded her husband in my youthful arms and, when she did, was she any good at Venus's gymnastics? The short answer is within the week and yes – and that is as much as I'm going to record whilst returning my readers to the business in hand.

La Montez had arrived in Dresden on 7th August 1843 and played there for just three nights. My judicious briefing of the scribblers, ably translated by Countess Mitzi, ensured that Lola was not well received and she moved from there to Berlin, announcing that she had received an invitation from the Queen of Prussia. Pure rubbish, of course. To coincide with her arrival, and perhaps as an omen, the Royal Opera House on the Unter den Linden burnt to the ground. But this did not stop her and – thanks to the intervention of Prince Albrecht, the King of Prussia's brother (God only knows how she secured that engagement: but I could hazard a good guess) – she was booked for a number of performances at the Schauspielhaus, culminating in a Command Performance at the royal palace in Potsdam.

I managed to get her booed off the stage at the Schauspielhaus on 10th September, but the private theatre at Sans Souci was beyond my reach and so La Montez managed to flaunt her knickers to the crowned heads of Prussia and Russia. That might have signalled the re-start of her career, had it not been for a grand military parade on the Friedrichfelde, a wide-open space on the western fringes of Berlin, which was scheduled for the Sunday following her Command Performance.

I had been tipped-off by the concierge of her hotel, whose co-operation I had secured with Baron Rothschild's gold, that La Montez had hired a horse and a suitable costume, *à l'amazon*, and was intending to attend the parade with a forged pass for the Royal Enclosure. Mitzi and I pre-positioned ourselves at the entrance and warned the guards what to expect. In due course, up rode the fake Spanish harpie to find, to her fury, that she was denied access. When she tried to barge her way through, the guards stood firm and then, to my astonishment, she went for them with her whip. Well, that was too much for the Gendarmerie and she was hauled off her horse and promptly placed under arrest. I decided to get a bit closer to watch the fun, but in the ensuing fracas – for she fought to break free like a woman demented – my tile and glasses were knocked off. At that very moment, I found her staring into my eyes. She screeched: 'You!' But, before I could hear any more, she was bundled into the back of a closed police wagon.

Needless to say, the papers were full of her arrest the next day, with some judicious briefing by Mitzi although – truth to tell – they didn't need much encouragement, and before you could have said 'drop your kegs, you brazen hussy' the story was being published around the capitals of Europe that Dõna Lola Montez had attacked a Prussian cavalry Regiment and driven them off with her whip!

Despite, or perhaps because of the coverage, La Montez decided that Berlin was too hot to hold her and, before I could get our coach harnessed, she had left for Warsaw announcing her intention of taking up an invitation from the Tsar to appear in Saint Petersburg. Well, I thought, it was time to drop my role of shadowing the bitch, for my cover was blown and, anyway, I could be reasonably certain that, following the Friedrichfelde incident, our friends in the Fourth Estate would do that job for me and I could settle down in Berlin for a month or two of well deserved rest, at the GB's expense, in the arms of my darling Countess. And that is exactly what I did whilst, over my daily *kaffee und kuchen*, I followed the antics of La Montez in the pages of the newspapers. These reported that the Governor of Warsaw, on the orders of the Tsar, ensured that her stay there was as short as possible and had her deported at the point of a bayonet back to Prussia from where, despite her treatment at the hands of the Tsar's officials, she made her way along the coast headed for St Petersburg. However, before she could even unpack there, she was thrown out of Peter the Great's Italianate city on the Baltic in early February 1844 and had to make her way back to Berlin, where in no time at all she had snared a randy, long-haired gypsy pianist called Littz – or some such.[58] Meanwhile, following a report that I'd sent to London in which I'd told the GB that I'd received a poisonous letter from the whip-wielding bitch swearing that she would 'see me in hell', I was given 'leave of absence' until Easter, by which time I was supposed to be back to London.

Whilst all this was going on, Johannes was himself ordered back to Munich to tend to one of his official charges, the seventeen-year old Princess Alexandra of Bavaria.[59] So, as I'd nothing better to do, I accepted Mitzi's invitation to stay with the Schwanstein *ménage* and take the train south. Now, at this stage in my life, I wasn't altogether taken by steam locomotion. Yes, it halved the time it took to get from A to B, but it wasn't exactly the lap of luxury and the wretched engines were then very prone to breaking down at no notice and usually in some damned out-of-the-way place. However, Johannes was completely obsessed with modern technology and so, instead of a comfortable and leisurely drive from Berlin to Munich in the Schwanstein's travelling coach, we were all bundled into a draughty wooden box on the Trans-Germania so-called-express where we had to make do with stone hot-water bottles, piles of furs and several baskets of provisions to stave off the cold and fuel the inner man.

Needless to say, on the second night the engine pulling the train decided to give up the ghost in the middle of snow-covered nowhere. Well, actually, to be fair, it ran into a large snow drift and, in its efforts to extricate itself, it managed to detach the last coach on which, of course, we were travelling. We first realised that something was wrong when we heard the engine's

---

[58] Lola Montez had an affair in early 1844 with Franz Liszt (1811-1886), the celebrated Hungarian composer and pianist.

[59] HRH Princess Alexandra of Bavaria (1826-1875) was the eighth child of HM King Ludwig I of Bavaria.

whistle receding into the distance and Johannes asked me to run down the window and see what was going on.

I did so. A veritable blast from the arctic hit me full in the face and fair took my breath away. There was a full moon – so visibility was not an issue – and, in the few seconds I had my head out of the carriage and saw a large gap in the snow drift where the engine should have been. We were stranded. I quickly withdrew my head and pulled hard on the window strap so as not to lose any more heat from the compartment.

"Well, my dear friends," I said, "I think we are going nowhere until those numbskulls on the box realise that they are one carriage short – and that won't be until they get to Bayreuth in a couple of hours' time. In the meantime, it looks as though we are here for the night, so I suggest we do the best we can to stay warm."

As soon as I'd finished speaking, I heard a quite ghastly sound that seemed to come from the depths of hell but was probably from the nearby wood: it was a wolf calling to its pack with a long-drawn-out howl that rose and fell. We could have had a fire blazing in front of us, but I would still have been chilled to the marrow by that hellish noise.

But the Schwansteins were obviously made of stern stuff and neither Johannes nor Mitzi turned so much as a hair. In fact, Johannes remarked that he thought the beast was probably a timber or grey wolf, but at that distance he couldn't be sure: I offered up a quick prayer that none of us would ever find out. To keep up our spirits – or, at the very least, mine – I broke out a bottle of cognac from one of our hampers and handed around three glasses. I'd just raised the glass to my lips there was a rough scratching on the compartment door. I nearly jumped a foot in the air, but Johannes merely leant across the hamper and gently lifted the corner of the blind that hid our compartment from the corridor. The next second he was up and sliding open the door, through which there appeared, first, the shaggy head of a large grey dog followed by a young, dark-headed boy with red-rimmed eyes and skin the colour of alabaster.

My German was still not good enough to understand what the lad was saying, and anyway he had a rather nasty hacking cough that punctuated his words, but Mitzi quickly told me that he was on his way to Munich in the care of an ancient forebear and the handsome hound. They too had heard the cry of the wolf and the elderly relative had sent the boy in search of other passengers. Johannes suggested to me, in English, that it would be a kindness to invite these two and their dog into our compartment, a course of action to which I readily agreed. After a further hurried exchange in German, the boy and his dog disappeared, to return shortly with a hook-nosed, wrinkled and hunched old crone who looked like a witch out of Grimms' *Fairy Tales*, a book that Mitzi had given me to read in Berlin to help improve my German. The old lady was dressed in a black, high-necked travelling dress that had been out of fashion for some two decades or more.

"Kind lady and gentlemen, may I on behalf of my grandson and myself thank you for your offer of hospitality? I am the Dowager Gräfin von Cernogratz and this is my grandson, Karl," croaked our new companion, in German that was so slow and pronounced that even I could understand it. "Your generosity of spirit will ensure your protection from the dangers that lurk outside."

At first, I thought that I hadn't fully understood this last bit but, after we had in turn introduced ourselves to the dowager, Mitzi assured me that I had. The old bat was either mad or we had fallen in with one of those ultra-religious Romans who believe that ten Hail Marys and a crucifix will save you from anything. I decided to reserve judgment and instead proffered the old girl a seat and a glass of brandy, both of which she willingly accepted. We had nothing to offer the boy, but he seemed content to curl up under a rug in one of the corners next to the window, with the dog on the floor beside him.

For several minutes, there was silence in the compartment, interspersed with a growing and deeply chilling serenade from the surrounding woods, at each sound of which the hound would prick his ears and emit a short, low growl. I'm sticking close to you, my hairy friend, I thought. After the third, or perhaps it was the fourth, chorus from the woods Johannes once again got to his feet, pulled down a small leather case from the rack and opened it to reveal a pair of beautifully crafted duelling pistols.

"I think, my dear Jasper, that perhaps we should prime these pieces just in case our friends outside decide to try and force their way in." He then loaded a pistol which he handed across to me.

"Those won't be necessary," croaked the crone without any warning. "I have already told you that for as long as you are with me you are quite safe." We all looked at her in astonishment, but it was Mitzi who had the courage to ask why.

"Why? Because the wolves are gathering not to hunt you down but to celebrate the passing of a Cernogratz. For generations, the death of one of my family has been marked by the wolves' chorus – and so it is tonight. A tree will fall and a Cernogratz will die as the wolves serenade the soul to Valhalla."

With that she fell silent. We were all too stunned to break it, for it was clear that the dowager had foretold her own end. The minutes ticked by and still the only sound was the dismal howling and wailing of what sounded like every wolf from the Ardennes to the Carpathians.

Suddenly there was a great crack, as though a tree in the surrounding wood had been split from crown to root, the window dropped open, an icy blast blew out the lamp in our carriage, our sanctuary was momentarily pitch black and then, as our eyes became accustomed to the dark, it slowly but faintly lit-up in the ghostly white glow of the moonlight. I lurched over to close the window and saw outside shapes and shadows loping near the carriage. Then, so loud was the noise that it seemed as though they were actually beside us in the carriage, the wolves once again took up their cry. It was a gross and hideous harmony that built to a deafening crescendo and then drifted away to nothingness.

I was frozen with fear as, I think, were Mitzi and Johannes, but we were startled back to reality by the sudden flare of a vesta. For a moment, it highlighted the deep craggy lines of the old lady's face and then she struggled to her feet and reached up to the oil lamp, which she relit. With the compartment once again bathed in a more human glow, I looked around to see what if anything had happened. But all seemed normal. Johannes sat with a loaded pistol on his lap, Mitzi was slowly blinking her way back to normality, the dowager had resumed her seat, and the boy and his dog were still by the window – but the dread music of the wolves had stopped.

It was only when I looked back at the two in the corner that it occurred to me that they were both unnaturally quiet. I was half out of my seat when I felt a strong, bony hand grip my wrist and force me back down.

"He has gone, and his faithful friend with him. It is as I foretold."

CHAPTER TWELVE: A GLASS PIANO

For most of the time I'm not easily shocked, but the sudden death of a little boy and his dog in a railway carriage, surrounded by slavering wolves in the middle of a snow field in Bavaria, did the trick and no mistake. In fact, the only person who appeared to be completely unmoved by the ghastly tragedy was the boy's grandmother.

"Would you be so kind, Herr Rittmeister,"[60] she said turning her rheumy old eyes on me, "to assist me in taking Karl back to our compartment? I would like to prepare him for his arrival in Munich – and the dog too."

I nodded and, without a word, I picked up the body of the boy, which was just skin and bone under his clothes, and carried it back to her compartment. There I gently laid him out on the seat, put a small bag under his head and covered him with a blanket leaving, as instructed by his grandmama, his face exposed. I then returned for the dog but could not manage him on my own, so Mitzi gave me a hand and we placed the still warm body gently on the floor beside the dead boy. It was a most touching scene and Mitzi was dabbing her eyes as we turned to go; the old lady thanked us for our help and then made it absolutely clear, without so much as a word, that she wished to be left with her dead grandson and his dog.

Back in our own compartment none of us could think what to say and it was only the shrill sound of a whistle that seemed to jerk us back to reality. The engine driver had clearly not had to travel as far as Bayreuth before realising that he was a wagon short of a full load. The carriage heaved and shuddered as it was reconnected to the rest of the train, but it was only when the familiar clickety-click had resumed that anyone broke the silence.

"Consumption," said Johannes answering an unasked question. "It must have been consumption – and either the shock of the wolves or the cold

---

[60] German for a cavalry Captain.

of the carriage finally killed him. The Cernogratz family live in Bohemia, so perhaps the old lady was taking the boy to a clinic in Munich."

"But, my dear, that doesn't explain the death of the dog, the fall of the tree or the sudden disappearance of the wolves," said Mitzi.

She had a point and we were still debating the mysteries of life and death when the train finally pulled into Bayreuth station. We watched through the window as the old lady climbed stiffly down from the carriage, called over the station master and started issuing instructions. Shortly thereafter she climbed back up and that was the last we saw of her until we arrived in Munich where a black and gold hearse, with two small brass-studded coffins, plumed horses and liveried footmen, was waiting on the low platform. Johannes said that we should wait in our compartment until the coffins had been loaded and the cortege got on its way, which we duly did.

We were a sombre party on our arrival at Schloss Schwanstein, my hosts' country estate a few miles outside Munich. But, with a blazing fire in the hall, a steaming silver bowl of *glühwein* (the Bavarian version of punch) and Mitzi once again in a low-cut gown we soon revived – although I will remember that queerest of nights to my dying day: the boy, the dog and the wolves.

But, if the trip to Munich deserved an entry in the next edition of *Grimms' Tales*, what happened over the next couple of weeks was so extraordinary that I don't think even their publishers would have touched it. For readers will recall that the reason for our trip to Munich was the summons Johannes had received to attend on La Princesse Alexandra, daughter of the august and extremely randy monarch who sat on the throne of Bavaria, His Most Catholic Majesty King Ludwig I.[61] I say 'randy' because, of all the then crowned heads of Europe, who else had nine children and a huge collection of specially commissioned portraits of those women whom he considered were the most beautiful in Munich, most of whom were reputed to have shared the royal sheets with the old goat? The collection was called the 'Gallery of the Beauties' and it was on public display at the

---

[61] HM King Ludwig I (1786-1868).

Wittelsbachs' summer residence, [62] a wedding cake of an edifice called the Nymphenburg Palace located on the outskirts of Munich. Talk about parading your conquests! Anyway, according to Johannes, Ludwig didn't give a fig what anyone thought and did just as he pleased, as I was about to find out.

No sooner were we settled into the baroque, if somewhat draughty comfort of Schloss Schwanstein than a messenger arrived from the Residenz (the Munich Court of His Randy Majesty) commanding Johannes 'to attend upon the King'. Now, in England such a command would apply only to the person summoned, but Johannes said that I could accompany him for my education, if for nothing else. In the previous twelve months, I'd experienced at first hand probably the grandest and the most insignificant monarchies in the world, so it was with some interest that I tagged along to see what the Bavarian version amounted to.

As there had been a fresh fall of snow since we had stepped off the train in Munich the day before, Johannes, resplendent in Court uniform, ordered his parade sleigh to be harnessed and, with two outriders in the Schwanstein livery ahead of us and two caparisoned horses in tandem pulling the sleigh, we swished off to Munich at some speed accompanied by the soft beat of the horses' hooves on the snow and the jingle of the hundreds of tiny silver bells on their harnesses. The sleigh was open-fronted but we were warm enough covered with fur-lined velvet rugs over our winter coats. All in all, it was a charming scene straight out of a fairy tale.

The sleigh pulled up outside the Residenz, which unlike the other two palaces I had visited recently, was embedded in the city rather than standing aloof from it. It was quite an austere building on the outside but, as Johannes told me later, inside it is a riot of extravagant interiors ranging from the medieval to the modern. But on this visit, I was not to set foot in the place for, as soon as Johannes's footman had given his name to the

---

[62] In 1843 there were 26 portraits in the *Schönheitengalerie*. By the time King Ludwig I abdicated in 1847 there were 36, including his daughter, Princess Alexandra, who was painted in 1845. All the portraits can still be seen today.

flunkey at the front door, a Court official came bustling out to inform us that the King had gone for a stroll in the city and he hoped that J would join him at his favourite beer cellar, the Hofbräuhaus on Am Platzl, not ten minutes' distance away.

"Let's walk," said Johannes taking my arm for support, "it's a beautiful day and it wouldn't be fitting for us to arrive at the *bierkeller* in a sleigh when the King has gone there on foot."

I think he could tell from the rather shocked look on my face that this was the last thing that I had expected.

"It's like this," went on Johannes in answer to my silent question, "although His Majesty takes himself and his position with the uttermost seriousness, and demands all the deference that is due to his rank, he feels that he is so secure in his position that he can, like Zeus but without the disguises, descend from Olympus without compromising his status.

"So, it is his custom to walk through the streets of Munich without any escort or ceremony and to take his pleasures as and where he finds them. To someone like yourself, brought up to expect monarchy to live on a closely guarded pedestal, this may seem strange but His Majesty believes that it keeps him in touch with his people and, judging from his popularity, he may well be right."

At that moment, we rounded the corner into the square in front of the opera and, a few snowy minutes later with Johannes puffing somewhat, we arrived at the inn. Pushing our way through the heavy curtains behind the door, I couldn't at first see anything in the smoke-filled gloom, but a white-aproned and red-faced publican, who bore an uncanny resemblance to Mr Theakston of none-too-sacred memory, bustled up to Johannes, who quietly ordered him to show us to the booth in which His Majesty could be found.

At first the publican was reluctant, as he was apparently under strict orders to preserve HM's privacy, but Johannes opened his coat. At the sight of the Court uniform, the publican attempted a deep bow and pointed us to the far corner of the room.

By now my eyes were accustomed to the gloom, but all that I could see, as we made our way across the crowded room to the corner indicated, was a rather scruffy late-middle-aged man with a prominent birthmark on his forehead, cradling a *stein* of beer – and with his nose practically wedged into the ample bosom of a *dirndl*-clad barmaid who had obviously just handed the drink to him. There must be a mistake, I thought, as we got nearer. But Johannes made a deep bow and His Randy Majesty King Ludwig I of Bavaria dismissed the pair of tits he was engrossed in and proffered Johannes the seat opposite.

"Ah, Schwanstein, how good to see you and how is your lovely wife? You know she really should sit for Stieler as she would be a considerable adornment to my collection."[63]

Johannes looked slightly pained and deftly ignored the remark.

"Sire, may I present Captain Speedicut of Her Britannic Majesty's Hussars? My wife and I met him in Berlin and he is spending his leave with us. He has recently provided signal services to Your Majesty's cousin, His Royal Highness Prince Heinrich of Reuss, about which I am sure he would be pleased to inform you…" Thanks for that, Johannes, I thought, but which version of the tale will be fit for the royal ears?

"Sit down, sit down, m'boy," intoned the King in English pointing at me, then indicating the space on the bench next to Johannes. "It is a pleasure to meet you. Now, you both look as though you could do with a drink."

He raised his other hand an inch or two from the table and, as if by magic, the beefy barmaid reappeared, took an order for two more *steins* (you take what you are given by Princes) and then the King turned back to us.

---

[63] Most of the portraits in the Gallery of the Beauties were executed by Joseph Stieler (1771-1858), Court painter from 1820.

"Captain Speedicut, I will be most interested to hear of the events in Ebersdorf, about which I remember reading, but first – if you will excuse me – I have business with Count von Schwanstein," and he continued on in a nasal German which was so clear that I was able to follow the conversation quite easily.

"Now, my dear Count, first my apologies for interrupting your holiday in Berlin, but I have need of your services in connection with my youngest daughter, Princess Alexandra. In August this year, it will be her eighteenth birthday and she will be of marriageable age. However, her health is frail and she shows no interest whatsoever in anything other than books and writing. Indeed, she has told me that her ambition is to be a published author, which, whilst entirely admirable, is a quite unsuitable occupation for a member of my House. I am, of course, most supportive of her literary ambitions but these she can pursue within the confines of marriage.

"As Hereditary Chamberlain to the Lesser Children of Bavaria – yes, yes, I know it is a purely ceremonial appointment – I require you to earn your honorarium and you will assist me greatly if you and your beautiful wife could take Princess Alexandra under your wing and into your house for a month or two, introduce her to some young people - I'm sure the Countess knows many such suitable persons – and see if you can't bring the girl out of herself. What do you say?"

What could poor Johannes say? There he was in the early evening of his life, commanded to nursemaid an apparently petulant and seemingly wayward seventeen-year old princess. He must be regretting, I thought, the day he inherited his Court appointment from his father.

"Sire," replied Johannes, "my wife and I are, as always, entirely Your Majesty's to command."

"Good, good," continued the King, "well I propose that you both present yourself at the Nymphenburg tomorrow to collect Her Royal Highness – and why not take this young man along with you?" he said pointing again at me. "He is exactly the kind of well set-up young fellow that my daughter should be meeting, although his rank, of course, precludes him from being anything other than an acquaintance." Johannes murmured his agreement as the King turned to me and once again broke into English.

"Is it true that my cousin Heinrich made a complete fool of himself with a Spanish dancer? The newspapers have been full of her exploits across the continent – although she has had the good sense not to set foot in my realm. But I hear she is a great beauty, so perhaps I would, after all, like to meet her…"

He rambled on in a similar vein for a few more minutes. When it was clear that he was ready for my story, I told him of my encounters with Lola both in Ebersdorf and after, although I was careful to make it appear that I had been a passive observer of her antics. By the time I had finished, I could see from a light in the King's eyes that he was rather more interested in La Montez than he wished to appear. His questions, particularly about her principal assets and her activities with her horse whip, were altogether too probing to be mere idle curiosity. If the bitch ever tired of her piano-playing gypsy she might do worse than set the compass to south and head for Bavaria, I thought.

In my experience of royalty, then and since, there is a moment when you know that the audience is at an end. Nothing is said, but you can sense that royalty's attention is starting to wander and you know it is time to make yourself scarce. Ludwig was no different in this respect to his cousins and it shortly became clear that he wished to be left to enjoy his beer and the big-titted barmaid. So, Johannes and I rose, bowed and made a discreet exit from the inn. To my surprise, Johannes's sleigh was drawn up outside waiting for us and we were soon flying back to Schloss Schwanstein and a lavish luncheon presided over by my darling Mitzi. Over the meal Johannes told her of his task.

"It's really too bad: why, at my age, should I have to spend time dealing with a spoilt royal child who quite clearly just wants to be left to her own devices? It's not even as though she's in the line of succession or is a particularly important runner in the royal marriages stakes. Surely her brothers and sisters are better placed to draw her out of herself?"

"Johannes, dear," replied Mitzi, "I understand from cousin Sophie, who was until recently her governess, that the other royal children are largely responsible for Alexandra's present state. Apparently, they do nothing but tease her about her literary ambitions and her increasing eccentricities. I think it would be a considerable kindness to try and help her. What do you think, Jasper?"

Actually, I didn't have a view on this subject, just an interest in whether Miss Alexandra was beddable material or not, but I replied:

"I think it would be a great thing if we could help the poor girl. I know little about royalty, but what I have seen convinces me that the life of a royal is by no means a bowl of cherries." Shortly afterwards, the conversation turned to subjects of more immediate interest, such as the prospects for hunting in the snow.

The following morning, togged up to the nines in our best kit, the three of us set off for the Nymphenburg Palace. As I've already stated, it was a confectioner's idea of a building set within a great courtyard at the end of a broad canal, which was covered in ice. The main palace had a central pavilion and two side pavilions, all in gilded white stone, topped with bright terracotta tile roofs and bounded by stables and servants' quarters. At the rear was an elaborate park, the outlines of which were clear to see, snow-covered though they were. Johannes's sleigh pulled-up at the main entrance to the central pavilion where we were met by saluting guards and the usual phalanx of palace servants and functionaries. With much ceremony, we were shown into the main entrance hall, which was an extraordinary space that rose the full height of the building up to an elaborately painted ceiling. Needless to say, it was freezing cold. The Princess's Private Secretary soon came bustling in and, instead of arranging for our coats to be taken, informed Johannes that HRH 'was at the Amalienburg'. It seemed, I thought, that the Wittelsbachs made a habit of never being where they were supposed to be or perhaps that was just the privilege of monarchy. Anyway, the Private Secretary led us across the hall, through a pair of doors onto a terrace with a double flight of steps into the park.

As we reached the bottom of the steps a closed royal sleigh pulled up, we climbed in and were swept off into the depth of the park to be deposited in front of a most handsome pink and white, single-storey pavilion. In a small lobby yet another servant took our coats and we were ushered into the principal room. If it was beautiful on the outside, the inside, which thank God was well-heated, was quite simply fantastic. The round saloon into which we had been shown was a riot of mirrors, silvered rococo plasterwork and blue damask. I had never seen anything like it and it made my head spin. Seated in the middle of the floor, dressed entirely in white and surrounded by books, dolls and with a Lady-in-Waiting lurking in the background, was a young girl whose striking beauty matched that of her surroundings. She had dark hair, a straight nose and full lips but it was her eyes which were her principal asset for they were deep pools of light framed by dark, arched eyebrows and full lashes. As we entered she rose and curtseyed to us, a compliment that we were quick to return as Mitzi took charge and presented us.

"I am greatly pleased to meet you," said Alexandra in a babyish voice that was belied by her blossoming bosom. "My father, the King, has told me to expect you and so here I am." There followed a moment of awkward silence, which was broken by Mitzi who enquired as to what Alexandra had been engaged upon when we arrived.

"I have been working through a story in my head," she said, "and I plan soon to put it on paper. It is to be the first of a series of short stories that I am planning to write. I draw inspiration from my dolls, who are my best and most constant companions," she said pointing to the dozen or so figures that lay scattered on the carpet. This would have been reasonable enough behaviour in a twelve-year old, but in a girl on the threshold of womanhood it was downright unnatural. However, I decided that it would be easiest to play along with her and so I asked her to tell me the plot of her story, which she proceeded to do. I soon wished I had not asked.

Some two hours later, a small convoy of sleighs made its way back to Schloss Schwanstein carrying the Princess, her Lady-in-Waiting, ourselves and about a ton of luggage, the Princess all the while wittering on to me about her stories.

Over the next couple of weeks most of the Thurn and Taxis gang aged under thirty were paraded at small luncheons and teas to entertain HRH but, despite our best efforts, there seemed to be no way to stir her out of her world of infantile fantasies and bring her into the orbit of adults. Her childish behaviour, to say nothing of the bevy of royal staff who guarded her every waking and sleeping moment, was more than enough to banish any lusty thoughts I might have entertained for her, had I had the energy to play away from Mitzi's bed.

However, at least Johannes and I could enjoy her beauty; not so Mitzi, who was finding the duty more of a strain and said as much over breakfast one day:

"Enough is enough; we are achieving nothing. What is required is for Her Royal Highness to be exposed to the wider world. Then, and only then, is there a chance that she may throw off this obsession with her dolls and her world of make-believe. Johannes, you must write to the King and ask him if we may give a party for Princess Alexandra."

We both agreed that this was a sensible course of action, so the long-suffering Johannes duly wrote to HM and, by return, received a letter in the affirmative. Mitzi swung into action and, in no time at all, had roped in the more eligible of the Bavarian aristocracy, a string band from the opera house and, at my suggestion, one Signor Brunoni, a mountebank illusionist who styled himself the 'Grand Turk' and was the talk of Munich. Apparently, his show, which he was touring around Europe, defied belief. If that was the case then he and Alexandra would be well suited.

The great evening arrived and Schloss Schwanstein was decked out in its festive best. A dining table that sat sixty had been set up in the great hall with a footman behind every chair. The table seemed to be about the length of a cricket pitch and was almost buckling under the weight of silver, porcelain and flowers. On a buffet, at one end of the room, gold plate glinted two yards high and, on a small stage at the other end, the band scraped its way through the latest popular melodies. Whilst Bavaria's *jeunesse dorée* quaffed the finest that Johannes's kitchen and cellar could offer, HRH sat demurely in her customary white at one end of the table, with her Lady-in-Waiting on one side of her and Mitzi on the other. Although before dinner HRH had chatted to those who were presented to her, the whole evening thus far was somewhat stilted and showed no signs of achieving our ends. However, there was time and Mitzi had arranged that the hall would be cleared after the last course and reset for Signor Brunoni's show, which was to be followed by dancing.

...

Brunoni was a great lard mountain of a man, clad in Turkish pyjammy trousers, a silk blouse, curled gold leather shoes and a truly absurd turban surmounted by an egret's feather. Sweating slightly from the heat of the thousand or so candles that illuminated the hall, he performed a series of tricks the like of which you can see any evening in Vauxhall: fire-eating, making doves appear out of a hat and so on. Pretty tame stuff. But then he had a large cabinet wheeled-on and he invited one of the audience to come onto the stage. Quite how he achieved the feat I don't know, but over the next few minutes he made his subject disappear from and then reappear in the cabinet. It was a sensational trick and the audience showed their appreciation, none more so than HRH.

Seeing that he had netted a big fish, Brunoni called for silence and then invited Alexandra onto the stage. With considerable reluctance, for she was chronically shy, she was eventually led up by her Lady-in-Waiting. Brunoni then signed to two footmen who carried a box piano from the orchestra onto the stage. Up-ending the instrument, they placed it in the cabinet and closed the door. Brunoni then put a wand into Alexandra's hand and, with him standing behind her and gently guiding her paw, she made several passes over it. He then invited HRH to open the door – and, lo, the piano had vanished. There was a storm of applause, but Brunoni was not finished. He asked Alexandra to move to the front of the stage where he then asked her where she had sent the piano. The poor chit blushed and, in a tiny voice, said she had no idea.

"Your 'ighness," said Brunoni in his fake Italian-accented German, "do you not feel a lump in your stomach? Something more than the excellent meal which you 'ave just eaten?" Alexandra clutched her stomach and gently nodded her head. "Well, I think we now know wherer you senter that piano... So sincer we know where it is, we canner bringer it back."

And with that he slapped her gently on the back, she coughed and Brunoni, who had passed his other hand over her face, opened his palm and there was a miniature piano in glass. There was another storm of applause, Brunoni bowed low and presented the little toy to HRH who left the stage clutching it with a puzzled look on her face.[64]

"Your 'ighness, milords, laydies and gentlemen, I bringer you now to the finale of my little show. But what I have presented to you so far are mere slighters of 'and. What I will shower you now is something far beyond mere tricks, something that 'as amazed the crowned 'eads of Russia, Prussia and the Grand Mufti in Constantinople – for I shall summon the dead!" There was a sharp intake of breath from the audience. "Is there somerone 'ere tonight who 'as recently suffered a bereavement or witnessed a death?" No one replied. Brunoni clutched the side of his head and started to rock to-an'-fro. "Come, come – the spirits tell me that there is at leaster one of you who 'as been witness to a recent tragedy... You, sir," he said pointing at me. "The spirits tell me that you 'ave seen death in the recent past. Pleaser to come upper to the stage."

There was no denying that I had been present at the death of little Karl Cernogratz, or that his death had been widely reported in the press, but so too had Johannes and Mitzi. However, not wishing to be a spoil sport – and with a little shove from Mitzi who was, I think, relieved not to have been selected – I made my way through the seats and stepped up onto the low stage. Brunoni turned, closed the cabinet door and then returned to my side where he took my hands in his.

---

[64] Editor's Note: It was one of the tragedies of the life of Princess Alexandra of Bavaria that, as an adult, she was convinced that she had swallowed a glass piano. This incident reported by Speedicut may at last explain why.

"Whater, plis, iser your name?" I told him. "Now, Capitano Speedicut, I wanter you to fixer your mind on the scene of death that you witnessed."

Almost against my will, I saw in my mind's eye the tableau in the railway carriage: the dead boy on the bench, the dead dog guarding him on the floor and the old lady presiding over the macabre scene.

Suddenly, behind us there was a flash, a bang and a cloud of smoke. Instinctively I turned and, as the smoke cleared, the door of the cabinet slowly swung open to reveal – the blood-drenched figure of Dora Empson. Someone in the audience screamed, I felt my knees buckle and I lost consciousness before I hit the floor.

CHAPTER THIRTEEN: NEMESIS

When I came to a while later, it was to find myself in a small saloon off the hall. My first thought was that I had had a bad dream but, with Mitzi fussing with my collar and Johannes fanning a napkin in my face, the awful truth came back to me: Brunoni had summoned the wraith of the dead Dora.

"Who was that?" asked Mitzi with real concern on her face.

"I have no idea." I lied. "What happened after I passed out?"

"Brunoni set-off another explosion and, by the time the smoke had cleared, the cabinet had gone. He then took a bow, Johannes paid him and he is now on his way back to Munich. If you are feeling up to it, the rest of the young are hard at work dancing and we can join them. Johannes, give Jasper a brandy."

As I pulled myself together, with the help of a large glass of Johannes's best Napoleon, I tried to push the image of Dora to the back of my mind. She was dead and had long since passed through the shark's digestive tract; it was quite impossible that she had returned. No, I thought, it must have been a combination of the heat, Johannes's excellent wines and a bad conscience that had made me imagine the figure was her. Brunoni was nothing more than a fake, just like the rest of his kind, and as capable of summoning the dead as flying to the moon. Fortified by this thought, I struggled to my feet and made my way back to the dance, with Mitzi still fussing around me. An hour later I had put the nonsense out of my mind altogether and it was in the small hours that I finally climbed into bed, to be joined minutes later by Mitzi. She snuggled up close, then used her tongue to lick the dregs of the memory of Dora from virtually every orifice I possessed, before getting down to work in earnest. I slept well that night.

But if I thought that was the end of the story I was mistaken.

After breakfast the following morning, an ancient and knobbly-kneed retainer informed me that there was a courier from London waiting for me in the hall. More than a little surprised, I went to investigate. The hooded and cloaked figure looked strangely familiar as I strode across the parquet towards him and, at my approach, he threw back his hood to reveal a most unwelcome face. A queasiness, that had nothing to do with the meal I had just eaten, gripped my guts but I nonetheless held out my hand in greeting.

"Where have you sprung from, Searcy?" I said, with as much steadiness as I could muster at short notice.

"I'm here, sir, on the orders of Lord Steyne who has instructed me to deliver to you this letter." He handed me a missive sealed with the Steyne coat-of-arms.

"How do you come to be workin' for Lord Steyne?" I asked as lightly as I could. "I had no idea that you even knew him."

"I don't really, sir, but I remembered you saying that you had been in India on some business of his." I certainly didn't tell him that, I thought. "And, as I needed to speak to you about Dora and no-one seemed to know where you were, I called on him – and he said that my arrival was timely as he needed to get this letter to you. So, I have been able to kill two birds with one stone, as it were."

Searcy was clearly lying on at least one point, but there he was, large as life and twice as unwelcome, bearing a letter from the GB. I told him to take himself off to the servants' hall whilst I read Steyne's note and said that I would summon him when I was ready. Back in the sanctuary of the breakfast room, and under the quizzical gaze of Mitzi and Johannes, I slit open the letter and read that 'my period of leave was at an end', and that my 'secondment to political work' was also terminated, as the Tenth Hussars were shortly returning from Ireland and my presence with them was 'required'. The letter went on to say that I should return by the fastest means possible and report to the Adjutant at the cavalry barracks in York. Quite why the GB had felt it necessary to use Searcy as a courier rather than entrust his missive to the mail, or even the diplomatic bag to which

I knew he has unfettered access, was yet another mystery to add to that of Searcy's presence in Bavaria. I handed the letter to Johannes who read it and passed it to Mitzi, who stifled a small cry on reading of my recall.

"Sadly, my dear Jasper, all good things must eventually come to an end and a soldier must obey orders. With considerable regret, I will make whatever arrangements you need in order to comply with this letter. But please be aware," and with this he reached across the table and took Mitzi's hand, "that we will *both* miss you very much indeed and that there will always be a welcome for you at Schloss Schwanstein should you ever return to Bavaria."

Then he got up and, displaying his usual tact, left me with Mitzi who was by then in floods of tears. The following day, my hosts' best carriage conveyed me – after many a tear shed on the steps of the schloss - for the railway station and my least favourite mode of travel in order to return to England *sans délai*. I had arranged with Searcy that he would accompany me and he was, in consequence, waiting on the platform. Although I could have told him to make his own way back to hearth and home he might, I thought, have his uses, if only to carry my bags.

Using my still ample supply of the GB's gold, I'd booked a First Class compartment for the two of us – 'keep your friends close and your enemies closer' is a Chinese proverb I've always subscribed to – and awaited developments. They were not long in coming. We had hardly left Munich's Hauptbahnhof when Searcy raised the subject that was uppermost in both our minds.

"Sir," he said clearing his throat and looking out of the window, "you may remember that when we last met in London, when I helped you compromise Mr Brown and Mr East…" How the devil did he know their names, I wondered, or that I had set them up? "I said that I could find no sign of Dora, Mrs Empson that is, in Rugby. Well, I couldn't find any trace of her in London neither, nor was her name on any of the manifests of the passenger boats that had docked in Tilbury or Southampton from Cape Town in the past three months."

"You have been busy," I drawled, examining my nails, "but, of course, we had agreed that she would travel under her maiden name, just in case the good Major Empson suspected that his wife had not ended up as fish food and had put out enquiries. So, you were searchin' for the wrong name."

"Actually, sir, if you recall, you told me in Cape Town that she had registered as 'Mrs Smith', so it was under *that* name that I searched for her – and there were a fair few 'Mrs Smiths', I can tell you, but none turned out to be Dora. So, I set to thinking that perhaps she had not left Cape Town when you said she had and that, for some reason," this said with not a little malice, "you were keeping her from me."

"Now why on earth would I want to do that?" I reposted. "Your sister is a sweet enough little thing, but she's hardly my style – or worth more than a quick rattle on a verandah or a poke or two below decks – activities which I seem to remember were undertaken to affect her escape from Major Empson and not for any love of me; her behaviour was no better than prostitution by anyone's reckonin'. So why on earth should I seek to conceal her from you? In fact, I was pleased to see the back of her when she got on the boat to England. And, for the record, she is a brainless hussy and a pretty average lay."

Not surprisingly, and as I had intended, this last remark angered him, for I could see his colour changing from common-white to turkey-cock-red and his fists were clenched. I would have liked nothing more than for him to have taken a swing at me, for a bloody lip would have been a small price to pay for having him arrested and carted off by the local constabulary after I had pulled the emergency cord. However, he too must have realised that that way lay my salvation, for he unballed his fists and, when he next spoke some minutes later, his tone was level, not to say – at least initially – pleading.

"Look, sir, let's not get off on the wrong foot on this one. I love Dora and I'm concerned that she seems to have disappeared off the face of this earth. All I ask is for your help in trying to find her. After all, it's not much to ask as the price of my silence, now is it?"

"Searcy, I have long since discharged any obligation that I may have been under to you in that regard. I have done more than I should have done to get your sister out of India, I cannot be responsible for her whereabouts after Cape Town and I am certainly not goin' to spend any more of my time lookin' for her once I get back to England. Do I make myself clear?"

He nodded, still staring out of the window and then, as though he had made up his mind to a course of action, he lobbed a grenade straight into my lap.

"That's as may be, sir, but if what you say is true – then why did Dora appear last night in Signor Brunoni's cabinet and why did you pass out at the sight of her?"

"How the devil do you know about that?" I asked before I could stop myself.

"Well, let's just say that Signor Brunoni is a friend of mine – leastwise, we got friendly yesterday afternoon in the Munich pub where we were both staying and, over a few pints of what passes for beer in this country, we got to talking. He said that he hailed from Brum and it turned out that we knew a few of the same people.

"Then we got to talking about his act. He told me that he needed some help with his finale and that, if I was free, he would be pleased to pay me a small fee for my time. Because of Lord Stein's letter, I knew you were staying at the castle and so I put a suggestion to George – that's his real name, sir, George Pennyworth – about how he might create a sensation and at the same time, although I didn't tell him that, test a theory I've been working on for some time. He did as I suggested – and you proved me right."

"What damned theory?"

"That Dora is dead – and that you killed her."

"Now look here, Searcy, what you claim is both outrageous and untrue. As I have told you until I am blue in the face, your sister left me in Cape Town and, as to her whereabouts, I know nothin' and I care less."

"So why did you pass out when you saw me in a frock, covered in chicken's blood and looking for all the world like Dora come back to life?"

"So, it was you! Well that just goes to prove that it was nothin' more than a cheap trick and of no significance."

"Trick or not, sir, you thought it was Dora – else why did you collapse in a heap on the floor?"

"Don't be absurd. It was hot," I replied, trying hard to think of a convincing excuse, "I was tired and I'd had a skinful of the Count's claret. And the shock of Brunoni's trick was enough to upset anyone…" I ended rather lamely.

"That's as maybe, sir, but you don't convince me. You know a lot more about what's happened to Dora than you care to let on and I'm not going to leave your side until I've found out what's happened to her – or what you have done with her, more like."

"Searcy, you are being absurd," I retorted, "I've told you everythin' that I know and doggin' my footsteps is goin' to do you no good at all and will get you no closer to findin' the wretched Mrs Empson. Once we get back to England, I'm re-joining the Tenth and you can return to the gutter or wherever it was you sprung from this time. And, if you continue to harass me, I will have you arrested." I finished with more firmness and confidence than I truly felt.

"As to the gutter, sir, I have already arranged for a more comfortable billet than that – and one that will ensure that I will be your constant shadow."

"What on earth do you mean?"

"Thanks to Lord Stein, sir, on our return I too am re-joining the Colours – or, to be more precise, the Guidon of the Tenth Hussars. You see, sir, Lord Stein wanted to pay me for delivering his letter but I said that it was permanent employment I wanted and, in particular, employment with you. He asked me why and I said that I had grown to admire you when we were out East together and that, if I was once again to 'take the shilling', I would want to serve with you. He liked that, congratulated me on my 'loyalty and devotion', and has arranged with the Colonel of the Tenth for me to be your orderly. I don't know how he does it, sir, but your friend Lord Stein seems to be a big cheese indeed, particularly around at the Horse Guards."

Thank you *very* much, GB, was all I could think.

"I see," I said gathering myself together from this latest shock, "well, if you are to serve with me, then you had better stop this nonsense about Mrs Empson. The likelihood is that she met some nabob on the boat home and is now lordin' it over a houseful of servants in Bournemouth – and she's covered her tracks as she doesn't want you and your father at the back door beggin' for her new-found bounty."

Searcy was clearly unconvinced but said nothing. Indeed, I think we hardly spoke another word to one another between there and Hamburg. This actually became rather a strain, as dumb resentment and disbelief proved to be somewhat more wearing than his previous rants, which was probably precisely what the bastard intended. If that was his intention, it worked, for I was nearly crawling up the carriage wall by the time we sighted the North Sea and, in a desperate attempt to bring a halt to his behaviour, I was about ready to tell him the truth about how Dora had fed herself to the fishes. The only thing that stopped me was a conviction that he wouldn't believe me. That's the trouble with the truth.

By the time we finally got a crossing to Harwich on the mail packet, I was ready to pitch Searcy overboard at the first opportunity. I think he sensed that and was careful to stay in the reeking box that was the passengers' saloon, whilst I paced the deck inhaling the salt air off the heaving foam. Safely landed, we sought out a train for London where, once aboard, I tucked myself into the window seat of the compartment and attempted to doze away the next few hours before our arrival in the great metropolis. By this time, I had had so much experience of cat-napping that I was 'off' in a matter of seconds and back in a sunlit, snow-encrusted landscape with Mitzi nibbling my ear and Signor Brunoni turning snowmen into naked dancing boys to amuse us.

All of a sudden, this delightful idyll was halted by a most appalling crash. I awoke with a start as the carriage seemed to revolve around me. I turned effortlessly in the air and then landed with a sickening and most painful crunch on what, moments before, had been the ceiling of the compartment. The whole thing had seemed to happen in slow motion, but can only have taken a fraction of a second and, although it was broad daylight, everything was dark until I realised that one of our bags had fallen off the rack and was now wedged over my face. Gingerly raising one arm, for I had as yet no idea if I had been injured, I pushed it off and took stock of my surroundings.

It was like a scene from hell. For a start, the world was disconcertingly upside down and at a strange angle, the benches had broken loose, the compartment door was hanging open and everything inside seemed to be covered in what looked like snow. Searcy was nowhere to be seen and, as I recovered my senses, I became conscious of smoke and screams coming from outside. Concluding, rightly as it turned out, that there must have been a collision and that I appeared to have broken no bones, I hauled myself upright, lacerating the palms of both hands on the broken glass that was everywhere. But for some reason, shock I suppose, I felt no pain. Then, half-walking and half-crawling, I dragged myself through the open door and slumped onto a grassy bank.

Moments later I looked back and the sight that met my eyes made the interior of the carriage look almost normal. To my right I could see two locomotives almost upright on their tenders, belching smoke and fire and locked in an obscene embrace. Behind our engine, the first three carriages – in the second of which we had been travelling – had been tossed and broken by the force of the collision and bodies were scattered everywhere on the trackside. Somewhat surprisingly, the carriages that made up the rest of our train were still upright, as though nothing had happened. Their occupants were leaning out of the windows to see what was up, but were frozen into inaction with their mouths hanging open. Behind the other engine there was what appeared to be a small hill of coal, which made no sense until I reasoned that it must have been a goods train carrying fuel for the steamers at Harwich. I realised all of this in far less time than it takes to write, which was another strange thing about the accident thus far. In fact, the whole experience seemed strangely unreal until I heard a voice that I recognised only too well. It was Searcy, obviously in pain and apparently trapped under the carriage. More out of curiosity than anything else, I think, I pulled myself together and stumbled back towards the wreckage.

At first I couldn't see him, but then I realised from his cries that he must be under the coach, so I fell to my knees and peered beneath it. Sure enough, he was lying on his back, his thighs pinned to the track by the roof of the carriage. He should have been cut in half, but must have been saved by a buckled wheel that was acting as a wedge between the rails and the woodwork. Now, under normal circumstances and if I had been thinking straight, I would have left him to his fate; but I wasn't and I didn't. What galvanised me into action was the realisation that fire, fanned by a spring wind, was rapidly spreading from the engines along the line of carriages. If I wasn't able to release him, he would burn to death and that was not an outcome that I wanted to have on my conscience.

"Hold on, old man," I shouted to him, "I'll go and get help."

It was immediately obvious to me that I had no hope of getting him out on my own, so I stumbled along the track to the first upright carriage and begged the occupants to come and help me, but no one moved. At this point I think I must have lost my mind. In a sudden red rage, I grabbed the two nearest men I could lay my ripped and bleeding hands on and practically dragged them out of their carriage and onto the embankment.

"You," I barked at the first, "go and find a spar or something that we can use as a lever and, you," I shouted pointing to the other, "grab as many men as you can and then follow me."

My assertion of authority, no doubt subconsciously developed in the Shiners' riding school, worked and moments later I had a team trying to effect Searcy's rescue. But it quickly became apparent that, if we weren't extremely careful, any attempt to move the carriage would almost certainly result in Searcy's legs being severed. I was squatting on my haunches and wrestling with the problem when I felt a hand on my shoulder and a young lad asked if he could help.

"My name's Charlie Gordon,"[65] he said in a voice that had only just broken, "and I'm going to be an engineer. Now I think the solution lies…" and, without even a nod from me, he proceeded with a precision and determination which belied his obvious youth. You'll go far, m'lad, I thought.

"The best thing that you can do, sir," he said, turning again to me having directed our team to fetch various bits of debris from the wreckage, "is to keep the trapped gentleman calm; then, when I give the word, haul him out as quick as you can."

So, with great care, and not a little fear for my own safety, I crawled under the carriage and made my way over to Searcy. He was by now only half-conscious but I cradled his head with my left arm and murmured encouragement to him, whilst fumbling with my right hand to find my brandy flask. I got it, levered off the stopper with my thumb and gently dribbled some liquid between his parched lips. Just then there was a curious roaring sound and I realised with horror that the fire had reached our coach and that it was going-up like a torch. Smoke started to billow around us and we both coughed in its acrid fumes.

---

[65] Editor's Note: It's interesting to speculate that this may have been the future Major General Charles Gordon (1833-1885), military engineer, future colleague of Speedicut and highly successful leader of colonial armies, who met his death defending Khartoum against the Mahdi.

"If you don't get the damned thing off him quickly," I called out to the boy, with what little lung power I had left, "we are both goin' to choke or roast under here!"

"Hang on," he called back, "we'll have the carriage off him in a jiffy." But there was no sign of movement and my head was starting to spin with smoke and fear.

"Don't leave me, sir, please don't leave me," whimpered Searcy again and again.

"Don't worry, old man, I won't – and we'll have you out of here in a second or two," I lied, for it was clear to me that it would soon be the end for us both. I don't really understand why, because I don't give a fig about religion but, all of a sudden, I started to recite the Lord's Prayer whilst gripping Searcy as tightly to me as I could. Arnold would have been proud of me at that moment, but he was far from my mind as I faced certain death. Well, I thought, switching swiftly from the sacred to the profane, if I have to go then at least I will arrive at the pearly gates with a good-looking man to share my time in eternity. And then, in succession, Molly, young Arthur, 'Scud' East, Brown, Mrs Wickham and Dora were all standing over me and I realised, as the flames licked around us, that I was headed for t'other place. Oh, well, my brain told me, at least it'll be warm…

CHAPTER FOURTEEN: PASSAGES IN INDIA

"Now! NOW!" I heard dimly in the background. "NOW, SIR – **PULL HIM OUT!**"

But, you know, I was rather enjoying the sensation of drifting away and felt no need to move. Then something clicked in my head and I snapped back to awful reality, grabbed Searcy by his collar and started to drag his inert form from under the carriage. It was agony. Every bone and muscle in my body yelled in pain. Then, just as I thought I couldn't move another inch, I felt hands grab me and haul us both onto the grass. The coach crashed back onto the track and, with a whoosh, it vanished in a ball of flame that singed the whiskers off my face and damned near blinded me. Then someone was trying to tip a cup of water down my throat, but I pushed the hand away croaking that he should look after Searcy first, whom I still had held fast

"Time to let go..." a gentle voice said in my ear, a short while later, "let him go... he's going to be fine... thanks to you."

I realised that I was still clinging to Searcy and that tears of relief, and I don't know what else besides, were rolling down my scorched cheeks and onto his smoke-blackened phiz. All I could think was what curious little white puddles they were making. I passed the next couple of hours in rather a daze. The unconscious Searcy was loaded by some locals onto a cart and I walked along next to him as we were led to the nearby village of Little Oakley. There we were deposited in what I suppose was the village hall, along with the other wounded from the crash, and in due course a couple of the local ladies and a rather harassed-looking sawbones cleaned me up, bandaged my hands and applied some evil-smelling salve to my raw face.

The quack then turned to Searcy, who was still unconscious, and told the women to strip off his trousers, through which blood was now seeping. Fortunately for their modesty, Searcy was wearing long under-garments but, without any ceremony, the doctor produced a large pair of scissors and cut them off him to reveal – well, let's just say that there was a muffled gasp from one of the old trots and the other leaned forward for a better look. In addition to the women's prurient point of focus, Searcy had some nasty cuts and ugly bruises on both his upper legs. The doctor poked and prodded and finally declared that no bones were broken, dressed the wounds and said that Searcy wouldn't be able to walk for a week or two and required peace, quiet, bed-rest, horse liniment and broth. One of the old girls looked as though she would be happy to administer this prescription and, given the chance, had an extra cure of her own to boot.

By the end of the day, and thanks to some of what remained of the GB's gold, I had managed to get us a room in Ye Olde Cherry Tree, the only pub in the village where, in due course, our trunks were brought from the luggage van, which, being at the back of the train, had survived the collision and the fire. All things considered, we weren't in bad shape: I could scarcely hold anything and my face was still on fire, and Searcy couldn't walk, but we were alive and had most of our kit.

Although unspoken, a strange bond had developed between the two of us in those minutes under the carriage. In particular, the dread subject of Dora seemed to have perished in the fireball for, in the following days, he never mentioned her again, his whole manner towards me changed from insolent deference to a puppyish and rather clinging kind of affection - of the brotherly rather than the carnal variety - which I too felt for him. Thinking about it now, I suppose we'd been to hell and back together and survived. It must have been what is called a 'life-changing experience'. Whatever had happened, after the past few weeks it was, for me at least, most welcome.

We stayed in Little Oakley until Searcy could walk without undue pain and then I booked us places on the London mail coach. There was no way that I was ever going to set foot again on a railway train. On arrival in London, we made our way to the Verulam, where I dropped my valises, and I then took Searcy to the 'Running Footman' where I secured him a room, despite the rather leery look given to us by the publican who seemed to think, quite rightly, that he'd seen us before.

With Searcy settled, I sent a note round to Steyne House and settled into the comfort of my club to await the inevitable summons from the GB. It came an hour later, not in the form of a note, but in the shape of the GB himself.

"When I heard of your accident, young Speedicut," he explained in front of the fire in the club's morning room, "I determined to put you to no further inconvenience. However, I am delighted to see that your injuries, whilst I am sure they are still painful, appear to be superficial." I nodded my agreement. "I am also relieved to hear that the excellent Searcy has suffered no lasting damage and that he will soon be able to fulfil his appointed role for you." There was nothing I could or indeed wanted to say to that.

"I have sent a note," he went on, "to your Commanding Officer informing him of your misfortunes and suggesting that you both be given a few additional weeks in London to recover fully. I am sure he will assent to my request. In the meantime, given your unique insight into the political situation in Bavaria, you would greatly oblige me if, once you are able to hold a pen, you could draft a confidential note for me on your assessment of the threat posed to European security by the inherent instability of that country where, since your departure, there has been a week of rioting in Munich against the King and his tax on beer."[66]

That was a poser and no mistake. It arose, I supposed, from my report to Flashman in Paris, but what I knew about 'the inherent instability' of Bavaria could have been written on the head of a pin: it was a great pity that the GB had not asked me about the inherent mental instability of the Wittelsbachs, about which I could have written a book.

---

[66] The Munich beer riots lasted from 1st to 5th May 1844. Calm was only restored when the King agreed to cut the price of beer by 10 per cent.

However, two weeks later I sent the report to the GB and then, before he had time to return it with 'unsatisfactory' scribbled in the top right-hand corner, Searcy and I took the mail to York and arrived there on the last day of May 1844. He may not have the oriental exoticism of Khazi, but by the time Searcy helped me into my Regimentals, he was proving to be a damned fine orderly and, I suspected, a trusted companion should I ever have the misfortune to undergo another adventure.

Meanwhile, little had changed *chez* the Shiners although there were some new faces in the Mess and some of the old and bold had retired to their estates. Routine was the order of the day, which was actually rather a relief after the previous eighteen months. Of course, I knew it wouldn't last – it never does - but for the time being Regimental soldiering was a rest cure from adventures on either side of the bedroom door. Indeed, life was wonderfully dull in York where there were no Fenians, no over-sexed widows, no upwardly mobile whores and, sadly, no beautiful Countesses. So, I able to idle away my time in mindless military pursuits until Christmas, which I spent back home in Wales.

When I got back to the Dower House the day before Christmas Eve it was to find a house party in full swing. My sister, Lizzie, who had recently got hitched to some City swindler son of a friend of Papa's, had invited a whole crowd of her new-found London friends up to Wrexham for the festivities. Frankly, I felt like a fish out of water, which was a bit strange in one's own home, but Mama was determined that we should all have a good time, so I went along with the whole wretched thing. Fortunately, amongst Lizzie's friends was a pert little piece called Lucretia Cazenove, who was married to some deadly dull ass from Leadenhall Street; she immediately caught my eye and I hers. Ho, ho, I thought, I wonder if she would like to view our horse with the green tail.

Like most families at that time we celebrated the birth of the bloke on the Cross not on the 25th on Christmas Eve. Mama worked the kitchen into a frenzy getting cook to prepare roast goose, plum pudding and all the usual trimmings. In addition, she'd had the gardener fell a fir tree and re-plant it in the hall where it was covered in ribbons, candles, sugared ornaments and other gewgaws. Apparently, so she said when I asked her, good Queen Vicky's mount, Prince Stuffed Shirt, had introduced the idea to the Royal Household the previous year and now everybody had to have these 'Christmas trees'.[67]

After a lengthy dinner, Lizzie's new husband Percy, who amongst other things traded furs from Russia, said that we should all go down to the stables because, according to a Russian folk legend that he had heard on a recent visit to the frozen north, the animals speak at midnight on Christmas Eve. Complete nonsense, of course, but we were all soused enough not to object, so we threw on our cloaks, Percy grabbed a lantern and we all trooped down to the stables to see if the story was true. Now, of course, Percy had omitted to mention that the Ruskies' Christmas Eve wasn't until 6th January, so whether or not the beasts did have a chin-wag to celebrate the birth of Christ, they wouldn't be doing so for another thirteen days, but... To make matters worse, someone suggested that, as it was Christmas, the servants should join us, but Mama didn't subscribe to such modern ideas and said 'no, it would be too much of a crush'. However, Searcy, who had come with me to Wrexham rather than return to Rugby and who had volunteered to fill-in as an extra footman for the duration, caught me as we were leaving and asked if he could come too. Of course, I said 'yes' as I was sensitive to his feelings and so he tagged along with me at the back of the party.

We all squeezed into the stables and awaited developments. A short time later the coach house clock struck midnight and a hush fell over us. Needless to say, nothing happened. Just as I was about to suggest that we would all be a damned sight warmer if we went back to the house, I felt a hand groping at my crotch. I was pretty sure that it belonged to the muffled figure in front of me, but it was too dark to see who it was until a shaft of moonlight broke out from behind a cloud and lit-up the lasciviously grinning face of little Mrs Cazenove. Just as things were about to get interesting, my Papa growled that Percy was 'a damned ass dragging

---

[67] Editor's Note: Christmas trees were actually introduced to the English Court from Germany by King George III's wife Queen Charlotte, but it was Prince Albert who popularised the practice of installing and decorating Christmas trees.

us all out on a fool's errand' and he led the way back to the house. I hung back but Mrs C didn't, which was a bit strange.

"I saw what she was up to, sir," whispered Searcy in my ear, "and I'm sure I can get her into your bed if that's what you'd like."

"Searcy, you are a rogue," I replied. "How could you have possibly seen what she was up to?"

"You forget, sir, that it's my job to look after you – and, if you want to give Mrs Cazenove the benefit of your experiences in the East Indies, then it's my job to smooth her path to your door."

"See what you can do," I said hurriedly, as I lengthened my stride to catch up with the party.

By the time we'd finished off the hot punch and exchanged presents it was heading for two in the morning and, with no further sign of interest from La Cazenove, I decided to call it a night. Sometime later, I was just dropping off into a delightful dream that once again involved Mitzi and snow, although this time without the slimy Signor Brunoni who seemed to have finally fled my subconscious, I was woken by the creak of my door opening. I vaguely discerned a candle and two figures, then the door creaked-to again and there was a soft padding of slippers across the rug, the rustle of silk dropping to the floor and I felt a warm, naked body slide between my sheets - with the hairy end heading straight for my midriff. If this was Mrs C she certainly knew what she wanted and, having got it firmly between her lips, she also clearly knew – in a rather straightforward, English sort of way - exactly what she wanted to do with it. Really there was nothing for me to do except lie back and enjoy her not inexpert attentions which, rather quicker than I hoped, brought me to the point of no return. Before I could even say 'thank you', the body had slipped back to the floor, I heard the sound of fabric being lifted, the door creaked again twice and, as there was nothing else to do, I drifted off into a deep and dreamless sleep.

The following morning, after the men had breakfasted in the dining room, we joined the women in the hall to walk to church. Mrs C gave me a friendly greeting, but no different to that which she'd bestowed on the rest of the bucks, and, gripping her husband's arm, she followed on behind my parents as though she was a completely devoted wife and as pure as the snow that had fallen overnight. I suppose it was possible that she was as innocent as she chose to look, and I had not had the opportunity to check the situation with Searcy who was having a well-deserved lie-in, but I was reasonably sure that the lips which now pecked her husband's cheeks had been wrapped around my pecker some eight hours earlier.

On our return from church, where Lady Cunliffe's brother (who had recently been given the living by her husband) had droned on and on and on about 'the baby Jesus, meek and mild' until I was ready to either throw-up or doze off (in the event, I decided that the latter was more suited to the season), Searcy was waiting for us in his temporary footman role.

"Meet me in the conservatory in a couple of minutes," I murmured to him as he took my tall tile and cloak. He nodded and a short while later I joined him there behind a large potted palm.

"I know what you're going to ask, sir, and the answer is 'yes'. But please don't ask me how or why because the lady in question has sworn me to secrecy."

"Well, she certainly brightened up my Christmas mornin' and no mistake. Do you think there is any chance of a second-round tonight?" I asked.

"To be frank, sir, I doubt it. I think, if Mr Cazenove can be encouraged to fill his boots as he did last night, then Mrs Cazenove has another experience in mind. But my lips are sealed."

"Searcy," I said, "you are incorrigible - but I trust you and I'm sure if you can arrange it you will. Now, you'd better cut along back to the pantry or Betteridge will be wonderin' where you've got to."

And that was that. Christmas night and the early hours of Boxing Day morning found me once again deep in the arms of Morpheus without the pleasure of being joined by Venus. As with the previous night, Cazenove had downed more than he could hold *and* stay awake, so it was with some interest that I scanned the faces of the men in the party over breakfast to see if I could spot a satisfied grin. But to no avail and Searcy, bless him, whom I tackled after breakfast, wasn't telling either. But that was not the end of the matter, for later in the day, I was passing the morning room when I heard the most unholy row taking place behind the oak. Not wishing to intrude, but also not wishing to miss any fun, I dropped to my knees by the door as though looking for something.

"Your behaviour is disgraceful!" I heard Cazenove rant. "Our friends I can understand – but a servant! Have you no shame? How could you so demean yourself?" The tirade was interrupted by a sob, but he went on. "You have gone too far this time. I'm sending you to my sister and her husband where you will be closely chaperoned. You will not return until I have been assured that you have reformed. Then, and only then, may I consent to take you back. Meanwhile, we are leaving this house today. Until I have made the arrangements, you will, madam, remain in your room and see no one. Do you understand?"

I decided not to linger, as the 'interview' appeared to be drawing to a close and I had heard enough. I made straight for the library and rang the bell. As I hoped, it was answered by Searcy.

"Come in and close the door," I said and he did so. "Well, you're a dark horse and no mistake." Searcy said nothing but affected an air of surprise. "I thought you only played for the opposition, so what's this I hear about you pleasurin' Mrs Cazenove?" He still said nothing but stared at the ceiling. "Look here, man, what you do in your time off is your own affair and I'm not goin' to pry, but I just want to know whether it was because of you that Mr Cazenove is about to send his wife to God knows where."

"Very well, sir," he at last responded with a cheeky grin, "it was me who gave the lady what she wanted last night, although why she should confess it to her husband this morning I have no idea. The gentleman was out for the count when, as she'd instructed, I went to fetch her. When she said she wanted to come to my room, what was I supposed to do?"

"How the Cazenoves live their lives," I said, "is their affair. But what I can't fathom is why you gave her what she wanted, given that the fair sex is not your style?"

"It's like this, sir: she was very insistent, it was late and, with the lights out, one pair of lips is much the same as another… Now, if you'll excuse me, sir, I think I have some duties to attend to." He gave me a broad wink, turned and returned below stairs.

So, all in all, it was a Christmas that was not entirely bereft of fun, games or surprises and Searcy and I both returned to York in the New Year of Our Lord 1845 where everything should have been rosy had the Horse Guards not lobbed a shell into the tranquil world of the Shiny Tenth in February with the news that in May we were to embark from Gravesend via the Cape to serve in India for the next *eight* years. It soon emerged that we were to be stationed in a prime dump called Kirkee,[68] some ten days' march from that ace manure heap, Bombay. What the hell had we done to deserve that we all asked? Anyway, Kirkee was said to be a 'healthy station', which probably just means that death struck every week not every day. Needless to say, I immediately applied for a transfer to the Second Battalion, but I suspected – rightly as it turned out - that it would fall on deaf ears.

Meanwhile, to bring us up to strength, we were busy absorbing assorted louts from lesser cavalry Regiments such as The Royals, The Greys and the 7th, 8th and 11th Hussars. They were a pretty motley gang as their parent Regiments had deliberately sent us their entire cast of rogues, cripples, malingerers and thieves. The worst news of all was that we would to leave behind our mounts – both the four-legged and the two-legged variety.

I was thinking of sending in my papers when I had, out of sheer desperation, a most dangerous brainwave. I wrote to Flashman proposing

---

[68] Kirkee is the present-day Khadki in Maharashtra State.

that he should hint to the GB that he put me back on the task of trailing around Europe on the rancid scent of that dangerous bitch, Lola Montez. Her name was on the lips of everyone in the Regiment for, having ditched her gypsy musician, she was now rogering one of our former brother officers, Francis Leigh, who readers may recall was also a friend of Mitzi's. Apparently, he'd met La Montez whilst on leave in Paris, got sucked into her circle of artists, newspaper hacks, tarts and debauchees, sent in his papers and, as his brains have clearly gone the way of his prick, was spending significantly more than his extremely generous allowance keeping the bloody woman in Paris frocks and vintage champagne. There was clearly no fool like a rich fool. Anyway, I told Flashy to suggest to the GB that, as the bitch was corrupting the morals of a scion of the British aristocracy in Paris, it ought to be 'Speed to the rescue'. Well, I was desperate to do anything to avoid the ghastly voyage to the land of inedible food, unbearable weather, flies, dirt, stinking natives and randy memsahibs – actually, I didn't particularly mind the last, but the price of the others was too much to pay for the occasional and rather inexpert bending of the bedsprings with the corps of amateur houris in Poonha and Bombay.

Needless to say, my cunning plan didn't work and, by September 1845, after a bloody uncomfortable voyage, I was in India where I found that, in the two or so years since I'd last been in the place, there had been no apparent improvements. It was still the arsehole of the world and it didn't improve with second acquaintance.

It took us ten days to march Bombay to Kirkee, which was no treat for a cavalryman, and we lost three good men on the way to cholera. This was not a very auspicious start and, despite the fact that we'd taken over from the 14th Hussars, we found on our dusty arrival that there were virtually no horses in camp. Parlby 'had words' with the pen-pushers in Bombay, who said that they had ordered a batch of Arab stallion remounts for us from Persia, but that they would take six months to get to us in Kirkee. In the meantime, the Orderly Room notice board announced that we were going to be playing a lot of cricket and volunteers were called-for to join an Amateur Dramatics Club. I wrote again to Flashy, this time in desperation, begging him to ask the GB to get me a job up-country: the prospect of a constant diet of 'amdram' and cricket, which has always been my least favourite sport, was likely to drive me into an early grave, if cholera didn't get me first.

Despite all of the above, I will concede that we were a sight more comfortably billeted than the last time I'd been in the hell hole; I had quite a decent bungalow that I shared with a couple of other Shiners. Searcy had a reasonable enough room at the back where, as our major domo, he lorded it over the half-dozen or so natives who made up our domestic crew.

Meanwhile, there was one light blinking dimly on the horizon. Baird, the Adjutant, announced that we were to host some 'lady' called Mrs Lombard and her 'companion', a Miss Maplin, who were *en route* to Singapore via Bombay, the Shiners, Delhi and Calcutta; apparently, they were 'sight-seeing', which in India was an oxymoron. Baird told us that they were due to arrive the following week and that a cricket match, a play and a ball would be staged in their honour. As the newly-appointed Mess Secretary, it was – so he said - my job to ensure that there was a suitably equipped 'powder room for the ladies'. So, I sent Searcy off to Bombay to purchase the necessary items, whilst I tried to make a dingy store room into something approaching a *boudoir* suitable for the gentler sex. Searcy duly returned from Bombay, laden down with chintz, frills, laces and pins but, despite the miracle that he worked with a floral wallpaper, he said that the women would have to make do with the long-drop dunnakin outside as there was no plumbing in the camp.

Speaking of Searcy, I had found that since our train crash I had been able to sense his mood without him saying anything - and his mood when he got back to the cantonment was subdued. As I didn't like to let matters fester with him, I called Searcy into the bungalow's sitting room the afternoon after he got back and asked him what was on his mind.

"Do you mind if I sit down, sir?" he asked quietly. I nodded my agreement. "It's like this, sir. When I was in Bombay I decided to have one further look for Dora." I should have expected this, but I involuntarily started forward. "No, sir, please don't be concerned. I know now that you had nothing to do with her disappearance." He paused. "But I had to find out what had happened to her, so I took myself down to the harbour to see who was about - and there was the *Pride of Poonha*, just returned from another run to the Cape.

"I went on board and asked for the Master, who soon came up on deck. I said who I was and he said I had better go below with him, which I did. In his cabin, he told me the whole story - about how she had slipped overboard, how you had jumped in to save her at the risk of your own life, and how the big shark got her." He paused again, now wiping tears away. "What I don't understand is why you didn't tell me, sir. After all, what you did was gallant and brave – nothing to be ashamed of or to hide. So why?"

"Searcy, if I knew that I could have saved both of us a lot of bother," I replied. "I truly don't know why I spun you the tale that I did, but I think that the shock of seein' you so unexpectedly in Cape Town, on top of what I'd just been through, brought out a defensive instinct in me to lie. I didn't know you as I do now – and I thought that you wouldn't believe me if I told you the truth. Tellin' you that she had left for home was a way of gettin' rid of you. But it didn't work, did it?" I smiled weakly. "Then Lord Steyne intervened and it now looks like I'm saddled with you for life…" I broadened my smile into a grin to let him know I was joking. "Well, there you have it. Had you asked me anytime after the crash I would certainly have told you, but you didn't. Anyway, I'm glad that you now know the truth. It wasn't a pretty end, but she can't have suffered much…" I ended rather lamely, knowing full well that Dora had spent at least a couple of agonising minutes quite literally being put through the mincer. But on this occasion, I knew that, for once, the truth was best avoided. Searcy said nothing for a minute, staring at the Persian rug with his hands clasped in front of him; then he sat upright.

"There's just one thing I want to do now, sir, before I get back to my duties. It's against regulations but I've got to do it. Would you please stand up?"

Is he going to belt me, I wondered? Well, I wouldn't have blamed him if he had and I certainly wouldn't have reported it. He closed the distance between us, his face set. Then he silently put his arms around me and, for at least half a minute, he gave me a brotherly hug. At last he dropped his arms, then, with a smile a mile wide on his face, turned and headed for the door. When he got there, he turned again and looked me straight in the eyes.

"We're really pals now, sir, and no mistake. So, don't you ever try and ditch me again!" With that he left the room and, from that point onwards, he seemed to be even more on the look-out for my welfare which, with what came next, was just as well.

A couple of days later everything was ready for the arrival of Mrs Lombard and her companion, Miss Maplin. A bungalow, with a clutch of native staff waiting for them, was ready and the Mess had been brushed and polished until you could have combed your 'tashes in the reflection from every surface. I was even quite pleased with the 'powder room', which Searcy had fitted-up in a close approximation to a French tart's *boudoir*, although Parlby started munching his whiskers when he inspected it, which was never a good sign.

"Well done, young Speedicut," he said, as he left to return for a snooze in his office, "it all looks top notch - although perhaps you could get your man to remove that candelabra from the ladies, err, room? As it is, it rather reminds me of the leave I had in Paris afore we embarked… And we don't want 'em thinking that the Tenth don't respect 'em eh, what?" He marched off with Baird the Adjutant in tow, who threw me a broad grin over his shoulder.

Just before luncheon, a tonga drew up at the steps of the Mess where we were all lined up as a welcoming party: actually, everyone except me, for I was still busy in the Mess checking the arrangements for luncheon. You can tell how bored we had become, and how welcome this arrival was, for Parlby had ordered that the band be drawn up on the verandah to play the old trots in.

As I was congratulating the Mess Serjeant on a job well done with the table arrangement in the dining room, I heard the band strike up, followed by the chirruping of female voices in the hall. Turning to join the rest of the boys, I saw Searcy standing in the doorway with a most peculiar look on his face, as though he'd just seen a ghost.

"Sir, sir! You won't believe this," he said, as he hurried over, "but Mrs Lombard isn't who she says she is. No, although she's veiled, I'm absolutely certain that she's Mrs Cazenove, that lady at Christmas last who, err, 'looked after' the two of us."

"Really?" I gasped. "Are you sure?" He nodded his head vigorously. "Well, I'd better go and see if you're right."

So, I went out to the hall and through into the ante room, where Mess waiters were already circulating with drinks. By this time Mrs Lombard/ Cazenove had raised her veil, as had her distinctly sour-faced companion, and there was no doubt about it: it was Lucretia Cazenove of the wandering hands and wayward lips. Deciding that I should play along with her *incognito* I sidled over, held out my hand and introduced myself as though we'd never met afore. She must have instantly decided that I was playing along with her game and greeted me as though this was the first time she had ever seen me. It was her call not mine. Eventually, we went into luncheon and, towards the end as the pudding plates were being cleared away, Parlby tapped his glass and cleared his throat.

"Gentlemen, the arrival on the Kirkee cantonment of two such fragrant reminders of what we have left behind in England is extremely welcome." There was polite applause around the table.

"In the three days that Mrs Lombard and Miss Maplin are to be with us, I have arranged what I hope will be entertainment that is up to the finest traditions of the Tenth. This evening we have a dinner party, tomorrow our guests will explore the local countryside in the company of Captain Speedicut," that was news to me, "there will be a cricket match in the afternoon between the officers and the other ranks, to be followed by a reception, the, err, play and a supper party for the garrison.

"On the last day, if they have any energy left in this dreadful heat, we will arrange something for 'em to remember on their onward journey to join Mrs Lombard's brother-and sister-in-law in Singapore." So that's where old Cazenove had banished her to, I thought. "Although," went on Parlby, "as Mrs Lombard's brother-in-law is – so she tells me – engaged in the suppression of piracy with Rajah Brooke, perhaps we should offer her nothin' too excitin', eh, what?!"

Once Parlby had sat down to more polite applause, Mrs Lombard/Cazenove leaned into him and I clearly heard what she said.

"*Dear* Colonel Parlby, Miss Maplin and I are *deeply* grateful to you for your kind hospitality and we will, I am sure, *much* enjoy what you have planned for us. But I wondered if it would be possible for us to experience a tiger shoot? We have heard so much about these fearsome beasts, and the sport that they offer, that were it possible to arrange such a thing for us on the last day we would be *most* grateful."

She said this last with a look down the table at the younger members of the Mess, myself included, that quite clearly said exactly how 'grateful' she might be prepared to be. Fortunately, Parlby didn't appear to have seen it.

"Mmm," rumbled the Colonel, "well it's not really the season, y'know, but I'll have enquiries made and see what might be arranged…" He allowed his voice to tail away, pushed back his chair and asked Mrs L/C if she would like to take coffee in the ante room.

"How delightful," she said.

Then, one-by-one, we all filed out after her and the Colonel. Later, once the women had been escorted by the Orderly Officer to their bungalow to take a nap ahead of the evening's festivities, Parlby sent for me in his office.

"Speedicut, m'dear fellow," he said, with his whiskers dangerously close to his lips, "I'm sorry to have landed you with the entertainment of our two ladies tomorrow morning but Baird told me, just afore they arrived, that he has to attend a Court Martial tomorrow and, after all your hard work getting the Mess ready, I thought you might like the job as a reward.

"Perhaps you might take 'em out for a ride on the maidan? The stables should be able to scrape-up enough screws for them, you and your orderly and I'm sure there are a couple of side saddles somewhere in this damned garrison."

As this was clearly an order, I said that I would be delighted, saluted and headed straight back to my bungalow where I hoped I would find Searcy. Sure enough, there he was.

"I've heard, sir, and I've already had an idea – that's if you fancy a return match with the lady?" I nodded slightly warily. "Well, if you are to have a gallop with Mrs Cazenove – and I don't mean on horseback, sir – it can't be around here. Far too many prying eyes, to say nothing of that ugly old tug boat who has Mrs Cazenove permanently in tow. So, here's what I plan." And he outlined a plot that was so bold it quite took my breath away.

Later that evening we sat through a formal dinner of the type so beloved by people like my Mama. The table was buckling under the weight of silver, we were in our best whites and, to try and keep the heat down, the punkas were being fanned into a frenzy by unseen natives. But, as I had planned an early start so as to avoid the worst heat of the day, the women rose from their seats in good time and pleaded the need for sleep.

The following morning Searcy woke me before the sun was up, gave me a quick shave and helped me dress, whilst a syce led four reasonably presentable horses, with food bags and panniers slung behind the saddles, around to the front of my bungalow. My screw's saddle had a leather holster, as well as the panniers, in which I stowed a standard issue carbine that Searcy had earlier signed out from the armoury. Mounting up, we 'rode and led' the ponies to La Cazenove's where we found the two women waiting for us, immaculate in solar topees, veils and khaki cotton habits. Soon we were trotting out of the garrison and heading for the maidan. We were about half way across it when Searcy called out.

"Hold hard, sir, one of ladies' horses has thrown a shoe." Sure enough, the Maplin woman's screw was starting to limp. "If the lady doesn't mind, I'll lead it back to the stables and she can take mine."

"Oh, I couldn't possibly do that," she said, "how would I ride? My saddle will never fit your horse." And, of course, she was right.

"It seems a pity to spoil the outin'," I said, "so how about if I take Mrs Lombard on to the spot we've picked for tiffin and you can both ride out and join us once the farrier's fixed that shoe?"

The Maplin woman looked even more sour than usual, but really there was little she could do except order that the outing be cancelled – and she didn't seem to have that amount of authority.

"Well, see you in an hour or so, then. We'll save you some food!" I called after them as Searcy, Maplin and the two horses walked back to camp.

Once they were out of earshot, Lucretia turned to me.

"That was clever, my dear Jasper. I presume that your man organised that little charade and that it will be at least an hour before they catch us up – maybe even longer? Quite time enough to renew an old acquaintance…"

Then she leaned across from her horse and her hand headed straight for a spot just behind the pommel of my saddle. Not wanting to be tempted to slide the woman off her horse and roger her there and then, I touched the spurs to my mount's side (the horse not her – yet) and it sprung into a canter. She soon caught up and asked where we were going.

"Not far - about a mile at the most. It's a ruined temple site that's rather a good spot for tiffin, as there's some shade under the old temple walls. Anyway, let's see what you think."

So, we rode on for another fifteen minutes or so with the sun rising behind us until I spotted the group of trees around a ruined building that Searcy had told me about. We dismounted, tethered the horses to a rotten wooden stump and spread a rug out on the ground. I didn't take the saddle bags with the food off the horses as, from the noise in the trees, there were monkeys about and there were kites circling above. There seemed no reason to take the carbine either.

"I'm told that this old temple is worth a look," I said, as the brazen hussy dropped onto the rug, her knees parted under her dress and a 'come and get me look' in her eyes.

"Well if I must…" she pouted, before getting back to her feet whilst I headed towards the ruined walls.

Searcy had told me what to expect, but the carvings took even my breath away: for there in front of us were tier upon tier of carved stone couples, frozen in 'the act' in literally dozens of different positions, some of which looked downright dangerous not to say impossible, unless you were equipped like a horse. Lucretia gasped, then moved in for a closer look, her eyes virtually popping out on stalks.

Some ten minutes later she was still deep in study when I coughed and reminded her that we didn't have all the time in the world to ourselves. Without a word, she broke away from the carvings, grabbed my arm and virtually dragged me back to the rug, where she proceeded to throw me onto my back – she was really quite strong for a small woman – bent over, ripped open my britches, lifted her skirts and lowered herself onto me with a cry that should have been audible back in camp. I told her to take it easy if she wanted matters to last and she moderated her rhythm from that of a jackhammer to a hand pump, all the while letting out a regular moaning sound.

Realising that nothing was required of me, beyond remaining at attention, I closed my eyes and let nature take its course. She was very experienced and, every time I was about to discharge my weapon, she took me off the boil only to raise the flame again and again. Just when I thought that the moment had finally arrived, I was distracted by a second noise in her love making: for her moans were now interspersed with deep grunts and, somewhat surprised that she could make such a noise, I opened my eyes.

It was immediately clear that the second noise was not coming from her. Just as I was wondering where it could be coming from, the monkeys in the branches above us set up an ear-splitting chattering which threw even Lucretia off her stride.

"What on earth's going on?" she asked, as she settled down on my lap.

"I've no idea," I said, "but the monkeys seem extremely vexed about somethin'." And then I realised.

"Oh, my God! Quick, get up. We need to get out of here fast. No, not the horses; let's get into the temple, it won't follow us there and it may even content itself with a horse."

Her eyes were wide with incomprehension as I leapt to my feet. Careless of my state of dress, I practically dragged the silly bint back towards the temple as fast as I could manage with my britches hanging open. As we made it past the outer wall that had so distracted Lucretia not ten minutes before, I heard the horses give a terrible shriek, there was a sound of splintering wood and a pounding of hooves; they'd obviously bolted and with them was our only means of protection.

Meanwhile, having reached the end of the wall of love, instead of an intact building and sanctuary we were confronted with nothing but piles of stones. There was nowhere to hide. Thinking fast, I dragged her back around the wall to the obscene carvings.

"Up, get up the wall or we're doomed!" I whispered as I proceeded to climb up using tits and pricks as my main purchase points. Lucretia followed and, thanks to the excited state of the carvings, we managed to make it to the top of the wall quite quickly. Puffing like a pair of blown race horses, we stared down to the clearing where only our rug remained – but it was not unoccupied. Lying in the middle of it, and licking one of its paws, was a very large tiger.

CHAPTER FIFTEEN: THE MOUNTAIN OF LIGHT

Now I'm no expert on the beasts, but it did seem to me that this tiger was either very lazy or very old, for the horses had clearly got clean away and the tiger didn't seem inclined to go in pursuit of them or us. It just lay on the rug, going through its morning *toilette*, whilst we tried to adjust our dress into some semblance of order. This was easier for Lucretia than for me as, in her hurry to get at my principal asset, she had ripped off several of the buttons on my britches. But that was the least of our worries.

"Do you think it could reach us up here?" she asked in a hoarse whisper. "I've heard that tigers can climb trees."

"Yes," I replied equally quietly, "I've read the same thing, but this one don't seem disposed to do anythin' other than to have a wash whilst stretched out on our rug."

As the sun rose higher in the sky, there seemed little that we could do except wait for the tiger to lose interest in us and go in search of a more rewarding spot. Then I remembered that, sooner or later Searcy, would be back, with or without the dratted Maplin woman. Just as I brightened at the thought, which I shared with Lucretia, she asked the question that I should have done.

"Will he have a gun on him?"

"No, why should he? The gun was on my nag. Christ Jesus, he'll ride straight into its jaws - what can we do? Let me think." but before I could say anything, she chipped in with considerably greater calm than I felt.

"We've got to distract the brute. Here, some of these stones are loose, if we throw them at him perhaps he'll go away."

"It's worth a try," I replied, prising loose the nearest bit of erotica. "On the count of three – one, two, THREE!"

Together we hurled an oversized pizzle and half a pert little tit at the old tiger. The first landed just in front of him and the second caught him square between the ears. Seemingly more offended than hurt, the tiger looked around him, then warily sniffed the curved tubular stone piece, scratched his ear and settled down for another snooze. So, we tried again, this time with a larger breast and the leering head of a temple dancer. Although they both missed, the tiger clearly now thought that there were better places to rest and raised itself wearily from the rug.

Just at that moment I thought I heard hoof beats, but I couldn't be sure as the monkeys chose the same time to start another rendition of the *Hallelujah Chorus*. The tiger had heard something too, for he looked around, sniffed, stiffened and then drew back on his haunches ready to pounce. A shot rang out, a monkey screamed and the tiger made a sort of lurching move forward, staggered and rolled over in the dust. From out of the long grass emerged first the smoking barrel of a carbine then, on the end of it, Searcy, closely followed by a brace of natives leading three horses.

"What took you so long?" I called over to him with more bravado than I truly felt. He looked up smiling, spotted the two of us at the top of the wall and strolled over to the tiger to check it was dead. Waving us down he helped us as we dropped the last half-dozen feet to the ground.

"You're a sight for sore eyes," said Mrs C, brushing the dust off her habit, "but where's Euphemia?" Searcy and I both looked puzzled until, at the same time, we realised she must be referring to Miss Maplin.

"I left her back in camp," Searcy replied. "When we returned, there was no one at the forge, so Miss Maplin urged me to ride back to keep you company and then legged it back to her bungalow for tiffin. As I was mounting-up, both of your horses came trotting into the yard. That didn't seem right, so I grabbed a couple of the syces and we galloped here as quick as we could. I already knew that you must be in trouble – but not that much," he said, pointing to the tiger.

"Well," I said, "we couldn't be more pleased to see you."

But before I could say any more, Lucretia grabbed the gun from Searcy, strode over to the tiger, kicked it in the ribs and then posed, gun in hand with one dainty foot on the poor beast's head.

"It's a shame that we don't have one of those Fox Talbot boxes," she said, "because this would look quite impressive on the front cover of the *Illustrated London News*. I can just see the headline: 'Society hostess bags tiger on trip to the Indies'. Yes," she went on, "if you'll both agree – and I can't think of a single reason why you shouldn't – we can get a local scribbler to interview me and sell the story to the *Bombay Times*, and they will be sure to sell it on to London.

"Of course, we'll need to bring back the evidence, so sling that smelly corpse between two of the ponies and let's get back to camp. I'll have the story quite straight in my head before we get there: I'll just need you two to go along with whatever I say. Jasper, you've already had payment on account: as for you, Searcy, there's a rather curious carving I noticed on the back of that wall, so if you'll follow me whilst Captain Speedicut supervises the loading of the tiger…" She strode off, gun still in hand, back towards the temple. Searcy looked at me, shrugged, gave me one of his boyish grins and followed after her.

Some thirty or so minutes later, the arrival back in camp of a dusty party in possession of a large, dead tiger caused a considerable sensation. The smelly beast was laid out in the road in front of the Mess, a journalist from the cantonment newspaper was rapidly summoned and Lucretia was interviewed at length. I only heard snatches of what she was saying, and it certainly bore no relation whatsoever to our actual experiences, but she had already secured the silence of the only witnesses on the subject. However, as we were all about to file into the Mess for luncheon, I noticed the Maplin woman making a close examination of the corpse. At the time,

I thought no more of it and, over luncheon, there was much talk about what Mrs Lombard/Cazenove was going to do with the skin.

"If it could be arranged, Colonel, I would so like to send it back to my family in England. It will cause a sensation and, who knows, my husband might even decide that the hazards of my journey abroad merit an early recall."

Maplin gave a loud cough and I could see that Parlby, from the expression on his face, hadn't a clue what Lucretia was talking about for, in the heat of the moment, she had clearly said more than she'd meant to.

"At least I don't have to lay on a tiger shoot for you, eh, what?" he said covering his confusion, "as you seem to have done a good job on your own!"

Maplin coughed again and, mistaking the cause, the Quartermaster, who was sitting on the other side of her from Parlby, offered her a glass of water which she refused.

"Ladies and gentlemen," said the Colonel in his best Commanding Officer's manner, "after the excitement of the morning I think we should now all repair to our bungalows for a rest. The cricket match will start at four p.m. and we have a long night ahead of us."

He then pushed back his chair, got up and eased back the women's chairs as they too rose. I was one of the last out of the dining room and was somewhat taken aback to be accosted by Miss Maplin, who I had assumed was on her way back to her bungalow.

"May I have a word with you, Captain Speedicut? Perhaps in here?" she said, indicating the writing room, the one place in a Shiners' Mess that was certain to be empty. She closed the door firmly behind me. "I am concerned that Mrs Lombard's account of this morning's adventures is not in exact accord with the truth." She paused and gave me a penetrating stare. I said nothing but tried to look stupid.

"You see, I've had a good look at your tiger and I can't see how it died. In fact, the only mark on it is a fresh hole drilled through its left ear which, whilst probably giving it some temporary discomfort, cannot possibly have been the cause of death. Are there, perhaps, any other facts that I should know which could explain this strange anomaly?" I said that I couldn't think of any. "I see or, rather, I don't see. Anyway, if you do think of any little fact that you might have overlooked, for example that Mrs Lombard fumbled the shot and the tiger died of shock, I would *so* appreciate hearing about it – that is, of course, assuming that you don't want me to point out to Colonel Parlby the obvious absence of most of the buttons off the front of your britches? You see, I have no illusions about my charge, but I do so dream of a small cottage by the sea – perhaps Tiger Bay in my home city of Cardiff would be an appropriate spot - once we return to England."

So that was it. Miss Maplin would keep her lips sealed on the subject of my probable activities with her mistress, if I would give her the necessary means to achieve an early and comfortable retirement at Lucretia's expense.

"I can't think what you mean," I retorted, with what I judged to be just about the right level of ironic indignation. "It's absurd to suggest that Mrs Lombard's tale to that journalist and my brother officers is anything less than the unvarnished truth; ask Searcy if you don't believe me."

"I intend to," she said and stomped out of the room.

Not before I've briefed him I murmured under my breath as I headed back to the bungalow, where I found Searcy bulling a pair of my boots. We quickly agreed that, to keep my reputation safe, he should confirm Miss Maplin's suspicions about the tiger's death.

The cricket match that followed in the afternoon was, well, another bloody cricket match and best passed over at speed, unlike the dreaded game itself, and there was nothing of note arising from the evening's entertainments beyond the distinct impression I had that Mrs Cazenove was determined to bag at least a couple more pelts before she left the following day. Quite how she was going to achieve was not my problem, but the distinctly rough appearance of two of the better-looking officers at breakfast the following morning confirmed my view.

On the last morning of the two women's visit, it was with some relief that the officers of the Tenth lined up on the Mess steps to bid the two women farewell as they set off in a tonga back to the railway station and Delhi. God help their next hosts, I thought. I was about to go and inspect my Troop lines when Baird came trotting over and said that Parlby wanted to see me. Fearing that perhaps the Maplin woman had left a slow-fused bomb with my name on it, I approached RHQ with caution, but Baird said I was to go right in, so I stepped briskly, if somewhat gingerly, into the Colonel's airy office.

"Come in, come in, m'boy," said Parlby. "Sit down. I have some news for you." He cast his hand across a pile of paperwork on the desk, finally reeling in an official looking letter.

"I have here a letter from the Governor General himself.[69] It appears that, based on your earlier service in Afghanistan, you have been recommended for political work on the North-West Frontier and Sir Henry has asked if I can release you to work with a Major George Broadfoot, the new Political Agent for that region. It seems to me that Sir Henry's wish is in all probability my command. So, unless you have any particular objections, you are to report first to Government House in Calcutta and then make your way to the Punjab. What do you say?"

What the hell could I say? It was a classic case of be careful what you wish for. With no option but to accept with a good grace I did just that but, as I got to the door I turned and asked if I could take Searcy with me.

"Of course, of course, m'boy. We'll miss you both, but I dare say we'll survive without you." With that he buried himself back in the paperwork on his desk.

---

[69] Sir Henry (later 1st Viscount) Hardinge GCB (1786-1856).

Was he pleased to see the back of me again, I wondered as I made my way over to break the news to Searcy? Parlby was a leery cove and I didn't think he had been entirely convinced by the official story of the tiger incident; and he certainly hadn't forgotten my spot of bother in Dublin, although he never mentioned it. But, whatever he thought of me, it was 'pack-up and fuck-off' time again and almost certainly back into the jaws of hell for, even in Kirkee, we had heard the stories of the fearsome Sikh Army, the demented Dowager Maharani who ruled the Punjab as Regent and the likelihood of bloody war.

Searcy took the news in his stride and asked when we would be leaving for Calcutta. Now, I hadn't thought about that, but the one thing of which I was immediately certain was that I had no intention of taking a train even part of the way there, so the alternative was either a long ride or the sea route. I decided that the longer it took us to get to Calcutta, and from there back across the country to the Punjab border, the better. If I could delay our arrival at Broadfoot's HQ by even a month, everything might be over before we ever had to set foot anywhere near danger. But, as is so often the case, fate intervened in the shape of an order to travel on a fast government steam sloop which got us from Bombay to Calcutta far quicker than I had planned.

If the former was a dump, the latter was just a bigger and smellier one without the benefit of a sea breeze. A swamp had been drained at great expense to create the British quarter, White Town, which looked like Piccadilly on a bad day, but unfortunately the memory and the mosquitos lingered on. As instructed we made our way to the Garrison Mess at Fort William and, with my kit and Searcy safely stowed, I sent my card over to Government House and sat back with a *burra peg* of brandy and soda to await developments.

My fate presented itself in the shape of Master 'Scud' East, smartly, togged-out in the uniform of Gardner's Horse,[70] a single pip glinting on

---

[70] Editor's Note: Although always referred to as Gardner's Horse, by this date the Regiment was officially known as the 2nd Irregular Cavalry and later as the famous Bengal Lancers.

his shoulders and the gold aiguillettes of an ADC swinging across his right tit. Not surprisingly, East seemed less than pleased to see me, but 'duty' was ever his watchword and, with the minimum of courtesy he could muster, he bade me to join him in a carriage that was waiting outside.

As we rolled over to Government House, East said not a word although I was sorely tempted to ask him how he had enjoyed his night at the Running Footman. But it was obviously on his mind too for, just as we arrived, he blurted out.

"Bye the bye, Speedicut, Tom - that is I mean, err, Brown - isn't here. He's been posted with his Regiment to the western frontier." Then he clammed-up tight, looking as though he wished he'd swallowed his tongue.

As I've already written, I'd experienced palaces great and small over the past couple of years, but up to that point I'd seen nothing to match the sheer bloody grandeur of Government House in Calcutta - or the absurd amount of bowing and scraping that took place there from the moment we stepped out of the carriage. There must have been at least a thousand assorted soldiers, servants and hangers-on placed there to impress visitors with the might of John Company and the Great White Queen. It was absurd, but it achieved its aim for I was feeling thoroughly cowed by the time I had been escorted through a series of ever larger ante rooms on my way to the Governor General's office.

After what seemed like a route march of over a mile, we finally ended up in his outer sanctum where East handed me over to the great man's Private Secretary who, I found out later, was his eldest son, Charles. Moments later the door to the *sanctum sanctorum* was flung open and I was marched in. Although Hardinge was a General he was in civvies, but there was nothing of the civilian about him. Tall, ramrod straight, with receding dark hair and the eyes of an eagle, he exuded an air of efficiency and precision as he stretched out his hand for the briefest of handshakes, then pointed me to a chair opposite his own on the other side of an enormous desk. Behind me the door closed and we were alone.

"Brother Speedicut," he said, immediately revealing in those two words the reason for my presence in Calcutta and his own affiliations, "I have asked for your services as I have a very particular task for you of the uttermost importance to the Crown." He paused to let this sink in and I assumed an air of the appropriate gravity. "Are you familiar with the present situation in the Punjab?" I said that, beyond what was common gossip in the cantonments, I was not.

"Well, my Private Secretary will give you a comprehensive dossier on the subject when you leave, the contents of which you will familiarise yourself with, before your departure to *rendezvous* at Umballa with Major Broadfoot, to whom, as you know, you are seconded for the duration.

"However, the resolution of our relationship with the Punjab is not your first concern. The particular task which falls to you and which is to remain completely secret between the two of us," I nodded agreement, "concerns an heirloom of this country." He paused again. "Have you ever heard of the Koh-i-Noor, which is known in English as the 'Mountain of Light'?" I hadn't and I said so. The old boy looked somewhat exasperated but nonetheless carried on in the same measured tone.

"The Mountain of Light is the largest diamond in the world and its worth is beyond calculation. Its history is obscure but bloody. What we do know is that it was mined in India, probably five thousand years ago and, since its discovery, it has become a symbol of power on this sub-continent, changing hands with the rise and fall of the ruling dynasties of northern India.

"Consequently, it is of vital importance that we own it for, in doing so, we make the most powerful statement that we can of our right to rule here. That it is currently in the hands of the utterly depraved and debauched Regent of the Punjab is just one more reason for it to be transferred to its rightful place on the bosom of our own dear monarch. It is *your* task to secure it for her."

If he'd dropped his unspeakables and asked me to lick his untouchables I couldn't have been more surprised and it must have shown in my face.

"Yes, yes, I know it's a tall order but the Great Boanerges has complete faith in you and has assured me that you have the skills necessary to achieve this great mission. There's nothing much more to be said at this point. Read the brief, return it to this office when you have fully digested it and you will then be given your travel instructions to Umballa, which is where your task will begin.

"You will, of course, send your general reports to the Brotherhood in the usual way – but you will report to *me*, and me alone, on the subject of the diamond and, once you have obtained it, you will deliver it to me here in this very office. No questions? Good. Well, be off with you then!" And that was it.

A couple of days later I took the dossier, which weighed about half a ton, back to Government House and received instructions to embark on yet another steam sloop for Karachi on the west coast, and from there – the method was unspecified – to Broadfoot in Umballa.

...

Editor's Note: There follows a gap of several months in The Speedicut Papers. I believe that, as with the previous omission of his dispatches on the retreat from Kabul, Speedicut's reports for the Brotherhood concerning his activities whilst working for Major Broadfoot and his involvement in the First Sikh War were destroyed after Flashman had plagiarised them for his own memoirs.[71]

For those who have not read this account, the story opens with Flashman (for him read Speedicut) being sent to Lahore by Broadfoot on a spurious mission to negotiate with the Regent, Maharani Jindan, for the rights to the so-called Soochet legacy.[72] His actual role was to ingratiate himself with the lascivious Maharani and to feed back information to Broadfoot about the intentions of the Khalsa, the European-trained and highly effective Sikh Army. After many somewhat fanciful and self-serving adventures,

---

[71] *Flashman and the Mountain of Light.*

[72] Editor's Note: Raja Soochet buried his substantial fortune in three large copper pots at Ferozepur, in British-controlled India, shortly before he died in March 1844. It was discovered by the British and then claimed by Lahore, but the British refused to return the gold, arguing that it should be distributed to Raja Soochet's heirs.

Flashman is instrumental (at least that's what he claims) in bringing about the defeat of the Khalsa at the hands of an Anglo-Indian force led by Sir Hugh Gough with,[73] somewhat incongruously, the Governor General serving as his second-in-command.

In the aftermath of the battles of Mudki, Ferozeshah and the decisive Sobraon, Flashman is sent back to Lahore to affect the capture of the Maharani Jindan and her son, the Maharaja Juleep Singh, then aged eight. He is not entirely successful in this endeavour but does manage to secure the Koh-i-Noor diamond, which he somewhat flippantly throws at Sir Henry Hardinge as he is leaving for England. This last assertion, as with much of the rest of Flashman's story, is pure fiction as the following two letters, which I have not rendered into memoir format, reveal.

...

Umballa Field Camp, April 1846

Dear Flashy

It's all over – at least for the time being for, as sure as God made little green apples, there will be a second round at some point in the future, but hopefully with me safely tucked-up in bed anywhere but on the Sutlej.

As Hardinge has directed, I have the diamond stowed safe with my kit and under the watchful eye of Searcy, who wouldn't let a button disappear off my tunic without his say so. He and Khazi have settled down into a sort of armed truce with the potential battleground always being myself.[74] Honestly, I thought that jealousy was supposed to be a female characteristic. I shouldn't complain, as having two cut-throats guarding your front and rear is a real bonus in these parts, particularly if it were ever known that I was lugging around a diamond the size of a small ostrich egg and worth the country's National Debt.

---

[73] General (later Field Marshal & 1st Viscount) Sir Hugh Gough (1779-1869). At the time Sir Hugh was the most battle-experienced General in the British Army.

[74] Editor's Note: It would appear that Speedicut had at some point after his first arrival in Umballa been reunited with his Kizilbashi scout and companion in Afghanistan, Muhamad Khazi, but there is no explanation of the circumstances.

But there is a problem. In the treaty negotiations Hardinge had to pledge to return the Koh-i-Noor to the Sikhs and, of course, that's the last thing he wants to do. So, whilst he haggles and prevaricates, I'm off to Bombay with the bauble to meet-up with a Jewish gem-cutter from Amsterdam called Ascher,[75] who's been rushed out here with all his tools in great secrecy and on the specific orders of the Governor General. The plan is that Ascher will make a copy of the stone in crystal, which will then in due course be surrendered back to the Sikhs. Meanwhile, I am to take the real one back to London and deposit it at the Bank of England. Quite what that will achieve remains to be seen, for my understanding was that it is the known possession of the jewel which is the thing that will con the natives out here into accepting the rule of the Great White Queen as the natural order of things.[76] As I've said afore, mine not to reason why – and I'm certainly not going to say 'no' to a government-funded, all expenses paid, first class trip to London via the Suez overland route, now am I? And I get to take Khazi as well as Searcy back with me 'for protection', although quite what I'll do with two orderlies once I return to Regimental soldiering heaven only knows – actually, thinking about it, Khazi can become my groom. So that's another problem solved!

If I can swing it, I'm going to try and return via Paris so that I can get in some proper R&R with you afore having to face the GB, Horse Guards, the Bank of England and the inevitable one-way ticket back to this accursed country for further service with the Shiners. If I were you, I would start laying in the champagne.

I'll write again from Alexandria when I know the final itinerary for the European leg of the trip. Thinking of home and les demoiselles françaises en route.

---

[75] Editor's Note: When the Koh-i-Noor was recut in 1852 in Amsterdam the work was carried out by James Tennant, under the supervision of Prince Albert. The firm of Ascher Brothers of Amsterdam was responsible for cleaving and cutting the Cullinan diamond almost exactly sixty years later.

[76] Editor's Note: Prior to the discovery of *The Speedicut Papers* it was believed that the real Koh-i-Noor was only surrendered to the British Crown under the terms of the Treaty of Lahore of 1849, which ended the Second Sikh War and established British rule in the Punjab.

Yours ever

Speed

...

Hotel El Gyppo Splendido, Alexandria, July 1846

Dear Flashy

Just a quick note to say that I hope your cellar's now well stocked, for I have persuaded the powers-that-be to allow me (and my party) to make the final leg back home via Marseilles and Paris. We land in France sometime in the next three weeks, so I may well see you before the start of September. The British Agent in Alexandria, who met me on arrival (just how many people do actually know what I have in my pocket, I wonder?) has arranged for us to stay at the Embassy in Paris on account of my 'special duties', so there is no need for you to make any special arrangements for me with your neighbour as you proposed in your last missive that was waiting for me on arrival here. Quite what the Ambassador's wife will make of Khazi remains to be seen!

When I last wrote I was just off to Calcutta to get a replica of the Koh-i-Noor carved to send to Hardinge for him to palm off on our turbaned friends across the Sutlej. Mr Ascher turned out to have all the wiles of his race and cunningly suggested that he should create two replicas: the first for Hardinge to give to Mrs Jindan and young Master Juleep, and the second for me to carry as a decoy. He proposed that I should carry the copy and entrust the real diamond to Searcy because, if the word got out that I was carting the Koh-i-Noor back to London to lay on the ample left tit of our Sovereign Lady, no one would be expecting me to be carrying a fake and my servant to be in possession of a Queen's ransom. The Chosen Race are bright and it was a clever plan. Only you and Ascher are in on the secret that I have a lump of glass in my waistcoat pocket and dear old Searcy has the rock in his britches. He's secured the gem in a silk sock which he has suspended from a string around his waist, from where it hangs next to his other bijoux de famille. By all accounts, the stone was frequently used in the erotic games played after hours at the Lahore Court, so it won't be offended by this proximity to Searcy's organ. Quite what our prudish Sovereign would think if she ever found out that her newest brooch had spent the best part of the last few years in such places doesn't bear thinking about, so I'm not! The only problem thus far is that Searcy has to be careful when crossing his legs.

Homeward bound and hoping for lots of mischief in the City of Sin.

Speed

CHAPTER SIXTEEN: A SLEIGHT OF HAND

Readers may remember that I mentioned a while back that a former Shiner called Francis Leigh had lost his balls, his brains and most of his patrimony to that hell-cat Lola Montez. Well blow me down but, after seeing Flashy onto the train for Brussels, who should I run into in the Faubourg but Leigh himself.

At first, I didn't recognise him for, to say the least, he was looking down at heel. However, it wasn't the unpressed state of his well-cut clothes, but the terrible hang-dog look that had replaced his once rather charming features which threw me. He was about my age but, on that Paris pavement he could easily have passed for my Papa on one of his bad days, and that's saying something. Leigh was shambling around just by our Embassy gates, head down, kicking the pebbles and walking slowly in a circle as though he couldn't make up his mind whether to ring the bell or not.

"It's Leigh, isn't it?" I asked tentatively as I got up to him, for there was no way around him if I was to get back into the building. "Don't you remember me? I'm Speedicut of the Tenth – we served briefly in Ireland together."

"What's that?" he said as though waking from a dream, "Speedicut? Oh, yes, I do remember you. Didn't you have to go and play the hero somewhere?" he added with a sneer. Snot-nosed aristos like Leigh didn't improve in adversity it seemed, but I was still minded to be friendly.

"Yes, that's right old chap – although in the end there weren't many heroics involved. So, what's up with you? You look like a man who's lost a sov and found a farthing."

"I'm finished, Speed, finished," and he started to blub.

"How so, old sport?"

"That Montez woman has kicked me out, taken everything I own and stuffed me with a stack of debts. My pater won't stump-up as he says it's my fault for carrying on with a shameless tart and that I have to learn my lesson or some such. So, I'm stuck here with the bailiffs on my tail. There's just one chance left, but I need a bag of chips to pull it off and I can't bring m'self to ask Cowley for the necessary tin.[77] I think I'm going to throw m'self in the Seine. It's the only answer…" and he sunk to his knees on the *trottoir.*

It was pathetic, but I hoped that if I ever found myself in similar circs that a Shiner would come to my rescue, so I patted him on the shoulder and said I'd give him a *burra peg* in the local *zinc.* He perked up a bit at that and rose wearily upright.

As we were about to set off, Searcy and Khazi, who had set out earlier to explore the Tuilleries Gardens, hove into view looking very pleased with themselves. Khazi was causing heads to turn as he was still in a rather elaborate native outfit that I'd bought for him in Bombay - if you're going to play the returning nabob, you need to do it in style - and Searcy, too, was causing not a little attention in his frogged tunic, busby and skin-tight Shiners' overalls, in which the addition of a couple of hundred carats of diamond had created an almost obscene bulge.

"Where are you off to, boys?" I called over to them as they both threw me a *pukka* salute. Searcy replied that they were headed back to the Embassy and asked at what time I would be returning to change.

"At about six I should think. Lay out my black coat, would you?" Then I took Leigh by the elbow and steered him around the corner to a smoky little café I'd taken to using.

"Now what's all this about?" I asked. "You can't have got in that deep with the Montez woman, have you?"

---

[77] Henry Wellesley, 1st Baron Cowley (1773-1847). He was the younger brother of the 1st Duke of Wellington and British Ambassador in Paris 1841-1846.

"Deeper than you can possibly imagine," he replied. "Y'know for the last year I've been sharing her with some Frog called Dujarier who owned a newspaper and had a pile of rhino. During that time, it seemed as though she was behaving herself, although I can't be sure that she didn't sleep with anyone else but the two of us, but if she did she was discreet.

"Then Dujarier got his head blown off in the Bois and she lost control, lifting her skirts to anyone who took her fancy - and the rougher the better. Meanwhile, in no time his family had reneged on all her debts, so the bootmakers, the furriers, the dressmakers, the glovers and I don't know who else came crawling to my doorstep. For it don't matter how much money she has, she always spends double and then some. She's worse than a sailor newly arrived in port – and with the morals to match.

"I wouldn't have minded so much if I'd had her to m'self, so to speak, but no sooner had I got rid of the first wave of duns than she was not only sleeping with *le tout Paris* but paying the younger ones with my money for the privilege..."

"So why do you want to touch Cowley?" I asked. "You must have got enough tin left to leg it back to England and leave your problems behind you, surely?"

"Would that it was that easy," he sighed. "If it was, I would have left weeks ago, but she's got something of mine and she won't let me have it without a substantial payment."

"And what might that be?" I asked, as I imagined a cache of embarrassing letters.

"All right, I'll tell you if you promise to help me *and* never to breathe a word of this to anyone." I thought for a moment and then nodded my assent.

"You see," and he paused again, "she's got our marriage licence. If I don't pay-up enough for her to take herself off in style to Munich, where she's got an engagement for the winter, she's going to send it to my pater - and I can then kiss goodbye to ever seeing home again."

And once more he started to blub. It was pathetic, so pathetic in fact that I decided to help him but I needed to consult with my other brain first.

"Pull y'self together, old chap," I said, "I'm sure there's a solution but I need an hour or so to work it out. Where's Signora Montez stayin' at present?" He said the Albany on the rue de Rivoli. "And d'you think she'll see you?" He nodded. "Good, we'll meet me back here in an hour." He nodded again.

I got up and, without a further word, but with a reassuring pat on his shoulder, I left him staring moodily at his absinthe and made my way back to the Embassy, where I found Searcy and Khazi hard at work on a pair of boots I'd bought that morning. The outline of an idea was starting to form in my brain that would both help a fellow Shiner in need and deal a nasty blow to the frightful Montez woman, without exposing myself to her in any way.

Over the next twenty minutes or so I went through the idea with Searcy and Khazi. The Kizilbashi's English comprehension may not have been one hundred percent, but what he lacked in understanding he more than made up for in unadulterated cunning and brute strength, whilst Searcy's finely tuned mind more than compensated for his lack of brawn. Within the hour we were ready and, with Searcy in my best black coat and Khazi in a sober *kurta*, we made our way out of the Embassy, across the Faubourg and back to the café. Leigh was sitting exactly where I had left him, head down over an empty glass, but he looked up and brightened somewhat at our approach.

"Here's the plan, old chap," I said, as I sat down next to him. "I want you to go over to the Albany and leave a note for Miss Lola tellin' her to meet you at the Tour d'Argent in an hour and to bring the certificate with her. I'll meet you back here tomorrow morning at eleven with the document and, if you take my advice, you'll then get out of town fast."

An hour later we were in position in the restaurant. I had my tile tipped well down over my brows and was sitting in the darkest corner in the room, nursing a brandy. Khazi and Searcy were in full view of everyone, having made quite a stir when they entered. The table I had reserved in Leigh's name was in a small alcove booth at the back, with a bottle of fizz chilling in a bucket. A few minutes later, in sailed the bitch herself in a scarlet velvet, low-cut gown that was so laced as to ensure that every eye in the room followed her progress to see if her boobs would break loose before she got to her table. I saw her look slightly surprised that Leigh wasn't waiting for her, but she took a pew and in no time at all I could see that my two boys were very much the centre of her attention.

As I'd hoped, given what Leigh had told me, it didn't take her long to catch Searcy's eye and, moments later or so it seemed, they had both been invited to join her in the alcove. A couple of hours and several bottles of fizz later the three of them left for her hotel and I followed. Once I was satisfied that they had successfully negotiated their way past the concierge, who anyway was probably used to far worse behaviour by the imperious 'Spanish' madam and was well-paid to hold his tongue, I sauntered back to the Embassy and a well-earned sleep.

As the sun was breaking through my curtains the following morning, there was a quiet knock on my door and, moments later, Searcy and Khazi slipped in. Khazi had a rather soiled looking envelope in his right hand and, once at the end of the bed, Searcy slipped a hand inside his britches and, with a quite enchanting grin, drew out the silk sock. It was empty.

"Sir, it went like a dream," said Searcy barely able to control himself. "Muhamad and I at first played hard to get. She bought the idea that he was an Indian prince and I was his 'confidential secretary and constant companion' with all that implied – and she immediately saw it as the challenge you meant it to be.

"Once we'd cracked the fourth bottle of champagne, Muhamad here - who'd told her that his religion forbade him touching alcohol - let slip that I was carrying a prized possession of his family. She then poured most of a fifth bottle down him and, so she thought, discovered where it was hidden. At that point, she just asked us straight out to come back to her hotel with her. There was no mistaking her: she wanted us in her bed and with no further delay.

"Being good boys, we did as we were told. We were hardly inside the door of her bedroom before she had removed all of her clothes and quite a few of ours.

"I won't trouble you with the details, sir, leastways not before you've had your breakfast, but she took what she wanted not once but several times. I'm not saying as I'm ready to play full time for the other side, if you take my meaning, sir, but I wouldn't be averse to more of that lady if she were ever on offer again. And I've certainly got to know Muhamad here a lot better, sir, and I hope you don't plan to split us up any time soon."

"As to *that* Searcy," I said, "you need have no worries. I may not be rich but, were push ever to come to shove, I'd rather go without food than say goodbye to you two. But, although I can see that Khazi's got the certificate, you haven't yet told me how you got it. Did it all go to plan?"

"Not *exactly*, sir," Searcy paused for a moment, clearly not wanting to show-up the flaw in our plan. "Of course, once I'd shed my britches there was no hiding the stone, but she seemed to find its presence exciting and insisted that I wear it. I think that she actually found it quite stimulating - leastwise, she moaned a lot. Anyway, after our third session, with Muhamad and I quite played out, she asked to look at it and to be told its story.

"I left that bit to Muhamad, but he made a grand tale of how it had been handed down in his family over the generations and of how it was a part of the various rituals that were part of his family's traditions. She couldn't get enough of it and kept cradling the stone in her hand, between her breasts and in other places no decent woman would put a finger, let alone a diamond. Finally, with the stone safely back in its sock, she turned down the lamp and we all got ready for sleep.

"Sometime later I felt her stir and roll over towards me. She started playing with the sock and the bits around it and, when I didn't appear to wake, I felt her slip the diamond out. Then, slowly, she slid from the bed, quietly gathered up her clothes and some jewellery and let herself out of the room. I gave Muhamad a nudge, but he like me had never gone to sleep and - once we were certain that she had gone - we both got dressed and made our exit via the back stairs."

"But how did you get the certificate?" I asked.

"You should thank Muhamad for that," said Searcy with a grin at my dusky, bearded orderly. "Your plan for me to pinch it from her bag whilst she was getting ready for fun and games didn't work, because she never did make any preparations other than getting us all stripped for action in double quick time.

"So, after round two, Muhamad here asked her for a cheroot: 'I thought that your religion didn't allow you to smoke,' she said, but Muhamad here just gave her a big grin, opened her handbag and palmed the envelope, which he held between – well, let's just say that she couldn't see that he had it and, anyway, she had more than enough to look at as Mo – Muhamad that is - got ready for round three. To be fair, I couldn't keep my own eyes off him either. Anyway, here it is. It's a bit crushed and we're neither of us quite sure if those marks were on it earlier in the evening, but I hope Mr Leigh will be pleased to get it back."

Now, dear reader, if you've been paying attention you may be wondering why I hadn't had apoplexy at the loss of the Koh-i-Noor: I didn't need to because we'd switched it earlier for Mr Ascher's spare fake. I didn't think that Lola would stop to examine it too closely and would leg it as fast as she could out of town, grabbing her spare luggage on the way out of the hotel and getting them to send on the rest after her. And, so I assumed, that's exactly what happened.

So, for once, it was a happy ending for me (if not for the Montez creature, who must soon have discovered that what she'd pinched was a worthless lump of glass); Searcy and Khazi were inseparable; Leigh was safely back in the bosom of his family; our Gracious Sovereign would in due course get another bauble with which to festoon her frumpy dresses; I was in good odour with the GB, to whom I delivered the diamond; and there was every prospect that I would be seconded as a reward to the Second Battalion at Hyde Park Barracks where I could sit out in comfort the remainder of the Regiment's tour 'in our Indian possessions', as I was sure Vicky was wont to refer to that dung heap of human misery.[78]

---

[78] Editor's Note: It will never be known if Speedicut's account is any truer than Flashman's highly fanciful story. However, it is certainly true that Lola Montez was in Munich by October 1846 and there is to this day a glass copy of the original, unrecut Koh-i-Noor diamond in that city's principal museum – although there is no explanation as to how it got there. In 1850, Queen Victoria had the real Koh-i-Noor mounted in a brooch...

CHAPTER SEVENTEEN: THE GRIM REAPER

The first day of January 1847 was a very happy New Year for me as it opened with the news that my ghastly Papa has finally gone to the great duck pond in the sky. There was a certain justice in the manner of his end, for he had choked to death on Boxing Day whilst gorging himself on roast quacker. Mama seemed completely unmoved by his passing, although when I went up for the funeral she told me that Emily the parlour maid had carried on as though the old skinflint had been married to her. Poor Mama, could she really never have known what had been going on all that time?

Somewhat to my surprise, given the state of play between us, I inherited virtually everything. I told Mama, who would otherwise have had to beg a bed from Lizzie, that I hoped she would stays on at the Dower House, as I had no intention of moving up to Wales any time soon. She prevaricated a bit, until I told her that I would pay the running costs: I could well afford to do this as our family lawyer had informed me that the old bastard had been hoarding cash for years and making some pretty astute investments with it. So, I had snagged more than enough to keep Acton going, to set up my own establishment in town and to allow me to take some time off from service to Her Majesty.

By the end of the month I'd tooled around to Horse Guards and put in my papers to go on half pay and, at the same time, I sent a note around to Steyne House requesting a meeting with the GB so that I could tell him that I would be unavailable to the Brotherhood for the foreseeable future. Then I started looking for a suitable house where I could set up a permanent base for myself and the home team, whilst I worked out what to do with my new found and very well-funded leisure.

A few days after I'd sent in my papers, Searcy showed me a report in *The Times* to the effect that the Montez woman was treading the boards in Munich. If she ever managed to get poor old Ludwig clamped between her thighs, I thought, he'd make her his Prime Minister before the year was out. Searcy also said that he'd seen a house at 25 Curzon Street that was up for sale, so I got an order to view.

I had only to step through the door of that house to know that I needed to look no further. The previous owner had rather overplayed his hand at Brooks' before Christmas and, in consequence, the house and all its contents were up for a quick sale so that he could cover his position. I closed the deal virtually on the spot and moved in within the week. Searcy took on the role of butler and Khazi was as happy as a lark lording it over the mews, for which I acquired a smart town carriage and a pair of nags. I blush to think of it now, but in keeping with my growing and entirely spurious reputation as a sort of military nabob, I decked the staff out in a rather dashing Indian-style livery.

So much for the good news of January 1846. Unfortunately, the bad news, which in my experience is never far off the good, caught up with me at my interview with the GB. He saw me in his study and I told him what I had in mind. It did not go down well.

"Brother Speedicut, I think that you have mistaken the nature and extent of the *obligations* that are attendant upon your membership of the Brotherhood of the Sons of Thunder. It seems, from what you have just said, that I must remind you that, in exchange for the Brotherhood providing you with quite unique opportunities for preferment, wealth creation, political power and advancement generally – benefits that, in the matter of your rank, you have already tasted – you place yourself at the *unreserved* disposal of the Brotherhood to assist me in the effective pursuit of our sworn aims.

"I also have to remind you, since it is clear that you have been labouring under a misapprehension, that having taken our oath it is not for you to pick and choose - in order to suit your own circumstances - those obligations that I may from time to time lay upon you. I hope that clarifies the position for you. Now will you take a dish of tea?"

Deciding that any attempt to mitigate this Jovian pronouncement would be so much wasted breath, I tried to repair the damage.

"Great Boanerges," I responded with my best attempt at noble humility, "as to tea, that would be most welcome." He reached across and pulled the bell. "As to the other matter, I had not intended to infer that I was no longer at the disposal of the Brotherhood, merely that – were it at all possible – I would be grateful if those duties and obligations which you may lay upon me could be, err, mitigated whilst I continue to rearrange my affairs followin' the untimely and tragic death of my beloved father." As I had intended, the GB seemed to soften at this blatant hypocrisy.

"Of course, of course, my dear Brother Speedicut; I did not know of your tragic loss, so please accept my sincere condolences. I, too, had not intended to infer that your obligations to our great undertaking had to be discharged without any regard to external circumstances, merely that your membership involves, shall we say, the concept that your privileges bring with them their own responsibilities?

"Now it so happens that, at present, I have no need of your particular skills or experience and so I trust that you will find the time to settle your affairs and, indeed, enjoy the benefits that have now – I hope - fallen to you.

"On a different and I trust altogether more pleasurable subject, you would oblige me greatly if you would accept an invitation – and I apologise for the late notice - to a ball that my wife is organising next week to introduce our daughter, Mary, to London Society; may I tell Lady Steyne to add you to our guest list?"

I said that, of course, I would be delighted. However, the thought of having to partner, even for one dance, a daughter of the GB filled me with trepidation: she would almost certainly be over six-foot-tall, moustachioed, flat chested and capable of drilling the Grenadiers.

But the GB was clearly not finished with me yet and he was about to go on when a powdered and liveried footman appeared with a silver tray the size of a flag, on which was laid an elaborate tea service. The flunkey fussed around, gave us our tea and retired backwards, courtier style, out of the room. Once he'd gone, the GB resumed.

"There is a second matter with which you could help *me* as opposed to the Brotherhood. It fell to me – for the government cannot be seen to be involved at present – to inform His Royal Highness Prince Albert that the great Indian diamond is now lodged within the vaults of the Bank of England. Somewhat inconveniently, for as you know it must remain a secret that we have the real stone, he has asked to see it.

"As not even the Governor knows what lies within his care – he has been informed that the box contains some highly sensitive State papers – there are only three people who can comply with this royal command: I am a Privy Councillor, so it would be highly inappropriate - and possibly inconvenient should the truth ever emerge - for me to do so, and Lord Hardinge is still in India. That just leaves you…" He allowed the news and its implications to sink in. "Will you agree to perform this small service for me?" What could I say? Of course, I said 'yes and willingly'. "Good, good," he went on in a rather more avuncular tone, "then there is only one other thing in this regard that I need to address with you.

"Whilst I would not wish you to minimise your part in its seizure, you would greatly oblige me - and the government - if you were to allow His Royal Highness to go away with the impression that the stone had in fact been *gifted* to Her Majesty by the Maharaja and that the deception plan, which you carried out so brilliantly, was merely a device to allow time for the necessary diplomatic moves to be completed."

If that was what the powers-that-be wanted the Stud Royal to think, who was I to say no? So, I said that it would be an honour to do as instructed. The GB then said that two weeks later I was to present myself at the side entrance of the Bank of England where, a short time later, a carriage would pull up and I would be joined by a certain 'Baron Windsor' whom I was to escort to the vault and, once we were locked inside, to show him the former contents of Searcy's britches.

But before this duty, I had to attend the Steynes' ball to mark their daughter's coming-out in Society. The evening duly arrived and Khazi drove me to Steyne House. Searcy had engaged a couple of darkies for the night as footmen, who rode in my flash livery on the back of the carriage.

We caused a mild sensation on arrival and my own appearance, when I stepped out of the carriage in the latest Shiners' skin-tight rig, merely helped to heighten the effect.

Once inside, under the blazing chandeliers, spectacular frescoes and a ton of gilding in the hall, I waited patiently in line to file up the staircase for the presentation on the *piano nobile* landing. Fiddlers were scraping away somewhere in the background, footmen emerged from behind giant palms to take our cloaks, hats and swords and the whole thing made Buckingham Palace look like a provincial town hall – indeed, I heard a woman in front of me saying that when The Queen first visited the Steynes, shortly after her accession, she said to Lady Steyne: 'I come from my house to your palace'. The way it looked for the ball, that was no exaggeration.

Eventually, I got to the head of the queue and there was the GB, the Garter star on his coat and a blue ribbon across his paunch. Next to him was the Marchioness, whom I had never met before but I knew to be a rich American. She was tightly laced into a green brocade gown that was sprinkled with diamonds and, in conseq   uence, looked like one of Prince Albert's Christmas trees. Her whole ensemble was topped-off by a diamond and emerald tiara the size of a club fender and a necklace of sparklers that covered her from chin to tit. These baubles must all have weighed half-a-hundredweight, but she had the shoulders to carry them and a chin to match. Not someone to meet unexpectedly on a dark night, I thought as I made my bow over her gloved and diamond-encrusted paw.

Next to her was a tall, slender, dark-haired beauty, all in white and pearls, who could easily have been a younger, darker version of my darling Mitzi. Perhaps that's why she felled me at that first encounter. For I couldn't take my eyes off her for the rest of the evening, which seemed to pass in a whirl that had nothing to do with the fashionable new waltzes being played. Of course, I had little chance to dance with her, for her card had been pretty well fixed in advance and anyway, who was I - a mere Captain of Hussars - compared to half the burks in the Peerage who were also her guests. But I did manage to book her for a mazurka and a waltz and, as we danced, we chatted away merrily about nothing in particular. It was difficult to know if I had made an impression, but I did catch her looking for me over her other dance partners' shoulders at least once...

Back home, I couldn't sleep for thinking of her and, when he came to wake me, I told Searcy that I was in love. He asked me with whom and, when I told him, I could see that he was less than pleased at the news and for the next few days he was distinctly in a sulk. Khazi, when he heard, said that I'd had too much to drink and would soon come to my senses.

Of course, I'd read in the cheaper type of fiction about 'love at first sight', but I'd always thought it was just so much romantic tosh. Well, that evening changed my mind and all I could think of was how to climb the walls of the Steyne fortress and carry off my beloved. Meanwhile, before I could work out a solution to that problem, I had my *rendezvous* with Baron Windsor to endure.

As planned, Khazi drove me to the Bank where I was met by Robinson,[79] the new Governor, a sickly-looking fellow who was clearly overwhelmed at the thought of meeting royalty. No sooner had I arranged with him that he would show us to the vault and then clear off, than a town coach from the Mews pulled up and out stepped HRH. I could see his duty Equerry lurking inside but, as this was all supposed to be unofficial, he remained there. Of course, this whole business of being incog was blown in the first second, for I lifted my tile whilst Robinson practically doubled up, although that could have been indigestion. He then led the way down to the vaults where we were confronted by a massive steel door with a Grenadier stationed on either side, weapons at the high port.

The Governor said the magic words, or whatever he needed to do to open the door, and it slowly swung open. Just inside I could see a table on which was a largish leather box and two oil lamps with, behind it, row upon row of racking stacked high with gold bricks; Aladdin's Cave would have looked like a market stall by comparison. Albert and I stepped inside

---

[79] William Robinson Robinson was Governor of the Bank of England for the shortest possible time, between April and August 1847.

and, as the door was closing, I heard Robinson say that he would return in ten minutes. Up to that time (nor since) had I ever been locked up alone with royalty in a room in which there was more gold than one could ever dream of spending. It was all curiously unreal.

"Captain Speedicut, I unnerstand zat it ist to you zat Herr Majesty should be tankful for ze safe deliverry of ziss great trreasure," he says pointing at the box, "ist zat correct?" I murmured that it was, although no great danger had been involved.

"*Nein, nein,*" he said, "ze tranzporrtation of zuch a prize *must* have entailed danger, zo pleaze do not be modest. I am only sorry zat, vonce again, your Sovereign *und* your countrry arre unable to rrecognise your service." Hey, ho, I thought, so no tap on the shoulder then for yet another service rendered to the Crown by J Speedicut Esquire.

"Zo, are you going to show zis jewel to me?" he asked, with just a hint of royal impatience.

I said that it would be my pleasure, stepped forward and lifted the lid. Inside was another box, and inside that another one in which lay, on a cushion of black velvet, the Koh-i-Noor. I was relieved to see that the GB had buffed off the grease and sweat that it had accumulated whilst nestling next to Searcy's temple decorations. Albert reached for the stone and, between thumb and forefinger, he held it up to one of the lamps to catch the light. I knew damn all about jewellery, but it seemed to me that there really wasn't much twinkle to it (I think the experts call it 'fire') and Albert, who I later heard was something of an expert, clearly thought so too.

"Hmm, ze size *ist sehr* imprrezzive, but for ze rrest it could be glass."

Oh, God, I suddenly thought, did we muddle the switch in Paris or perhaps even in Bombay? Just as my guts were about to discharge themselves into my linen, Albert fished a small magnifying glass out of his waistcoat pocket, placed it practically on his eye ball and then held the diamond up close.

"Vell, although ze table *ist flach* ze colour *ist gud und* zer are no incluzions – but if Her Majesty ist to vear ziss stone it vill have to be rrecut."[80]

Then he put it back in its box and turned towards the vault door which was still shut, leaving me to complete the job of re-encasing it in the other boxes. I had not looked at my fob when we entered, but I calculated that at this point it must have been close to the ten minutes which we had been given by the Governor. At that moment first one, then the other lamp flickered out and we were plunged into darkness that was so profound that I thought I'd been struck blind. Both Albert and I called out in surprise, but we might as well have been tapping on the door with a feather.

What happened next will forever remain in my memory: it must have been a reflex reaction to the sudden dark, but I felt impelled to reach the door and the Prince was obviously driven by the same instinct. I groped my way in the total darkness to where I remembered the door was located but, instead of the handle, I found myself grasping the royal arse. Albert let out a yell of surprise, I backed off at full speed and there was an appalling crash as I collided with the table which went flying, along with the lamps and the box. Deciding that the safest thing at this point was to stay put, I lay there – but seconds later I felt the Carcass Royal trip over my legs and crash down next to me with an obscene German oath.

It's hard to judge time in total darkness, but I swear we lay there for at least another five minutes. In all that time Albert said nothing to me, but the string of German swear words which he was muttering to himself grew in intensity as time went on. When, finally, the door opened to reveal the Governor he was nearly knocked flat by the explosion of words from HRH as he leapt to his feet and dashed out of the vault. I thought the poor man – the Governor that is – was going to have a seizure, for he turned deathly white and once again doubled up, although this time it really seemed to be from pain rather than obsequiousness.

---

[80] Editor's Note: When the Koh-i-Noor was recut in 1852, under Prince Albert's supervision, it was reduced from 186 carats to 105 carats to improve its brilliance, but he was reportedly less than pleased with the result.

Albert stormed up the stairs, his right hand bleeding profusely and his brow covered in sweat. He tried to stem the blood with a kerchief, which he then absent-mindedly used to mop his brow. The result was that his face looked as if he was the victim of an anarchist's bomb. When, finally, we emerged into the fresh air, Albert paused, took a deep breath, tucked his kerchief back into his pocket and gave me a very particular stare. Then, with a Herculean attempt at royal *sang froid*, he spoke.

"I haff no love for enclozed spazes, Captain Speedicut. I dank you for rremaining calm down there – and I vill rremember your service not only to ze Crown but to me. I may haff need of your skills in ze future. For ze moment, *auf wiedersehn.*"

Then, completely ignoring the Governor, he stepped into his coach and it was bowling away past Mansion House before I could even lift my tile in salute. What Vicky would think when he emerged from the carriage at the other end didn't bear dwelling on. So that was that. I had had no opportunity to convey to the Prince the lie that the diamond had already been gifted to our diminutive monarch, but it's difficult to raise a subject when royal protocol demands that you only speak when spoken to. That's particularly so when you're in complete darkness and lying on a heap of broken glass with the royal personage in question on top of you uttering a stream of untranslatable German. The GB should have thought of that.

When, after a stiff drink at the Verulam to steady my nerves, I returned to Curzon Street I convened a council of war with the 'home team', sulks or no, to devise a strategy for me to win my fair maiden or carry her off without undue risk to my more sensitive body parts. Well, the GB was quite capable of having me 'Aberlarded' with a blunt knife and I'd already been too close to that operation in Bokhara to risk it again.

However, before we could devise anything resembling a risk-free plan of action, I received a letter from Mitzi telling me that Johannes had died and begging me to come to her. My campaign to capture the heart of fair Mary Steyne would, under these sad circumstances, have to wait for I had no choice but to speed (no pun intended) to Bavaria as fast as I could. Anyway, the subject of Mary was causing not a few problems with Searcy and Khazi, who didn't appear to relish the prospect of having a mistress as well as a master and were being less than helpful in devising a plan to secure her.

As soon as I could arrange matters, I left Searcy in charge of the house but I took Khazi with me because, if I was to venture anywhere within the orbit of the dreaded Montez woman, then I had to have close and ruthless protection to hand.

CHAPTER EIGHTEEN: CROWNED & UNCROWNED HEADS

Thanks to my father's gold, the post chaise system and reasonable weather, I managed to get to Munich in under a fortnight, to find that Johannes had long since been laid to rest in the family vault, Mitzi was in the deepest black, her household at the Palais Schwanstein in central Munich was plunged in gloom and the Bavarian Court was in uproar.

I was soon made aware of the latter over *kaffee und kuchen* with one of Mitzi's Thurn und Taxis relatives and, for the cause, one needed to look no further than the Countess of Landsfeld. Who? Well, the Countess of Landsfeld was a recently naturalised Bavarian citizen, whose portrait had just been hung in the Gallery of the Beauties at the Nymphenburg Palace and who had been elevated to the nobility with a large State pension on the King's birthday,[81] in 'recognition of her charm, political sagacity' and, doubtless, considerable dexterity in the Royal bed linen. Have you got there yet? No? Here's a clue: I mentioned a few pages ago that the Montez woman had got herself an engagement in Munich the previous October and I somewhat flippantly remarked that she would soon be made Prime Minister. Call me Cassandra.

From what Matilda Thurn and Taxis told me,[82] in the wake of Lola's capture of the King's prick the Munich Court resembled nothing so much as a comic opera in which all the principal players were living on laudanum and the bit players wished that they were too.

"My dear," she said to me as she devoured a slice of *kirschtorte*, "it all started when that woman, whom Mitzi tells me you knew in London, used her wiles to secure from dear Heinrich von Maltzahn a Letter of Introduction to the King. Half of Munich already knew what she was up to at the

---

[81] 25th August 1847.
[82] Mathilde Sophie (1816-1886), née Princess zu Oettingen-Oettingen und Oettingen-Spielberg, was the wife of Maximilian Karl, the 6th Prince von Thurn und Taxis.

Bayerischer Hof where she had installed herself, doubtless at Heinrich's expense, for the duration of her 'engagement' with the Court theatre. Of course, it was inevitable that His Majesty would see the woman there and, given his obsession with beauty, it was equally inevitable that she would catch his eye. So, when she presented Heinrich's letter at the Residenz she was shown straight up to the audience chamber.

"The dear King – and I blush to tell you what happened next – was so struck not only by her beauty but by her... now how can I say this delicately? err... her chest, that he asked her if it was 'nature or art', at which the shameless harlot leaned over the royal desk, seized a pair of His Majesty's scissors and cut open her bodice to reveal the truth. The story was all over Munich in minutes and many chose not to believe it, but I heard it direct from the King's Private Secretary – so I know it's true.

"It was straight to the royal bedchamber after that and, in the twinkling of an eye, the King had installed his 'Lolitta' - for that's what he calls her, can you believe it? - in a small, fully-staffed mansion on the Barerstrasse. There she has gathered around herself a large following of good-looking young officers and students, who have the dual function of escorting her in public and, and... well you know what I mean. Oh, yes – she's also acquired a large black mastiff by the name of Turk which follows her everywhere."

Hmm, I thought as Princess Matilda went on, if the hound ever seemed likely to cross my path, I would either shoot it: one encounter with a Lola-controlled Turk was quite enough for me.

"All should have been well, for we Bavarians and the Munichers are fairly tolerant and the dear King is popular. However, whilst we are happy for him to kiss her feet in private – yes, that's what he does - we draw the line at a royal mistress meddling in politics or making a nuisance of herself in the streets.

"But in no time at all she had done both and was at loggerheads with the Police Chief, Baron von Pechman and the long suffering First Minister,

Karl von Abel.[83] By February this year she had persuaded the King to sack von Abel and his entire cabinet for opposing her naturalisation and, since then, she has frozen-out the nobility, the Ultramontanes and the Jesuits.[84]

"There is, however, a glimmer of light: the latest word from the Residenz is that His Majesty has closed his bedroom door to her, although he shows no signs yet of wanting to close the gates of Munich behind the strumpet!"

So much for the State of Bavaria, I thought, but I didn't say so.

"Tell me, Princess, why does no one speak to the King about the woman? Surely if he realised the anger and discord she is fanning amongst his loyal subjects - or indeed if he knew the truth about her past - he would soon be rid of her?"

"You ask a most interesting and difficult question, my dear, for many people have tried. My own Max has himself spoken to the King, but to no avail. He will hear not a word against her and, indeed, seems to think that the problems are of his own making and that he is honour bound to protect her. Such rubbish of course, but His Majesty has always had a rather, shall we say, 'eccentric' view of the rights and duties of monarchy. But I tell you in all seriousness, if he allows the situation to continue I fear for his throne. Of course, if there was any way in which you could help – for Mitzi tells me that you know much of this woman's past – the people of Bavaria would be forever in your debt."

This was definitely dangerous ground for me and so I edged the conversation away from Ludwig and Lola and onto the behaviour of other members of the Royal Family, including my old 'friend' the Princess Alexandra. As those most loyal to a crown are the first to gossip about it there was no stopping Matilda, who by now had got the bit firmly between her teeth.

---

[83] Editor's Note: Despite being in Paris at the time, in *Royal Flash* Flashman claims that he was seduced in Munich by a Baroness Pechman, held by the police on false charges of rape and only released when he agreed to help Bismarck.

[84] The Ultramontanes believed in the supremacy of the Pope over secular rulers.

"I know, Mitzi, that you tried to help the dear King to draw out Her Royal Highness – and of course, Captain Speedicut, you too had a hand in that noble project - but it was bound to fail as Alexandra's quite mad, you know," opined Matilda. "Well, perhaps mad is too strong a word, but she is certainly more than a little *distrait*. She now only wears white, is obsessed with cleanliness, refuses to socialise with any of the eligible Princes of the Blood and tells anyone who will listen that she has a grand piano in her stomach!" I'm definitely *not* taking the blame for that, I thought.

"And it's not even as though she is fat – in fact she has the most graceful figure. You know, there are times when I fear for the Wittelsbachs. Too much inter-breeding has led to a complete absence of common sense: the Crown Prince is rebuilding an ancient ruined castle in the Schwangau into a fairy tale gothic mansion,[85] and Duke Max in Bayern is obsessed with folk music and spends every moment he can at the circus.[86] And he allows Elizabeth to run wild,"[87] she ended, on a rather downbeat note.

Mitzi and Matilda chattered on in a similar vein until the light was starting to fade. Just as she was sweeping herself together to leave, Matilda turned to me again.

"You know, Captain Speedicut, if there was anything you could produce as evidence that the Landsfeld woman is nothing but a whore and a fraud, I am sure that Max would be able to get it to the King. Do please think about it – for all our sakes."

Determined though I was to ignore this request, Mitzi returned to the subject over dinner that evening. We were in the small family dining room that overlooked the garden, at the end of which there was a low wall that separated the property from the city. We were tucking into a plate of *schweinshaxe* when there was a simply appalling racket from the other side of the wall, as a great crowd of students marched past chanting, blowing

[85] The Crown Prince Maximilian created the castle of Hohenschwangau – a precursor to the prolific building of such follies by his son, the future King Ludwig II.

[86] HRH Duke Maximilian in Bayern (1808-1888) was the head of a cadet branch of the Wittelsbach dynasty. The main branch carried the title of Dukes von Bayern.

[87] The future Empress Elizabeth of Austria (1837-1898).

horns, throwing their caps in the air and waving banners. I couldn't make out what was going on and said so.

"It's the Alemannia," said Mitzi. I must have looked blank, for she went on, "They are a group of students who have become that woman's self–appointed bodyguards. They fill her salon by day and night, and her bed most likely too, when they are not getting drunk at their *bierstube*, Rottman's; the Munichers call them the 'Lolianer' or 'Lola's harem', which makes them even bolder and more partisan. Really, they are almost more of a menace than the woman herself.

"You know, Jasper, if there *was* anything you could do… Johannes always said that the King thought most highly of you and I am sure he would listen if you could present him with the truth." Tears started to fall silently down her cheeks.

I think it was the tears that did it for, at bottom, I'm a sentimental idiot and I can't bear to see a woman cry, particularly not one as lovely as Mitzi. So, I took a deep breath and said that I would draft a document setting out all that I knew about Mrs Rosanna James, sometimes known as Lola Montez and at that time going under the title of the Countess of Landsfeld.

As I picked up my pen to write a demolition job of heroic proportions, I thought of calling it *The Life and Times of the 19th Century's Biggest Liar.* Anyway, because the document was not for publication, I was able to lay on the dung with a pitch fork. Far from being a Catholic widowed Spanish aristocrat-turned-dancer, I stated quite unequivocally - and upon my oath as a British officer - that the Countess of Landsfeld was in fact Irish by birth and Protestant by religion, had been married, divorced and later remarried, probably illegally as it was by no means clear that she had divorced her first husband. In the meantime, she had become a Dublin brothel-keeper and a collaborator with dangerous Irish anarchists, before arriving in London with an entirely fictitious new persona. I went on to relate, in highly explicit language, my first-hand knowledge of her horizontal progress through the capitals of Europe, starting with her extraordinary behaviour at the Court of the Prince of Reuss and progressing through her series of evictions from Saxony, Prussia, Poland

and Russia. I ended with a colourful account of her later sojourn in Paris as a high-class tart and bigamist. By the time I had completed the document it amounted to such a damning indictment of the woman that not even a love-blinded king could have ignored it.

I gave it to Mitzi, who read it through with her eyes widening further and further with every line.

"Is this really the truth, Jasper?" she asked, to which I replied that I thought it was 'not the half of it'. "I will send it to Matilda, and Max will see that it gets straight to the King without being intercepted by that woman's agents." And that's just what she did.

A couple of days later, whilst Mitzi was out visiting relatives, I saw from my bedroom window a carriage pull up and a dapper, elderly gent stepped out of it. A few minutes later, Mitzi's butler tapped on my door, entered and said that there was a gentleman asking if he could see me. I pulled on my coat and, when I got down to the hall, the visitor introduced himself as Baron von Heideck,[88] 'personal confidant to His Majesty the King'.

The name meant nothing to me, but I was on my guard for Lola's agents were everywhere. Would I accompany him, he asked, to the Residenz where I was to be given a private audience with His Majesty in connection with a certain paper recently delivered to His Majesty by Prince von Thurn und Taxis? This was not a request but a royal command and I had no choice but to accept. However, I felt confident that it was not a trap, as the number of people who knew about my dossier was small and none of them, so I thought, was connected with Miss Montez. However, you don't spend time amongst the heathen without acquiring an ingrained cautiousness so, slipping away to get my cloak and hat, I quickly told Khazi to let Mitzi know what had happened and where I was bound.

---

[88] General Baron Carl Wilhelm von Heideck (1788-1861) was a soldier, amateur painter and lifelong friend of King Ludwig I, who appointed him to 'look after' Lola Montez.

Returning downstairs, I re-joined von Heideck and we sped off in his coach in the direction of the Residentz, arriving there some fifteen minutes later. By now my guard was well and truly down, for what ill fate could await me within the baroque splendour of the Wittelsbachs' seat of power? As in so many palaces before, from Bokhara to London, I was shown up a grand staircase and then through a seemingly never-ending succession of chambers, each with its own complement of palace guards, until we finally arrived at a tall set of closed doors in front of which was a richly uniformed Court Chamberlain flanked by yet more guards.

"Captain Speedicut and Baron von Heideck to see His Majesty," intoned my escort.

The Chamberlain bowed, confirmed that we were expected, the doors opened and we were ushered into the Presence with the Chamberlain stating our names in a loud voice for the old boy was as deaf as a post. Across the other side of the room, positioned in front of the fireplace and with tall folding lacquer screens to either side, was an ornate desk with, behind it, the familiar figure of His Most Catholic Majesty King Ludwig I of Bavaria.

"Come in, come in," he half shouted in his nasal *hochdeutsch* and we bowed and scraped our way to the front of his desk.

Somewhat surprisingly, since I knew from my previous meeting with HM that he disliked formality, he did not ask us to sit down. Instead, he picked up a small dagger, which he probably used as a letter opener, and started tapping its sharp point on what I quickly realised was my dossier.

"Captain Speedicut," he said looking up at me briefly and then turned to stare at the paperwork, "we know from our previous meeting, and from your associates here in Munich, that you are an honourable man, respected in your own country and received by your Sovereign." He paused for a moment as though considering what to say next.

"That such a man should have even considered placing on record, let alone actually doing so, this account of the previous history of a lady who is well respected in Munich, whom we have recently raised to the higher ranks of the Bavarian nobility and who is close to our person is scarcely to be believed." He paused again and I felt my guts move uncomfortably from relaxed to emergency position.

"So, before taking any further action, we must ask you to confirm that you are indeed the author of this paper." He dropped the knife and picked up the paper which he handed across the desk to me. I had already seen that it was my manuscript, so as I handed it back to him.

"Yes, Your Majesty, that is indeed the account of the life of the Countess of Landsfeld that I wrote not two days ago."

"And are you willing to swear to us that this account is wholly truthful and written without malice."

"Yes, Your Majesty, I would be willing to swear that," for what else could I say? And with that there was a loud bang off to one side and as I saw, out of the corner of my eye, one of the lacquer screens crash to the ground. There, in its place, stood the figure of Mrs James, Countess of Landsfeld, her face livid with rage and her eyes almost popping out of her head.

"He lies," she hissed. "He lies!"

The shock of her sudden appearance had the same effect on me as being punched hard in the stomach: it left me winded and speechless and I felt my breakfast heading south. But before I had time to recover, she strode forward, seized the dagger from off the King's desk and, with one hand grabbing my lapel to hold me steady, she brought the point up under my chin.

"Given the chance I will use this knife to cut out your tongue, something that I should have got Mrs Lovett to do back in Dublin," she whispered to me in her bog trotter's English. Then, she switched to her appalling German.

"Sire, what this man says is nothing more than evil propaganda devised by my enemies who are jealous of the confidence that you repose in me." She let go of me and dropped the knife back onto the desk.

"He also omits to tell you, Sire, that he is a secret agent of the scheming Palmerston,[89] sent here to sow discord and foment rebellion in Your Majesty's kingdom as part of a fell British plot to create chaos in Europe." She paused, as I wondered where she'd dreamt up that fantasy. But before I could take the thought any further she went on. "His lies I can ignore, but you should not allow his motive to go unpunished, for it is nothing less than *treason.*" The King looked down at his desk, then across to the window and finally back to me.

"Is what the Countess says true?" he asked me.

"No, Your Majesty, I am a private citizen staying in your capital to be with my friend the Dowager Countess of Schwanstein in her hour of need. I am not, nor have I ever been, an agent of Her Majesty's government. I am a simple soldier on half-pay whose sole motive in submitting that dossier to Your Majesty was to place on record what I know of this lady," I said, pointing to the bitch. "I did so at the request of some of Your Majesty's most loyal subjects."

There was a moment's silence, before Mrs Landsfeld put in another three ha'pence worth.

"I think," she said, "that Your Majesty is already aware that, far from being here to comfort the Dowager Countess, Captain Speedicut is in fact here to continue an illicit relationship with her, which he started in Berlin and has conducted ever since behind the back of the late Count. You cannot trust the word of a man who would so shamelessly betray the trust of a friend."

Well that was a bit of a poser, for it was common knowledge amongst Mitzi's friends that I was indeed something more than a friend, although the irony was that, since I had returned to Munich, my role had been

[89] Henry John Temple, 3rd Viscount Palmerston (1784-1865), British Foreign Secretary 1846-1851 was known to be sympathetic to the democratic movements that were starting to unsettle the absolutist monarchies of continental Europe.

nothing more nor less than that of chaste comforter. The King thought for a moment.

"There are some things in this matter that are clear, but many - including your motives - that require further investigation. It is our wish that you remain here in Munich whilst these matters are examined in further detail. Will you give us your parole as an officer and a gentleman that you will not attempt to remove yourself out of our jurisdiction until these matters are resolved?"

What could I say? I decided that the best thing was to say nothing but to nod my assent. This seemed to satisfy the King, although I could see that Lola was not at all happy at this turn of events. She had doubtless been planning that I should be heaved into a deep and dank dungeon and the key thrown into the nearest lake.

"Baron von Heideck, you will escort this officer back to the Palais Schwanstein where he will remain at our pleasure pending the resolution of this matter. He is not to be permitted to communicate with the outside world nor is he to be allowed to receive any of his countrymen. That is all."

And with that he went over to La Montez, took her by the arm and disappeared behind the one remaining screen, from where — despite the rumours to the contrary - he doubtless took her off to the royal bedchamber for another bout of Venus's press-ups.

The Baron then led me, shaken to the very core and in a complete daze, out of the palace, into his carriage and returned me to Mitzi. I don't think I uttered a single word for an hour at least as I contemplated my position. That I was under house arrest was clear; that I was also probably facing a trumped-up charge of treason was a reasonable assumption; and that, in the meantime, I stood a real risk of being injured or killed by the all-powerful Montez, or one of her henchmen, was all too likely. Worse still, I was forbidden to communicate with anyone outside the house, which meant that the British Minister in Munich was beyond my reach and, with that, any chance of disproving the claims that I was a British spy. The future looked distinctly bleak.

CHAPTER NINETEEN: IN TRADE

And there I remained for the next eight months. Suffice it to say that I had given my parole not to escape, which the King – probably at the urging of La Montez - insured by having armed guards posted outside the exits to the Palais Schwanstein. I may have been comfortably housed but I was effectively imprisoned in Munich with Khazi, whose house arrest was also, so it quickly emerged, included with my own. I may have been comforted by Mitzi in ways that only she knew, but I was unable to tell anyone of my fate or to seek outside assistance and, as I was being held *incommunicado*, I was wholly unaware of what if anything was being done to affect my release.

From time to time I was visited by the police, but as the weeks went by they were so preoccupied with the growing unrest on the streets of Munich that it became clear that the investigation into my motives was becoming a low priority and getting lower by the day. Mitzi kept me informed of what was happening in the outside world, where revolution was in the air, but I felt like nothing more than a bird in a gilded cage, unable even to stretch my wings. It was hell. But not as much hell, so I was to learn, as the problems facing Ludwig and Lola.

It is not for me to judge whether Ludwig was the victim of Lola's increasingly demented role in the affairs of Bavaria or if the wider tide sweeping across Europe was his undoing. But the fact is that on 20th March 1848 he was faced with the choice of accepting a constitution or abdication. He chose abdication whilst Lola fled to Switzerland with just the clothes she stood up in. In fact, she was lucky to escape with her life for, so Mitzi told me, the mob was ready to tear her limb from limb. But, in an act either of madness or bravery, she faced them down and made her escape.

With Ludwig's abdication and Lola's enforced departure to Switzerland it suddenly became clear that I was free to go. Max von Thurn und Taxis got the new King to give me a *laissez passer* and Mitzi gave me Johannes's duelling pistols for personal protection and as a keepsake. Then, with many a tear, she saw Khazi and me off on the long journey home. After seeing what the mob could do in Munich, I had no intention of returning by coach (the railway was, of course, out of the question) through Europe which, so I'd read, was *en flames* in what was later to be dubbed 'the revolutions of 1848'. Accordingly, I decided that we would travel via Lugano to Genoa, where we boarded a steamer to take us the long way back to England.

Using the new telegraph, I had sent word to Searcy from Munich that Khazi and I were on our way home and when we finally got back to Curzon Street it was to find that everything was much as we had left it, but with one major development. When we had left, I had told Searcy that we would probably be away for two months and I had left him in funds for three. However, as time went by, this money had started to run out and there was neither sign of our return nor any word from me.

Fortunately, Searcy was an enterprising fellow and so, rather than lay off the staff, he decided to use them to produce cooked food for the rash of bachelor sets that were opening up in neighbouring Mount Street. Not surprisingly, given his skills, the idea was an immediate success with the profits more than funding Curzon Street. Needless to say, on my return Searcy said that he was keen to continue with the enterprise, but I was reluctant both to turn our kitchen into a business and, more importantly, to lose his services. So, we reached a compromise: he would find alternative premises and a manager for his business, which would free up our kitchen, and he would give me at least ninety percent of his time in his role as my butler. I wasn't sure what Khazi thought about it all, but I wouldn't have been at all surprised if I'd found out that he was ferrying the prepared food around London in our wagonette. However, as I had no intention of being branded around the clubs as having gone 'into trade', I told Searcy that he must put his own name over the shop,[90] although I was happy to take shares in the enterprise in return for waving my rights to the profits he had made before my return.

---

[90] Editor's Note: Searcy's catering company was established in 1848 and continues in business to this day.

Despite the length of my absence, there were only two matters of any note that I had to address on getting back to London. The first was a letter from the GB asking me to present myself at St James's Square 'on my return' and the other was a heavily embossed missive from Prince Albert's Private Secretary also asking me to make contact 'at my earliest convenience'.

As the date of the second letter was some three months previous, I thought that I had better send an apology and an excuse to the palace by hand, which I gave to Khazi to deliver and, as he had the coach, I tooled around on foot to Steyne House to see the GB, with the thought uppermost in my mind that I might get a glimpse of the delightful Mary. With everything that had happened to me since the Steynes' ball the previous year, I had not given much thought to Mary, but with my return to London she was starting to dominate my every waking moment. On arrival at Steyne House, I sent in my card and, moments later, the GB's slimy secretary, Barrett, was oiling his way across the hall in my direction.

"Ah, Captain Speedicut," he said, rubbing his hands, "His Lordship has been concerned about your whereabouts this month or two back, but he will of course be delighted to hear of your safe return from...?"

"Munich," I replied.

"Munich, yes, so many troubles there - and elsewhere on the continent. Revolution is in the air, is it not? Although fortunately everything *appears* calm here."

I'd never liked Barrett and this encounter was no exception. He must have known perfectly well that Flashy had, in all probability, told the GB at the very least where I'd been all those months, but for his own reasons he maintained this charade of surprise and ignorance.

"Is His Lordship at home?" I asked, ignoring Barrett's observations on the state of the world.

"At home, yes, sir, but – I fear – not presently available. If I may, I will tell him of your safe return and he will, I am sure, send you word when it would be convenient for you to call again."

At that moment I saw, over Barrett's stooped and rounded shoulder, two figures descending the stairs. It was Mary and a woman who I thought I had seen before but could not immediately place. Ignoring Barrett, who was still prosing on about the GB's future availability, I stepped to one side and swept off my tile with a flourish whilst executing my most stylish bow. Mary paused on the stairs, turned enquiringly to her companion, who gave her an almost imperceptible nod and then skipped lightly down the last couple of steps with her hand extended.

"It's Captain Steadycut, isn't it?" she asked in her delightfully tinkling voice. "Are you here to see my father?" I replied that I was and was about to correct my name when her companion interjected.

"The gentleman's name is Speedicut, my dear. We have met before as I used to look after the Captain's dear sister, Elizabeth." With a start, I realised that Mary's companion was none other than Miss Prism, who I had last seen when she had brought Lizzie to Northampton for the Shiners' ball. At this point I couldn't decide whether the Prism woman's presence was an advantage or a disadvantage, so I decided to take a neutral line.

"Miss Prism, what a pleasant surprise and how good it is to see you after all this time. I trust you are well?"

"Very well, Captain Speedicut, and yourself?" Well these inanities could have gone on for hours, so I decided to cut them short.

"As a matter of fact, I have just returned from an extended visit to Munich where, for the last few months I have been the guest – if that is the right word - of the King. It is for that reason," I said turning to Mary, "that I have been unable to call upon you since your ball last summer. I hope you will forgive my rudeness but, as I can explain should you be interested, my time has not been my own since we last met." I hoped this would stimulate an enquiry from Mary and I was not disappointed.

"Captain Speedicut," she said rather hesitantly, apparently still unsure whether or not she had got my name right, "I should like nothing more than to hear of your adventures in Bavaria. However, Miss Prism and I are now on our way to call on Lady Bessborough, but," and she paused for a moment, raising a gloved hand to her lips, "my mother will be 'at home' tomorrow at noon and, should you be free, you would be most welcome to her salon where you can tell us about your time in the Alpine kingdom."

Then she bobbed a curtsey and floated out of the hall to a waiting carriage with Miss Prism fussing around behind her. As she swept through the double doors, she quickly turned her head and caught my eye and I could have sworn that I saw her purse her lips in a most coquettish way. Thunderbolts and lightning crashed around my ears in the hall of Steyne House.

"I will, of course," said the unctuous Barrett, "inform His Lordship that you will be attending upon Her Ladyship tomorrow – assuming that is your intention?"

I said that it was, gave him the briskest of farewells and sped off back to Curzon Street with my head in a whirl. Outside the house was a smart carriage and, waiting for me in the hall, was Searcy, a look of some concern on his face.

"Sir, there is a Mr Anson waiting for you in the drawing room, sir.[91] I believe he has come from the palace."

That's quick, I thought. I wonder what's up? Tossing my tile and cloak to Searcy, I headed for the drawing room. As I entered, a tall, quite good-looking man, not ten years older than myself, turned from the window and extended his hand.

---

[91] George Anson (1812-1849) was Prince Albert's Private Secretary.

"Do please forgive me, Captain Speedicut, my name is Anson and I work for His Royal Highness Prince Albert. His Royal Highness has been anxious for some time to see you and when he finally learnt from Lord Steyne of your enforced detainment in Munich, he instructed me not only to do whatever was possible to secure your release but also to present you with his compliments immediately upon your return. As soon as I received your note earlier this morning, I dropped everything and came around here in person. I trust that this is a not inconvenient moment."

"My dear Anson," I said, "I am delighted to be able to thank in person the agent of my release…" Pure hogwash, of course, for it was events not the long arm of Buckingham Palace that had done the trick; but it never hurts to toady and flatter when there's no cost involved: "And how can I be of assistance to His Royal Highness?"

"As to that," said Anson, "I know that His Royal Highness would prefer to speak to you himself and I am accordingly commanded to invite you to meet with him on Monday next at the palace at eleven o'clock. Would that be convenient?" I said that it would and then followed up with a question of my own.

"It would be most helpful, Anson, if you could give me at least a clue as to what His Royal Highness wishes to discuss with me, so that I can arrive prepared." Anson shuffled his feet and looked a bit uncomfortable at that.

"Shall we just say that His Royal Highness's concerns relate to matters of trade."

Oh, my God I thought, as I showed him back to his carriage, Albert had somehow or other heard about my involvement in Searcy's business and was going to demand the resignation of my commission on the grounds that no officer and gentleman can or should be involved 'in trade'. Perhaps, even, this was pay-back for my grappling with the royal posterior all those months before in the vault of the Bank of England. If it came to a choice between the Shiners and Searcy, there was no question in my mind as to the choice I would make.

Meanwhile, the door at Steyne House appeared to be open to me for further 'engagement' with Mary, so I pushed any thoughts of my future as an officer and a gentleman to the back of my mind and focused them instead on the task of how to get Lady Mary Steyne up the aisle and into my bed, preferably - but not necessarily – in that order.

The following morning, I dressed in my best and had Khazi drive me around the corner to Steyne House. By the time I got there, Lady Steyne's salon on the ground floor was already quite full, mostly with rather intimidating looking women of the Almack's variety. Other than Her Ladyship, Mary and Miss Prism, all of whom were seated at the far end of the room, I didn't know another soul there. But I needn't have worried for, spying me as I entered, Lady Steyne waved an imperious hand in my direction and bellowed my name to the room in a voice that would have done credit to a Guards Serjeant Major.

"Welcome, Captain Speedicut! My friends, may I introduce Captain Justin Speedicut who has just escaped from the clutches of the revolutionaries in Munich and has promised to tell us of his adventures."

I wasn't going to correct her just yet, particularly as I saw Mary's eyes widen somewhat at this introduction, so I took the chair to which I was directed and awaited events.

Over the course of the next hour or so, I found myself very much the centre of attention as I regaled the assembled dowagers and Duchesses with a highly edited and lightly coloured – but essentially accurate – account of my time in Munich and the part that the Montez woman had played first in my enforced 'holiday' and then in the downfall of the King. I could see that I had caught the attention of the lovely Mary, who seemed to hang on my every word, but I also noticed that a young fellow in the uniform of the Second Battalion, whom I hadn't spotted when I first arrived, was also more than a little interested in my story. I thought nothing of it at the time, beyond the fact that he appeared to be rather young to be attending such an august gathering, but this was perhaps explained by the old bird who appeared to have him on the end of a leash. Ah, ha, I thought, here's a young'un with a taste for well-aged meat.

The following Monday, once again in my finest I was driven to the palace for my audience with HRH, at which I was expecting to be ordered to hang-up my spurs for transgressing the social code of the age and 'engaging in trade'. My fears could not have been wider of the mark. Far from ordering me to abandon Searcy's business, or else face a firing squad, the bewhiskered German sausage wanted to talk to me about an idea he's had of staging a 'grreat interrnational exhibition of manufacturring and industrry' to rival the one the Frogs had held four years previously; and, for some reason, he 'discerrns' in me 'a man with the charracter, education and initiative' to help him bring off this project. I was not at all sure about any of that, particularly the education bit, but who was I to deny royalty its every wish and, if it meant that I could steer clear of India for another three to four years, I was all for it. Anyway, what it all amounted to was this: Albert wanted to stage the exhibition in Hyde Park in the summer and autumn of '51 but, as he said, there were many 'mountains of prrejudice and ignorrance to climb' before Parliament would sanction anything of the kind. Meanwhile, I was to be 'available' to him 'to assist in moving the prroject forward', which meant – although he didn't put it this way - that I was to be arse-kicker-in-chief for HRH.

Fortunately, news of this trickled back like a tidal wave to the Steynes where it was very favourable received. So, the time I was to spend trying to get the powers-that-be to agree to Albert erecting a big tent in the middle of the park, and filling it with steam engines, looked as though it would be time well spent.

That was the good news. The less good news concerned the young Cheesemonger who was lurking at the back of the first of old Lady Steyne's salons that I attended. As I've said, I paid him no notice at that first meeting, beyond remarking on the fact that he had an aged trot in tow who was senior enough to be his mother. Well, she turned out be his aunt and this was how I found out: I was at the Verulam enjoying a prose with some of the bucks, most of whom were about to ship out of town the next day in pursuit of pheasants and foxes, when Johnny Dawson of the 9th Lancers, who I knew well from Rugby, asked me to tell them the true story of what La Montez had been up to in Europe since she'd been sacked by the Theatre Royal.

In the past, particularly after my experiences in Munich, I'd always been careful to leave out the bits that had taken place behind the bedroom door. But this time, I thought, to hell with it: I was in privileged company and anyway I'd been gagging to tell the 'warts 'n all' story for some time. So, I spent the next hour – lubricating my throat all the while with the Verulam's best French firewater - regaling the bravos of St James's with the unexpurgated story. Just as I was getting to the bit where Ludwig developed a taste for Montez's toes, there was a ruckus at the back of the smoking room and a tall young fella came lurching forward through the crowd and the smoke and, without so much as a 'by your leave', clipped me across the phiz with a pair of gloves which he then threw at my feet along with a card.

"You have insulted the woman I love and intend to marry," he said, "and I demand satisfaction!"

Then he staggered out, as the room descended into chaos and uproar. There were cries of 'outrageous', 'disgraceful' and 'that's no way for a gentleman to behave' - but whether these were directed at me or my challenger it was impossible to tell. Recovering my poise, I picked up the card, although I was careful to leave the gloves where they lay, and went over to the fire the better to read it. It bore the legend: George Trafford Heald Esquire, 2nd Life Guards.[92] And then the penny dropped: he was the young Tin I'd spotted at Lady Steyne's. Scribbled on the back was a short note: 'My second is Mr Rupert McMurdo, White's'. I was about to throw the card in the fire, when Johnny joined me.

"You can't do that, Speed. You were challenged in public and if you don't fight you'll have to resign from here, the Tenth and I don't know what else besides." Of course, he was right so I asked him what he advised.

---

[92] George Trafford Heald (1828-1856) was the son of a rich and successful barrister, George Heald.

"Appoint me your second and I'll go around to White's and try and sort this out with McMurdo. I know him a bit and he's a sensible fellow. Meet me back here tomorrow at ten and I'll let you know what's going on."

As he left, I joked that I preferred pistols to swords but, whilst I was and I am no coward, the thought of cold-bloodedly facing a loaded pistol at twenty paces was enough to turn my guts to water. Accordingly, I prayed that Johnny would be able to make the other side see sense but, the following morning, he didn't.

"It's like this, Speed. Heald met the Landsfeld woman earlier this year in Switzerland. He fell instantly in love with her and has persuaded her to come and live with him in London - and she's due here any day now." My stomach lurched downwards at these words.

"Apparently, he intends to marry her and, as he's got at least eight thou' a year,[93] I would have thought that she would accept, wouldn't you? So, when last night he heard you blackening the name of the future Mrs Heald he saw red... and he won't now back off. I've agreed with McMurdo to pistols at dawn tomorrow under the Serpentine bridge on the south side."

"Is there nothin' to be done?"

"Possibly. Your one chance is to go and speak to his aunt who's staying at Mivart's Hotel. She's an old spinster, but if you were to tell her what her nephew is letting himself in for, then she might be able to get him to withdraw. Frankly, I think it's your only hope. Meanwhile, I'll make the arrangements for tomorrow morning."

I slunk back to Curzon Street with my heart in my boots. Searcy as usual greeted me in the hall.

"Is there something wrong, sir?" he asked

---

[93] £8,000 a year in 1848 was roughly the equivalent of £1,600,000 in today's money.

"You could say that," I replied wearily, as I made my way to my study. "Bring me a bottle of Napoleon, would you?"

Minutes later he appeared with the brandy and Khazi.

"Now come along, sir," he said, as he placed the salver with the bottle and a glass on my desk, "a problem shared is a problem halved."

"Not on this occasion, I'm afraid."

"Perhaps you had better tell us what is going on, sir, and let us be the judge of that." So, I told them.

"I will cut the infidel's throat," said Khazi when I'd finished.

"I don't think that would solve anything," I said. Khazi growled, fingered the dagger in his belt but didn't offer any more suggestions.

"It seems to me, sir," said Searcy rubbing his chin in thought, "that Mr Dawson is right and you should speak to Mr Heald's aunt, tell her the facts of the matter and get her to make her nephew see reason. If she won't – well, there's more than one way of skinning a tiger..." Whatever that might mean, I said to myself.

Anyway, as two people seemed to think that speaking to the old bat was a good idea, I sent a note around to Mivart's asking for a meeting with Miss Heald. I got a reply by return instructing me to join her there 'as soon as possible', so I pulled on an ulster and tooled around the corner to see her. On arrival, I was shown up to a large suite in which the venerable dame was ensconced in front of a blazing fire in a high-backed chair, her feet up on a stool and a shawl around her shoulders. As I entered she raised an old-fashioned quizzing glass to one eye, stared at me for a moment and then invited me to sit.

"Captain Speedicut," she opened in a surprisingly strong voice, "as you know, I have heard at first hand your account of the history of the Countess of Landsfeld, a lady whom I have not yet met and, whilst it seemed to me that you were highly critical of her influence over the late King of Bavaria, it also seemed to me that your comments were balanced.

"My nephew now informs me that, in altogether different company, you made allegations against the lady which no right-minded gentleman of her acquaintance could possibly allow to pass unchecked. That my nephew has formed an affection for this lady made your comments all the more serious in his eyes and, whilst I do not approve of 'affairs of honour', I nonetheless recognise that there are times when one is unavoidable. I am loath to intervene in this matter unless you can convince me that my nephew is mistaken in his defence of the honour of the lady in question."

So, I told her what I knew, laying emphasis on the fact that Montez was a divorcée and that her subsequent liaisons were widely known and had been reported extensively in the press. She appeared to be unmoved by this, so I gave her some additional information which had not been in the newspapers about the lady's moral code or lack of it and I hinted that she had remarried (I knew for a fact that she was hitched to Leigh) and was, therefore, in no position to do so again. This too did not seem to either shock or influence Miss Heald, for she stared in silence at me for several minutes with a look of considerable distaste on her face; whether it was distaste at the story or the fact that I had delivered it, I couldn't tell. Finally, she drew the shawl a little tighter around her shoulders, took her feet off the stool and leaned forward in her chair.

"Captain Speedicut. I have listened carefully to what you have told me and I have pondered as to what should be done for the best. I have already said that I do not approve of duelling but I am of the view that there is a certain natural justice in its practice. If what you have said to me is true, then the good Lord will direct your aim accordingly and you will spare my nephew the pain and disgrace of a *mésalliance*. If what you have said is untrue, then I believe that my nephew will become the instrument of divine retribution. Tomorrow we shall know. I bid you a good night."

It was clear that the old bat had nothing more to say so, I put on the best face I could. Whilst cursing the influence of the church and romantic fiction on feeble minds, I left the room and returned home where I ensconced myself in my study with a large brandy. With as steady a hand as I could, I wrote a letter to Mary and then took it down to the servants' hall where I found that Searcy and Khazi had unearthed Johannes's duelling pistols. It was not a reassuring sight. I gave the letter to Searcy with instructions to deliver it – if necessary - after my *rendezvous* with fate.

Realising that there was nothing further I could do, I took myself up to bed where I tried to reconcile how, after all the care I'd taken to stay clear of the damned woman, I was probably going to be facing my Maker in the morning because of that bitch Montez.

. . .

To be continued...

APPENDICES

APPENDIX A: The Speedicuts & the Flashmans

APPENDIX B: Rugby School & *Tom Brown's Schooldays*

APPENDIX C: The Brotherhood of the Sons of Thunder

APPENDIX D: *Dictionary of British Biographies*

APPENDIX A: THE SPEEDICUTS
& THE FLASHMANS

Until the present day, almost nothing has been known about Speedicut, the shadowy accomplice at Rugby School of the amoral coward, bully and, later, much decorated hero Brigadier General Sir Harry Flashman VC KCB KCIE, whose life story has been extensively covered in *Tom Brown's Schooldays* and the publication of the thirteen volumes of *The Flashman Papers*. Indeed, Speedicut's first entry in the *Dictionary of British Biographies* only appeared in 2011 and was based on my researches. In order fully to understand *The Speedicut Papers*, it has been necessary to establish the facts about Speedicut.

I started my search at Rugby School but, as neither Speedicut nor Flashman excelled at anything other than drinking, bullying and rogering the local barmaids – activities at which, by all published accounts, they were experts - there was no mention of either of them on the school's honour boards, and the other school records were curiously silent about the two reprobates.

The first clue I found to Speedicut's identity was the embossed heading on some of the later letters in the Ashby find, which displayed a baronet's coronet and the address The Dower House, Acton Park, Wrexham. Neither *Debrett's* nor *Burke's Peerage Baronetage & Knightage* currently lists a Speedicut baronetcy. However, a trawl through back copies confirmed that a Jasper Jeffreys Speedicut was granted a baronetcy in 1902 but, although married, he appeared to have died 'without male issue' as there was no mention of the baronetcy in the post-First World War editions of either publication, but a back copy of *The Times* recorded the death of Sir Jasper Jeffreys Speedicut Bart KCVO on 1st April 1915 in Paris.

As Speedicut is only referred to in previously published material by his surname, or the nickname 'Speed', there was no certainty that the baronet and Flashman's friend were one and the same. For confirmation, I travelled to Wales and commenced a search in the Wrexham county records and the local library. This uncovered the fact that a family, initially referred to in the records as Seedcut, had held the lease of The Dower House, Acton Park from the late 17th century until 1918, when the lease had been bought out and the property reintegrated with the adjacent Acton Hall and its 1,000-acre park.[94]

A further search of the parish records revealed that The Hon Virginia Jeffreys, a daughter of the notorious Judge Jeffreys,[95] had married one Seth Seedcut in Wrexham Parish Church on 30th March 1689. Seedcut is described in the Register of Births, Marriages & Deaths as a gardener; this bland description probably indicates the not unusual tale of a randy rustic, lust run riot and virginity lost amongst the bushes. It seems reasonable to assume that the grant to the newly-wed Seedcuts of a perpetual lease of the Dower House at a peppercorn rent was some form of dowry provided by Virginia's bloody father, who died, universally unlamented, nineteen days after the wedding.

Virginia and Seth produced a son, Robert Jeffreys, who was baptised on 15th June 1689 in the church where his parents were married. Judging by the dates, it had been a shotgun wedding and Virginia's Christian name had been nothing more than a piece of baptismal bluff. The Seedcuts remained at Acton, father to son, through succeeding generations with the name Jeffreys being given to all the male children, either as a chilling reminder of their monstrous forebear or, more likely, a determination to

---

[94] Acton Hall and its park were acquired in 1918 by the millionaire diamond merchant and philanthropist Sir Bernard Oppenheimer (1866-1921). The Hall was demolished in 1954 but the grounds have recently been restored and are now open to the public.

[95] George Jeffreys, 1st Baron Jeffreys of Wem, (1645–1689), better known as Judge Jeffreys or 'The Hanging Judge', was born in Acton. He became notorious for the severe punishments he handed down at the trials of the supporters of the Duke of Monmouth, following Monmouth's unsuccessful armed rising to depose his uncle, King James II. Monmouth himself suffered a grisly end being inexpertly beheaded on Tower Green – it took the amateur executioner 3 blows of the axe to render the Duke unconscious and a further five to part sever the head. In the end, under threat of immediate death himself, the executioner finally severed the head from the body using a butcher's knife.

maintain a link with the gentry 'up at the Hall'. Sometime in the late 18th century, presumably with an improvement in the family's fortunes, the surname had been gentrified to Speedicut. The birth of Jasper Jeffreys Speedicut to Algernon Jeffreys and Honoria Speedicut is recorded on 20th December 1821, the same year as the birth of Harry Flashman.

This seemed to me to be fairly conclusive evidence that Jasper Jeffreys Speedicut and 'Speed', of *Tom Brown's School Days*, *The Flashman Papers* and the Ashby letters, were one and the same man. Certainly, if they were, then the viciousness and general licentiousness Speedicut later displayed at Rugby could be explained as an undiluted inheritance from his variously bloody and randy ancestors. However, there was still no actual evidence that Jasper had been sent to Rugby School.

I was pondering this last missing piece of the jigsaw one afternoon in Wrexham Library, when the assistant librarian, a mousy spinster of uncertain age who had been most helpful to me over the preceding weeks of research, came over to my workstation. She hovered for a moment, then cleared her throat to get my attention.

"Excuse me, sir, but I can't help having noticed that you are taking an interest in the Speedicut family of Acton. Well…" and she paused for a moment, looking for all the world as though she was about to take a shower with a room full of naked rugby players, "…the fact is that I am descended from the Speedicuts through my maternal great-great-grandmother. Indeed, I believe that I am the only remaining member of the Speedicut family – although, of course, I don't bear their surname."

Clearly the reading room of the library was no place to continue this conversation, so I asked her if she would join me later for a cup of coffee and a sandwich in the library's café. She hesitatingly agreed.

An hour later we were seated in the neon-lit café. Miss Pole, for that she told me was her name, was clearly still reticent, so I encouraged her with a smoked salmon sandwich, which, to judge from her reaction, was a luxury bordering on wanton extravagance.

"Err, sir…"

"Do please call me Christopher," I interjected.

This familiarity was clearly too much for Miss Pole, but she rallied and did at least drop the "sir".

"Well…", she paused again, "… knowing of your interest in my family I thought you might be interested to see some journals and letters which I have in my possession."

This was said in a great rush without a pause. Having taken this bold first step, she drew breath and then went on in more measured tones. "I have no idea whether or not they will be of any interest or help to your researches, but – although I have only read bits of the journal and some of the letters, you understand – I do know that they date from around the middle of the 19th century and belonged to Honoria Speedicut. On her death she left them, along with some jewellery which I still have, to my great-great-grandmother who was her sister."

"How interesting, Miss Pole. Would you be willing to lend me these papers?" I asked tentatively, barely able to conceal my excitement.

"Well, before I approached you, I, err, realised that you might ask me that question. After a lot of thought, I, err, have decided that no possible harm can come from letting you read them…of course, it would not be *appropriate* for you to come to my home, so I will bring them to the library tomorrow and you can read them here."

I thanked her and persuaded her to indulge in a second smoked salmon sandwich, which she proceeded to eat in tiny bites, as though to prolong the reckless experience for as long as possible.

The following day I got to the library as the doors opened and there was Miss Pole behind the desk, her thick glasses balanced, as usual, on the end of her long nose. However, the wisps of mousy grey hair that had escaped from the severe bun at the nape of her neck betrayed the fact that she was not entirely her usual self-effacing and utterly restrained self. Looking to left and right, as though she was about to commit a minor crime, she surreptitiously and with some effort handed me a bulging and rather elderly Tesco shopping bag.

"I would be most grateful, sir," - clearly my stricture of the previous day had been forgotten - "if you could return these papers to me whenever you have finished with them, but may I ask you not to take them out of the library?"

I readily agreed and immediately decided that, if the contents of the bag were of any relevance at all to my quest, I would be spending several hours with the library's photocopier.

Over the next couple of hours, I reviewed the contents of Miss Pole's shopping bag. What I found there was beyond my brightest hopes. For not only was there the thick, hand-written journal of Honoria Speedicut, but also several bundles of letters to her from Jasper, an assortment of letters from other correspondents, cuttings and other paperwork. At the end of the day I returned the bag and its contents with many thanks to Miss Pole.

"Have you found anything of interest in my family's papers?" she asked quietly, to which I responded that they appeared to confirm my belief that Jasper Speedicut was the same person as the Speedicut in Hughes's and Flashman's published works.

"Oh, I'm so glad that they have been of use. Perhaps, err, when I have the time, I will read them properly myself. Meanwhile, err, if you would like to borrow them again, do please let me know – a note to the library will always find me – and, err, should you publish anything about the Speedicuts, I would be *so* grateful to know." I promised her that, if any publisher was foolish enough ever to allow me into print, I would certainly send her a copy and include a fulsome acknowledgement in the text. She simpered and said that would not be necessary – or *appropriate*. I suspected, at this point, that Miss Pole had perhaps read rather more of the papers than she was willing to admit.

The following day I returned to my house in Shropshire in a state of considerable excitement and the burning need to get to grips with Honoria Speedicut's journal, to say nothing of the letters and the other assorted documents with which the journal was interleaved. Over the next two weeks I read, annotated and sorted. For what Miss Pole had shown me, and I had shamelessly copied, was not just the proof that 'Speed' and Jasper Speedicut were one and the same person, but there was also a wealth of information about his childhood and time at Rugby.

Honoria's journal, which ran to over two hundred, tightly written pages, was largely a somewhat naïve account of her daily life and much of its contents were records of trivial incidents: the problems of managing staff, the illnesses of her children and relations, some record of events beyond the bounds of the Dower House and so on. In other words, a typical Victorian country lady's diary or commonplace book. However, from my point of view, there was much else besides. For Honoria was clearly not a woman who felt she could discuss things with her husband, Algernon, who, it became rapidly apparent, was an unreasonable and intolerant man with a quick temper and a propensity to take out his anger (and probably other needs as well) with physical attacks on his servants and verbal assaults on his long-suffering wife and children. So, Honoria's journal was also her confidante and friend.

Although infrequently dated, the journal opens in 1819, probably shortly after her marriage to Algernon, and describes her arrival at The Dower House. There she found the need for extensive refurbishment and reform of what had clearly been a bachelor residence, in which the female servants seemed to treat the house as their own, and the difficulty of extracting cash from her parsimonious but apparently reasonably well-heeled spouse. A typical entry reads:

> *The coachman and footman both require new liveries, but Mr Speedicut says that their existing coats are perfectly good and that I should get Emily the serving girl, whose attitude to me has not improved, to turn the cuffs on them. What good that will do is beyond me, for the coats are in truth hanging in tatters, which is not surprising as they were made in Mr Speedicut's*

grandfather's day. Meanwhile, Mr Speedicut has just bought two new hunters at Wrexham fair.

Another early entry illustrates Algernon's temper:

> *Cook is in tears and threatens to <u>leave</u>. Mr Speedicut, who had been in an <u>ill</u> <u>humour</u> all morning after receiving a communication from London, summoned her to the dining room and confronted her with the pheasant, saying that he had specifically ordered duck, for which he has a <u>preference</u>. Cook fled before Mr Speedicut's wrath and I fear we must find another, for she will <u>not</u> be <u>reconciled</u>. At least, this time, he did not take his whip to her, as he did last evening to the under footman. If this goes on we will have to cook and clean for <u>ourselves</u>, for Emily is with child and must leave, although Mr Speedicut - for no reason that I could discern - <u>insists</u> that she must stay.*

In the early years of the journal there is much more of the same, although the tone lifts somewhat with the arrival, first, of Master Jasper on 20th December 1821 and, some two years later, his sister, Miss Elizabeth.

The first entry of any significance about Master Jasper records a discussion between Algernon and Honoria in late 1832 about the future schooling of their son:

> *Mr Speedicut will not listen to reason. He insists that J must go away to school to 'grow up'. He says that J will attend Rugby School as it is <u>highly recommended</u> and is the institution to which his business associate, Mr Flashman, is sending his son. If he must go away for his schooling I would prefer to send J to Shrewsbury, which has a <u>most excellent</u> reputation, whilst that of Rugby is such that it has even reached the pages of the newspapers.*

Lady Cunliffe,[96] at the Hall, tells me that not so very many years ago there was a revolution at the school and the militia had to be called![97]

This entry is of great significance for, not only did it make the conclusive link in my search for the identity of Speedicut, but it also made a business connection between the Flashmans and the Speedicuts, a fact that was previously unknown. Fortunately, Honoria returned to the subject of the Flashmans at some length several pages further on:

I have told Mr Speedicut repeatedly that my father thinks ill of the Flashmans. For, although Mr Speedicut's friend Mr Flashman has married well, my father says that his father was virtually a pirate! Dear Sir Foster, who knows about these things, also says that Mr Flashman's reputation in the City is far from the finest. After luncheon last week, when Mr Speedicut was hunting – at least that is what he said he was doing, but his horse returned quite fresh and with bark on its bit, as I heard the new stable boy telling Percy the under footman – Sir F revealed to me that Flashman père is not at all the thing. It seems that he was originally called Fleissman, or some such, and was employed by a Mr Rothschild, who is I believe a banker, in maritime activities that Sir

---

[96] The Acton Hall estate passed through several hands after the death of Judge Jeffreys and was acquired in 1785 by Sir Foster Cunliffe (1755-1834). Sir Foster's grandfather, another Foster (1682-1758), had made his fortune in the slave trade and purchased a baronetcy. His heirs and successors spent much of their time covering up these facts.

[97] In 1797 a group of Rugby school boys exploded a bomb outside the Headmaster's office, ransacked it and burned all his books on the school Close. The boys then withdrew into the main school building and barricaded themselves in. The local militia arrived, armed with pikes and muskets, the Riot Act was read and only then did the rioting boys surrender. Some were subsequently expelled and, as the school history states with more than a hint of pride, a number of those expelled went on to become, in the unintentionally ironic words of the school history, "renowned military leaders".

F would not enumerate.[98] But there is more, for Sir F also vouchsafed to me that there is some <u>scandal</u> about the untimely death of the late Mrs Flashman, who was a friend of Lady C - for they were <u>Presented at Court</u> together. He would tell me no more but, as I left, Lady C said that she would call in to the Dower House tomorrow, for she is verily <u>concerned</u> at how this friendship between Mr Speedicut and Mr Flashman is so <u>influencing</u> Mr Speedicut's decision to send my dear boy so far away from home.

The next entry reveals all:

Lady C called upon me this morning on her way around the parish where she had been dispensing charity. When she was certain that we were alone and would be <u>undisturbed</u>, she told me that her friend, the late Mrs Flashman, had entrusted to her care a letter that she was <u>sworn</u> to deliver to the Flashmans' boy on his 21st birthday. As the letter was unsealed she had read it and now felt herself <u>duty bound</u> to show it to me. Although I must return it on the morrow, it lies before me now and I can do no better than to record it.

My Dearest Harry

By the time you read this letter I will be in Heaven, free of the toils and tribulations of this world and free, too, of your father. That he may also be dead by the time this letter is delivered to you, gives me hope in the justice of God, as too does my firm belief that he and I will be spending Eternity in very different places.

If you are more than just a babe-in-arms when I pass to my just reward, you will already be aware that the warm, loving and supportive relationship that is the hope of all women at the time they marry is sadly

---

[98] Derek Wilson's official biography of the Rothschild family states that, very soon after his arrival in England in 1798, Nathan Meyer Rothschild (1777-1836) established a fast and efficient cross-Channel service for couriers and cargo and that, as a result of this, he became involved with the Kent maritime community whose way of life included smuggling, blockade-running, privateering - and piracy. The N M Rothschild & Co archives list amongst the staff on Rothschild's London payroll from 1799 to 1809 a J H Fleichmann, whose duties are noted as "clerk to the maritime fleet".

absent from my own union with the drunken and philandering beast who calls himself my husband and your father.

But enough of these sorrows and to the point, my darling boy.

Though this may come as a shock to you, it is my sad duty at the last to vouchsafe to you the terrible fact that I am not your mother. Indeed, the circumstances of my marriage to your father, who confessed to me on our wedding night that he was afflicted with a terrible disease, means that I could never permit myself to be placed in the situation where I could have been your mother.

However, despite my disgust at your father's condition, which was without doubt the result of extreme depravity from an early age brought about by an excess of wealth and an absence of parental care, I agreed to consent to a subterfuge. So, I made it appear that I was with child by your father and I took the infant offspring of my French maid, whom your father had repeatedly debauched before, during and after our wedding, as mine own. That child was you, my dear Harry.

I do not need to tell you that, aside from your father and my maid, you are now the only person who knows the true circumstances of your birth. I could of course never vouchsafe the dreadful truth to my parents, but I have demanded and received a promise from my brother that he will always take care of you should I not be there to do so. He knows only too well the ways of your awful father and so did not press me for an explanation.

From my seat in Heaven I send you my love and my hopes for your future career and happiness. You may not be the child of my flesh, but I have always loved you as though you were.

Your loving, but sadly traduced, Mother

I was so shocked that I could hardly <u>breathe</u> and would indeed have rung for Emily to bring me my salts, had not Lady C <u>restrained</u> me. She also had with her a report from the Leicester <u>newspaper</u> which I also record:

It is the writer's sad task to announce to his readers the tragic death of the Honble Mrs Flashman of Ashby Lodge, née the Honble Alicia Paget, wife of H B Flashman Esquire, mother of Master H Flashman and cousin of the Most Noble Marquess of Anglesey, whose body was today found in the ornamental lake that borders the south terrace of the late noble lady's home. The circumstances of Mrs Flashman's death are not known.

Lady C believes that <u>poor</u> Mrs F must have decided that life with her husband was no longer tolerable and <u>threw herself in the lake!</u> That I should be required to send my dear boy to consort with the child of such an <u>ill-fated</u> union is more than I can bear. After Lady C left I wept a full half hour until I rang for Emily, who entered the room looking rather flustered and was quite rude to me. Despite what Mr Speedicut says, she will have to go.

However, despite these appalling revelations - including the ones that Harry Flashman was both of Jewish blood and a bastard, which will come as a considerable shock to all Flashman aficionados - it would appear that Honoria was unable to shake her husband's resolve. Or it may be that she simply did not try. After all, the evidence she had been shown by Lady Cunliffe would probably have been unlikely to move a man of Algernon Speedicut's disposition, indeed it would almost certainly have stiffened his resolve - or made him reach for his horsewhip.

Whatever happened, it seems that Master Jasper was to go to Rugby School, whether Mrs Speedicut liked it or not, as there is a tone of resignation on the subject in later entries in her journal.

At about this time too, there enters into the journal a note of concern about the character of Master Jasper himself, which may also account for Honoria's decision to give up her battle to send him to Shrewsbury. I have abbreviated and selected these entries:

Cook has threatened to resign, again, as Mr Speedicut upbraided her in the most <u>violent</u> terms for the absence of stilton at luncheon today, but Cook told me later that J used the stilton to try and lure Mr Speedicut's ducks into a trap he had set-up in the stable yard....Emily in tears, again, but she will not *tell me why...Mr Speedicut <u>furious</u> that his prize Indian Runners are dead and insists it was not a fox...Emily has given in her notice...Mr Speedicut now furious that Emily is leaving – apparently J has been pestering her, but for what or why he would not tell me...<u>dear</u> Dr Chasuble, who has just moved in to the Rectory, tells me that he saw J <u>running wild</u> with the boys from the village...Mr Speedicut must speak to the boy or there will be a scandal...J quite rude to me today when I told him not to visit the village again. How have I so <u>erred</u> with my first born?*

In due course, the journal goes on to reveal that Master Jasper Jeffreys Speedicut was put on the Wrexham mail coach on 28th September 1834 and packed off (possibly with some relief on his mother's part) to Rugby School where he was destined to join Harry Paget Flashman, the son of his father's friend, who had arrived at the school a term earlier.

APPENDIX B: RUGBY SCHOOL, TOM BROWN'S SCHOOLDAYS & THE RUGBY LETTERS

Although not as ancient as Eton or Winchester, Rugby is nonetheless an old school having been founded, so the school's official history tells us, in 1567 by Lawrence Sheriff 'as a free grammar school for the local boys'.[99] The transformation from a free grammar school into a private fee-paying boarding school was a process that started in the late 18th century. It arose from a growing demand from the officers of Britannia's spreading empire for somewhere to educate and house their male offspring whilst they were busy in foreign climes slaughtering the natives and impregnating their wives and daughters. Scions of the aristocracy, and the sons of upwardly mobile merchants and bankers, who recognised - as they still do today - a purchasable social cachet when they saw one, swelled the ranks of such pupils. It was into this latter category that Flashman probably fell.

Discipline at Rugby in the early 19th century was either non-existent or excessively harsh, resulting alternately in anarchy or a running confrontation between pupils and staff. It was to this simmering hotbed of pimply teenage discontent that the Reverend Dr Thomas Arnold was appointed Headmaster in 1828. Prior to this appointment, Arnold had taught at Rugby as a tutor and what he experienced in that role had appalled him. Once in charge, he set about a programme of reform driven by a set of muscular Christian principles.[100] In order to deliver his personal manifesto, he made radical changes including instituting the practice of being available to any of the boys in private, treating the senior boys as gentlemen (whether or not they qualified – and a lot of them didn't) and giving them power and a share of his moral responsibilities and disciplinary duties, which – given the innate viciousness of teenage

---

[99] Lawrence Sheriff (1510-1567) was born in Rugby, moved to London and became a wealthy grocer and spice merchant. He was Purveyor of Spices to Queen Elizabeth I, which doubtless accounts for his ability on his death "without issue" to leave his estate to found and endow a school and several alms-houses.

[100] "First, religious and moral principle; second, gentlemanly conduct; and third, academic ability."

boys – was probably taking a big risk. It was into this partially reformed environment that first Flashman, then Speedicut, arrived in 1834.

Much of what is known about Rugby in the 1830s under Dr Arnold, and what little is known about the schoolboys, Flashman and Speedicut, is recounted in *Tom Brown's Schooldays*, published in 1857. The author, Hughes, was himself at Rugby from 1834 to 1842 and so was an exact contemporary of Flashman and Speedicut, but Tom Brown is generally thought to be Hughes's younger brother George (lightly disguised) and this is borne out by the fact that Flashman and Speedicut were already well established at Rugby by the time Brown arrived there, probably in 1837.

For those who have not read the book – don't, it's a tiresome read - the story recounts, in the most pompous prose, the childhood and schoolboy experiences of the eponymous hero, his interaction with his fellows – particularly the brilliant but vulnerable George Arthur - and his and their ultimate translation, under Dr Arnold's benevolent and wise guidance, from callow youths to God-fearing Christian gentlemen, who will make model satraps for the Empire. In the first quarter of the book, the character of Brown is forged, almost literally, in the fire of Flashman's and Speedicut's relentless bullying. The tone of the book throughout is a moral, not to say priggish one, but with distinctly homo-erotic undertones. As Hughes himself reposted, when accused of preaching through the pages of the book, preaching was his purpose- although the homo-eroticism was probably unintentional.[101]

It is not my task to judge the moral precepts of *Tom Brown's Schooldays* but rather to examine the facts as they apply to Flashman and Speedicut. However, before looking at the book, there were four years prior to

---

[101] "Several persons, for whose judgment I have the highest respect, while saying very kind things about this book, have added that the great fault of it is too much preaching; they hope I shall amend in this matter should I ever write again. Now this I most distinctly decline to do. Why, my whole object in writing at all was to get the chance of preaching! When a man comes to my time of life and has his bread to make, and very little time to spare, is it likely that he will spend almost the whole of his yearly vacation in writing a story just to amuse people? I think not. At any rate, I wouldn't do so myself."

Brown's arrival at Rugby that were covered, at least in part, by Speedicut's letters to his mother and her corresponding entries in her journal. These years are of only passing relevance to the bigger story, so I include just three examples. For ease of reading I have corrected Speedicut's immature spelling and grammar.

Rugby School

Dearest Mama

Rugby is a big school. I am in School House with a lot of other boys. Lessons are not fun; the beaks are strict but football is good to play. We go to chapel every day and I am sharing a study with Flashman, who is nice. We have to fag for the older boys, but Flashman says that he will show me what to do. The house Dame says I need more hose, so can you please send me some?

My best wishes to Papa

Jasper

Extract for Honoria Speedicut's journal:

I am much relieved, for dear J seems to have settled down and the Flashman boy appears to be a <u>beneficial</u> influence, despite the <u>warnings</u> from Lady C.

Rugby School

Dearest Mama

We went to chapel twice today. Dr Arnold's sermons last for a long time and I am not sure that I always understand what he means. What are the 'vices of the Greeks', which are a frequent subject of his? Flashman told me afterwards that he will explain.

Lessons are boring and fagging is awful. I can't wait until I am old enough to have a fag. Today we played the rest of the school at football and we won! My trousers were torn but the Dame says they can be mended.

Best wishes to you and Papa

Jasper

Extract for Honoria Speedicut's journal:

> *J seems <u>not</u> to be <u>enjoying</u> his education, which <u>concerns</u> me greatly – after all what is the <u>point</u> of education if it is not the <u>pleasure</u> of learning, as dear Miss Brodie always told us? I am <u>puzzled</u> by the good Doctor's reference to the Greek vices as I know not what they are. Perhaps Master Flashman helped my <u>dear</u> boy to an understanding. I asked Mr Speedicut for <u>enlightenment</u>, but he uttered a <u>most</u> uncouth phrase with which I am not familiar – it sounded like 'b****y odd' – but I <u>cannot</u> be sure. I must ask Lady C at the parish council meeting tomorrow.*

Rugby School

Dear Mater

> *It's perfectly splendid to be back at dear old Rugby after the Christmas hols. Nothing has changed, Flashy is still as reckless as ever and spends much of his time either giving the young 'uns something to think about, or is off in Brownsover where he's friends with the publican's family. He promises to introduce me to them this half.*

> *Must stop now as some new bugs have just arrived and will need to be taught their manners. One of the ticks is called Brown and has already cheeked me. Wait 'till Flashy and I introduce him to footer, we'll learn him!*

Yours

Jasper

Extract for Honoria Speedicut's journal:

> *During the recent holidays, J was <u>restless</u> to be back at Rugby and his conduct to the servants was most <u>inappropriate</u>. The stable boy absconded without*

reason and Emily was strangely silent. What can it all mean? I fear that the Flashman boy, who J speaks of all the time, is a most pernicious influence upon him.

Speedicut's progression over four years from new boy to old hand is clear from these examples, which are, as we can see, recorded with increasing concern in Honoria's journal. But the awful reality of her fears emerges only as Flashman and Speedicut first appear in *Tom Brown's Schooldays* on the day that Brown arrives at Rugby. The scene is a football match played to Rugby's unique rules. In describing the scrimmage, Hughes mentions Speedicut and Flashman 'the School House bully' as giving the impression that they are playing hard whilst really shirking.[102] From the outset, there is no doubt about what Hughes thinks of Flashman and Speedicut and it is clear from the tone of his prose that he is on a mission of revenge, although the reasons for this only emerge later.

For the reader's next titillation, or more probably the next chapter of revenge, Hughes describes the Rugby practice of senior boys tossing junior boys in blankets:

"No catastrophe happened, as all the captives were cool hands, and didn't struggle. This didn't suit Flashman. What your real bully likes in tossing is when the boys kick and struggle, or hold onto one side of the blanket, and so get pitched bodily onto the floor; it's no fun to him when no one is hurt..."

This is followed by a lengthy passage that I have paraphrased:

"One morning after breakfast they [Tom and "Scud" East] were seized upon by Flashman [and Speedicut] and made to carry down his books and furniture into the unoccupied study he had taken.....From this time they began to feel the weight of the tyranny of Flashman [and his friends]...But that blackguard

---

[102] "You don't really want to drive that ball through that scrimmage, chancing all hurt for the glory of the School House, but to make us think that's what you want – a vastly different thing; and fellows of your kidney will never go through more than the skirts of a scrimmage where it's all push and no kicking. We respect boys who keep out of it, and don't sham about going in; but you – we had rather not say what we think of you."

Flashman, who never speaks to one without a kick or an oath…twisted his arm and went through the other methods of torture in use.….Flashman was an adept in all ways, but above all in the power of saying cutting and cruel things, and could bring tears to the eyes of boys in this way…Flashman [and Speedicut] left no slander unspoken, and no deed undone which could in any way hurt his victims."

Although the bullies' behaviour is vicious, it is actually not much worse than that which most men of my generation would admit to having committed at some time during their school days. But Hughes kept his most damning prose to the last. Flashman, supported by Speedicut, has tried, thus far unsuccessfully, to get Tom Brown to part with a winning lottery ticket:

'Very well then, let's roast him,' cried Flashman, and catches hold of Tom by the collar; one or two boys hesitate, but the rest join in. …[Tom's] shoulders are pushed against the mantelpiece, and he is held by main force before the fire, Flashman drawing his trousers tight by way of extra torture…

'I say, Flashy, he has had enough…'

'No, no, another turn'll do it,' answers Flashman. But poor Tom is done already, turns deadly pale, and his head falls forward on his breast.

The story of Flashman's expulsion for drunkenness, a couple of pages further on and presumably – for there are no definitive dates in the book - around the end of 1838, is positively tame by comparison with this and there is no further mention in the book of either Flashman or Speedicut. The rest of Speedicut's time at Rugby is described in the letters which he started writing to Flashman after the latter's expulsion.

Rugby School, Spring Term 1839

Dear Flashy

Gad, life is different here without you! Of course, all the ticks are now completely out of control. Brown, and his smug little friend East, are impossible and show no respect whatsoever. The beaks too, doubtless taking their lead from 'the dear Doctor', have changed their attitude to me and the rest of the old crowd and seem to think that we are here to learn Latin and Greek! That's all they know! That drivelling idiot Raikes, who you may remember teaches French, tried to gate me for not returning his prep on time, but I legged it over the back wall of School House and spent a most pleasant afternoon with Molly.

I'm glad to hear that you may have got your Pater to buy you a set of colours, do let me know which Regiment the old skinflint stretches to. Molly tells me that there is a Dragoon Regiment recently arrived in Coventry and it would be such fun if you ended up stationed near this dump. Bye the bye, I think there may be trouble brewing in that quarter, Molly's I mean, for she has become uncommon broody of late and complains that I don't spend enough time with her at Brownsover. She just won't accept that I risk having the arse tanned off me every time I sneak out from school. That said, she's a damned fine romp and infinitely preferable to the fun to be had with young Arthur.

Must dash as there is a game of footer to be played and I can't wait to take a hack at Brown's shins if he is stupid enough to get in my way.

Pip, pip!

Speed

…

Rugby School, Summer Term 1839

Dear Flashy

You will be mightily pleased that you are not here when you learn what happened yesterday.

I was just settling down last eve in our old study to teach Arthur a couple of new tricks I had learned from Molly, when there was a furious rap on the door. Buttoning up, I pushed Arthur out the window and tried to compose myself. Despite his cries I don't think he hurt himself too much, it's only one floor up and the roses probably broke his fall, but he'll probably be picking thorns out of his bum for a day or two yet...

Arthur safely out of the way, there was a further cannonade of knocks and the voice of the house beak demanding that I open up, which I did - to be confronted by the wizened visage that you must remember. "You are to go to the Doctor's study immediately, Speedicut! Immediately, do you hear, sir?"

From the look on his sour old face there was trouble in the wind so, without even grabbing my tile, I ran down the stairs, across the Close and up to the Doctor's tower. When I got there, the door was half-ajar and I could see that the Doctor was not alone, for there were Molly and her fat father. I tell you, Flashy, had the Doctor not caught sight of me I would have turned on my heels and not stopped running 'till I got to your house in London. But, too late, he espied me and, in that quiet but menacing voice we both know so well, ordered me into the room.

"Mr Speedicut," he said, "I believe you are acquainted with Mr Theakston, the publican of the Old Brown Cow in Brownsover, and his daughter, Miss Molly?" I said that I was, for what else could I say?

"Well, Mr Speedicut, Mr Theakston has made a most serious accusation about you and it seemed only fair that you should be confronted with it and allowed to offer up a defence." He paused, looked over his glasses at old Theakston, who nodded assent, and went on.

"To put not too fine a point on it, Mr Speedicut, Mr Theakston believes that you have been having, ahem, improper relations with his daughter and that she is now in a condition that means that no right-minded Christian man would feel able to associate with her in future. In short, sir," and his voice rose somewhat at this point, "and I will not mince my words, you are accused of violating her and, as a result, she is now with child! What do you have to say to that?"

Frankly, Flash, all I could think was that if there was a God the floor would open beneath my feet and swallow me up. But no such luck. So, with the old brain box in a complete spin, I did the only thing I could think of – I fell to my knees, put my head in my hands and blubbed my heart out. At least I did my best to make it look as though that was what I was doing, which wasn't difficult as I was about to shit my britches anyway.

I'm not sure that this is what the Doctor had expected for, instead of telling me to get up, he gently ushered the Theakstons out of his study, saying that he would get in touch with them shortly, came back from the door and stood over me. "Now compose yourself, Mr Speedicut. Whilst this is a most serious business, you have the right to tell me if these accusations are unjust." I carried on blubbing for it seemed to be doing the trick.

"Now, now, my boy, get up and take this chair," he said rather more kindly, so I did so, but I kept my fingers firmly over my phiz and allowed the snot to trickle between them onto his rug. "Mr Speedicut, I must tell you that this is not the first time that I have had to deal with this sort of complaint and you would not be the first boy in my care to have been led astray by the wiles of an older woman."

Here was a ray of light in the encircling gloom, but I still said nothing – although I allowed my blubs to subside somewhat – as it seemed to me that the old ass would show me the path to salvation, and not in the way that he intended neither.

"Speedicut – Jasper, listen to me. You are but a callow youth, not yet turned eighteen and wholly untutored in the ways of the world. If this accusation is baseless, or if the fault lies not on your part, you have only to tell me and we shall seek a way to your redemption."

Yes, I thought, and if I tell you the truth you will see me on that path with twenty lashes on my bare bum in front of the whole school and a note to my Pater informing him that my 'presence will no longer be tolerated at Rugby'.

I was not damned fool enough to make that mistake and my blubbing had allowed me to collect my thoughts. So, I blubbed some more to see if he would take the cue, which he did.

"Tell me, my boy, were you led astray by Miss Theakston? Was it she who persuaded you onto the path of sin and damnation?"

Damn right she was, or at least you were, Flashy, by getting the three of us together in that hayrick last half, afore the old fool threw you out for being drunk. "It's not at all as you think, sir," *I started,* "and...and...I don't understand the accusation that has been made against me...for all that I have done is to be friendly with Miss Theakston...in the ways that she asked...I had no idea that there was any vice in it and I certainly had no idea..." *I allowed my voice to trail away. Would the old fool take the bait?*

"Now, Jasper, take a hold of yourself and tell me everything. You know, when I lift the lid on a sewer I like to have a good smell of its contents."

I bet you do, I thought, you sanctimonious old bastard – and, whilst your pecker's still pushing its way out of your unspeakables, you'll probably roger your scraggy wife stupid. "Sir, it's like this...it was...", *and then the answer came to me,* "it was...it was Flashman who introduced me to the..."

"That rogue and scoundrel!" roared Arnold. "Why is he always at the centre of anything that is base or ignoble in this school? I thank Heaven that he gave me the reason last half to cast him into outer darkness. Not content with abusing the God-given gift of the grape, you tell me he has also abused the sanctity of unblemished virginity. Why am I not surprised?"

So, you see, Flashy, your memory still lingers on here! Anyway, the mention of your name seemed to distract him from the charge levelled against me by old Theakston, who presumably had noticed that Molly was putting on weight and thought to extract some cash from the school. If he only knew. For he'd do better knocking on the door of the Dragoons in Coventry, as Molly has spread her legs for them as wide as she ever did for you or me, and not just two at a time neither, as I found out t'other day. Anyway, back in the gloomy confines of Arnold's study I could see the edge of the wood, but I was clearly not out of it yet.

"Mr Speedicut, what you tell me comes as no surprise. I have known for some time that you had a weak and pliable nature. Whilst you must shoulder some

part of the blame for this deplorable incident, in light of your confession and your disclosure of the involvement, nay the leading role, of that scapegrace, Flashman, I will content myself with flogging you and gating you for the rest of the half. I will not, for the present, bring this matter to the attention of your parents but, and mark this well, sir, if there is any further wrongdoing on your part, you will be sent back to your family with a full explanation of my reasons, including this deplorable incident. Now, sir, remove your britches and bend over that chair."

Well, Flashy, it could've been worse and, in the event, he only gave me six with the birch which, although they hurt like hell, were as nothing to the havoc that my guv'nor would have inflicted on me. Can you believe it, though, Arnold actually recited the Lord's Prayer whilst raising the welts on my arse? If you ask me he was confessing his own sins, for the bulge in his unspeakables was plain as a pike staff when I was pulling myself together afterwards. Saintly schoolmasters! I tell you, it's no wonder that in the Middle Ages they whipped themselves on a daily basis… Dirty old bugger!

Anyway, after thanking the bastard for tanning my hide, I slouched out of his study and back to School House where who should I spy but young Arthur skulking around with rather red eyes.

"Come here, boy" I shouted over to him, "we've got some unfinished business" and I spent the next hour in my study none too gently prising rose thorns out of his backside, afore… let's just say that with Molly off-limits I'm not one to 'abjure the vices of the Greeks'.

Not exactly in clover,

Speed

. . .

Rugby School, Summer Term 1839

Dear Flashy

I think I told you in a recent letter that, as I was now gated and so deprived of the comforts of dear Molly, young Arthur had provided me with much needed consolation after my interview with our esteemed head man.

But even those delights were soon to be denied me for young Arthur, despite the removal of the rose thorns, now seemed to be in a perpetual state of tears. Just as I was starting to think that I would have to look elsewhere for my pleasure for what remained of the half, I received a visitation from that sanctimonious prig Brown and his half-back East.

Barging their way into my study one day after tea, they closed the door and stood with their back to it – a firm set to their spotty chins and a couple of cricket bats dangling from their hands. This means business, thought I, swiftly calculating if there was space enough through the mullion for me to copy young Arthur's enforced escape route, but decided that there wasn't.

"What do you want?" I barked.

"We want to speak to you about Arthur," Brown replied. "We do not like the way you are using him, and we are fairly certain, although Arthur won't say, that you are going well beyond what the house beak permits with fags."

"What I do with Arthur is none of your damned business! Now get out of here!" I reposted with more confidence than I felt.

"We have no intention of moving until you sign this..." and East handed me a folded note. I won't bore you with all its contents, for it was written in the churchy style that these two bravos had learnt from the dratted Doctor, but – in essence – it was a confession on my part that I had 'gone beyond the bounds of what was considered proper in the manner of my dealings with Arthur'.

"I'll be hanged if I'll sign that paper," I said, and thrust it back at East. He did not take it and it fell to the floor between us.

"Let me make this clear, Speedicut," said Brown. "If you don't sign it we will take Arthur to the Doctor – and I don't mean the sawbones down in the town – and you can be certain that he will tell him how you have dealt with him."

"And if I do sign?"

"If you do, I swear on my mother's grave that I will hold this letter as a pledge of your good conduct. Should you abuse Arthur in any way, I will give the note to the Doctor. When you leave this school, and as far as we are concerned that can't be too soon, we will burn the note."

So that was it. Damned if I did and damned if I didn't. It was a nasty spot, Flashy, I can tell you…

"And who else knows about this?" I asked.

"No one," said East.

"Alright," I said, "leave it with me and come back tomorrow at this time – you'll have my answer then." For I needed time to work this one through. My first thought was to arrange for the two of them to have a nasty accident over the next twenty-four hours. But, hard as I racked my brains during the rest of the evening, I could think of no way that wouldn't implicate me. I even thought about setting fire to the building, but decided that was too big a risk. Then it came to me.

The following morning, I feigned sickness in the classics class, found the porter's boy, slipped him sixpence and told him to deliver, in one hour's time, a letter addressed to Arnold – and I threatened the little bugger that I would thrash him to death if he ever revealed who had given him the letter. The scruffy little urchin slipped away and I legged it over to the sanatorium, feigning a stomach ache to establish my alibi.

Later that day, with m'self returned to good health – despite the administration by the Dame of a deeply unpleasant purgative that had me running to the water closet — as luncheon was drawing to a close the Doctor pushed back his chair and called for quiet.

"It has come to my attention that certain boys in this school have been GAMBLING! My informant has not identified the miscreants, but I give you all fair warning that I will not tolerate this vice in my school and I will expel, on the instant, any boy who it can be shown has so depraved himself as to commit this sin. You have been warned!" And with that he gathered up his cap 'n gown and swept from the room.

At around tea time Master Brown and Master East returned to my study. "Well, Speedicut, have you signed?" whined Brown. "Oh, yes," I said, "I've signed all right — but not the note you gave me yesterday, but this…" and I handed a sheet of paper across to them. They both went white, for what it said was this:

> *Dear Headmaster,*
>
> *After our most painful meeting, and your recent announcement in Hall, I can no longer reconcile my Christian conscience with your rightful demand for me to confess all my sins.*
>
> *The enclosed lottery ticket, made out to Messrs Brown & East, was issued by me to them at their request. I know now that it was wrong and I am prepared to suffer the consequences. All I would ask you to note, in mitigation of my crime, is that I was only responding to their demand.*
>
> *Sincerely*
>
> *Jasper Speedicut*

"That should ensure your hasty departure from this venerable seat of learning, don't you think?" I leered, brandishing — well out of their reach — the lottery ticket[103] you persuaded Brown to give you last half thanks to my holding his arse in front the common room fire. By the way, I'm sorry I never gave it back

---

to you, but you vanished so quickly and dramatically that it quite slipped my mind; anyway, I've been able to put it to good use, as I hope you will agree.

"…and you'll be expelled too," stammered Brown.

"Just what I had in mind," I re-joined, "and don't think for one moment that my guv'nor will care that the school fees have stopped because of a damned lottery ticket!"

"Speedicut, you are a fiend!" bleated East.

"Better an expelled fiend for gambling than a humbled gentleman forced to lick your filthy boots," I whispered with considerable satisfaction – for the bluff had clearly worked as I thought it would, the two of them being mealy-mouthed little pricks who couldn't imagine a worse fate than being driven from the school.

As they left, Brown threw over his shoulder: "I will be revenged, Speedicut, I will!"

"I'm quaking," I drawled, throwing a cricket ball at his head. Sadly, it missed. Mark you, Flashy, with Molly and Arthur off limits, I shall have to take care to look elsewhere for my pleasures during the rest of this half. And I don't plan to return when the term is over, but more on that anon.

Yours aye,

Speed

APPENDIX C: THE STEYNES AND THE BROTHERHOOD OF THE SONS OF THUNDER

References to 'the Brotherhood' occur early on in Speedicut's post-Rugby correspondence although, presumably because Flashman was also a member, there is never a specific description of the organisation, its origins or purposes. In order to complete the background to *The Speedicut Papers*, and because it rapidly emerges that 'the Brotherhood' was - and possibly still is - a very significant organisation, I decided to find out what I could.

I started with the fragment of what appeared to be an oath that I had found with the Ashby papers and the name of the Marquess of Steyne, which occurs frequently in the letters.

> *The Brotherhood of the S…*
>
> *I swear upon pain of my…*
> *will at all times take any act…*
> *by any means necessary th…*
> *undesirable unions by line…*
> *that might affect the succ…*
> *Royal House. I further sw…*
> *Great Boanerges, the enem…*
> *Finally, I swear, with my lif…*

Despite reading it several times, initially I could make nothing of this, beyond the fact that it was almost certainly the oath of 'the Brotherhood' that Speedicut signed on joining and was probably one half of his copy. It was clear that it referred to royalty and might also refer to Jesus's disciples, the brothers James and John.[104] But to which royal house it referred was a mystery I could not penetrate.

---

[104] Mark 3:17 "…and James, the son of Zebedee, and John, the brother of James, and he gave them the name Boanerges, which is Sons of Thunder"

So, I put it to one side and turned to the Steynes.

The Steyne Marquessate died out with the death of the Lord Steyne mentioned in Speedicut's letter. The fabulous Steyne collection of furniture, pictures and other works of fine art was left to his illegitimate son, Algernon StAlbion. On StAlbion's death in 1921, he had bequeathed it and his London house in trust to the nation.

Judging from the dates, it was the 3rd Marquess of Steyne who ran the Brotherhood of the Sons of Thunder, that members or Brothers were bound by an oath and that Steyne himself held the title of the Great Boanerges, which presumably was reserved for the head of the order. A later letter discloses that at least one objective of the Brotherhood was the guardianship of the 'nation's honour' – and that some of the members or Brothers were leading players in the 'Great Game'.

In order to establish not only the link between the Steynes and 'the Brotherhood' but also to uncover the identity and purpose of this organisation I decided to make further enquiries. A search in the Public Records Office threw up a Mrs Mona Norris, who was a distant relation of the last Marquess through his illegitimate son, and was living on the wrong side of Wimbledon with, as it turned out, a large number of cats.

I wrote to Mrs Norris and she agreed that I could call on her, which I duly did. I can't say that I warmed to her or that my initial impression improved over the short time I was with her. About sixty, with crudely dyed reddish hair, she was also short, fat and rather toad-like in appearance. She opened the door to me dressed in a frilly blouse that might have been fashionable in the 1950s, a rather soiled skirt and fluffy bedroom slippers. There was a reek of cat in the dingy hall and it grew stronger as she led me into her sitting room.

"Do please take a seat," she said, indicating a rather grubby, threadbare sofa on which perched an overweight tabby cat consuming what looked like the remains of Mrs Norris's luncheon. "Now, how may I help you?" she queried with about as much enthusiasm as a call centre operator.

Significantly, she had not offered me so much as a glass of water, which was rather a relief given the state of the house.

I explained that I had become interested in the life and times of the 3rd Marquess. She pursed her lips and absentmindedly scratched the side of her inexpertly rouged cheek with her none too clean fingernails. This was a physical characteristic that, in the minutes that followed, I quickly came to loathe.

"As I am sure you know, I am only distantly related to the Steynes through my late father and I do not possess any of the family's effects, records – or assets," she said rather tartly. "I don't know if any such things still exist outside the Steyne Collection and Trust, but my father used to say that if the last Marquess's natural son hadn't left everything to the nation then we might not have been reduced to living in Wimbledon."

It didn't seem tactful to point out to her that she was hardly living in Wimbledon, nor did there seem much to be gained from prolonging the interview. However, as it had taken me over an hour to get there, I carried on with a set of questions that I had rehearsed on the drive out to the suburbs. "Did your father ever mention to you an organisation known as 'the Brotherhood' in connection with the Steynes?" I asked.

"No," she snapped.

"Did he ever mention whether or not the Steynes were freemasons?"

"No – and as far as I know there were and are no freemasons in my family." This was said with a pronounced sniff.

"Does the name or word 'Boanerges' mean anything to you?" She blinked and scratched the side of her face again.

"Of course, it's in the New Testament. It was the collective name for two of the disciples, James and John. But everyone, at least those that have been educated - which is not many these days - knows that." This, with an even more pronounced sniff that implied I probably fell into this category.

Meanwhile, the cat had abandoned its meal and decided to make itself comfortable on my lap. My initial attempt to get it off, for I don't like cats at the best of times, resulted in it digging its claws into my thigh. I winced and started to sniff as well.

"Is there any information that you do have which might be of some help to my search?" I asked in desperation.

"I think not," she said with the most pronounced sniff of all and, with that, she shoed the cat off my lap as though it, rather than me, were likely to catch something unpleasant. The interview was clearly at an end. But, as she showed me to the door, I noticed a rather poorly framed piece of manuscript hanging in the hall over a pile of dusty and faded berets on top of a cheap dresser. All that I could read in the gloaming, for she had not turned on the lights despite the fact that the sun was nearly down, was the heading:

'The Brotherhood of the Sons of Thunder'

Before I could ask her if I could look at it, she had pushed me out of the front door, slammed it shut and I heard the lock click firmly behind me. Clearly there was no going back and, short of breaking and entering, it looked as though I had hit a dead end. Besides which, I thought, the old witch would probably take down the manuscript and hide it. I was deeply frustrated, for a possible key to unlock this mystery had been just within my grasp and then, for no apparent reason, snatched away. I drove home in a bad mood that was not improved by the throbbing of my left thigh. The next morning, I woke up uncertain as to my next move but even more determined to get to the bottom of the mysterious Brotherhood.

Over breakfast I decided to contact my old friend Desmond Duveen, the deputy chairman of Christie's International the auctioneers and a man extremely well connected in the art world. Desmond suggested that I should trawl through the Steyne Collection archives and, an email later, I had the name and contact details of the curator of the Collection. A couple of days later, such is the influence of Christie's, I was on my way to St James's Square to meet up with Mr Robert Symonds the curator.

On my arrival, and with much ceremony, I was ushered into Symonds' somewhat austere office, although a quick glance around showed me that it was lined with the most exquisite treasures. Symonds, a tall, slightly stooped man in an elderly but beautifully cut three-piece suit approached with outstretched hand, guided me gently but firmly to a leather armchair, offered me tea and settled back in a chair opposite me. "Now, how may I help you?" he asked courteously, whilst peering at me quizzically over his half moon spectacles.

I told him that I was researching the life of the 3rd Lord Steyne and his possible involvement in, or connection with, a mysterious organisation called 'The Brotherhood of the Sons of Thunder'. I gave him a copy of the oath fragment that I had found with the Speedicut letters and the description of Speedicut's induction ceremony, but I did not tell him much about Speedicut or Flashman, beyond the information I had uncovered about the Brotherhood, as I thought that they were unlikely to be of interest to him - and he studiously avoided probing my exposition.

When I had finished there was a pause and, between sips of tea, he asked me - in a way that was designed not to be insulting - if I had yet made use of the Internet to see if I could pick up a clue to the Brotherhood. I confirmed that I had - and that I had drawn a blank.

"Well, not even Wikipedia is omniscient – yet! So, let's review the facts. You have good evidence that the 3rd Lord Steyne, the son of the great Lord Steyne who started the collection that I have the enviable privilege to curate, was involved in some way with this Brotherhood and your theory has been confirmed by reason of the curiously defensive behaviour of his sole descendant. For Mrs Norris is, indeed, his only known living descendant...and a great thorn in my side, I may tell you...well, you have met her and can easily guess her interest in this treasure house. Sad to say, she thinks she has some claim upon the Trust that established the gift and, despite being told by the most learned jurists acting for the Government that she has no such entitlement, she persists in bombarding me with letters and demands. But, that is not your problem!" he finished with some asperity.

"However, before we go any further," he went on, "I have to tell you that I can't, at first sight, relate the induction ceremony you have described to the layout of the house. That doesn't mean that it is a fiction, for there were major structural changes made to the interior of the house in the late 19th century. It does however make it difficult to verify. Second, although the last Lord Steyne's illegitimate son, Algernon St Albion, bequeathed his house, its entire contents and all the Steyne archives to the nation, our librarian has never found any of the personal family papers. There are no memoirs, no letters, nothing that tells us anything other than the business affairs of the family. So, great is the task of conserving, cataloguing and restoring the Collection that I tell you, frankly, that neither I nor my predecessors have ever made any attempt to delve into this curious omission. But, if you wish to avail yourself of our archives - and on the sole condition that you disclose to me anything that you may unearth – I am willing to open them to you."

I thanked him profusely but, privately, I thought that what he was offering me was a task so great that it would take a lifetime of research with no certainty of uncovering the result I was seeking, which was to find the truth about the Brotherhood. I think that Symonds sensed my mood, for he went on.

"Let's look at this conundrum from a different perspective. You are, I am sure, aware of the science of iconography – the interpretation of symbols and other images included in art from the Middle Ages onwards." I nodded.

"Well, many of those artists collected by the Steynes were skilled practitioners of this science. I'm sure you are aware that the works of Hieronymus Bosch, for example, are practically a three-volume novel on canvas – and that Poussin, in particular, is thought to have included codes in his paintings that will point the cognoscenti in the direction of the fabled treasures of the Templars. Probably rubbish, of course, but who knows for sure? We can, on the other hand, be sure that the famous group portraits of the members of the Society of Dilettanti by Reynolds, now hanging in the Great Subscription Room at Brooks, are thinly disguised pornography with each of the members demonstrating either the size of their own male member or the dimensions of their mistresses' pudenda!

"It is my experience, as an art historian, that there are only few people who want to rub out their private lives completely. Certainly, there are plenty of examples of the burning of personal archives before death or by loyal relatives after death – H H Munro's sister made a bonfire of his indiscretions, John Ruskin almost succeeded in destroying all J W M Turner's 'adult' drawings and watercolours, to say nothing of the editing job done on Queen Victoria's diaries by her daughter. But such events are usually recorded in one way or another – and there is no such record, anecdotal or otherwise, that this happened in the case of the Steynes. If we assume, for one moment, that this is correct and we further accept that what most famous or prominent men seek to do is to hide or disguise their true selves but not erase them, then the possibility exists that the missing records do indeed exist, if only the clue to their whereabouts is uncovered. In other words, the Steynes' have set us a quest!" Again, Symonds sensed my mood.

"Cheer up, my dear chap, I think that it is possible that this quest is not nearly so complex as you fear, for knowing what I do about the Steynes, I think that the secret will be a matter of intelligence applied - not endeavour undertaken." I brightened somewhat.

"Let's look at the known facts. First, you have made a connection between the 3rd Lord Steyne and a shadowy group that goes by the name of 'The Brotherhood of the Sons of Thunder', about which there is nothing published. Second, we also know that members of this Brotherhood paid a subscription, took an oath – of which you have uncovered a rather unhelpful fragment – and provided each other with financial and possibly other support. We do not know if there were conditions attached to this benevolence. Finally, we also know that the 'Sons of Thunder' were the Apostles James and John... I think that you might start this quest, therefore, by having a look at our collection, for it is possible that Lord Steyne left a clue not on paper but on canvas..."

I spent the next three days meticulously examining every picture in the public galleries of the Collection, which was arranged over four sumptuously appointed floors in the St James's Square house. But none of the paintings were of the Apostles I was looking for, or seemed to have any bearing on them. From time to time Symonds would appear beside me enquiring, quietly, if I was making any progress, but my answer was always the same. Finally, on the afternoon of the third day, I was drinking a coffee in the Collection's café when Symonds appeared again.

"Still no luck?" I shook my head wearily. "If you still have the stamina for it, there is - of course - the reserve collection, which is stacked in the basement. It's been catalogued, so we know what's down there, but it's mostly second or third-rate pictures or those still waiting for an attribution. But they might be worth a look..."

So, the following morning I made my way into the bowels of the house. Standing in front of a heavy steel security door was Symonds, immaculately dressed as always, and with an impish grin on his face.

"Enjoy!" he said as he pulled the heavy door open, "here's the inventory and ring the bell on the left there, when and if you need to be released from durance vile," he chortled as he swung the door to. It closed with an ominous clunk.

In front of me, in serried and tiered racks from floor to ceiling ranged to the distant end of the room, were hundreds of picture canvases, most of them unframed. What I had imagined might take me a morning of sifting through was clearly an altogether bigger task. Taking a deep breath, I started to examine the pictures in the nearest rack. Fortunately, they were all on numbered slides, and the lighting was good, so it was quite easy to pull forward a picture, examine it and mark it off on the inventory Symonds had given me. By the end of the morning I was suffering from fine art indigestion and, by the time the Collection closed that evening my indigestion had turned to nausea. And I had drawn another complete blank. Later, in my London flat, I seriously questioned whether or not I wanted to return to the Collection's basement the following morning – the idea of breaking into a cat-infested house on the shabby side of Wimbledon was starting to have its own appeal. However, some ten hours later, I took a deep breath and decided that a basement full of fine art was actually preferable to a houseful of smelly moggies and I set off once again for St James's Square.

In order to break up the routine, I decided that I would abandon my systematic search by inventory number and, instead, home-in on those pictures that were described as portraits. I also decided that I would start with the eighteenth- and 19th century canvases as I liked these images far more than the earlier depictions of saints and sinners.

Around lunchtime, I pulled forward a tall canvas that, according to the inventory, was a 'portrait of a young man in military dress attributed to the school of Sir Thomas Lawrence'. I recognised one thing immediately: the figure was wearing the late-18th century uniform of a Life Guard. It was quite an arresting image although the painting seemed curiously unbalanced in its composition – and it reminded me of another picture that I had seen recently, perhaps in the National Gallery. I was still tussling with this problem later in the café when Symonds once more came into view.

"How are you getting on in our basement?" he enquired amiably, so I told him about the portrait I had just uncovered and that it reminded me of another - but that I was reasonably sure that the one I had in mind had been a double portrait and by an earlier artist.

"You don't by any chance mean the van Dyck of the Stuart brothers, do you?" Symonds asked. "If you wait here a moment I will get the National Gallery catalogue and show you the one I mean." And he disappeared off to his office, returning a short time later with a fat and obviously heavy volume under his arm.

"Now let's see…. yes, is this the fellow?"

He handed over the book to me with his finger holding back a full-page colour image of the famous double portrait of Lord John and Lord Bernard Stuart by Sir Anthony van Dyck. The brothers are portrayed opposite each other, full length and in three quarter profile. Lord John on the left, who is dressed in a golden doublet, is resting his right arm on a plain rectilinear stone pillar, while the younger brother, Lord Bernard, who is dressed in a blue cloak and britches laced with silver, is half facing him with his left hand on his left leg, the foot of which is placed on the base of the pillar.[105] As the Gallery catalogue states: 'The simple background sets off the aquiline features, confident poses and rich clothing' of the two brothers who were the younger sons of the 3rd Duke of Lennox.

"Yes, that's the one!" I said. "But it's by van Dyck, it's not in your collection, yours is a single portrait and it's attributed to the school of Lawrence. So, we are no further forward."

"I'm not so sure," replied Symonds. "I'm not very familiar with the picture you have found, but why don't I come down with you and take a second look?" Five minutes later we were standing in front of the large canvas I had unearthed earlier.

"Yes, the pose of the figure and the setting is curiously like the van Dyck double but, as you say, the composition is oddly unbalanced with only a single figure... I wonder... I wonder. You know, I think it's time to call in an expert." And with that he swept out of the room leaving me somewhat bewildered.

An hour later he was back with the familiar figure of Philip Mould, the renowned art dealer who has an enviable record of unearthing or re-attributing historical portraits. I had met Philip several times previously, initially over dinner with David Mellor the former Cabinet Minister, football pundit and classical music specialist, and more recently in his gallery in Pall Mall, just around the corner from St James's Square. "What do you make of that?" asked Symonds of Mould.

---

[105] There is a second version of this portrait, in the National Portrait Gallery, in which the brothers are dressed in red and blue respectively and the stone column is somewhat obscured.

"Hmm, well, Robert, it certainly looks like a Lawrence, but as you say the composition is all wrong and there is some clumsy brushwork across most of the right side of the canvas. Let's see what this tells us," and he took out of his pocket an ultra-violet pen torch. "Yes, as I thought, this is an over-paint and a pretty crude one at that. So, what do you want to do about it?"

For a minute there was complete silence, then he said: "In your opinion, Mould, could this be a Lawrence?"

"It's hard to judge down here, but I certainly think that's possible..."

"In that case I don't think that my trustees will have any difficulty in financing a complete restoration and an investigation into its history and the subject matter. As for your quest, Joll, I suggest that you suspend your labours whilst Mould and his team see what they can find." And with that he swept from the room taking Philip Mould with him. I called Philip later and asked him how long he thought the restoration and research would take.

"I think you should allow at least three months and possibly longer – and the research will largely depend on whether or not we uncover any clues during the restoration. Sorry, but this isn't a quick process."

With the prospect of no further progress in that direction for the time being, I turned back to my analysis of the Ashby find and the other documents. A couple of weeks later the telephone rang in my study. It was Philip Mould.

"Good news, Christopher!" he said with some enthusiasm. "I have just been on the telephone to Symonds and I have told him that, in my opinion, the Steyne Trust is definitely the owner of a hitherto uncatalogued double portrait by Sir Thomas Lawrence."

"Double portrait?" I asked.

"Oh, yes, sorry - I should have said that when we removed the overpaint there, sure enough, was a second military figure and a pillar. The composition is remarkably similar to the van Dyck double portrait of the Stuart brothers and I think it's safe to assume that when Lawrence painted it he must have had the van Dyck in mind – or it was a pose requested by whoever commissioned the painting in the first place. Anyway, my team are busy researching the subjects and are optimistic that they will be able to put names to the sitters. The fact that the original figure is dressed, as you know, in the uniform of a Life Guard and the other, revealed figure is dressed as a Blue[106] - and the fact that the two look quite similar, indeed are probably brothers - will narrow our search considerably. But you may have to wait a little while yet. In the meantime, and this should make you happy, the cleaning revealed two rather curious inscriptions on the plinth."

"Really?" I queried, sitting-up rather straighter in my chair.

"Yes, these inscriptions are curious for three reasons. Firstly, one was clearly painted contemporaneously with the subjects whilst the other was an overpaint, albeit that it was in its turn overpainted when the right-hand figure was obliterated. Secondly, although the later inscription is in Latin, the original inscription, whilst written in Hebrew script, is in a language that neither my assistant nor I recognise. Thirdly, the last sentence of the Hebrew inscription may have been added later, possibly at the same time as the Latin inscription. I have taken close-up, high resolution photos of both and, if you let me have your email addresses, I will send them to you and Symonds. Anyway, next time you are in Pall Mall, do drop in and have a look at the picture."

I gave Philip my email address and, a few minutes later, the two images duly popped up in my email inbox. At first, I couldn't make head or tail of either of them and, as they were not easy to read on screen, I downloaded them onto a memory stick and set-off for a professional print laboratory in Soho. A couple of hours later I was back at my desk but still none the wiser. Clearly the Latin inscription was a list of names, but the Hebrew script defeated me, so I decided to call Symonds to see if he could shed any light on it.

---

[106] The Royal Horse Guards were usually known, prior to their amalgamation in 1969, as The Blues by reason of their blue tunics. The 1st & 2nd Life Guards, by contrast, wore red tunics.

"My dear chap, how nice to hear from you," was his instant reply to my call.

"Yes, I too have been puzzling over the Hebrew script and I have already forwarded it to a friend of mine at the British Museum, who is something of an expert on Middle Eastern languages. I don't think that the Latin inscription is too much of a puzzler, however, as it seems to me that it is a straight transliteration of people's names — and it's mostly their first names - from English into their Latin equivalent. So, I'm sure you will have noticed that the name heading the list is Gulielmus Steinius Primus Frater, which I think we can correctly translate as William Steyne First Brother.

"Well, we know who William Steyne was: he was your friend the 3rd Marquess! Given what you have uncovered already, I think it is safe to assume that the Latin inscription is, therefore, a list of members of the Brotherhood although, from what Mould has said, it would seem that the list is not contemporaneous with the original painting, so it's probably not the original membership - at least not all of them. It shouldn't take you too long to translate the names back into English and find out who and what they were. Do let me know… and I will, of course, call you as soon as I hear back from the BM." Then he hung up.

Symonds was right. It didn't take me long, with the help of a Latin-English dictionary, to translate the cod Latin back into English and to uncover the names, which were as follows:

William Steyne
William Alvanley
George Brummell
Charles-Henry FitzCharles
Richard Croft
David Dundas
Edward Ellenborough
Thomas Erskine
William Grenville
Rees Gronow
Everard Home
George Spencer

Was it significant, I wondered, that there were twelve names - like the apostles?

As to the names themselves, Steyne I already knew about, and the addition of Primus Fratis – 'first brother' - after his name was clearly the rough equivalent of 'Great Boanerges', which of itself doesn't easily translate into Latin. However, it was not necessary to be a student of early-19th century English social history for many of the other names to jump out of the page – and they also, I realised once I had looked-up each of them, fell into three distinct but connected groups.

For a start, George Brummell was clearly the celebrated 'Beau' Brummell[107] and William Alvanley his friend, Lord Alvanley,[108] a noted buck and dandy. The inclusion of Brummell on the list might also help to date it, for Brummell went into debtor's exile in France in 1816, so it was reasonable to assume that the membership list – if such it was – pre-dated his enforced departure for the continent. There was also one other, probably tenuous, connection with my quest: Beau Brummell had served in the 10th Light Dragoons (later the Tenth Hussars). Rees Gronow[109] was the noted Regency diarist and gambler, thanks to whose writing we know in some detail the goings-on of the Regency social scene. Charles-Henry FitzCharles was the 6th Duke of Whitehall; King Charles II had granted the dukedom to the bastard son of his mistress, Belle de Poitrine.[110] What these four names had in common was a reputation for being at the heart of society and their friendship with various members of the Royal Family.

The second group were all politicians or senior members of the Establishment. In addition, and perhaps of greater significance, my

---

[107] George Bryan Brummell (1778-1840)

[108] William Arden, 2nd Baron Alvanley (1789-1849)

[109] Rees Howell Gronow (1794-1865)

[110] Because, at the same time, Belle de Poitrine produced a twin daughter, Charlotte, the title was granted the privilege of being able to pass through the female line as well as the male – and the Whitehalls' adopted the confusing habit of naming all their children Charles or Charlotte, hyphenated with a second Christian name to distinguish one from another.

researches quickly uncovered the fact that Grenville,[111] Erskine,[112] Ellenborough[113] and Spencer[114] were the four 'wise men' who, in 1806, carried out an investigation into the private life of Queen Caroline,[115] the wife of King George IV whom he cordially loathed from his first meeting with her.

The third group, it emerged, shared a common involvement in a national tragedy. Sir Richard Croft[116] was Physician-in-Ordinary to King George III and was the doctor whose botched delivery of Princess Charlotte of Wales'[117] still-born baby led to her death five hours later and his apparent suicide three months after that. At least that was the received wisdom. Of interest, but probably of no significance, I uncovered the fact that Sir Thomas Lawrence had made a posthumous sketch of Croft in his coffin. Home[118] was the doctor who carried out the post mortem on the Princess, which was supervised by Dundas.[119] Both men reported that she had died a natural death and that the child, a boy, had been still-born.

Armed with this knowledge I made an appointment to see Symonds at the Steyne Collection the following day to see if he could add anything to my own efforts.

"So, you conclude that this is a membership list of The Brotherhood of the Sons of Thunder and that the names on the list are, by and large,

---

[111] William Wyndham Grenville, 1st Baron Grenville (1759-1834). Prime Minister 1806-1807
[112] Thomas Erskine, 1st Baron Erskine (1750-1823). Lord Chancellor 1806-1807
[113] Edward Law, 1st Baron Ellenborough (1750-1818). Lord Chief Justice 1802-1818
[114] George John Spencer, 2nd Earl Spencer (1758-1834). Home Secretary 1806-1807
[115] Queen Caroline (1768-1821) was born HRH Princess Caroline Amelia Elizabeth of Brunswick-Wolfenbüttel. She was known for her garrulousness and lack of attention to personal hygiene. On first meeting her the future King George IV is reputed to have said "bring me a glass of brandy".
[116] Sir Richard Croft, 6th Baronet (1762-1818)
[117] HRH Princess Charlotte Augusta of Wales (1796-1817) only child of King George IV and Queen Caroline.
[118] Sir Everard Home, 1st Baronet (1756-1832)
[119] General Sir David Dundas, 1st Baronet 1735-1820). At the time of Princess Charlotte's death Dundas was Governor of the Royal Hospital Chelsea

members of an early-19th century London society. You also believe that the names fall into three distinct groups: friends of The Prince Regent; the commission that investigated Queen Caroline; and a group involved with the death of her daughter. You also conclude that, because Brummell had to leave for France in 1816, this membership list is of an earlier date as he would have been unlikely to have joined once in exile.[120] Furthermore, because it was an overpaint, the list is not contemporaneous with the original painting." I agreed that this was a good summary of the list as I saw it.

"I agree with you and, if you had seen me yesterday, I would have said that I couldn't add anything more until I had heard back from the BM. But just before you arrived I received an email from my friend there which, as I haven't had the time to print it off, I will read to you:

My Dear Symonds

The answer to your question is relatively straightforward. The language of the inscription you sent me is Aramaic, a Semitic language of Syrian origin dating from approximately 1000 BC. Aramaic script evolved into Hebrew, which is why you recognised the script but could not translate it. I have effected a translation for you as follows:

The Brotherhood of the Sons of Thunder

I swear upon pain of my very life that I, a Brother of the Sons of Thunder, will at all times take any action that the Great Boanerges directs to protect by any means necessary the Monarchy and the Realm against any undesirable unions by lineal descendants of His Majesty King George III that might affect the succession to the Throne or lower the status of the Royal House. I further swear to seek out and destroy, as directed by the Great Boanerges, the enemies of our Sovereign wherever they may be. Finally, I swear, with my life's blood and on my life to hold these secrets secret.

---

[120] It is significant that Flashman joined the Brotherhood before he had to leave the country.

I hope that is helpful. It is worth noting, however, that whilst the English translation of the Greek word Boanerges in the Gospel of St Mark is correctly rendered in English as 'the sons of thunder', the Greek word is possibly a mistranslation from the original Aramaic. This is an academic point, still subject to much learned debate and probably of no interest to you.

Sincerely

David Schayek

"Accordingly, it would seem that the painting contains the Oath of the Brotherhood, which was concealed to the casual observer through the simple but effective device of writing it in a largely unknown language – and, by the way, it matches the copy of the fragment you left with me. The painting also contains a list of members and, probably, an additional clause to the oath that was added in the next generation and that, sometime later still, all these clues were painted over. Now what do we think we can conclude from that?" I let him go on, which he did.

"I think it might be reasonable to assume that our painting contains a reasonable amount of iconography, which the 3rd Lord Steyne decided subsequently – for reasons we don't know - to obliterate. The two figures look like brothers and the composition is remarkably similar to a picture - from an earlier period - of the brothers Stuart, so they probably are brothers. And they are also dressed in the uniforms of brother Regiments – one of the Regiments of Life Guards and The Blues. On the pillar against which the right-hand figure – or shall we assume brother - rests are two inscriptions. The first is an oath rendered into Aramaic and mostly painted at the same time as the main picture. The word Boanerges is usually – although possibly wrongly - assumed to be the Aramaic for 'Sons of Thunder', which is perhaps why the oath was hidden in that language. But the name itself is significant and I think we can conclude that the brothers portrayed are indeed 'the sons of thunder' – although 'thunder' may of course have been their father's nickname rather than surname."

"So far, so good. This then is a portrait of a pair of brothers whose father's name has some association with the word 'thunder'. But it is also a record of an oath which binds together a society or 'brotherhood', so there is now a triple connection with the word 'brother' — and triple connections, of which the best and most potent example is the Holy Trinity, are powerful stuff. Now let's look at the oath itself. The wording is completely unambiguous: the Brotherhood exists to enforce some specific terms from the Royal Marriages Act, which, if my memory serves me correctly, was passed in 1772 and — probably of a later date - to seek out and destroy the enemies of the State. The members are also sworn to silence. So, there are three parts to an oath — another triple connection, although probably not original. Now, in 1772 Lawrence was only three years old and, although he started drawing at the age of four, the Act predates even his skills. So, would it be fair to conclude that the Brotherhood was formed sometime after the Royal Marriages Act but before 1816 when Brummell left England?" I agreed that that was a reasonable conclusion.

"If that is the case, what event do we think might have brought about the creation of this 'brotherhood'? How about when King George III was first seriously incapacitated, which I believe was in 1788? Perhaps, with the King not in his right mind, his closest friends formed the Brotherhood to ensure that his wishes were carried out — and the painting exists to commemorate its formation and to enshrine its oath of membership. Lawrence started painting society portraits in 1787, so that lends added weight to a formation of the Brotherhood and the date of the picture at around that time. However, we now have a problem. For the members of the Brotherhood listed are mostly, if not all, the friends of The Prince Regent and so hardly the kind of people to band together to defend the wishes of the King against his eldest son. But I think that the answer to this apparent anomaly is staring us in the face." I looked suitably blank.

"You see, we know that the second inscription is of a later date; possibly as late as 1816. That means that between the formation of the Brotherhood in, say, 1788 and the latest date for the list of names, say 1816, there was some twenty-eight years — that is a generation, which is more than enough time for the membership of the Brotherhood to have evolved along with a re-interpretation of, or addition to, its aims. Do you agree?" I nodded weakly.

"I think that we should pass our deductions on to Mould as they may help to advance his researches. I'll give him a call now." Which he proceeded to do, telling Philip that the painting was probably of two brothers, possibly called James and John, whose father's name or nickname was 'thunder' and that it was probably painted sometime around 1788.

A couple of days later I received an email from Philip Mould headed 'Eureka!'

Gentlemen:

Thanks to your positively Holmesian powers of deduction, my assistant has traced the subjects of the Lawrence double portrait. They are Their Royal Highnesses Prince Johann (John) and Prince Jacobus (James) of Saxe-Weimar-Eisenach, born in 1758 the younger twin sons of Duke Ernst August II Konstantin of Saxe-Weimar-Eisenach,[121] who was known during his lifetime as 'donner und blitzen' - thunder and lightning - probably because he was alleged to have had a vile temper. Their mother was Princess Anna Amalia of Brunswick-Wolfenbüttel, the sister of George IV's estranged wife Queen Caroline. The boys' father died shortly after they were born and they were virtually adopted by their godfather King George III, who brought them to England and, at 18, gave them commissions: John in the 2nd Life Guards and James in The Blues. George III also appointed the 2nd Marquess of Steyne as their private secretary. The only known portraits of them are in the Liechtenstein Collection in Vaduz.

I hope that helps,

Philip

---

[121] Duke Ernst August II Konstantin of Saxe-Weimar-Eisenach (1737-1758) married two years before his death.

No sooner had I read this email than the telephone rang. It was Symonds and he sounded excited.

"I think we can safely say that the riddle is explained! The young princes John and James were the 'Sons of Thunder', they were probably members of the Brotherhood which was founded by the 3rd Marquess's father, their private secretary, to enforce the terms of the Royal Marriages Act. Quite what the Brotherhood got up to, if indeed it was anything more than a Masonic-style drinking club, I don't suppose we will ever know. Anyway, I am most grateful to you for uncovering this picture – I will now have to think where we are going to exhibit it. Do stay in touch - good-bye."

Well, I thought, I may have helped solve your riddle but I'm not a great deal closer to understanding the Brotherhood as it was constituted in the mid-19th century. Or was I? Perhaps, as Symonds had said, the answer was staring me in the face. The more I thought about it, the more it seemed to me that I should focus not on the picture as originally painted, but on its second and somewhat altered state. For, whilst I agreed with Symonds' interpretation of the meaning of the picture in its original state, that meaning didn't fit with what the Speedicut letters revealed about the Brotherhood in later years. Clearly, the original purpose of the Brotherhood was to enforce certain terms of the Royal Marriages Act, but everything that I knew about the Brotherhood from Speedicut's letters referred to its later aim of destroying the enemies of the Sovereign, which could be interpreted – as Symonds had inadvertently done - as 'enemies of the State'.

I went back to look at the list of members and realisation started to dawn. There were linking historical themes to the list of names: The Prince Regent later King George IV; his running battle with his wife Caroline; and the life and death of his daughter Princess Charlotte. Steyne, Alvanley, Gronow, Whitehall and Brummell were friends of The Prince Regent (not yet King George IV), who ordered Grenville, Erskine, Ellenborough and Spencer to investigate Caroline's private life and Croft, Dundas and Home were all involved in the death of Princess Charlotte…who was the heir to the throne.

Was it possible, I wondered, that the Brotherhood – a society also dedicated to upholding the royal bloodline - was somehow implicated in her death? What if the four wise men who headed the parliamentary Commission had actually uncovered the fact that The Prince Regent was not Charlotte's father but had then covered it up? George, who was well known to be jealous of his only child, had himself claimed that Queen Caroline was not a virgin when he married her. And what if they had taken it upon themselves – or been ordered by The Prince Regent - to ensure that the succession did not pass to Princess Charlotte and her children? Was it possible that the Brotherhood could have encompassed her death and that of her child? The subsequent overpaint of the double portrait seemed to indicate that Lord Steyne had something to hide. It was a completely outrageous theory – but it fitted with the facts.

When I sat back and pieced together all the information I had uncovered, and then reduced it to simple statements of fact or propositions, I arrived at a set of linked conclusions: The Brotherhood of the Sons of Thunder was clearly a dangerous and determined secret society at the heart of the British establishment; it existed to root out enemies of the state and to protect the royal bloodline; Flashman and Speedicut were both members of the Brotherhood and Speedicut had certainly acted, as evidenced by the letters in Book One, on the orders of its leader in defence of the nation's honour and/or its own purposes - and earlier members of the Brotherhood were almost certainly implicated in the untimely deaths of Princess Charlotte and her child.

APPENDIX D: DICTIONARY OF BRITISH BIOGRAPHIES

(This extract first published in the 2011 edition)

Speedicut, Sir Jasper Jeffreys, Baronet of the United Kingdom, KCVO (1821-1915), soldier and courtier, was born on 20th December 1821 at The Dower House, Acton Park, Wrexham, the eldest son of Algernon Jeffreys Speedicut and his wife Honoria. The Speedicut family claimed descent from George, 1st Baron Jeffreys, the 17th century Lord Chancellor also known as 'The Hanging Judge', and enjoyed the status of minor gentry from the 18th century onwards.

Education, 10th Hussars & Central Asia
Jasper Speedicut was educated at Rugby School (1834-1839) where he was befriended by Harry Flashman *(ibidem)*. In mid-1839, Speedicut's father purchased him a commission in the 10th (Prince of Wales's Own) Royal Hussars and he initially served with the Regiment at Hounslow, Northampton and Dublin. In October 1841, following an incident with the Irish Nationalist group, the Young Irelanders, Speedicut was posted to India where he joined the staff of General George Pollock for the relief of Jalalabad. Later the same year, he was part of the force led by Captain Sir Richmond Shakespear formed to rescue the survivors of the retreat from Kabul held in Bamian. Speedicut was then tasked with assessing the fate of Lieutenant Colonel Charles Stoddart and Captain Arthur Conolly, who were being held by the Emir of Bokhara and was himself imprisoned by the Emir.

Early military career – India, Crimea, China & USA – and marriages
Following his escape from Bokhara, Speedicut spent time in continental Europe before re-joining his Regiment in late-1844 prior to its posting to India in 1845. From 1845 to 1846 Speedicut was involved in the Sutlej campaign. On the death of his father, he took leave of absence from his Regiment and went onto half-pay. He returned to Europe for the period 1847-1848 and assisted Prince Albert with the planning of the Great

Exhibition (1851). In 1849, whilst in America on Great Exhibition business, he eloped with and married Lady Mary Steyne, the only daughter of the 3rd Marquess of Steyne, and in late 1853 he joined Lord Cardigan's staff for the Crimean War. Whilst he was away in the Crimea, his wife died in childbirth along with the child she was carrying. After involvement in the Anglo-Persian War of 1856, by 1857 Speedicut was back in India where he became embroiled in the Mutiny. In 1860, he served with Captain Charles Gordon in the Second Opium War in China, returned to London in 1861 and married Lady Charlotte-Georgina FitzCharles, younger daughter of the 7th Duke of Whitehall. From late-1861 to 1863 Speedicut was in North America, where he fought on both sides of the Civil War. He was again in the United States in 1865, the year of the birth of his only child, Dorothea, and was present at the assassination of President Lincoln.

Overseas royal service – Mexico, France & Germany

In 1866, Speedicut was seconded by the British government to act as Equerry to the Emperor of Mexico and was involved in the downfall of the Mexican Empire and the execution of the Emperor Maximilian. He was appointed a Commander of the Imperial Order of Guadaloupe for his services to the Mexican Imperial Family. In the period 1870-1871 Speedicut served as an official government observer of the Franco-Prussian War and, somewhat unusually, received honours from both governments (Commander of the Legion of Honour and Knight of the Order of the Black Eagle). With the fall of the French Second Empire, Speedicut was instrumental in effecting the escape of the Imperial Family to England.

Further royal service – India and the Zulu War

Returning to Regimental duty with the 10th Hussars in 1871, Speedicut came to the attention of the Prince of Wales, the Regiment's Colonel, and was invited to join the Prince's staff for his tour of India in 1875. In 1879, Speedicut served in South Africa on Lord Chelmsford's staff and was present at the battles of Isandlwana and Rorke's Drift. He also witnessed the death of the Prince Imperial, son of Emperor Napoleon III.

Ongoing military career - Egypt & Sudan

From 1882 to 1885, with a brief interlude in Austria in 1883, Speedicut was for the most part in north Africa where he took part in the suppression of the Egyptian Revolt and witnessed the rise of the Mahdists in Sudan. In 1884, he was seconded to the staff of Major General Charles Gordon, with whom he had served in China, for the evacuation of Khartoum and spent a brief time in captivity as the sole survivor of Lieutenant Colonel John Stewart's party, which attempted to break through the besieging Mahdist forces. Speedicut managed to escape from the Mahdists and joined the relief force under the command of General Sir Garnet Wolseley.

Prince Albert Victor of Wales

On his return to England, Speedicut was appointed an Extra Equerry to HRH Prince Albert Victor of Wales (later HRH The Duke of Clarence & Avondale), eldest son of the future King Edward VII, with whom he served until the Prince's death in 1892. During this period, Speedicut's daughter married Prince Dimitri Lieven in Saint Petersburg. Speedicut was briefly in Bavaria in 1886 and in Austria in 1889 on detachment to the Austrian Imperial Family, service for which he was appointed a Commander of the Order of Franz Josef. From October 1889 to April 1890 Speedicut was "in waiting" to Prince Albert Victor during the latter's tour of India, before temporarily leaving royal service on the Prince's death in 1892.

Sudan & South Africa

In the period 1895 to 1896 Speedicut, on half-pay, spent time on private business in South Africa but from 1897 to 1899 he was once again in uniform for the campaigns in Egypt, the Sudan and South Africa, during which he was involved in the battles at El Teb and at Omdurman. In South Africa, he was captured by the Boers and escaped with his fellow captive, Winston Churchill (*ibidem*).

Boxer Rebellion & the siege of Peking

On his return to England at the end of 1899, Speedicut resigned his commission and in 1900, whilst on private business in China, became caught up in the Boxer Rebellion and was besieged in Peking. He returned to England in time for the death of Queen Victoria, re-joined royal service and had a minor but crucial role in the Queen's funeral and the coronation of King Edward VII, for which he was appointed a Baronet of the United Kingdom. In 1903, he accompanied the King on his State Visit to Paris and, following the death of the King in 1910, he finally left royal service and was appointed a Knight Commander of the Royal Victorian Order by King George V in recognition of his past service.

Death

The closing years of Speedicut's life were not without incident as, on a visit to his daughter in Russia in 1910, he had an unfortunate entanglement with Rasputin, and in 1912 he survived the sinking of RMS *Titanic*. Colonel Sir Jasper Speedicut died at the Ritz Hotel in Paris on 1st April 1915; there is some evidence that he was there on government business.

Recent information

In 2011, written evidence emerged that Speedicut had been a lifelong member of a quasi-masonic group called The Brotherhood of the Sons of Thunder, an organisation operating at the heart of the British establishment, and that many of his exploits listed above were connected to this organisation. Known collectively as *The Speedicut Papers*, these documents also allege that Brig Gen Sir Harry Flashman VC was a fraud. *The Speedicut Papers* are currently being edited with a view to publication.

Made in the USA
Middletown, DE
06 April 2023